BOUND TO DESIRE

A WARLOCK OF KAMVASANA STORY

BOUND TO DESIRE

A WARLOCK OF KAMVASANA STORY

CLEA SALAR & TALLIS SALAR

BOUND TO DESIRE
First Edition.
May 1, 2025

Periapt Press
PO Box 25693
Colorado Springs, CO 80936
www.periaptpress.com

ISBN: 979-8-9903639-4-6

To our English teachers, who surely never saw this coming.

Content Notes:

Bound to Desire is what happens when the player characters have too much chemistry and the GM only encourages it. Well, okay, not quite that bad. But this romp was inspired by familiar TTRPG settings and is full of open door descriptive encounters between our plucky pansexual heroine, three strapping men of various ages and fantasy races, and one primordial deity who defies gender. Be prepared for explicit and descriptive scenes.

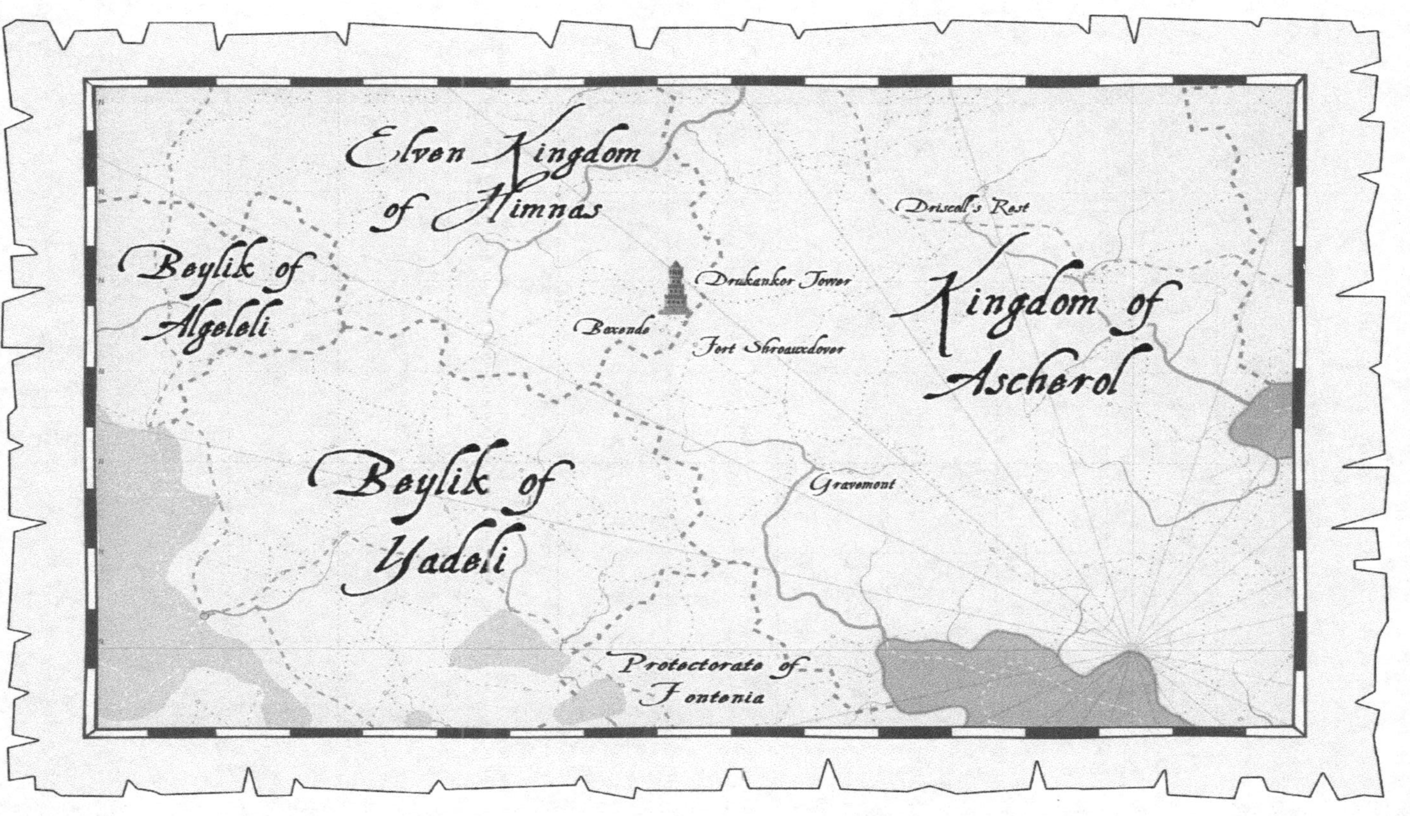

Elven Kingdom of Himnas
Beylik of Algeleli
Beylik of Yadeli
Kingdom of Ascherol
Driscoll's Rest
Drukankor Tower
Boxendo
Fort Shroauxdover
Gravemont
Protectorate of Fontonia

ONE

Gravemont seemed well named at first, then horribly so upon reflection. A farming village that was located at the bottom of a hill, it was a pleasant enough place, with a popular harvest festival and one of the area's lead producers of sweet wines. However, it was overshadowed by a massive mausoleum that sat at the top of a hill, surrounded by a cemetery.

In the best lit corner of The Broken Headstone tavern, right by the enormous open windows that were letting in a gentle late summer breeze, Octavia grumbled to herself, picking at a currant scone while bent over two books and four maps that were spread on the table before her. The largest map was of the whole of the town of Gravemont.

She tossed back her mass of silver blonde curls and sighed. "There has to be another way in," she muttered, pulling another map out and looking it over. She tapped a manicured nail on the table as she pondered.

Further frustrated pondering was interrupted by a loud, boisterous voice declaring, "Come, lads, I heard she should be here."

The group that came through the doors of the tavern seemed as out of place here as Octavia did herself. The first, and certainly loudest as he called to his companions, was a massive creature of draconic descent almost too large for the doorway. A dragonkin, most likely, though she'd never seen one in person. Silver scales shimmered in the low sunlight with three large horns arcing gently upward from his head. He was heavily clad in plate armor adorned with engravings of vines and leaves spiraling across the pauldrons and greaves. It was beautifully done, but

Octavia couldn't match the symbols to any group or order. A kite shield hung on his back and a mace swung from his belt, clanging harmlessly off his chausses as he walked.

Following the dragonkin was a man who was almost jarringly normal compared to his companion. He was about Octavia's height, something in the vicinity of five and a half feet, maybe a little over. His frame was lithe and athletic, his shoulders a little broad, and the form fitting black leathers he wore caused a number of inappropriate thoughts to trip gaily through Octavia's brain. By his warm skin and almond shaped eyes, she would have guessed he was from the far west, somewhere near the Salt Empire, but those eyes were a bright jade and his hair was yellow-blond and tied up in a neat bun. He hissed slightly at his large companion and quickly locked those jade eyes with Octavia's sky blue gaze. She felt something animalistic behind them. And…did he have a cat's pupil? It was hard to see from this distance.

The stare was broken by the final member of the group stepping inside and walking up to the blond. He was between the other two in height, at about six feet if she was any judge. His skin was a pale porcelain white, his eyes pink, and if it weren't for the raven black hair, tousled from their journey, she might have mistaken him for an albino. He had small point to his ears, but it wasn't quite enough for an elf. He looked like a noble, his traveling clothes well made and of rich materials in reds, blacks, and dark purples with an ornate bag hanging from a cross belt. He wore an odd contraption that looked to be a complicated spear, but instead of a point it was just a tube with a thick, bent wood base over his shoulder.

"How do we know if we see her?" the pale man asked.

"Oh, I think we'll know," the blond said, smiling broadly as his eyes looked back at Octavia.

She set her hands on the table and leaned forward, her head tilting slightly to the side as she studied them. She didn't bother pretending she wasn't. She probably shouldn't be leaning forward—she was wearing a low cut shirt and had cleavage that had been described more than once as breathtaking—but she had also been standing there milling over her notes long enough that she needed to stretch out her back.

"And who are you looking for?" she asked, her voice musical and clear as it carried through the room. It was early, there wasn't much of a din to be heard over. Yet.

"Greetings, incredibly fair maiden," the massive dragon-person said as he stepped over to her. The other two moved to flank him. None of them looked threatening at all, in fact they felt downright casual and the dragon kept smiling in a warm fashion. "We seek a sorceress," he started.

"Warlock," the pale one corrected.

"Are you sure she's not an enchantress?" the dragonkin asked, raising his brow ridges to Octavia. She straightened up and set her hands on her hips, a faint smile curling her lips. This one was a flatterer.

"Yes. Alces, please," the pale man said, a touch embarrassed. Just a touch.

The dragonkin nodded. "Of course, yes, a warlock to help us on a quest we have. I have no doubt you are she. I am Ser Alces Brightrain, Knight of the Spree Spirits. These are my compatriots, Sumner Taery," he continued, gesturing to the shorter man in black leather, "Master of the Guiled Shadows, and Durante Calabria," he said, turning towards the pale one. Alces noticed Durante was farther back and reached behind him, giving him a friendly push towards the foreground, which caused him to shrink a little on himself. "Inventor Extraordinaire. Have we found the right person?"

The dragonkin was larger than life, and hard to believe. She did her best not to giggle at the introductions.

"I am the only warlock in town, so I must be the person you seek," she said, still eyeing them with caution in spite of the smile. "I am Octavia Baudelaire. Though maybe you should tell me why you're looking for me. Here—" she marked and closed up her books, and stacked the maps neatly. "Grab chairs and get comfortable, this looks like it might be a conversation. Ami! You have actual customers. Get out here!"

"Most gracious, my lady, you are as kind as you are beautiful," Alces said as he sat down carefully on one of the stools. It creaked a little in protest but held strong.

"You giant, scaled ham," Sumner commented as he sat down as well, glancing at Octavia and rolling his eyes as if to commiserate with her.

"Yes, thank you for hearing us out," Durante said, a little quietly, as he sat down as well.

Before more conversation could be had, Ami, the tavern-keeper's daughter, tripped lightly out of the back room. There was a short moment where she paused, taking in the sight of the four of them, before nodding to herself and stepping up to the table. Ami was a lovely young creature who filled out her work attire nicely and was certainly one of the draws at the tavern. The other being it was one of only two taverns in the village and the other only served grain alcohol and roasted corn.

"Oh, my, good evening gentlemen. Tavi," she said, greeting the three newcomers then batting her eyes a little at Octavia. "How can I help you?"

"Drinks and a feast, my sweet girl," Alces said, "Whatever you think is best, I trust your taste. Unless, Miss Baudelaire, do you have a request?"

"I'll have my usual, Ami," Octavia said with another faint smile. "Jed has been roasting a boar today, hasn't he? We'll pay for the haunch, and everything that comes with it. I'm sure the big boy here can finish it," she added with a nod to Alces.

She looked back at the three. "Will mead be acceptable? Or do you prefer something...bolder?" Her eyes flitted between the three of them as she spoke, finally resting on the quiet one, Durante.

"Mead is excellent," Alces said with Sumner giving her an agreeable shrug.

Durante glanced up, "Do you have any sort of wine, perhaps?"

"I know just the thing. And I'll have Jed start carving up the boar," Ami said with a sweet smile. She turned and walked away with a little extra sway in her hips.

As Ami walked away, Octavia briefly considered how long it had been since she and the barmaid had a tumble. Almost two weeks. Might be safe to spend time with her again. Ami was a lovely girl, and had an adventurous spirit, but also struck Octavia as the type of person who would get attached. And she was only there until she got that damn book out of the mausoleum.

"Now, should we eat first," Alces asked, "our treat, of course, or would you like to get down to business?"

"We can begin, if you wish," she said, looking back to Alces, uncrossing and crossing her legs as she tried to get comfortable. Honestly, she mostly stood because her rather generous backside was a little bigger than the seat and it wasn't pleasant to sit on for too long. "But it will also not bother me if you wish to wait. The three of you are new to Gravemont, yes?"

"Just arrived," Sumner said. While his eyes always came back to Octavia, or parts of Octavia, they never stayed. He was constantly looking around. Durante seemed lost in thought for the moment, holding his uncurled fist to his chin and tapping his lip with his thumb.

"I feel discussions are always better on full stomachs," Alces said.

"So, before we do move on, what can you tell us about yourself, Miss Baudelaire, if you don't mind sharing?"

"Well, as you know, I am a warlock," she said and looked at the dragonkin warily. "Bound to a Power, not a fiend. I am here attempting to breach the mausoleum, with permission from the ealdorman." She wrinkled her nose a little. "He keeps asking me if I can level it. I keep telling him I'm not that kind of warlock."

"Plenty of warlocks are bound to benevolent creatures of power, I wouldn't hold your claim to strength against you," Alces said, brushing that off.

"Known a couple of relatively upbeat and downright friendly types," Sumner said.

"Merchants!" Durante suddenly blurted out with a grin, then shrank a little into himself once more. "Sorry, I remembered where I heard your name before."

Alces chuckled, which rolled deeply, and patted him on the back. "Well, share the wisdom with us, friend."

"Oh, yes, sorry. There was a merchant family, out near the Valley of Driscoll, by the name of Baudelaire a decade ago. I don't know if they are any relation. Sorry, it just stuck in my mind," Durante said gently.

Octavia arched an eyebrow. "No, you're correct. Though I believe that was my uncle in the valley. Presumably he is still there. My father made his stake in the city, Driscoll's Rest. And did well. For a while." She smiled wryly at that.

"Ah," Durante said with a nod. "I believe my family had some dealings with them, but I don't know what it was about."

. There was a brief uncertain silence, but thankfully Ami broke it by arriving with a full tray of drinks. A pair of delicate glasses for Octavia and Durante, and a set of heavy mugs for Alces and Sumner. "I'll have the food out soon. Anything else I can get you in the meantime?"

"Your shining presence is enough, dear," Alces said with a broad smile that made Ami blush a little and she glanced over at Octavia.

"This is lovely, Ami, thank you," Octavia said, amused. She liked that Alces was also flirting with the girl, mostly because he seemed like a gentleman. Bombastic, but probably wouldn't grab the barmaid's ass as she went by.

"Well, if that's all, I'll be back in a moment." Ami scampered back to the kitchen.

"Every time," Sumner muttered, but he seemed amused more than upset.

"So what brings you three to Gravemont?" Octavia asked as she picked up her glass. She wanted to get the subject off of her. At least until she knew what they wanted.

"You, actually," Sumner interjected as Alces watched Ami walk away. The talking did grab his attention once more and he grinned.

"Quite so, miss," Alces said. "Our business is elsewhere, but we were at an impasse and needed someone of your skill." For some reason, this conversation was making Durante even quieter, and he sipped at his wine. Alces' mead was almost gone after one drink. Sumner was taking his time with his.

Arching an eyebrow again, Octavia rotated her wrist, giving her wine a light swirl in its glass, and then took a sip. "Well, I have been here a little over a month, I suppose that makes me more findable than I usually am." She took another sip, and set the glass down. "Though now I'm curious as to which skill, precisely, sent you looking for me."

"We've heard you can read anything," Sumner started.

"Regardless of the language or the antiquity," Durante added, hopeful.

"All those things," Alces said, then finished his mead.

"Oh!" Octavia smiled more genuinely than she had since they came in. While Octavia had made a number of friends and even more acquaintances over the years that valued her various abilities, it was usually her patron, not her skills, that sent strangers looking for her.

The change in mood certainly caught all three of their attention. So much so that no one noticed when Ami returned, hefting a surprisingly large tray on one shoulder and holding three mugs of mead in the other hand. She dropped all the mugs before Alces, then carefully maneuvered the tray down and onto the table, leaving it for them.

"Enjoy, folks," Ami said, resting a hand on Alces shoulder and winking to Octavia before sashaying away.

"I do have the skill you're seeking," Octavia said as Ami walked away. "And I will respect your want to wait until after food to dive into the meat of it."

"It appears as though the meat is right here," Alces declared with a laugh that filled the small drinking hall. Upon the tray was the haunch of a boar, surrounded by roast potatoes and ears of corn. It looked like enough food for a squad of soldiers. Sumner went to reach for a piece when Alces placed a hand on his shoulder and smiled at Octavia, waiting.

"Oh! You didn't need to—I mean—," she stumbled a little in her surprise, but quickly took some of the boar and sides for herself and motioned for the rest to go ahead. Picking up her wine, she waited until they had all served themselves before she began eating.

"Sorry," Sumner said with a grin that had a hint of fang, "we don't usually have a woman in our group." A not entirely appropriate thought involving Sumner and his teeth flitted through Octavia's mind, but she locked that down immediately. These three had come seeking her aid. She could remain professional.

Alces patted Sumner's shoulder and motioned. Sumner went after the piece he wanted and Durante took a small bit of meat and started to nibble on it. Once everyone had gotten a share, Alces ripped a chunk of the boar off and started to happily munch on it. It was fascinating how he ate ravenously but in a way that also seemed well mannered. Almost. He was doing his best. She quietly wondered what the three of them were to each other. They had clearly been traveling together for a little while based on their ease with one another. Sure, Durante looked uncomfortable, but she would almost guarantee that she was the one making him uncomfortable.

As they ate, the three chatted with Octavia about adventuring, things they'd encountered and conquered, a couple of laughs and comments about Alces' requirement for raucous victory celebrations. She was able to determine that they had been traveling together for at least a couple years. Durante looked at ease as the three of them talked, but still avoided too much interaction with her. She didn't think he had a problem with her. She was beginning to think he was shy. Perhaps, specifically, shy around women.

Between the four of them, especially Alces who seemed bottomless, they destroyed the boar and the trimmings. Alces stood as the stool creaked again and decided it was best to stay standing, which led to him towering over the table, as he finished his fourth mug of mead.

"Now I'm sure you'd like to know what we're up to, eh?" Sumner asked Octavia, taking a sip of his second mead.

"I would, yes," she said, leaning forward. "So do tell, what is this task that you require my assistance with?"

Turning, Sumner raised a brow to Durante. "I think that's where you come in, mate," he said.

The pale man cleared his throat and sat up straight, smiling awkwardly. "Um, yes. Well, I, um... I'm trying to fix—"

"Concoct a powerful new elixir," Alces interjected but let Durante continue. That was a redirect if Octavia had ever seen one.

"Right, make a new elixir, and we think we know where I might be able to find an old tome on components, where to find them, how they're used, and so on. But, well, we don't know what language it's going to be in, but we can be sure it's not going to be in common."

"Or draconic," Alces laughed.

"Or even elven." Sumner added.

"There's also a good chance it's protected under spells or enchantments. So, someone who can read any language to make sure we have the right book, and knows magic, would be invaluable," Durante was finally able to work out.

"Hmm." She picked up her wine, and took a drink as she considered. "How far away is the tome you need?"

"We, um, we believe it's about forty or so leagues to the northwest, in a tower in the mountains," Durante answered.

"Over a week each way," Sumner said.

"Rather advantageous that you were on our way," Alces said with a grin and finished the last of his mead.

"Not a short trip, then," she reflected, and considered for another moment. "What is the compensation?"

"Why, the payment of adventure! A cut of whatever we find, the sense of doing good, and a celebration of victory afterwards," Alces said soundly.

"We're negotiable," Sumner said with a chuckle. "What's your asking price?"

Octavia looked down into her wine cup as she thought it over. She knew she looked successful, but the truth was she was just getting by. Some habits were hard to curb, like a taste for well made clothing in sensual fabrics, and some of those habits hit harder now that her father was no longer paying for her lifestyle. It had been years, but still.

"A quarter of what we find is acceptable," she said after a moment, and she saw Sumner nod cautiously. "And additionally, knowledge is important to me. I would like first choice of what tomes remain after we have secured what you require. And there is one more thing."

Straightening up, she reached over and set a hand on the small stack of books and maps that were still on the end of the table between her and Sumner. "I am at an impasse with the reason I came to Gravemont. I need to get into the mausoleum. I have found the way, but the doors are quite locked and even if I could unlock them I don't think I'm strong enough to move them. The locals don't care about the mausoleum. We can take whatever we want from it. I only need the book. And maybe to grab a few things to cover my expenses."

"So what do you think? You help me, I'll help you?"

Sumner was about to speak and was immediately cut off by Alces. "It would be our immense pleasure, Miss Baudelaire. We will light the darkness that covers your path," the great dragonkin knight said, holding his hand aloft where a ball of light did, indeed, appear. "No lock can withstand Sumner's deft hands, and should the mechanism bar our way, I have no doubt Durante here can conjure up a counter. Once that is dealt with, I will toss the doors aside with ease. Your quest is now ours."

Sumner rolled his eyes but shrugged. They were contracted now, or as good as they could be minus a handshake or a writ. Durante almost spit up the wine he was drinking but kept it in as he held back a chuckle. Clearly they were used to and amused by Alces' antics. Leaning forward on the table once more, Octavia smothered a laugh in her hand and then made it look like she was resting her chin on her palm.

"Well, if we're in agreement, we can head into the mausoleum tomorrow," she said, gaze flitting between the three of them. "You should know, it's still very haunted. I've cleared out the path to the doors, but we will encounter more once inside."

"Excellent," Alces said, holding out his large, clawed, scaled hand to Octavia.

Straightening up, Octavia took Alces' hand and they shook on the deal. Another not entirely appropriate thought chased through her mind involving the size of those hands and how strong he likely was. She squashed that one as well. She was not going to potentially ruin this job. Besides, she still wasn't completely certain what the three of them were to one another. Sumner seemed to appreciate her assets, as it were, though he was also doing a very good job of not leering. Octavia pointedly ignored the part of her brain that said he should be rewarded for that. When taking her hand, Alces bowed towards it but made no motion of kissing it or the air above it, honoring her and the agreement.

"I look forward to working with you," she said, genuinely.

"Tomorrow, then. We'll pay for dinner. Sumner, pay sweet Ami. Can you recommend an inn? Is there an inn?" Alces' train of thought verbalized out of him. Durante dabbed gently at his mouth with a napkin before going back to working on his wine. Sumner got up and headed towards the bar to talk with Ami about payment.

"Yes, there is an inn. I can show you where it is when we're done here, I'm also staying there." She shrugged, and smiled. "Things have been fairly quiet, so there should be room for you."

"There is rarely room for me but they're welcome to try," Alces said with a laugh.

A sudden giggle caught Octavia's attention, the source being Ami as Sumner chatted with her, slowly counting out some coins from a pouch. The thought that Octavia might have some competition for Ami's affection almost made her giggle. She'd have to warn Sumner, though—while Octavia had not been Ami's first time, the barmaid had yet to be with a man.

With his drink done, Durante stood up and gave Octavia a little bow as well. "Thank you, Miss Baudelaire. I really appreciate you joining us on this. Should everything go right, I may be forever in your debt."

Taking the cue, Octavia also rose and smiled at Durante. "If we're going to work together, please call me Octavia or Tavi. I am glad I was available to assist."

She picked up her wine and drank off the rest of it, then proceeded to start gathering up her things. She was glad the books had been on Sumner's side of the table. Alces did his best, but she suspected she'd have some grease stains on her maps if they'd been closer to him. Almost as if reading her thoughts, Durante pulled out a small bottle and Alces held out his hands. A few drops on each, and the massive knight rubbed his hands together, all the remains of the boar and corn disappearing and his scales shimmering once more.

She smiled at Durante again. An alchemist, then. But what a simple yet clever thing to devise. She wondered if it worked on other substances. She'd certainly gotten covered in a number of muddy, grimy, sticky things at different points in this adventure of hers.

Sumner came back and smiled. "All settled, then? Shall we head out?"

"But of course. We'll drink the place dry when we return victorious," Alces said. "Miss, forgive me, Octavia, would you like some assistance with your materials?"

"Hm?" Octavia looked from Alces to the pile of books she was currently attempting to carry in one go. "Oh...well, if you don't mind..."

"Not in the least," he said. Reaching over, Alces carefully hefted the items in one hand with ease. Despite his outward appearances and his boisterous attitude, the knight seemed to understand when to be mindful of delicate things. "Onward!"

Durante picked up his strange device and slung it over his shoulder as Sumner slid past all of them and opened the door, waiting for everyone to pass.

"This way," Octavia said, leading them down the cobbled road towards the looming edifice. "It's not far." She briefly considered attempting to keep the natural sway out of her step, but decided they should get used to it now. She was not going to magically become less provocative on the road, that was for certain.

To their credit, the gentlemen did not make any comments or lewd noises despite being behind such a lusciously swaying rump. No, they were relatively quiet save the occasional comment about the scenery. She would have to tell them who she was bound to eventually. If they were going to be traveling together for weeks, it would have to come up at some point. But maybe it could wait a while.

The evening air was starting to cool and the mausoleum loomed in the sunset, like it did every evening. It was understandable why the farmers wanted the place gone. Unfortunately, it was a large complex and anything short of an entire mining company was barely going to put a dent in it. That, however, was none of their concerns. She turned down a little path with dozens of flowers lining the walk, up towards the Shining Lantern Inn.

Once more, Sumner somehow got in front of Octavia without a sound and opened the door for the group to let them in. The Shining Lantern was one of the only good things that had come out of the old noble family descending upon the village. The nobles had grand parties and events which required space for guests, so a sizable inn was built and established.

Heavily under utilized these days, the Shining Lantern was still kept up by the modern owners. It was mostly used for housing seasonal help, when needed, and hosting the harvest festival, which was a grand event many traveled to the small village for. So, most of the time, it was empty save for the occasional traveler and the locals felt fine with donating here and there to make sure the building remained in good shape.

"More surprises from Gravemont," Alces said as they walked in. "What wonderful lodging!"

The proprietor, an elderly man by the name of Paul, had owned the place for the past 50 years and took pride in it. Seeing the massive knight step in, voice booming, did give him a moment of pause.

"Um, th-thank you, ser. How can I help you this evening," he was able to get out.

"Three rooms, please. Basic as you have but big enough for him," Sumner got out, sliding to the front of the group and motioning towards Alces.

"Oh, yes, we can do that. Oh, hello, Octavia," Paul said, giving her a friendly smile.

"Hello, Paul," she responded with a warm smile. He'd always been kind to her, and old enough that while he could tell she was quite lovely, he had no illusions about doing anything about it. "Is Mariah in the kitchen? I won't need dinner tonight, but I was hoping for some tea."

"I believe she was prepping for tomorrow's breakfast. Think she was waiting up for you anyway. Go ahead," he said, waving her in the direction of the kitchen. Octavia had been there nearly a month, he wasn't worried about her causing any trouble.

Paul retrieved three keys and handed them to Sumner. "There you... gentlemen are. Breakfast is at dawn until the food is gone. If you need anything, be quick about it, I'm going to bed soon myself." The old man laughed at himself and waved them off as well.

"Excellent! Thank you, sir. I'm sure the rooms will be without flaw," Alces said and started to head upstairs. "See you in the morning, Octavia. Busy day ahead of us."

"See ya then," Sumner said, giving Octavia a wink and a smile, then followed Alces up.

"Have a good night," Durante added with a little wave, then nodded to himself and followed the rest of them up the stairs.

"See you all in the morning." She waited until they had ascended enough to be out of sight, then headed towards the kitchens. It was easy enough to get tea and a plate of biscuits. Octavia warned Mariah that they had more guests, and Mariah heavily implied that she could sneak up to Octavia's rooms that evening. Octavia sighed and smiled, but said she had an early morning.

"I need to stop sleeping with the staff," Octavia muttered to herself once she was heading back up the stairs.

Three healthy lads, yours for a few weeks. What a treat, Octavia heard in her mind as she headed towards her room. *I can't wait to taste that.*

Kamvasana didn't have a lot of warlocks under their bond, so they tended to take particular interest in their goings on. Especially when lust was in the air. Thankfully, by this point, Octavia was used to the voice of her patron randomly popping up, and so didn't startle or falter, but she did grumble as she set her tea down on the desk in her room.

"We have a working relationship," she said to the air—Kamvasana would hear her. "I don't even know if they fancy girls. Well, other than Sumner, he's definitely interested. But that's besides the point!"

Oh, they all do. That damn paladin, however. Chaste he is not, but principled he definitely is.

"Oh Gods, not *principles*," Octavia shot back dryly.

Well, best of luck keeping things professional. Don't forget your vow... those long trips on the road do get ever so lonely.

Octavia recognized a threat when she heard it. Sighing, she opened up her journal and flipped to a series of pages that was full of dates, names, and hashmarks. It had been three days since she'd satisfied her side of the pact. She had four more days. She was safe for right now.

"Tonight I am getting sleep," Octavia said firmly, closing the journal. "And tomorrow we breach the mausoleum. Alces made a comment about a raucous celebration once we were done. I'm sure I'll be able to pull someone aside to keep you satisfied then."

For now, of course, the voice came, sultry yet dangerous, *I only want you to have a good time, my dearest. Sometimes you need a little push.* Octavia could feel the presence disappear. They'd said their piece, they'd prodded happily. It was enough for now.

Sighing again, Octavia tucked the journal away and sat down at the desk. It was then that she realized her books were still sitting at the front desk where Alces had set them down. Groaning again, she got back up and headed downstairs. It was fine. She would go over her notes, finish her tea, make sure she was ready for tomorrow. This was a chance. She wasn't going to screw this up.

TWO

The next morning came sooner than Octavia was used to as Alces' booming voice echoed through the inn. She could only blame herself. After all, the best view was the room right over the front entrance. It let her examine the mausoleum from her room and examine the energies swirling around it in relative comfort. But noise traveled and the windows were currently open.

"Gods help me, they're early risers." Rolling out of the bed, Octavia dragged herself to her luggage and pulled out fresh clothes, her sturdier pants that could take a beating and one of her less delicate shirts. The pants still looked painted-on, like all her pants did, and the neckline of the shirt plunged far enough to see the protection amulet that nestled between her breasts. She swept her hair up into a bun to keep it out of the way, but curls practically teased themselves out around her face and at the back of her neck. Bracers, shinguards, and she grabbed her gloves before shoving the maps into her satchel and heading downstairs.

Paul was behind the counter again, and he smiled up at Octavia as she came down the stairs. "It's a good thing we don't have any other guests. We're about out of breakfast already," he chuckled and nodded his head towards the dining room.

Adjusting her pack, she smiled back at Paul. "If it's any consolation, I'm certain they'll pay you extra for it," she said. "Though speaking of, I suppose I should get in there while there's something to eat." She nodded to the innkeeper and headed into the dining area to see the carnage.

They had definitely put a dent in what was offered at breakfast. Of course, they didn't have many guests so Mariah didn't typically make that much. She had made more, given the sudden influx, but it appeared to be barely enough. Alces was awake and chipper. Sumner did not seem to agree with mornings as much as Alces did, and Durante seemed to be asleep in his chair. To Octavia's surprise, however, there was a plate at the table that had a napkin resting atop it, right in front of an unoccupied chair.

"Ah, there's our alluring warlock," Alces said and Sumner turned. "Come, we've saved you a meal." Alces' outburst woke the pale man and he looked around, dazed. His pink eyes landed on Octavia and he gave her a soft smile and a little wave before seeming to nod off again.

"You're a surprisingly considerate group," Octavia remarked quietly as she sat down and removed the napkin. There were pots of tea on the table, and they seemed fresh. She poured herself a cup. "And good morning."

"I did not want you to start the day hungry," Alces said, smiling at her.

"I hope you all had a pleasant night," she remarked, not wanting to completely forgo the semblance of civility.

"Good night, loud morning," Sumner said, rubbing his eyes. He did not have any of the signs of someone with a hangover, just someone who would rather be sleeping right then.

"Oh yes, I heard you upstairs," she remarked with a faint smile. "It's how I knew you were up and I should probably join you."

Durante stirred awake again and blinked, looking over at Octavia again. "Oh, Octavia, good morning," he said followed by a large yawn. Octavia saw fangs, sizable ones, there was no second guessing. They disappeared when his mouth closed. "When did you get here?"

It didn't seem that Durante had caught Octavia's surprised expression as she looked at him. The eyes and skin certainly suggested vampirism, but he wouldn't be able to survive the day. A halfbreed, maybe? She had heard of such things. Another inappropriate thought bubbled up in Octavia's psyche—she had a thing for being bitten, and with teeth like his, she would very much feel it.

"I only just came down," she assured him, snapping out of it. "It's nice to know I'm not the only one who isn't much of a morning person."

"I usually let them sleep in, but not today. Today, adventure is afoot," Alces said, still grinning. "So, they can blame me, I'm quite excited to see this mausoleum, and the daunted door that blocks your path."

She let out a small laugh. "I hope it's not too disappointingly simple for you."

"He's a cheery fellow," Sumner said, sitting up and picking at his breakfast. It looked like they had, for the most part, finished eating. Only Durante had nearly as much food as Octavia left. "He wakes with the light, I don't think he can help it."

"Serving the Spree Spirits certainly has its advantages," Durante added with another yawn, then shook his head to try and wake up some more.

Mariah came back in, pouring cups of coffee for Durante and Sumner. "Morning, Tavi. Did you sleep well?" she asked, something in her tone a touch petulant.

"Yes, thank you," Octavia sipped her tea and refused to look apologetic or sheepish. It seemed the girl was officially no longer a safe bed partner if she was getting pouty.

Not wanting to be the one holding everyone up, she set in to breakfast. She ate with a healthy appetite, and did not do so lightly like one might expect from a woman of her standing. She wasn't sloppy, but there was a certain amount of delicacy she had abandoned while on her own. She still used the right fork. Some things were too ingrained.

When breakfast finally concluded, Sumner produced a sum of coin and paid both Mariah and Paul, and Octavia knew it was more than enough. Not excessive, they weren't flaunting wealth, but certainly a percentage above board. Enough to compensate for the increase of food the dragonkin needed. By now the sun fully faced the mausoleum, and it was time to be on their way.

"Any advice for this hall of the dead?" Alces asked. "Traps you've encountered, spirits not yet laid to rest, glyphs to be wary of?"

"Um...," Octavia waited until they had all drifted out of the inn and were on the path in the sunlight. She motioned for them to follow her. "The warding I've encountered so far is very typical, and I think I've broken most of the wards. They're the usual guard dog style glyphs that would have let the old gravekeeper know someone was breaking in. The spirits, though..."

She adjusted her pack as they turned and headed up the winding path towards the cemetery and the mausoleum beyond. "There *are* some angry spirits. But there are more...hungry ones. The last generations of the Venebore family became involved in a particularly interesting magical cult. One with a very heavy focus on... well... let's say the pleasures of the flesh. And that is the wing we need to get to." She let out a small laugh. "You can hear them at night, if you're near the right wing of the mausoleum. I don't know how much they can actually do to the living, but may as well be ready for it."

"Well, that's certainly going to make for an interesting challenge," Sumner said, rolling his head back. "D, you got any of that spectrebane left?"

Opening his bag, Durante shuffled through it for much longer than the size of the bag would suggest, his arm reaching in further than should be possible, but he did produce a bottle that was pale blue in color, its contents seeming to glow. "Yes, still have some left. I always keep at least two bottles since the Bonny Fair incident."

"Fantastic! Their incorporealness will not protect them should we need to defend ourselves," Alces grinned.

Sumner took the bottle from Durante and tucked it into his own pouch. "I'm going to assume your magic works on the spirits?" he asked of Octavia.

Nodding slowly, Octavia quickly did a mental inventory as they crossed through the gates into the cemetery. "Yes. One spell in particular has been most effective so far, but I have a couple others that I believe will also do the job. There is always the hope that the daylight will keep them at bay, but, well....I don't know how haunted the inside of the mausoleum is. I don't think it's enough to warp the area. If nothing else, there's no bleed over into the outlying buildings; I haven't encountered any spirits, any weather phenomena, nothing like that. It's just the main mausoleum."

"Contained within, good," Alces said as they strode past the gates of the cemetery. "Unfortunately we would not be able to lure them into the light. That's fine, we bring our own!"

The old graveyard, pristinely maintained by the town, had a sweet peacefulness to it. As they climbed the hill, however, the grounds quickly became far less maintained. They could still make out the old path, and followed the crumbling bricks up to an intimidating structure of marble and sandstone. The building was overgrown and some of the parapets and grotesques had fallen and shattered on the ground below. Even if the townsfolk had been interested in reclaiming this place, there was no bringing it back without great expenditures of magic.

As they passed through the doors into the vestibule, Alces held up his hand and a bright ball of light appeared, like he had last night. This one was far brighter and functioned easily as a torch. Even with the light, the hall was dark and the air heavy. The first step in and anyone would tell you it was haunted. It was far colder than outside, and they could already hear the first stirrings which, for now, sounded like wind. Cobwebs, dust, and intruding vines were everywhere. If the old noble family had made any attempt to make the place cheerful, it had rotted away generations ago.

"I'm guessing we're not going to encounter anything until we get to that door of yours, or after?" Durante asked as he took a small vial and attached it to the top of his strange device. Flipping a small switch, the vial lit up and there was the distinct sound of a seal being released. This time he held it in both his hands, the long metal barrel pointed away from him, the wooden handle braced as one would hold a crossbow.

"I would be very surprised if we did," Octavia said, adjusting her satchel once more. "Though I didn't make it past the vestibule, so we may have plenty to occupy ourselves with very soon."

They crossed the large room, and it was easy to see where Octavia had already been. A few piles of ash, a streak of slimy residue that ended in a scorch mark. The doors in question were before them, stone and quite large. There was another scorch mark across the one door that looked fresh. There was also a noted lack of dust or cobwebs in the vicinity.

"Sumner, my good man, have a look," Alces said, moving towards the door so that the orb in his hand illuminated it. Sumner stepped up and cracked his knuckles.

"I'll have it open in a shake, Tavi," Sumner said with a grin, then started to look the door over. Meanwhile, Durante produced an eyeglass with a strap that he placed over one eye, adjusting which lens was in place. It took a little more than the shake promised, and soon grumblings were coming out of Sumner.

"Ah, fuck," he exclaimed with a sigh and Alces put a hand on his shoulder. "Yeah, sorry, this is just frustrating. It has six locks and they all need to be turned at the same time. Problem is…" he explained, standing up for a moment, then spread his arms out as wide as he could. "I need to pick six locks," he continued, a growl still in his voice, "set the pins, then we need to figure out a way for us to turn all six at the same time." Stepping up to the door, and following his fingers, one could make out the hidden keyholes he had exposed - just out of reach. They were on opposite sides of the great door.

"Oh, fun." Octavia considered for a moment. "Hm. Alces, if you have the wingspan to get two at once, then Comicha could help."

"Who?" the three of them asked at the same time as Alces shined the light on Octavia.

"Ah, yes. Alces, don't smite my familiar." Octavia reached out and swirled her right hand. A glyph appeared on the ground, the same vibrant blue as her eyes, with symbols unlike any wizard runes one might find in the schools. The glyph glowed and then mist rose up from it. With surprising quickness, the mist coalesced into...an imp? It wasn't any type of imp you'd see in a grimoire. Blue skin that deepened to indigo at its hands and feet and horns, with matching indigo hair. Rather than the craggy exterior you expected from an imp, this creature was as soft and smooth as its mistress, and also as feminine looking. In fact, the imp was exaggeratedly feminine in feature. Little wings that didn't look big enough to work snapped out behind it, and its eyes opened to reveal a kaleidoscopic range from blue to pink.

"Mistress!" The imp's voice was cheerful and chiming. "I am here to help! Whatever you need, whatever your desire, I—" the imp stopped, seeing that there were others in the room. "NEW FRIENDS!"

The little imp zipped around from Alces, to Sumner, to Durante, each of whom looked a touch bewildered, and back again. "Eeeeee, she never lets me meet anyone! Hi! I'm Comicha! If you need anything, anything at all, I would be so happy to help you!"

Octavia sighed. "Comicha..."

The little imp zipped back over to Octavia, dropping to the ground in front of her. "Yes, Mistress!"

Alces crouched down and held the ball forward to get a closer look at the familiar. His head tilted to one side, then to the other, then he started to chuckle. The chuckle rose as Alces did to a stand, becoming a full bore laugh. Sumner was only slightly better in that he concealed his laugh behind his hand, but his face spelled amusement all over it. Durante's eyes grew wide and his jaw went a little slack in amazement.

"By the spirits." Alces exclaimed when his laugh had peaked, "she's as adorable as her conjurer! There is a clear reason the spirits sent me here!" Adorable wasn't a term Octavia had heard used to describe herself before. Technically it was describing Comicha, and including her by comparison, but she would take it.

Sumner cleared his throat and removed his hand, but was still smiling. "Okay, I'll just, uh, get on those pins. D, pick up your jaw."

Durante snapped out of it and closed his mouth, letting out a short chuckle. "Well, I'll be. Hello, Comicha."

The imp took to the air again, smiling, and waved to Durante. "Hello! Need anything? A drink? A massage? Do you want me to go—"

"Comicha!" Octavia's tone was a little sharp, but not mean. "You're here because we're going to need your help turning a lock."

The imp drooped a little bit, and lost some altitude. "That's it?"

Octavia sighed. "That's it for now. If you're good you can stick around and maybe help us once we're in."

Durante looked between the two then cleared his own throat. Slinging his contraption over his shoulder, he moved to one side of the door, next to where Sumner was currently working. He had a brief conversation with him, and Durante held onto the pick Sumner had in place. Alces stepped up to the door and reached out, getting the same talk. As Sumner knelt down to work on the lowest lock, he glanced over his shoulder.

"Okay, which one of you two wants to take this one?" he asked.

"Comicha could do that, unless there's a higher one that would be hard for the rest of us to reach." She reached out and ruffled the imp's hair, which made the imp squee happily again. "She's a very steady flyer. What do you think?"

"I think Alces has the top ones, otherwise I'd have a problem picking them," Sumner grinned. "Alright, cutie, come here and I'll explain what we're doing."

Comicha zipped over. "Anything you want, handsome!"

Sighing again, Octavia made her way over and hoped her imp wouldn't say anything too revealing too soon. She was enjoying this, working with a team that needed her expertise rather than her...well.

Sumner finished setting the picks as they both got in place. When he was done, Sumner explained how it would work. The picks weren't quite like keys, and they had to be held in a particular way so they would keep the pins held in place and could be turned. He gave a brief explanation, then moved out of the way and headed towards the other side of the door.

"Alright, Tavi, give me a minute to get these set up," he commented as he went to work on the three locks on this side.

It was hard not to smile a little. She'd invited them to call her Tavi, but it was nice to have Sumner actually do it. She walked over and patiently waited. She didn't have to worry about Comicha - once given a task, the imp did it thoroughly and to completion, whatever the task was.

Each lock went progressively faster as Sumner learned how they were made and what made them click. She and him were the same height, so it didn't matter which took which lock, so when all was said and done, he was crouched down in front of her, hands on the last pick.

"Alright, everyone, we will turn on 3. Those on the left, clockwise, those on the right, counter-clockwise. Does anyone have any questions?" Sumner asked, looking down the line, then up at Octavia.

Octavia looked down at Sumner, a curl falling in her eyes as she did, smiled and nodded. "Ready when you are."

"Okay," he said, looking back towards the lock, "One, two, three!"

Each person did their duty, Alces having the hardest part as his massive hands were scrunched up around the picks and he had to turn in opposite directions. Not impossible, just awkward. Sure enough, there was a series of clicks followed by one more massive click. The door, it seemed, was unlocked. Everyone save Alces stepped back and he placed both of his hands on the large double-door, pushing. Nothing moved for a moment, then cracking sounds started to fill the vestibule, along with dust falling out of the cracks and joints of the door. The immense portal hadn't been tended to or oiled in hundreds of years, it wasn't surprising that it was sticky.

Finally, movement started to occur. Alces growled, the leather straps of his armor creaking as they were pulled taut by his muscles flexing under the padding. The door gave way, both sides easing open until Alces stepped forward and shoved, both doors snapping and most of the joints of rust that were once hinges popped off with dangerous velocity. One door fell off entirely, the other hung on by a single hinge. Neither would ever close again. There was a fit of coughing as the door that had fallen kicked up a considerable amount of dust.

As the dust cleared, Octavia looked from the doors over to Alces and back. "Damn."

"We have penetrated the depths of this mausoleum," Alces proclaimed in victory.

Comicha flew up, giggling, and perched on the dragonkin's shoulder. "Wow, you're strong! That's amazing! I mean, everyone is stronger than me, but you're really strong! I bet you could pick up Mistress easily!"

Octavia was also very confident that was true, but did not want to get into that conversation just now. No effort was made to hide the glare Octavia aimed at her imp, who remained happily perched on Alces' massive shoulder.

"With one hand," he said resolutely, "but not unless she asked. Now then, let us see what there is to see." Alces made no motion to shoo Comicha off. Bringing back the ball of light, he cast it into the room.

Grumbling to herself, Octavia pulled out one of the small maps, the original architectural plans in fact, and looked over it. "All right," she said, "let's go in."

The inner sanctum was the size of a small manor. They were now in the main hall, which had three wings branching off to the north, east, and south. The main hall would have once been a comfortable place to lounge, and perhaps reflect on those who had passed, based on the remains of the furniture. There was a skylight here, allowing some faint light in, but it was mostly overgrown by the vines that covered the outside of the mausoleum. There were no windows. As they moved into the room, the sconces and chandelier flickered and flared to life, cheerfully mundane flames illuminating the hall.

There were steps down into a lower level of the main hall, with more places to lounge, the short wall lined with low bookcases filled with books. Various trinkets also sparkled in the candlelight, covered in dust but carefully displayed.

"This is the main hall," Octavia mused, looking at the plans. "What I am looking for is to the left, in the North wing. Straight ahead is the trophy room, which could be worth looking at. To the right are the oldest tombs."

"This is your quest, Octavia, you decide," Alces said, turning towards her, fists on his hips.

"I figured we'll grab your book, right, then we can raid the rest of the place," Sumner suggested, pulling his picks out of the busted doors and tucking them away.

"Be really careful," Durante said, stepping in and unslinging his device. "There's a presence here."

Alces pulled the shield off his back and the mace from his belt, readying them and adjusting them in his grip. Sumner unsheathed his long sword and took out the bottle Durante had given him earlier, drizzling the liquid onto the blade. Tucking the bottle away, he gave it a gentle wipe with a thin cloth, spreading the oil out.

"To the left it is, then," Octavia said, tucking the plans back in her satchel. She didn't bother taking out a weapon—she hadn't even brought her crossbow with her, it wouldn't do any more to a ghost than the dagger at her hip. She would rely on magic if she needed it. And she probably would.

It seemed they had only gone a few steps in the direction she wanted them to go when the candles started to flicker. All around them, the flames whipped around on their candles and seemed to go out, only to burst into green flame. Moaning started to fill the room from all sides, but it was confusing. It sounded like the usual noise of haunted spirits but it was mixed with the more recognizable moans of pleasure.

"This is going to scar me, isn't it," Durante said, leveling his contraption, bracing it against his shoulder as he looked around.

"Oh, more than likely," Octavia said, a touch wearily. This wasn't her first exposure to such a thing.

"Steady, Durante. They're but spirits, nothing we can't handle," Alces said, the mace in his hand starting to glow with bright yellow light.

The deeper they went, the louder the sounds got, and soon the green light started to expose the haunted spirits occupying the halls of the dead. Ghostly forms of men and women, misty white tinged with a glowing green similar to the candle flames, seemingly occupied with each other in all manners of copulation. As they moved down the hall she sighed. She wondered vaguely what had left the spirits here trapped in such a manner. Surely after centuries they were tired of it. The ghostly figures faded in and out at first, but they became more solid and easier to perceive the longer the four adventurers walked through the hall.

Sumner waved his sword around carefully, narrowing his eyes. The spirits weren't moving yet, like they hadn't noticed the group. Then he made eye contact with one, who paused its activities to leer threateningly.

"Oh, fuck me," Sumner growled.

"Happily," the spirit suddenly exclaimed in a voice that was far more menacing than excited. The party of debauchery disbursed from their coupling and tripling and started to advance towards the group.

"Um, shoot, yes," Durante said, trying to figure out which ghost was coming for him first, "shoot, yes?!"

"Oh, Gods damn it all," Octavia muttered. "Comicha! See if you can find an anchor!"

"Yes, Mistress!" The imp leapt off Alces' shoulder and zipped around the room in her quest. Octavia had learned early that Comicha was useless as a combatant but still very good at many things.

"Hold," Alces said, pressing his shield in front of him, "they may not be able to do anything."

"We sure we want to test that," Sumner said as the one that started this whole thing flew at him, and through him. The leather-clad thief shuddered and grunted, almost doubling over but held his ground. Looking over at the spirit who had run through Sumner, Octavia brought her hand, which briefly crackled with blue energy then shot out at the ghost in question. The ghost let out another moan, a rather loud one, but dispersed into faint mist.

"They can definitely fucking do something," Sumner said through gritted teeth as his growl became much more animalistic.

The fight initially seemed one sided. With so many ghosts, it was impossible to keep track of them all, especially since they weren't limited by the barriers of physical objects. Alces learned his shield was useless as one passed through him. He made an interesting grunt of a noise, but turned and smacked it with his mace. The mace pulsed with a burst of light when it hit the ghost and it, too, dispersed. Sumner grinned ferally, his teeth becoming points and round black marks formed on his skin, on the sides of his face and down into his leathers. His eyes narrowed and his arms and legs lengthened. As the ghost dived for him, he seemed impossible to hit. Twisting, turning, bending in ways that were very impressive to move out of the way while swinging with his sword, the oil seemed to do the trick as the ghosts split then disappeared. Durante finally used his contraption, squeezing his hand around the handle and there was a loud boom that filled the room. The ghost he was aiming at seemed to pop as a blue streak emanated from his odd weapon, impacting into the spirit. As he swung around to look for another target, a ghost came up behind him and flew through him as well. He folded slightly and whined.

"Oh, that's not fair," he grumbled but was able to right himself again, firing off another shot.

The ghost of a man in an acolyte's robe came up from under the floor and flew straight through Octavia, sending surprisingly powerful shivers of excitement through her body, causing goosebumps and the hair on her neck to stand on end. Moaning, Octavia fell to her knees, making her an easy target for a second spirit. The sensation was delicious for all its strangeness, and an unfortunate side effect of her pact was sensitivity. Panting, Octavia reached into her satchel for a vial of dust, which she cracked and poured in a sloppy circle around her. Tendrils of blue energy rose around her. As a third ghost came for her, it was ensnared by the tendrils, and cried out before disintegrating.

Comicha zoomed to her mistress's side. "I can't find anything! They're just...here! And ooooo, are they tingly!" The imp was impossible to phase.

Protected, Octavia sent bolts of energy at another ghost as more attempted to come for her but couldn't cross the barrier. The battle adrenaline wasn't helping her body to calm down, but now she could concentrate enough to cast. Durante smacked something on his jacket and dozens of small metal shards burst out, then hung in the air no farther than five feet from his person. They were enchanted, at least enough to disperse any ghost that tried to get through to him. His contraption fired off again and again, each time popping another ghost. Alces was doing his best, but he was a big target. He would strike down two or three, but another ghost would get in and fly into him. His nostrils seemed to be hissing out white puffs of frozen air and he was slamming his mace against his shield to work himself up. Sumner moved in, quickly slicing and stabbing the ghosts that Alces didn't get. The way they moved demonstrated that they'd been fighting together for a while, and instinctively knew where the other was.

Between the four of them, the spiritual population dwindled to the point the restless spirits felt it wiser to disturb a different corner of the mausoleum. Once it felt safe, or at least calmed to the point they didn't have to be on edge, Alces collapsed to one knee, chuckling deeply.

Sumner seemed to shift again, back to the handsome gentleman Octavia had seen before, and patted the big knight on the shoulder. "I know, big guy, I know. Fuuuuuck," he muttered.

"Well, that was," Alces started with a grunt, "well, yes. Miss Baudelaire, Little Miss Comicha, are you alright?"

"Oh, I am fiiiiiiiiine," Comicha sang out, perhaps a little too enthusiastically, flying up into the air above the writhing circle that still surrounded Octavia.

Durante swung around again, looking all about before he finally hit the tab on his jacket and the metal shards reattached themselves, hidden under the folds of cloth. He set his device down on its wooden brace and stood behind it, grumbling as he adjusted his clothing as discreetly as possible.

Clear that the battle had ended, Octavia let the circle drop. No longer concentrating on the spell, she suddenly felt her body very keenly and couldn't hold back a whimper. After another breath, she got up off her knees.

"I'm all right," she finally managed, dusting the sand off her pants. "Let's....ohhhhh, gods, I shouldn't have stretched." The tensing of her muscles had almost made her orgasm. "Ahem. Let's press on before they decide to try again."

"Go on ahead," Alces said, waving in the direction Octavia's prize was, "I need a minute."

"I hear that," Sumner said, needing to adjust his pants with a grunt. Octavia's eyes flicked over before she could stop herself, and she got a very good idea of the size of what currently strained Sumner's leathers. He didn't put his sword away, however, and stepped towards where they needed to go, but waited for the others.

Durante had to do much the same, but made sure his back to Octavia when he did. Shuddering again, slightly, he sighed then slung the device. "So, what're we looking for now?" he asked, turning back towards Octavia.

Dragging her gaze away from Sumner, Octavia looked up in Durante's direction. She could feel that her cheeks and lips were still flushed, and knew there was something exceptionally hungry in her gaze. Durante was as pale as he ever way, but his eyes were wide and almost hypnotic. The two of them were caught for a breath. She wet her lips, and then came to her senses and looked away.

"We, um," she dug in her pack for a minute, "we're...it's a book, it was probably...probably buried with Darellia Venebore, it...it should be this way." She headed down the hallway, all the more aware of the exaggerated sway to her hips, and unable to do anything about it.

THREE

As Octavia led them into the next room, each glance backward was rewarded with the guys walking awkwardly behind her, looking everywhere but at her bubble butt swaying in front of them. Her amusement at their discomfort was cut short when they heard a roar from where they had left Alces. Sumner and Durante ignored it and kept walking forward, clearly not something they were worried about. Octavia elected to do the same.

They came to another set of doors. These had blessedly been permanently set open, with heavy ornamental chains holding them in place. Beyond it was a room where instead of more traditional tombs there were three immense, deep seated thrones, with three long decomposed skeletons regally posed in them.

"The Venebore triplets," Octavia said as they approached the macabre display. "Darellia, Evangella, and Baris. Leaders of the Faithful of the Azure Flame. They gave themselves over to selfish pleasure, so much so that they forgot to have heirs, forgot to see to anything other than their immediate wants. Their estates were left in disrepair, they squandered their fortunes, and when they died not a single cousin wanted to come clean up the mess. The estate fell into decay and crumbled years ago. Only the mausoleum remains."

"At least they had fun," Sumner said with a shrug, finally putting his sword away.

There was a table before the three, laid out as if before a feast with empty candelabras and jeweled goblets for wine that would never be poured. There were a few pretty if dusty baubles, and a book. Octavia approached the book carefully, studied it for a moment, and then picked it up. Nothing happened.

Durante adjusted the glass on his eye piece and looked over the table. He made a small noise of satisfaction and pulled the piece up onto his forehead. "No curses, glyphs, or magical traps that I can see. Sumner, want to take a look for something more... traditional?"

Sumner gave a shrug and looked over the table, then slowly crouched, adjusting as he did so, and looked under the table. "Oh, that's interesting," he commented.

Octavia took a moment to examine the book—it was magically locked, but she was fairly certain she knew the charm to open it. "Good, this is it," she said at last, tucking it into her satchel before looking up at Sumner. She was briefly overwhelmed by the reality that he was, in fact, very handsome, and from what she had seen in the other room, possessing of catlike agility. She hoped it didn't show on her face. It probably did.

Reaching under the table, Sumner patted around with his hand until it hit something, then he pulled, and they heard a click. "No traps, but check this out," he said, standing back up and sliding free a small hidden tray. Inside was a key with an absolutely pristine ribbon tied around its bow.

"Know what that's for?" he asked Octavia.

"No, I don't...wait." She paused and dug out a different book, this one looking like a very old beaten up journal, flipping through it to find the section where she'd read about the book she'd come for. "It...might unlock something in the trophy room. Though if it does, you may need to be the one to unlock it. What little I have speaks of a 'wondrous cabinet' that 'confounded thieves but held their greatest treasures.' It makes sense that the key would be here."

"Sure, that's not cryptic or ominous," he said, smirking and rolling his eyes. With a quick swipe, he gathered up the rest of the items from the table and held his hands out for Durante. The pale gentleman pulled out that cleaning solution of his and dabbed it on the jewelry and baubles. A little rubbing from Sumner and the items were sparkling like new.

"Did we find your book, Miss Baudelaire," Alces said as he walked towards them, seemingly fine now.

"Alces, please, Octavia or Tavi," she gently corrected, tucking the old journal away.

"I'm sorry, I meant no disrespect, Octavia," Alces said, the dragonkin said, placing his fist against his chest and giving her a bow.

"It's…it's all right," she said, a little flustered by his gallantry. "Ah, I found what I needed. And Sumner found a key, which hopefully unlocks something interesting in the trophy room."

"Good, I'm glad." Alces smiled his brilliant smile. The dragonkin was impressively huge; she thought back to his comment about being able to lift her with one hand. "I suppose we should move to the trophy room then if there is nothing else here."

Sumner gave him a shrug. "Saw what I saw," he said.

Durante nodded in agreement. "I didn't see anything else either. Spirits have also seemed to have calmed down."

Comicha tugged lightly on Octavia's sleeve. "Mistress?"

Adjusting her satchel, Octavia looked over. "Hm?"

The imp leaned in and said very quietly. "You were staring."

"Gods," she muttered, and brushed that damn curl from her face. "Thank you."

She looked over the table one last time, then nodded to herself and started back towards the main room. "All right, shall we?"

"Let's," Alces said and turned back the way he came. It did, indeed, feel like they had given the spirits enough of a thrashing that they may need a full night to recover. With it still being morning, that gave them plenty of time to check the rest of the mausoleum. Alces made sure he was close by Octavia's side. Their little band may have thrashed the ghosts, but that didn't mean there wasn't something else lurking about.

It was a relief when they made it to the trophy room without further incident, though Sumner had to deal with a comparatively simple lock and Alces had to force the doors open once more. This room, strangely, was in slightly better shape than the throne room, though that might be attributed to the fact that it had been additionally sealed and no corpses had been left to rot in here.

For all that it was dubbed the trophy room, aside from a very well-preserved dragon head and an entire equally well preserved wyvern in the center of the room, this was more a place full of strange antiques and treasures that were on the larger size.

Alces looked up at the dragon head, tilting his head to the side. Considering it fit in this room at all, through the doors, it hadn't been terribly old. "Did they fell you, cousin, or was it true hunters and you were merely brought here?" he asked, mostly to himself, which was about the softest the knight had spoken since they'd met.

There was a large ornate mirror, an ebony cabinet with complicated inlay and no discernable door, two suits of armor that were so ornamented that they couldn't possibly be practical, a number of statues from various stones, and the remains of an odd chair that almost looked like it belonged in a water closet but wasn't quite right. Octavia snickered when she saw the chair.

Sumner walked up to the cabinet and started looking it over. His hand gently caressed over its surfaces, fingertips tracing the inlay as he felt over it. "I'm going to wager that this is the 'wondrous cabinet'?"

"It's the only cabinet, so probably a safe bet," Octavia commented dryly. Comicha flew around the room, but more lazily, taking everything in and, Octavia could tell, getting a little bored and sleepy. She would be ready to dismiss soon.

"Riiiight," Sumner said with an equal amount of dryness and continued his work.

Durante adjusted his eye piece once more and started to look around. When he, too, looked at the chair he couldn't help but snicker as well. "Mi-, uh, Octavia," he said, finally able to manage a casual smile at her, "want to guess what the only magical thing in this room is?"

Looking over, Octavia smiled. "I'm honestly surprised any of it is magical, given that they lost everything by the end, but do tell."

"That, right there," Durante answered, pointing to the chair. "Cleaning spell with a jasmine and vanilla enchantment."

Giggling, Octavia reached out and set a hand on Durante's arm. "Are you serious!? Ha!" Durante smiled back and looked like he felt a little better, standing up a little straighter.

With a heavy sigh, Alces shook his head. "Anything you'd like me to carry back, Octavia?"

Glancing over at Alces, the laughter died off. He was sad. Probably for the dragon and the wyvern, but he was so boisterous and cheerful all the time it seemed all the more heartbreaking when he wasn't.

"Ah, no, thank you," she said as she released Durante. "Aside from the fact that most of this is ridiculous, I... well, I don't have a home to put any of it in anyway."

Across the room, Sumner was muttering to himself excitedly, and the three of them turned to see what he was about. Slowly and surely he was moving segments, flipping latches, placing hidden pegs into discrete recesses. Fingers nimble from picking locks and sensitive to light pressure from checking for traps danced over the polished wooden surface, and the cabinet opened like a flower unfolding.

"There!" He exclaimed triumphantly as three doors swung open to reveal something that initially looked like a very elaborate jewelry stand. "Alright, you wonderous pain in the ass, what's my prize?"

Stepping up near the cabinet, Alces regained a smile. "It appears we've found our payday," he said, still without quite the volume but he was getting there.

Octavia and Durante followed. Octavia had been in this business long enough to know that "treasure" meant different things to different people, and there was a chance that nothing in this cabinet was worth much, but she was still hopeful.

The interior of the cabinet was lined with a slightly moth-eaten velvet. Within each door of the cabinet was a portrait indicating which triplet that particular section belonged to. The door closest to Octavia contained a painting of an attractive man with long black hair and a sardonic expression. That would be Baris. Baris' area had the remains of his personal jewelry, a very lovely grooming kit made of silver inlaid with some shimmering blue metal and precious stones, and... locks of hair. Each one tagged with a jeweled metal plate and a name. Past lovers, it seemed.

Delicately, Octavia lifted one of the tags attached to a still golden curl of hair. She turned it carefully, examining it. "These are certainly worth something," she commented, then set it down. "We can snip the ribbons and take the tags. Should be easy enough to find someone to melt them down and save the gems."

Nodding, Durante extracted a pair of surprisingly delicate shears out of his bag and got on it, handing the tags off to Sumner as he did. Alces moved around to the next open door and made a small sound of surprise. Reaching in, he picked up a short, fat baby dragon carved from a vibrant jade.

"A sweet surprise in all this strangeness," he commented. Octavia left the other two to their task and looked around Alces at the portrait of a woman with a face like Baris's but softer in feature, and dark hair in intricate braids.

"Darellia Venebore," she commented as they looked over the tiny shelves absolutely filled with little carved animals. Some from valuable stones, a couple from gems, and some made of metal with more intricate ornamenting. There was nothing strange or twisted about the figures.

Most of them were a fat, cute version of more exotic creatures, from dragons to unicorns to gryphons, though a few were heavily detailed replicas of more common woodland animals.

There were a few drawers that also held jewelry, and several memento mori—mostly thin braids set in rings or brooches, but at least one tooth suspended in what looked like amber. A rather pointy tooth, at that. As Octavia held it up to the light, Durante glanced over and suddenly looked a little squeamish.

Sumner was the first to reach what had to, by default, be Evangella's cupboard, and he let out a laugh. Curious, Octavia stepped over to see what he'd found. This final collection seemed to be the winner in bizarreness and expense. More personal jewelry, a row of tiny dolls with disturbing eyes—they had clearly been enchanted to follow whomever was in front of them. They weren't the star of the show, however, as Evangella had a rather extensive collection of exquisitely carved male genitalia. Most crafted from semi-precious gems and rare stones, some spun from glass with gorgeous swirling colors, and three in rare metals ornamented with even more precious gems. On the base of each one was carved "Inspired by" followed by a name and a date.

Still snickering, Sumner glanced over at Octavia. "Well, do you know a collector that would buy them? Or maybe you want to keep some yourself?" Octavia snorted, and Alces smacked him.

"I'd say that really ornamented one, for posterity, but it would be worth a fair bit to pop off the gems and melt down the…is that platinum?" She paused, picking up the cock in question, and examining it. "Oh, wow, that's heavy. Um, I'm sure there is a collector for such things, how long do you want to hold onto them to try to find one?"

"Got plenty of space in the sack," Sumner said, holding it open for Octavia, "if I'm not thinking about it, I'm not gonna see it." These were seasoned adventurers, they all had bottomless bags. Good chance Durante even made them.

Shrugging, Octavia started tossing the various cocks into Sumner's bag. "If you ever make it back near Driscoll's Rest, I'm pretty sure you could turn a fair profit on these. Any city of a good size, really."

She dropped the last one into the bag and dusted off her hands. "Not a bad morning, gentlemen. I don't think there's much point in delving into the last wing. It's very old, and any lingering spirits are likely to be angrier. I have my book, and we have a decent haul. Are we content to return?"

"This was your delve, Octavia. If you are done, then we are done. Treasure was had," Alces said, placing his shield back on his back and the mace to his belt.

"Yeah, bit of silliness aside, I'm still not a fan of this place," Durante said, tucking his eye piece away and straightening his jacket.

"Let's bolt, then," Sumner said, and tucked his bag away. It seemed to disappear among the leather. "Good haul, only a little trauma."

Nodding, Octavia adjusted her own satchel. "A strange one, certainly. All right, Comicha, time to go back."

"Okay!" The imp flew back to Octavia.

"You did very well today," Octavia said with a smile, ruffling the imp's hair. "Good girl."

Comicha smiled blissfully and disappeared with a pop. Octavia nodded to herself and turned around, heading back out of the mausoleum with the three gentlemen in tow.

Leaving the shrouded darkness of the mausoleum, the late afternoon sun washed over them and eased some of the lingering discomfort. Octavia shielded her eyes and squinted suspiciously at the setting sun. She didn't think they'd spent that much time in the old crypt, but there had been many reports of the locals losing the day near the mausoleum. Ghosts and time magic were a frequent pairing. It was something to take notes on later. For now, Alces had taken the lead and it seemed the Broken Headstone was their target.

Bursting through the door, it looked like Alces had regained his composure completely. "Sweet Ami, we have returned triumphant! Feast and drink as soon as you can," he called out, heading for a larger table this time, one hopefully ringed with more durable chairs. The initial burst caught Ami off guard, but she recovered quickly and laughed, nodding and headed back into the kitchen. The couple of locals in the tavern looked up curiously, then went back to their drinks.

Rather than sit, Alces started to remove his armor. Octavia realized she hadn't yet seen him out of it. The heavy plate came off a piece at a time, and Sumner offered some assistance here and there. The armor did not at all exaggerate Alces' size. Beneath it he wore a linen shirt and simple breeches, the neck of the shirt open enough for light to catch on the scales of his chest. Once the heavy plate was tucked carefully in a corner, Sumner undid the tight lacing of his jerkin far enough to let his chest breathe. Durante unbuttoned the top two buttons on his linen shirt and opened his vest. Following suit, she popped off her bracers and shoved them in her pack. That way she could push her sleeves up and make sure she didn't get any food on her blouse. And there certainly wasn't anything to undo. Octavia's blouse was always open at the neck. Always.

As they settled, Ami came back out with another massive tray loaded with what Octavia guessed was a leg of venison this time. The barmaid had found a larger tankard somewhere in the back, which she filled with mead and set before Alces. Sumner got a regular sized mug, and Durante and Octavia were given glasses of wine.

Picking up the glass of wine, Octavia knew she had a problem. The day still had her aroused and wanting, her cheeks softly flushed, her nipples pressing obviously against the fabric of her shirt. She had been Kamvasana's warlock long enough that things like the ghosts didn't unnerve her the way they did the others. She did silently reflect as she stared into her wine glass that it probably wasn't really a good sign that the whole experience left her horny rather than feeling off or violated. Sighing, she drank off the entire contents of her wine glass and signaled Ami for another before she started to eat.

It seemed like the previous comments about Alces' love of a victory celebration were true. Drink was unending for as long as the tavern had it available, food was spread and torn into, and more than once Alces asked for a bard to play a tune. Sumner was slightly better, drinking more slowly and only hitting on Ami when she came to the table. Durante lit up a little, sipping on his wine but laughing at Alces antics. The few locals milling about the tavern also appeared to enjoy the dragonkin's rambunctiousness.

Octavia got the clear impression that if this had been a more significant victory, if they had felled a great monster or saved a town, the carousing would have been something to behold. As it was, Alces only broke a little furniture as he spun around, and he quickly repaired all of it with a simple spell. Octavia hadn't expected the massive warrior to know a mending spell, but she imagined he often needed it.

It was a nice evening, and Octavia found herself smiling a lot more than she usually did. She was a little drunk, but it wasn't too bad. Ami came out to serve drinks again, and Sumner was a little less subtle in this flirting this time. Laughing, Octavia leaned forward.

"Hey, Sumner," she said with a grin. "Can I bend your ear for a second?"

Sumner laughed, clearly something that happened regularly as well, but turned back to Octavia. "Yes, Tavi, what's up," he said, at ease and enjoying the night. He'd had a few in him, but much more responsibly than the clearly, entertainingly drunk dragonkin. Behind Sumner, Ami suddenly got picked up and twirled around by Alces, who immediately put her back down and apologized. Ami giggled and said it was okay, so she got picked up and spun again.

Still smiling, Octavia leaned in so her voice didn't carry. It did mean her breasts were pressed up against Sumner's arm, but she was certain that wasn't a new sensation for him.

"So if you're planning on sealing that deal," she began, "she's never been with a man before, but will absolutely tell you she has. Be upfront that you're not coming back and you won't break her heart - she's after the blacksmith's boy, anyway. So be patient, show her a good time, and the backs of her legs are very sensitive." She stepped back a little and tapped her glass against his tankard. "Happy hunting."

Sumner paused for a moment, groaned, then turned. "Fuck," he exclaimed, maybe a little louder than he should. "Fuck," he said once more, sharply. He then took his mug, drained it, and stomped outside. Alces paused in his spinning of Ami, holding her aloft relatively easily and blinked, looking at Octavia for context. Slowly he set the barmaid back down and looked, trying to piece what happened together. Durante was curious, but also didn't move, taking a sip from his wine.

Blinking in surprise, Octavia stood there for a moment in shock, then set her drink down and followed him. "Sumner, wait!"

Sumner was pacing outside, shaking his hands out and huffing slightly. She scrambled down the tavern steps after him and then came to an awkward stop. "Wait, I'm sorry! I thought... I thought I was helping! I didn't mean to upset you!"

"Look, Tavi, no, it's fine," he said, clearly trying to calm down. "You didn't do anything wrong. In fact, you saved me a lot of guilt."

Growling again, he smacked himself in the head, then laughed sardonically. "You're fine, you're fine. It's just, I wanted to have some fun. We're not saying anything but we all know what those ghosts did to us, but I'm not going to take it out on a lovesick virgin," he said, gesturing back towards the tavern. "We make assumptions about barmaids, especially pretty ones like Ami, but I'm not going to be her first. Some weird half-breed adventurer that came into town then quickly left. Few years ago, maybe, but now... no, I'd feel awful."

"I'm sorry," Octavia repeated, wilting a little. "I mean, if it's any consolation, she's definitely not a virgin," the emphasis with which she said that was very telling, "she's just never been with a guy."

"Well, glad you had your fun with her," he said snarkily, but it seemed his anger had subsided at this point, he wasn't mad, maybe a little jealous.

Sighing, she spread her hands. "Look, I've been here for over a month, and you don't look like *me*," she emphasized her figure with her hands, "without people asking. At this point I have been so many girls' first time with a woman that it's more remarkable when I'm not."

"Fair point," Sumner said with a laugh. "But she's also not pining for a girl, that's the difference. No, I told you, you did me a favor, don't apologize."

"I... look, I know the ghosts were a thing," Octavia persisted, shifting her weight a little uncomfortably, "which is why I was trying to help. That...I've run into that sort of thing before, so it doesn't bother me like it used to, but you weren't expecting it." She sighed. "And Gods, you're not weird, you're gorgeous! But I also don't want you to feel awful. Um..." she considered for a moment. "Not Aleia, she's looking for a way out. Oh! Mariah! Definitely been with men, but also not looking to ride one out of here. And quite frankly she needs someone other than me to be fascinated with right now."

Sumner looked at her for a long moment, then laughed again. "All right, I appreciate the pep talk. But, do you think Mariah's even interested?"

"Do that thing when you smile and show a little fang," she said honestly. "She'll be interested." *I was,* her tone implied, though she didn't say it. She walked up to Sumner and put a hand on his arm. "I am sorry. You just... looked happy, and I thought I could help you. But I don't know any of you very well, and it was presumptuous of me."

"By the moon, Tavi, stop apologizing," he said, a little exasperated but chuckling again. "You did me a favor. Trust me, it would have been much worse for me if I found out later. Okay, I'll go, chat up Mariah, see if it works out. If not, well, not the first night I've gone to bed alone, it's all good."

"I'll go back in and leave you be." She gave his arm a squeeze and started to step away. With surprising speed, he grabbed her hand before she could and gave her a squeeze back.

"You tried, wasn't your fault. If it wasn't for that one little piece of information, it would have been a great play. Go, have fun, just tell them that I bit my tongue. That shit hurts," he said, giving her a grin with a mouthful of sharp teeth.

It took intense willpower not to tell him that she would be happy to make sure he didn't go to bed alone. Not trusting herself, she nodded and smiled. She lingered perhaps a moment longer than she should have, then let him go and headed back inside.

As she walked back in, she smiled reassuringly to everyone and picked her drink back up. That seemed to satisfy the other two and Alces shouted, tossing Ami into the air once more.

Durante turned to Octavia and waved her over. "Everything okay?" he asked.

"Yes." Octavia sat herself next to Durante and nodded. "Apparently it was a bit tongue and a misunderstanding. He's heading back to the inn."

"Oh, yeah, that can sting," he said, and she got the immediate impression that a bit tongue was code for something. He took a sip of his wine and watched Alces, shaking his head. "You know, I honestly believe the spirits possess him. He has boundless energy."

That was a welcome subject change. "Does he, now? He's a little unreal." She turned and looked back at Durante. "His enthusiasm and fervor is endearing, but it's also hard to believe at first." She sipped her wine. "How long have you all been traveling together?"

"Three or four years now," Durante said, thinking about it. "Sumner and Alces were traveling together before they met me, but I think that was only a couple of months before. What about you? How long have you been out on your own?"

"Eight years," she answered, looking down into her glass. "It took me a while to figure things out. I spent everything I had getting out of Driscoll's Rest and landed in Rupaiya for...a while." She laughed a little and looked up at Durante again. "It turns out, money doesn't go as far when your parents aren't supplying it. It took a while to learn what I could and couldn't spend, and the consequences thereof."

"I'd believe it," he said, sighing and nodding, clearly empathetic. He took another drink. "The guys scooped me up after I got disowned, so I've had to make some adjustments as well. Sumner's a stickler, but it's taught me real quick what's important. Well, mostly."

Laughing again, Octavia clinked glasses with Durante. "I knew it! That we came from similar places, I mean. Also disowned. I was told I could either offer myself to my father's partner's sons as their 'secretary' with every horrible thing that implied, or go it alone. But it made for a heck of a learning curve." She was a little drunk at this point, but not recklessly so.

"I didn't get an offer. Of course, I did also destroy a wing of the estate, so I suppose that was fair. Family didn't much like me anyway," he said, taking a sip. She could see his eyes starting to shift a little, the pink color darkening and becoming noticeably red.

"Hungry?" she asked with a sympathetic smile.

Startled, he turned away. "Ah, yeah, sorry," he stuttered, pulling out his bag and frantically shuffling through it. He produced a frost-covered bottle that he quickly uncorked and drank. Another long moment and he tucked the bottle back away before turning back towards Octavia.

"Um, yeah, I'll probably get a little bit of meat here in a moment, sorry," he said a little more shyly. His eyes, she noted, had faded back to pink again.

Reaching over, she grasped Durante's hand and gave it a squeeze. "Don't apologize, kitten. If you ever need something fresher, let me know." She stroked the back of his hand with her thumb, then let him go. She needed to head back to her room. With every glass of wine she was becoming less reserved, and she wasn't terribly reserved to begin with.

"I, uh, wait. You know? Are you sure?" he asked, quite surprised.

"White complexion, pink eyes, and when you yawn it's very fangy. And adorable." She smiled again and gave his shoulder a squeeze. "And yes, I'm sure."

"Alright," Durante said quietly. He was clearly processing something.

"I think I'll head back to the inn before I can't walk there," she said with what she hoped was a disarming smile, not wanting Durante to think he'd driven her away. She finished her wine and set a hand on his shoulder. "How early tomorrow are we heading out?"

He held his own hand and shrugged. "Usually after a victory, Alces lets us rest up. He'll be awake with the dawn. Rest of us, probably not so much."

"If I'm not downstairs by the time you're all ready to go, you're welcome to send someone for me." She offered, and turned, only to almost walk straight into Alces.

"Octavia, loveliest of the warlocks," the dragonkin boomed, smiling, "you're leaving already?"

"I've had a lot of wine, and I want to make sure I'm at my best before we take to the road tomorrow! You all said you came here just for me, I don't want to hold you up any longer." She pushed her hair back and looked up at him. Gods, he was big.

"It's just our party this time, so without us, there is no party," he said, a soft drawl of an accent creeping into his speech. Maybe this was how he got when he was drunk.

He wasn't wrong, though. If she left, it would be Durante and Alces and poor Ami and Jed in the back. The few other locals had disappeared. "So, I escort you back, we all go to sleep, wake up, healthy, head out, yes?" Durante got up at that point and moved to collect the various bits of armor and gear they had strewn around the tavern, tucking them into his magic bag.

Octavia smiled. "I was reluctant to stop your revelry, but maybe that's for the best. I—" she started to step to the side, but caught her foot on the chair that Durante had left pulled out and stumbled right into Alces, who caught her and laughed again.

"Yes, time to go back, I think," he said, cheerful as always. "Let us go." He made a motion to scoop her up, then stopped and smiled. "Of course, ask first. Shall I carry you back, fair enchantress?"

"Oh, why not. If you please, Ser Knight." Octavia couldn't remember the last time she'd smiled so much in one evening. "Oh! But don't forget my bag!"

"But of course," Alces said, laughing as Durante passed by, handing him Octavia's bag.

That was their cue, then. The three of them headed out of the tavern, and Octavia swore she heard Jed sigh in relief. Once they'd stepped out, Alces did exactly what he promised he'd do, scooping her up with one hand under her rump and hefting her up to sit on his shoulder where Comicha had been previously that day.

"Comfy?"

"Oh, wow," was all she could say for a moment as she got settled. She didn't fit on his shoulder as neatly as Comicha had - her bottom was way too big - but she could lean in towards his head and stay put. She briefly grasped one of his horns as she got used to the position, then let go and caressed his head in apology. "This is incredible. You are so astoundingly strong."

"I am blessed to be the spirits' strength in this world," he said, patting her thigh as he held her steady.

FOUR

It was a pleasant walk, with Alces carrying Octavia easily and Durante catching up with their stuff in tow. Coming back to the sizable inn, Alces reached up with both his hands, grasping Octavia around the waist, and picking her up to place her back down on the ground gently. "You have been delivered, fair maid," he said, still chuckling and grinning.

"Thank you, Ser Knight," Octavia said, giggling. "And bless you for calling me a maiden. Oh, wait!" She reached into her bag and pulled out a scarf. Still giggling, she tied it around his arm. "A sign of my favor. Thank you for your service." She curtseyed with surprising grace given her inebriation, then started giggling again. "Gods, I need to go to bed. But it was a lovely evening. I think I'll enjoy traveling with you."

"Sleep well. I will be here in the morning," he said with a grin, patting the scarf.

"Goodnight, Octavia," Durante said with a little wave, turning back to Alces to talk to him about the pile of armor he was currently carrying.

Not so drunk that she couldn't walk, Octavia made it up the stairs to her room. As she went down the hall she could hear Mariah's tell-tale "By the GODS!" and she smiled brightly. Good for Sumner. And it sounded like the boy knew what he was doing.

Getting into her room, she closed the door with a happy sigh before she realized that she hadn't actually managed to bring anyone back with her. "Oh, shit." She ran a hand over her face and sighed again.

Four more days, Octavia heard her patron taunt in her head. *Which one are you going to go after first? Maybe the blond boy? That should be you in his room right now. I bet he's an animal in bed.*

Groaning, Octavia worked on getting undressed. "Let me be, Kami, I can't deal with this right now. I have four days, I'll find someone."

I feel like you've found three someones. Tick tock, my dearest. Kamvasana's nagging presence disappeared and she was left to sleep alone.

"It's fine," she murmured to herself as she put her things away. "There are other towns around here, I have four more days. We'll probably stop somewhere."

She poured water into the basin and washed her face, then also wiped herself off to make sure she hadn't brought any grit back from the mausoleum, and finally fell naked into bed. She'd have Comicha help her pack in the morning.

Grumbling, Octavia burrowed into her blankets. She was physically frustrated, but now also grumpy enough that she didn't want to do anything about it herself. And she definitely didn't want to think about how Kamvasna was probably right about Sumner, because letting her mind wander down that possibility would only make things worse. Nope, time to sleep, if she could.

Octavia heard a little popping noise then a gentle poke at her head. "Mistress," Comicha's voice came. "I can help! I know I don't count for the thing, but if you wanted..."

Sighing, Octavia rolled onto her back and looked up at Comicha. "I'm in a grump now, so not tonight. Come here, I'll give you a snuggle, and then you need to let me sleep, all right? I don't want them waiting on me."

"Yay," the little imp said, seeming happy to be offered some way to help. Hopping down off of the nightstand, she scurried under the covers, snuggling up against Octavia and nuzzling into her cleavage.

Yawning, Octavia ruffled Comicha's hair. "I like them, I want them to see me as valuable. For more than keeping beds warm. If this works out, maybe they'll want me to travel with them for a while. It's been me and you for a long time, I think I'd like not being on my own."

"They're nice," her familiar stated. "I like 'em too. They didn't yell at me or anything."

Octavia pulled the covers up. "No, they thought you were quite cute. Which you are. All right, time to sleep now."

They cuddled close, and Octavia fell asleep relatively swiftly, all things considered. Her dreams were on the graphic side, and involved her newfound companions, individually and together. Alces holding her against a wall, Sumner growling in her ear as he railed her from behind, Durante sinking those teeth of his into her neck. She woke up moaning and overheated, and with the feel of an eager tongue licking at her sex.

"Wha—" she looked down to find Comicha between her legs, happily sucking at her clit. She was going to say something, but then her orgasm hit, and she fell back with a shudder and muffled cry.

"Good morning, Mistress," Comicha chimed happily, launching herself up off the bed and hovering above Octavia's head. "You were moaning in your sleep and squeezing me. It was nice, but I could hear the large dragonkin in the hall and figured you would want to be woken up! And since you were having fun dreams, this seemed like the best way!"

Another moan, and Octavia pushed her hair back from her face. "It probably was. I'll be less distracted, if nothing else. Thank you, Comicha. Can you help me pack?"

"Yes, Mistress!" The little imp was utterly delighted.

In less than an hour, Octavia was completely packed up and back in her traveling clothes, which was more protective and less low cut than most of her clothes, but also so form fitting that an observer might wonder how she managed to move in it. She slung her satchel over her shoulder and snapped her fingers. The chest in the room that looked a tiny bit like a small, fat dragon started to move, following her out the door and down the hall. It might not have infinite storage like the boys' enchanted satchels, but at least she didn't have to carry it.

She headed towards the dining room. It was early enough, she probably didn't need to worry about Alces having finished all the breakfast. As she reached the dining hall, she was greeted by a beaming Alces and a slightly more awake than last time Durante.

"Good morning, lovely Octavia. I do hope the drink last night did not upset you upon waking," Alces said, seated comfortably and back in his armor. It looked as though breakfast was just getting served. Durante gave her a little wave, a measure of his shyness returning with sobriety.

She smiled and nodded to them both. "Good morning. No, I'm fine. I had enough to giggle and stumble, but not so much that I made myself ill." She sat down and poured herself a cup of tea. "Everyone else sleep well?"

"As well as ever after a successful quest," Alces said, smiling to Mariah as she appeared with some bread and cuts of meat and cheese. Octavia glanced up at Mariah as the young woman came out, curious to see if she looked happy and content or hurried and uncomfortable. She certainly had sounded like things went well last night. Based on the quick smile Mariah flashed Octavia, it seemed like happy but hurried. If the night had gone well enough, she might have overslept. After all, Sumner hadn't arrived yet.

"Just fine," Durante added with a nod, much quieter than the night before.

Once the food had hit the table, Alces made a plate for Sumner, then waited for both Octavia and Durante to serve themselves before devouring everything else.

"So, fair warlock, are you ready for a lengthy journey to the northern mountains? Are you equipped for the snow," Alces started to ask, then glanced over her shoulder at her chest. "Do you like dragons?" Alces grinned, but he wasn't leering, just very amused.

"I do," Octavia said, answering his last question first, "though I've had Matilda here since I was a child. She's old, and I've done my best to condition her wood, though the enchantments are a little simple and I think they might be fading. I used to be able to ride her when I was tired, but now she won't move forward unless she's following me."

She poured herself another cup of tea. "As for the rest, I am equipped for snow. I'm equipped for most everything other than wet swamps and the driest deserts."

"Good," Alces said as he sat up straight. "And should you tire, I can summon Nutmeg, he'll carry you. He would be honored."

Glancing over at Alces, she arched an eyebrow. "I can walk a lot further than I used to before getting tired, but I also don't know what your pace is like. It's nice to know there is an option so that I don't have to worry about falling behind."

"Say the word, he's at your call," Alces said.

"I, um, I could take a look at it sometime," Durante said, glancing over. "Your chest. I mean the chest. Matilda. Given some time, could probably make her better than new." Durante looked a little embarrassed and took a sip of his own tea.

Octavia smiled. "That would be lovely, thank you!"

Durante gave her another nod, this time with a little smile, and went back to sipping his tea.

Sumner finally descended down the stairs, stretching and yawning. He had his leather pants on, his jerkin was in his hands, and the light shone through his undershirt as he stood for a moment in the doorway of the dining area. Octavia fought back a sigh.

"Good morning, everyone," he said, plopping down at the table and taking the plate Alces handed him. Mariah came back out with a new pot of tea and some scones with fresh preserves. Octavia caught that she put her hand on Sumner's shoulder when she placed things on the table and gave his ear a slight tug before disappearing back into the kitchen. It was impossible not to smile at the exchange. So Octavia had been right, and it looked like it had been a very good night for both of them. She was only a little bit jealous. Well, maybe more than a little bit, but she was far happier that it had gone well and that she hadn't ruined Sumner's night after all.

"Morning," she said, and leaned over to grab a scone.

"We're all here," Alces said, tearing into a piece of meat, "what's the plan?"

"So, I've been looking over the map," Durante said, pulling the object from his bag and laying it on the table, "and while it's a long trip, I think we can avoid the worst of it by heading mostly north, here, through the Gramblethorn Woods then over the Mistmorrow Plateaus. If we follow the road, we'll end up in the Southmist canyon—the southern side of the Mistmorrow Plateaus—which is winding and has a couple of dead ends. It could slow us down. However, there is no town on the plateaus, while there is one on either side of the canyon."

Picking up her tea again, Octavia felt a prickle of panic. "Are we sure there's nothing on the plateaus? Can we pack enough supplies for that long if we don't know we'll have somewhere to stop?"

"That won't be a problem," Alces said with a wave of his hand. "Sumner and myself are expert hunters, and we have a few days of rations if we really need. But, if you're unsure, I don't want to pressure you into taking unnecessary risks. The three of us tend to enjoy being off the beaten path."

"While I understand not wanting to be so far out from a town, Southmist Canyon has been a bit of a hotspot for bandits and the Grummork tribe," Durante added, "and while I don't think they're much of a danger to us, it's still wasted time if we get in a fight." Durante leaned towards Octavia and did his best to whisper, "More so if they've captured someone. Alces will not stop until they're rescued."

Octavia nodded slowly and did her best to keep her concern from showing on her face. "No, that's fine. I... I don't venture too far from civilization that often, so I have my own... biases there. But I've also never travelled in a group before." A group that would soon find out what sort of warlock she was, if they didn't come across a town or a camp or something. She could almost feel Kamvasana smiling smugly.

"If you ever feel worried, say something. I will not have you feel like we're dragging you around against your better judgement," Alces said, and the others nodded and shrugged in agreement.

She took a sip of tea and cleared her throat. "If we are to travel together, I should trust you. If you think that is the best path, then that is the best path."

"We can take the longer route if you'd feel better," Sumner said, "I don't think the tower is going anywhere, but that would mean you doing far more than we hired you to do. Bad look if you feel like you're getting shafted."

"I promise, I'm not worried about the journey," Octavia said, firmly enough that they would know she wasn't lying. "I'm also not worried about running into more than we arranged. I'm sure we could negotiate if we needed to. But truly, I am not worried about the route."

"Alright," Sumner said, raising his hands in defense, "point taken."

"Your courage was never in question, Octavia," Alces said proudly, "you stood resolute against the spectral horde yesterday, I trust you. But do speak out otherwise."

A nod, another sip of tea, and Octavia managed a small smile. She wasn't ready to explain that what worried her was what they would see, or what she would need to eventually ask of them. And how it might change their opinion of her.

"Very well, we head for the plateau," Alces declared, the matter settled. "Eat up, my friends!"

The rest of them tended to breakfast and packed up a little to go to snack on the road. Mariah came in once more to make sure everyone was doing alright and to make sure they had enough food. After they had cleared out, Octavia slipped quietly into the kitchens to say goodbye to Mariah, cheerfully congratulating the girl on her night with Sumner and wishing her the best. She then headed up front to find Paul at the desk as always.

"Thank you for everything, Paul," Octavia said as she counted out her coins at the desk. "I don't know that I'll be back anytime soon, but if I am, I would be thrilled to stay here again."

"Well, it is the only place in town," Paul said, finishing the transaction with a smile. "We'd love to have you. Be safe out there."

Nodding, Octavia gathered her things and headed out to where the others were waiting. They all turned to look at her as she stepped out of the inn, the morning sun gleaming from Alces' scales and Durante's gadgets. Alces smiled. Sumner looked her over appraisingly. Durante's gaze flicked away shyly.

"Ready when you are," she said as she came down the steps.

"Then let us be off," Alces said, and Sumner whistled, circling up his hand and heading out. As they passed by the tavern, Sumner did run in real fast to settle up their tab, but aside from that, it was time to travel on.

Gravemont was in the middle of some gorgeous farmland, and it took them most of the day to leave the village and get out of sight of the lush plains. Octavia was definitely used to a more leisurely pace, but she kept her teeth together and toughed it out. These three were seasoned adventurers. Even with Durante's rather tame demeanor and lack of muscle definition, it was clear he could walk right along with the rest of them. She might have to take up Alces offer of summoning Nutmeg - whatever that was - eventually, but she most certainly wasn't going to the first day. She did make for a quiet traveling companion, though, as she was putting most of her focus and energy into keeping up.

The road wanted to veer west, heading down into a valley and towards the canyons. This was where they had to take a less traveled path and make their way through the Gramblethorn Forest. There were some worn horse trails and footpaths, it wasn't completely virgin trekking, but it was certainly slower than taking the road. When the sun started to set, they were reaching the edge of the woods.

Looking at the setting sun, she then glanced back to Sumner. Surprisingly, he seemed to be in charge. Well, not exactly—Alces was the leader, such as one existed, but it felt to Octavia like Sumner was the one that kept everyone on track. Alces spoke boldly and urged them on to glory and light, but Sumner paid the bills and kept the schedule. He was the ringmaster of this little circus.

"Are we camping before nightfall," she asked, "or continuing into the woods?"

"Oh, definitely before nightfall," Sumner said, laughing a little as if it were an amusing or naive question.

"While we don't fear what may be in the woods," Alces said, setting down his bag, "they are wrought with tripping hazards. Better to see where one is going. And sure, we wield the light," he demonstrated by forming that bright ball in his hand, "but no reason to chance it when it can be avoided."

"Oh, sweet Goddess of Mercy, thank you." Octavia stopped Matilda and took off her satchel.

Sumner laughed again. "One day, I'll tame a roc, then we won't have to deal with this ever again," he said as he started to pull out tent parts from his back.

"I'm telling you, I can make a self-propelled wagon," Durante commented as he worked on his own items. "I just need a workshop and, well, a couple of months and a few... thousand... gold worth of parts... but I can do it!"

"I know, D, I know," Sumner chuckled, shaking his head.

"Greatest inventor of our time, we have no doubt," Alces said without the slightest bit of sarcasm, his belief and conviction clear in his voice.

"So are you in the habit of taming wild things?" Octavia asked as she opened her trunk and bent over for a moment to dig through it. After a minute she pulled out a cube and looked around for a flat bit of land.

"I learned a bit from our tamer in the circus," Sumner said, stopping to look at Octavia curiously as she strode across the clearing and set down the cube. "So, not to that level, but I'll get there." He trailed off at the end as she pulled the little tag on it, then backed up quickly.

There were sounds of fabric rustling as a tent very quickly unfolded from the cube. A tent that had a surprisingly wide entryway for all that it didn't look very big. It looked rather nice for as small as it was, made of heavy canvas with a glass lantern that flared to life.

"Is that one of Caradelle's Comfy Canvas Coops?" Durante asked, amused. Alces also paused in his preparations. Her presentation had everyone's attention at this point.

"Probably," Octavia said, putting her hands on her hips. "Wizards have an unhealthy fascination with alliteration. I bought it when I first struck out, so I don't remember what the merchant called it. I don't use it much, but it's pretty great when I need it."

Looking back at the three of them, Octavia made a quick decision. "Um, you're all welcome to stay in it, if you like. It's significantly bigger on the inside and it's not like I'll have time to swan around the central area in my dressing gown. But there are multiple curtained-off rooms and five beds. And the lounge area. But more importantly, there's a bathing room and a water closet."

"Are you absolutely certain you will not mind sharing your space with us?" Alces asked, stepping closer to examine the odd tent.

"I'll take a bed over sleeping on a palette on the ground any day," Sumner said, "I've had a lifetime of cold floors and cots."

"Only if you're positively sure," Durante added. "We do have tents. We're used to sleeping outdoors."

"No, absolutely," Octavia said, sincerely. This was an easy thing to share, and she hadn't been body shy in years. "You are very welcome. It's pretty nice."

There was a small pop as Comicha appeared in the middle between all of them. "Slumber party!"

Alces threw his head back and laughed. So booming was it, it startled a flock of birds out of a nearby tree. Octavia sighed and ran a hand over her face, but smiled indulgently at her familiar. Sumner and Durante started putting their tent parts away.

"I'll warn you," Sumner said, grinning at Octavia, "I sleep in the nude and tend to sleepwalk."

"Oh, you do not," Durante said, hefting up his gear. Octavia snickered.

"Spoilsport."

"Can we aim not to make our companion uncomfortable after she invited us in," Alces said as he picked up his own bag, "if that bothers her."

Octavia motioned for everyone to head inside and set their things down. "I am unbothered, Alces. It's all right."

Inside the tent was much bigger, and much more luxurious. The lounge area had a chaise, a small couch, and chairs that were all upholstered with sable fur. There was a chandelier that illuminated the main area. Heavy draping curtains cordoned off the sets of beds. And the entire tent seemed to maintain a very pleasant temperature.

"Now, there are three rooms," Octavia said as she moved to the center area, out of the way enough that they could easily move around her. "One of them is definitely mine. If you see lingerie, you're in the wrong room. The other two rooms each have two beds. Sumner and Durante, you can share one, and Alces you can shove the beds together in the last room so that you actually fit."

"We really need to get one of these," Durante said as he looked behind one of the curtains, trying to find the appropriate bedroom.

"If we find a market that actually has one, we can look into it," Sumner said and looked at one of the other rooms.

"I believe I've found your room, Octavia," Alces said after peering around one of the curtains. "Your underthings look like their color would be very complimentary."

"Thank you, Alces, I've found pink to be very complimentary on me as well, though it also stains too easily, so I don't include it in my outerwear often," she said, smiling. She went back to the entryway of the tent and whistled for Matilda to follow her in.

"She looks good in purple, too," Octavia could hear Comicha telling Alces. "Oh, and she prefers silver to gold, though she looks very nice in both. It works out, because I look good in gold, and she lets me have the rings for my horns." Octavia tried not to roll her eyes and led her trunk over to her room.

"Right, I guess we're in this one," Sumner said to Durante, pointing to the room he was currently looking in.

"We still have the food we packed from this morning; shall we rejoin here and eat?" Alces asked.

"I think so. Right, changing. See you all in a bit," Sumner said, disappearing behind the curtain.

FIVE

When Octavia returned, she paused for a moment to take in the three men lounging in her tent. The packed meats and cheeses with some bread had been spread out on a handkerchief on the floor and most everyone had on more comfortable clothes. Alces was wearing the least, as he only seemed to have some loose pants and nothing else. The dragonkin was a solid wall of muscle, and she briefly wondered if he wore the armor for ornamental purposes. She also realized in that moment that he also never wore boots, his clawed feet being impossible to shoe properly. At the moment, he was rubbing that cleaning lotion on them.

Sumner was in less loose pants, though still not as tight as the leathers he worked and traveled in. He also wore a comfortable looking vest, though nothing underneath. Spread out comfortably on the chaise, he carefully balanced a ball that seemed to roil with orangey liquid, moving it from his palm to the back of his hand by way of his fingertips.

Durante was sitting on one of the chairs in delicate slacks and a laced shirt. His device was across his lap, and he was carefully tinkering with some fine tools on it. A lock of his raven hair kept falling into his eyes, no matter how many times he paused to smooth it back.

Standing there, she suddenly regretted her offer, simply because it meant there was no escape from them or the desire they stirred up in her. Giving herself a shake, she moved out to join them. Her lounge clothes clearly reflected her time in Rupaiya. Billowing pants similar to what Alces wore, but set low on her hips, dipping below her belly button, and a cropped shirt with three quarters sleeves that crossed in front and tied off in the back - as in other than the tie, the back was completely open. As she crossed the room, all three of them looked up in open admiration, though they all averted their gaze politely after a moment—Alces first, then Durante, and finally Sumner, whose gaze lingered the longest before he pulled himself back to what he was doing.

Coming around the couch, Octavia picked up a thick slice of bread and piled meat and cheese on it, then sat herself on the couch with her feet up. "Comicha! Foot rubs, please!"

"Yes, Mistress!" The little imp zipped over and happily got to work.

"Have to admit, this is the best way to do camping," Sumner said, taking a piece of meat and dangling it over his head before dropping it into his mouth.

"Don't get soft on me, Sumner," Alces said with a chuckle, "we can live like this when we retire. Or, rather, when you retire."

"There has to be a compromise," Octavia said with a smile. "A way to roam and adventure without sacrificing all comforts. I like soft things. There's nothing wrong with soft." She took a bite.

"Oh, nothing wrong with soft," Alces said, focusing on her, his eyes sweeping over her. She was the picture of softness, with her hair down, in her soft clothing, lounging on the fur upholstered couch. "I'm very much a fan of soft, but soft needs protection. Too soft and you need too much protection. True, that is why I am here, to protect all those who have need, but I cannot always be."

Duranted cleared his throat. "Um, O-Octavia?"

"Hmm?" Octavia looked over, mouth full.

"Did you want me to look at your che-um-walking storage?" Durante asked, fidgeting a little. She wondered if he needed something to do with his hands, since he didn't really seem to be eating. She nodded and held up a hand, indicating that he should wait a minute. After she swallowed, she whistled, and Matilda trundled out of her room, stopping on the other side of the couch.

"If you need me to empty it, let me know."

"It should be fine, I'm just going to look it over," Durante said, scooting off the couch and sitting next to the chest, doing as he said. Durante seemed quite content right there, using his eye glass to look it over and prodding it from time to time with his tools.

"All I'm saying is when you've been living rough the whole time," Sumner said, dropping a piece of cheese into his mount, "there is nothing wrong with a change of pace. I bet I could sleep on a bed of silk and down every night and still be able to shank anyone that crossed us."

Finishing dinner, Octavia dusted off her fingers. She then scooted herself down on the small couch so that she would put her feet up over one arm and stretch out over the rest of it, which she did with a content sigh. Comicha obligingly moved over and went back to rubbing Octavia's feet.

"So what is your goal, Sumner?" She rolled her head to the side to look at him. "What does retirement look like to you? Or I suppose, if money were no object, what would you do?"

"Not really sure," he said, looking over at her. "Just... I want to be happy, I guess. Dunno what that means. Safe home with a family, maybe? My own business? Not sure. I guess it's one of those things where I'll know it when I see it."

"Being happy sounds like a simple goal, doesn't it? The hard part is figuring out what happy looks like, I suppose," she mused, smiling softly at Sumner. She looked past him to the dragonkin lightly snacking. Alces nibbled on the food that was there but wasn't ravenously eating like he did normally. Maybe he was waiting for everyone to finish. "And what of you, Alces? What are you hoping for?"

"Bringing the Light to any who want it," he said proudly. "But, like many, I seek the brightest light of all. Do you know what that is?"

"I confess, I do not." She picked her head up a little, curious.

"Love," he exclaimed. "It will shine its way through the darkest parts of our hearts and guide us through the worst shadows of our lives. One day, I will find my own. But until then, and even after, I will be the light that others need."

"I mean, you got us," Durante said with a shrug.

"Yes, and while I do love my compatriots, you know that's not what I mean," he said, then huffed at the pale young man, which caused Durante to shiver. A cool breeze also wafted past Octavia—Alces had frost breath, it seemed. It stirred her skin and caused little goosebumps to rise on her arms.

Letting her head drop back against the couch again, Octavia looked up at the chandelier. "I don't...think I've ever known love, if I'm being honest. Kindness, certainly, but...well. It's always been a beautiful thing in stories. I'm sure it exists. And I have every faith you can find it if you wish."

"If I can, it will be easy for you, sweet Octavia," Alces said firmly.

"Anyone would be lucky to have your love."

She shifted a little and cleared her throat. "All right, Durante, what about you? What do you hope for?"

"Oh, I don't know," he said, pausing in his examination of Octavia's walking chest. "Just want to be a better person. A better me, I suppose. I don't know." He didn't yet have the skill to hide that he was being evasive. She'd have to dive deeper to get something out of him. "What about you?"

"You know, I really hadn't thought about it much," she said, stretching as Comicha finished with her feet and then zipped over to convince Alces that he also wanted foot rubs. Alces had no reason to deny the imp her activity, but did warn her that his feet were significantly tougher, more firm, and with a different muscle structure than her mistress'.

"And I promise, I'm not trying to deflect. The last eight years—the first year was about survival, and then I made my pact. It's…let me see… another eight years before I have the option of ending it. I do miss having money," she admitted with a laugh, "but after that…maybe I also need to figure out what happy looks like."

"Any reason you can't be happy while in your pact?" Durante asked, curious as to what all that entailed.

For a moment Octavia considered her response. "Technically, no," she said, and sat up again. "There are some complications, but for the most part my patron isn't terribly demanding. Provided I uphold my end." She reached above her head to stretch, arching her back for a moment. "But again, what does happy look like? This is nice, though. I really can't remember the last time I've sat around, relaxed and chatting with people. Happy might look something like this."

"Whatever your burden, if we can help, we will," Alces commented from over his shoulder. "I do know the power of facing our problems alone, but if you ever need assistance, it is my duty to do so. These lads are good people, I'm sure they'll be happy to help." They both nodded in agreement.

Octavia fought hard not to laugh. A small giggle slipped out. There were so many ways she could think of that they could help her, but… what if it ruined moments like this? She was pretty sure this moment was worth more than asking any of them for a convenient tumble.

"I am sorry, I'm not laughing at your offer, or your sincerity," she said, looking at Alces so he could see that she meant what she said. "I… ah. We'll be traveling together for a while. You'll learn soon enough why

I laughed. Thank you, though."

She stood up, a little awkward. 'I think I'll retire for the night. Comicha, don't offer anything other than foot rubs, do you understand me?"

The imp pouted. "Fiiiiiine."

"As you wish, Octavia. Comicha is doing a fine job despite complications," Alces said, reaching over to pet the imp's head gently. Comicha beamed at the praise.

"Staying out of juju I don't understand is something I pride myself on, but you know we'll help you," Sumner commented.

"Sometime I'd like to chat with you about pacts. Much later, though," Durante said, barely looking up from her trunk. "Have a good night."

"Yes, sleep well. When do you wish me to wake you?" Alces asked.

"If I'm not up by the time Durante is awake, feel free to wake me," Octavia said. "I hope you all sleep well." She felt bad about retreating, but she wasn't ready to tell them, and she wasn't entirely certain why it was making her so nervous.

The curtains between the rooms were heavy and would cut the noise a little. They weren't enchanted, unfortunately, so she could still hear them talk but she couldn't make it out. This did mean, however, that she would not be pleasuring herself while they were in the tent. Or at least not while she knew they were awake. She stripped and slid into bed, listening to the quiet murmurs from the main area.

The guys didn't stay up much longer. Comicha completed her rounds of foot massages, Alces probably finished any remaining food, and everyone went to their respective beds. Sleep was had; somehow Kamvasana found it in their heart to not pester Octavia despite everyone being under the same roof and lightly clothed, separated by only a curtain. She was woken up once more by familiar voices. They were relatively soft, but not so that they didn't stir her. She wasn't used to traveling with company, after all.

Blinking, Octavia sat up, and the lantern next to the bed illuminated as she did. She yawned and got dressed and pulled her boots back on. Her feet were a little sore, but Comicha rubbing them down last night helped a lot. She'd probably need it more that evening. She made sure she was completely ready before pulling back the heavy curtains and heading out into the main room. She had braided her hair back that day, but as always curls had managed to pop out and gently frame her face, softening the overall look.

"Ah, there she is. Good morning, glorious Octavia," Alces said as he turned to look at her. Durante was standing on one of the chairs behind him, strapping Alces plate mail on and rolling his eyes.

Durante did manage a little smile. "Good morning, Octavia. I'm still working on the enchantment on your... trunk, but I cleaned it up. Should at least look near new."

"Thank you, Durante," she said, and yawned. "That was very kind of you. Oh, before I forget, don't leave anything more complicated than clothing in the tent when I collapse it. Clothing, food, those things are fine, but anything with an enchantment, well, breaks."

"We figured we'd pack up our things as normal," Durante said, pulling on the last strap and slapping Alces on the shoulder. "There you go, all strapped in."

"Thank you, Durante. Gentleman and a master scholar," Alces said, rolling his shoulders and flexing his arms to test the fit. He looked to Octavia again. "Incidentally, let me know if you wish me to stop with the qualifiers."

Yawning again, she regarded Alces. "Are the qualifiers sincere?"

His vibrant violet eyes widened. "My dear, if they weren't sincere, I would not say them."

"Then if they are sincere, you may continue," Octavia replied. "Such things only bother me if they're insincere or manipulative. You do not have to change who you are for me. Speak as you would." Her words were soft, gentle, partially from waking up but also because she, too, was being sincere.

"Most gracious," Alces said with a bow, then settled himself down on the couch.

"Where is Sumner? All things considered, I had assumed that Durante would be the latest to rise among the three of you." She smiled apologetically at him.

"Sumner is out getting breakfast," Alces said. "Well, he got breakfast, he's cooking it right now."

"Yeah, I am always the last one to get up," Durante said, casting his gaze down, his shoulders dropping a little.

Octavia walked over and hugged Durante's arm. "And I am grateful for that, because it means I am not the only one."

He turned aside a little and cleared his throat. "Thank you," he said quietly. She let him go and stepped back.

Any more conversation was halted as Sumner came in with a flat stone piled with shaved meat. "Ah, good, you're up," he said to Octavia, setting the stone on the ground. "Eat up. There's more outside, but I cut this off before it got too crispy." Given how the strips weren't terribly large, it was a good chance it was rabbit or some other critter.

"We don't have a lot in the way of spices, and Alces is a better cook, but hey," Sumner added with a toothy grin. It was impossible not to return Sumner's smile. She was starting to really like that grin of his. She picked up a piece and blew it on lightly before popping it in her mouth. Definitely rabbit.

"Ish good," she said, holding a hand up to hide the food in her mouth as she spoke, then went back to chewing.

Alces picked up his bag and headed for the door. "You always do a good job, Sumner. It'll just take practice. I shall tend to the meat. Eat up, come out when you're ready for more."

Sumner sat himself down and started eating. Durante did the same after setting his bag and his contraption down next to them. Octavia darted back and forth, grabbing things from her room to toss in the chest that had been left by the couch, and grabbing bits of meat in between. This did mean she was leaning down and not quite pointing her cleavage in Sumner's face every time she did.

"So, into the forest today?" she asked between bites.

"Yup, quick as we can. I'll, ah, wait for you guys outside," Sumner said after Octavia's third trip, "see how the meat's doing."

Durante watched him leave, shrugged, and took another few bites. There wasn't a lot left on the stone. Once it was cleared, Durante picked up his things, then the stone, then motioned out. "Ready to go?"

"Yes, ready," she said, getting back up and slinging her satchel over her shoulder. She wasn't used to such a rushed morning, but they had a ways to travel, and she imagined they might be at this tower they hoped to find for a little while, depending on what was there and how easy it was to access.

Outside it was a clear and promising morning. Alces and Sumner had, at some point before Octavia could be bothered to get up, set up a small campfire and had been roasting three rabbits. It should be enough meat for the rest of the day, at least. She went around to the corner of the tent and pulled on the little tag again. Within minutes it was once more a small cube that she could tuck back in Matilda. In short order, they were ready to go.

The forest wasn't terribly bad, as things go. True to its name, there were a number of brambles that had to be cut through and would snag occasionally. Octavia managed to have her shirt rip seductively not once, not twice, but five times during their trek. It was mostly humorous—Octavia was not particularly body shy, and her three companions walked into more brambles and the occasional low hanging branch in their efforts not to look. A quick mending spell fixed it every time, though she swore her shirt got a little tighter every time they repaired it.

As they walked, Alces began telling stories, with Sumner and Durante chiming in. He told of how he and Sumner had met, back when Sumner was still traveling with a circus. The old owner had retired and sold the circus to a shaytani. Shaytanis were an unusual race, with fiendish ancestry, and a sometimes deserved reputation as a result. Things had seemed fine at first, but the shaytani quickly started using the travelling show for smuggling and endangering the performers. That was when Sumner chimed in to describe how Alces had helped the performers and workers to rise up against the shaytani and cast him and his lackeys out, securing the writ of ownership before sending them down the river.

After a few lighter stories, Durante told of how he'd blown up a wing of his family estate and was cast out, all but disowned, only to stumble across Alces and Sumner a town over. Durante's tone was light, and he even laughed a little, more relaxed in Octavia's presence than he had been since they'd met. Alces then took the story over again, describing how the three of them had taken down a monstrosity known as a Hope Devourer, a flying beast that toyed with its prey before consuming it. Durante knocked the creature out of the sky, Sumner snared it in one of his traps, and Alces sent it back to the abyss from whence it came.

This then led to Sumner telling Octavia about Alces' victory parties, the proper ones. How both bar and brothel alike would be turned upside down in a raucous celebration. While they'd been run out of town a few times by guards for disturbing the peace, it was never at the behest of the establishment owners. Sumner always made sure everyone was properly paid, and Alces fixed anything that had been broken with his mending spells and Durante's help.

Octavia smiled and let them spin their tales. Alces was a very good storyteller with the proper amount of flourish, Sumner kept things tighter, and Durante had a good memory for detail. It was a fun way to learn about them, and it certainly made the day go faster. She expressed excitement over being able to attend the inevitable victory party once their journey was done.

The next day they exited the forest and started making their way up the slopes towards the plateau. Weather was getting noticeably cold, but the late-summer sun was a saving grace. Without dodging through brambles, they were able to make better time.

As the sun started to get low, Octavia grew quieter. She usually grew quieter as the day drew on and her energy flagged. But she could feel a tension in her shoulders, a tightness in her bearing as they came to an early stop for the evening, on a broad stretch of flat terrain ideal for camping. She kept glancing towards the setting sun trying to gauge how long until night fell.

"Are you alright?" Sumner asked. He was always the most observant. Of course, at his question the other two turned.

"Technically," Octavia said with a sigh as she fished the tent out of her chest. "I'm sorry. Yes, I'm all right. I'm just...out of time." She was resigned, not frightened. Pensive and uncomfortable, but it definitely wasn't fear. She set down the tent and pulled the tab so it could unfold and looked over at the sun again.

"Is there anything we can do, or do you wish to face it alone?" Alces asked, brushing himself off and standing to his full height.

Laughing a little, Octavia shook her head. "I should have asked for your help days ago, but I couldn't bring myself to. At this point I will very much have to face this alone." She looked at the sun one last time, and shook her head, then looked back at the three of them. "I... have not fulfilled my half of the pact. So my patron will be here soon. To take what I owe them. I am going to apologize now for the noise."

"As you wish," Alces said, but no one immediately moved. They hovered near the entrance to the tent, looking around, as if they might still help her with whatever was coming.

The sun slipped below the horizon, and the sound of laughter filled the camp. It wasn't wicked or malicious, it was mirthful and very amused. Octavia ran a hand over her face. The area around the camp shifted, a fire in a stone pit forming, surrounded by carpets strewn with pillows. It all looked very comfortable, which was at odds with Octavia's obvious discomfort.

It was then that Octavia's patron arrived. A beautiful, very feminine creature as tall as Alces, perhaps taller, appeared before them. Their skin was the blue of a summer sky, their eyes fairly glowed, and their long hair in shades of pink floated about them like a swirling cloud. They wore a very abbreviated version of Rupaiyan fashion, their cropped shirt barely holding in breasts that dwarfed Octavia's generous bosom, and a flowing skirt that sat low on the hips and was split on both sides.

Comicha popped into existence, right next to the three by the tent. "Show reverence to Kamvasana, Essense of Desire."

"This explains quite a bit," Durante said, his eyes flicking from the being to Octavia before finally turning to look at Comicha. He dropped down to one knee—one did not just stare slack jawed at a primordial being.

"Ah, wha, huh," Sumner responded, gawking but having enough sense to drop to his knee as well. For the most part he'd been respectful with his gaze at Octavia. He was finding it impossible to do so with Kamvasana.

Alces was the last to kneel but did so the most grandly. "Ah, the Spree Spirits have spoken of you, I believe you know them well. Let it be known your pact-bound is an admirable and stalwart woman," Alces said, also moving to one knee with a fist to his chest.

Octavia groaned, her gut twisting with embarrassment. "Hi, Kami."

"Do not 'Hi Kami' me," the creature said, folding their arms and glaring at Octavia. Their voice was accented but also strangely resonant, sounding both male and female at once. "You had multiple warnings, Octavia. You had opportunities! Three of them, every night, in your own tent!"

For the first time since she'd joined their strange troupe, Octavia blushed. "I was trying to be professional!"

"You were professionally stupid!" Octavia winced as Kamvasana raised their voice, and Durante and Sumner exchanged raised brows. "You knew the price, you know they will have to carry you tomorrow as you recover!"

"I—" Octavia began angrily, but looked over at the three still down on one knee and wilted a little, her cheeks going from pink to red. "I wanted them to like me..."

"Of course they like you! You have been perfected!"

"I meant as a person, not an object!" Octavia shot back, holding onto that sliver of anger. It was better than the sting of humiliation.

"Your acolyte has more than proven herself competent, intelligent, talented, and kind," Alces said, trying not to raise his voice but it came naturally to him, it boomed. Both Octavia and Kamvasana looked at him in shock. "She is a wonderful person and, if you accept my mortal opinion, not deserving of ridicule."

"It's true," Sumner agreed, and Octavia's embarrassment bled off of her in the face of these men rushing to her defense. "We've only been travelling together a few days but she's great." Durante was quiet, but the look on his face made it very clear that he could not believe either of his companions were attempting to chastise the entity before them.

Kamvasana pinched the bridge of their nose. "The gall. Three hundred years ago—" They took a deep breath, and looked at Octavia again. "Nevermind. I'm not mad, I'm just disappointed. You cannot serve me and deny yourself."

Octavia sighed. "I understand."

"Good!" She gestured to the three again. "And, obviously, they like you, if they are determined to talk back to *me*!"

Glancing over at them again, Octavia smiled a little sheepishly, then looked back up at her patron. After a long moment, she took a deep breath. "I am sorry I did not listen, Kami."

"You are forgiven."

Octavia arched an eyebrow. "Does that mean you'll stop before dawn?"

"Absolutely not," Kamvasana said with a malicious smile, "and you were a fool to even ask. Now then."

The Essence of Desire patted Octavia on the head, and the warlock was abruptly transformed. Instead of her travelling clothes she was wearing an ensemble out of the old stories of concubines and pleasure palaces.

The tight but functional top that Octavia had been wearing was replaced by a cropped halter top of a sheer material. Fabric panels that were a little smaller than the breasts they strained to hold in place. The fabric was so sheer that it was easy to see that her nipples had been gilded. An elaborate pectoral piece hid where the fabric circled her neck, a heavy silver disk festooned with sapphires in countless shades of blue. The same sheer fabric wrapped her hips in a skirt that only hid more than the top because of how the fabric was gathered, complemented with another heavily bejeweled belt. Silver armbands, bangles, rings, and anklets set with more sapphires decorated her arms and legs, and her hair was elaborately done up into a high ponytail with beads and gems twined and pinned into her cascading curls. Her make up had also been done, heavy kohl lining her eyes and an inviting pink stain on her lips.

Sumner's lips pursed as if he were about to whistle, but a knowing glance from both Alces and Durante halted that before it happened.

Putting her hands on her hips, Octavia looked down, and then back at Kamvasana.

"Are you quite serious!?" Octavia glared at her patron. "Tell me you didn't destroy another pair of boots! Please say they are in the tent!"

"They are. Now then," Kamvasana turned towards Octavia's slightly bewildered companions. "Octavia is in forfeit of her pact. She is to encourage and participate in acts of desire and passion, and she has elected not to do so. To pay her forfeit, she is mine until dawn. I invite you to view her punishment, if you so wish."

Alces stood and sighed. There was nothing to be done, a pact was law with the primordials, to go against that would bring all sorts of calamity. "I only wish to do what Octavia wants," he said, then turned to Octavia, "do you wish us to stay or leave you with your patron?"

Octavia looked sheepish again. "It... won't bother me, but... I think you all have a fair idea of what's going to happen, and...," she glanced at the three of them, her eyes flitting from Durante to Sumner and finally to Alces, "if you are going to see me in such a manner, I'd rather it be because we chose each other. At least the first time. And again, I'm sorry about the noise. The tent will muffle some of it."

"That is what I needed to hear," Alces said. He turned, bowed to Kamvasana. "I serve to spread the light. There is no light for us here, simply payment due. I will greet you when you are done, Octavia." With that said, the massive knight headed into the tent.

Sumner lingered for a moment, looking deeply conflicted. However, a swift swat to the shoulder from Durante and a glance back to the tent made him think better of it. The other two followed Alces inside, leaving Octavia alone on the great, cool plain in relative silence.

SIX

K neel before me, Octavia," Kamvasana demanded.

"Um, I'll let Alces know that if they're really mad at you they might leave you on the ground," Comicha said quietly. "Good luck, Mistress!"

"Thank you," Octavia murmured. She took a breath, then turned and did as instructed. The primordial waved a hand, and their clothing disappeared, revealing that beneath the faint skirt, Desire's incarnation also had a very sizable shaft that was swiftly growing erect.

"I can never be too disappointed with you," they said, smiling as they stroked themself briefly. "You are one of my best warlocks, after all. Open your mouth."

There was a tightness in Octavia's posture, a faint twist in her stomach, but she did as directed, mouth open with her tongue slightly extended, and Kamvasana placed the head of their cock on that waiting tongue. Octavia immediately began to lick and suck at the head, fitting her mouth around it as best she could, getting her jaw used to the size. She knew what was coming.

"Yesssss," they hissed, petting the side of her face. "You could have done this for them, you silly girl. I'm sure they would have loved it. I'm sure the dragonkin would have roared at your talent."

Though Octavia would never admit it, the praise did send a flush through her as she slowly worked to take more of the primoridal's cock. She could feel it bumping at the back of her throat now. Seven years as Kamvasana's warlock had, thankfully, gotten rid of Octavia's gag reflex.

"See, you are already prepared for more," they continued, caressing her face again before reaching back to cup the back of her head. Suddenly gripping Octavia's hair, they thrust themselves in down her throat, fucking her mouth as she whimpered. It didn't take long before Kamvasana came, spilling seed into Octavia before letting her go. Octavia fell to her hands, catching her breath. Lack of a gag reflex aside, she still needed to breathe.

"An excellent start, sweet girl. Stay as you are. I think I'll enjoy you like that."

Octavia nodded and stayed in place as Kamvasana walked around and knelt behind her. They stroked her thighs and pushed up the short wrap before sinking into Octavia with a solid thrust, followed by a relentless fucking. Kamvasana didn't care about Octavia's pleasure—that wasn't the point. Octavia's penance was to provide Kamvasana with enjoyment to make up for having denied the primordial the experience of her joy at another's hand.

Gasping, Octavia struggled to keep herself upright as the primordial pounded into her. It still felt good. Part of being Kamvasana's warlock had included changes to the body, which meant that sex almost always felt good, even with an inconsiderate or inexperienced partner. That said, it wasn't what it could be with someone who was invested in her enjoyment.

The primordial pulled out abruptly, shooting cum across Octavia's lower back and ass. "I think I am interested in your less explored assets tonight," Kamvasana said, sliding their cock between Octavia's full, jiggling asscheeks. "Not enough of your partners go delving back here. You should ask for it more."

Their positions meant the primordial couldn't see Octavia roll her eyes. "Yes, Kami," she said, shifting a little and doing her best not to tense. She squeaked as a cum-covered thumb pushed into her tight back entrance.

"There, see?" The thumb worked into her, Octavia moaned, and Kamvasana tsked. "Too tight. You almost feel untrained. That's fine. We'll get you loosened up again."

The thumb withdrew, but before Octavia could move or speak the primordial's cock was pressing into her ass, stretching her as they grabbed that ponytail and pulled Octavia's head back.

"That's my good girl," Kamvasana purred, and Octavia gritted her teeth even as her sex started to drip. Her body was well conditioned after all these years. Then the essence of Desire was thrusting into her again, and she was bracing herself as well as possible to take it.

The test of Octavia's sexual endurance went on for hours. When she could no longer hold herself up, Kamvasana manifested pillows, cushions, and padded furniture much like what they had seen in the Treasure Room to keep her in place. As dawn rose, Kamvasan was pleased enough with Octavia's performance that they did bring her into the tent. They laid her on the floor in the lounge and left her there, still swathed in her provocative finery, hair and makeup mussed.

"This is how you should look every morning," Kamvasana said, nodding to themself. "Well done, dearest. Let's hope I don't see you soon." Octavia managed not to groan and decided to give herself a minute before attempting to move.

As the Essence of Desire left, Comicha flew over to the curtains to Alces' bed. "Um... Alces? You... you can heal, right? It will help."

The curtain parted immediately. Alces was already awake, and seemed to have been waiting. "Of course. I will tend to our exhausted warlock," he said, petting Comicha gently.

He walked to the center of the tent and knelt beside Octavia. "Adorable Comicha, would you fetch a blanket for her? I do not know if she would like to remain in this manner," Alces said, looking Octavia over. "Our strong Octavia, let me share my light with you."

"Oh, yes!" Comicha said, cheerful as always and ready to serve.

Alces rubbed his hands together, then very gently placed them against her chest and her stomach. Closing his eyes, his throat opened and an ancient chant resonated throughout the tent. It was low, soothing, with power behind it. His hands began to glow and Octavia could feel soreness and weariness leaving her body. While there was only so much to be done about the fatigue and muscle ache, there had still been some damage to heal. Kamvasana did not *try* to hurt Octavia, but they did not hold back either.

As the spell worked through her, Octavia groaned softly and became capable of more than just laying there. Comicha came back into the room, dragging Octavia's blanket.

"Thank you," Octavia said as the chant died away, her voice soft. "I'm sorry I will be a burden today. If you carry me to my room, Comicha can help me dress. And... we will all talk over breakfast."

"You will never be a burden," Alces said. Laying the blanket over her, Alces scooped her into his arms and stood up, careful with his steps so she was not jostled. With utmost care he placed her on the bed.

"Take your time. Sumner and I will prepare breakfast, I'm sure Durante will awake at some point," he said, giving her a half smile and tilting his head. This was the most soft spoken she had ever heard Alces. Standing, he carefully brushed her hair out of her face and gave her a nod, then stepped out into the main room, calling for Sumner to get up.

After waiting for a breath, Octavia groaned and pushed the blanket off. "Comicha, please help me get this off."

"Yes, Mistress," the imp fluttered around Octavia, removing everything from her hair first, then working down her body. "You must have done very well, Mistress! They let you keep this pretty outfit, and I can tell it's worth a lot. And they brought you inside! I know they were mad, but they hate it when you deny your desires."

It was a strange mix of emotions as Comicha helped Octavia undress and then get cleaned up. Octavia felt a thread of pride in that she could still delight Kamvasana after all these years. She was worried about what she would see in the eyes of her traveling companions when she came out for breakfast. It had only been a few days, but things had been going well. It had felt like, maybe, they might be friends in time. But she wasn't sure anymore.

It took longer than usual, but Octavia finally made her way back out into the lounge, dressed and as clean as she could get for the moment. She had wanted to use the bath, but she didn't dare delay them that long. She would see if she could manage it tonight before bed. She hoped she wouldn't need assistance. But for now, clean enough, dressed, boots on, ready to... probably be carried.

Durante was in the main room, looking over her walking trunk again. He smiled as she walked in. "Hi," he said softly. "Are, um, are you okay? The others are outside cooking. Should be ready soon." He didn't seem that phased.

"I... yes, thank you." She sat down in one of the chairs, carefully— Alces had healed the damage, but her ass was still pretty tender. "All in all, I am in far better shape than I was last time. Um... I am sorry if I kept you up."

"Only a bit with worry," he said. "We didn't know exactly what was going to happen. I've read about deals with ancients going, well, not well. But I should have remembered that you've been doing this for years, so you're used to it...? Kind of?"

A laugh bubbled out of Octavia. "As much as you can get used to it. I don't... have to do that often. I travel enough that it's easy to find passing dalliances. And I'm not above paying for a brothel, if one will let a woman in. I've been turned away before." She shrugged.

He stood up and patted her trunk. "I think I can fix her up. Not here, I'll need to stay in one place and work on the enchantments a little, but I think it'll only take some tweaking. Did you want to come outside, or should I go get you some food?"

Looking over at Durante, she smiled. "Thank you. I appreciate the work you've put in. And...I think I can come outside. Walking around a little is good to keep my muscles from getting too stiff, but...I won't be capable of keeping up with you all today."

"It gives me something to do, so I appreciate you bringing me a challenge. Here, you won't have to walk," Durante said, wiping his hand on his pants then offering it to her. She let him pull her out of the chair, and stretched with a groan. At least stretching still felt good, even if it reminded her of all her sore spots.

"Alces already called for Nutmeg," Durante said, averting his eyes, a measure of his shyness returning. "He's outside as well. Let's get you fed, we really didn't have dinner last night."

Octavia blinked. "No, I suppose we didn't."

They stepped out of the tent, and Octavia shielded her eyes in the morning light. The plain lacked tree cover and the sun was up and insistently shining. Her hair had been left down for once and a breeze played through it. She pushed it back from her face and looked for Alces and Sumner. They weren't far, tending a small fire pit and cooking eggs on the stone from the other night as well as a few birds roasting on spits. As Octavia and Durante approached, she could hear them discussing something about spices.

She also noticed an immense elk standing nearby, with a rich brown coat around its ruff that faded to a dark cream farther down its back. There was an otherworldly sense to it, from the way it calmly observed them to the color of its eyes, which were a brilliant violet much like Alces'. It turned as she walked out and stepped towards her.

Durante patted it on the nose, "this is Nutmeg."

The elk nudged him and walked right up to Octavia, bowing its head down enough so she could do the same without fear of the huge antlers. Eyes wide, Octavia gently petted its nose, but the little girl in her took over and the gentle nose pat turned into head pets, scritches around the antlers, and finally a hug and nuzzle into his great neck.

"Oh, he likes you," Alces laughed, standing and turning towards them. The elk cuffed and nuzzled into her. "He says that he will happily carry you wherever you need, and that you are a most welcome change of pace."

"I think I love him," Octavia said, muffled by the elk's ruff.

"Oh no," Alces said, laughing again. "Keep that up and he'll become your problem." The elk chuffed and Alces shook his head. "No, and be good. I mean it." She finally let go and gave Nutmeg one more nose pet.

"Food is almost ready too," Sumner added. "How're you holding up?" Yeah, everyone was going to ask that question, but thankfully it was just the three of them. This time. There wasn't a whole audience that she had to reassure.

"I'm all right," she said, smiling sheepishly at Sumner. "I am grateful to have a healer this time." She looked to Alces, then back to Sumner. "I was telling Durante, it was worse last time. Um...I would like to explain things to you all, if that's all right. Over breakfast, maybe. While I'm sure you've deduced a fair bit I... would like to know we all understand each other."

The others nodded, and they all settled down to eat. Durante produced some tin plates from his bag along with knives. Nutmeg settled himself down behind Octavia, effectively giving her a fluffy couch to lean against. Sumner put a couple of eggs on a plate, then cracked one of the small poultry in half and set that on it as well, before handing it over to Octavia. She could smell rosemary, thyme, and pepper on the bird.

"If we are to travel together, we want to know everything you wish to tell us," Alces said.

Octavia nodded, and ate her eggs first, then picked at the bird while she started talking. "All right. So... a little history. Maybe more than you need. My father, as Durante mentioned, was a merchant. My grandfather had been very successful, but after he died it became clear that my father lacked his acumen. My mother was a socialite. My brother and I were both raised by our nanny, essentially. It wasn't an unusual childhood among my peers. My brother left when I was fourteen, and I still don't know why. No one would speak of it. And at 18 my father lost everything."

She took a few bites, considering. "His 'partner' swooped in and bought all of our businesses, and kept my father on as a figurehead. My mother was in his bed by the end of the week. I was told I could provide the same services for his sons, or I could leave. So I left. I ended up in Rupaiya and tried to find work. But... I wasn't good at a lot. I had been trained to society, they had hoped to wed me to a noble family. Those skills aren't worth much to a woman with no money. So I taught voice lessons, tutored children, tried to find work as a clerk. The life I was building was nothing I wanted. So... I performed a ritual. I would make a pact with anyone who answered, so long as we could agree on the terms. To my utter surprise and amazement, Kamvasana answered."

"There's stories about getting out of pacts made under duress—," Durante started to say.

"Not with a primordial," Alces interrupted. "Those are sealed. But, it has worked out for you, yes?"

There was a moment of quiet as she ate some more. Sumner didn't comment, but it was clear that he was listening. They all waited for her to continue.

"Honestly, most of the time it isn't so bad," Octavia admitted at last. "The terms of my pact are very straightforward. I serve Kamvasana for a minimum of 15 years. They provide me with power and abilities I wouldn't have otherwise, things that I could leverage to live the kind of life I wished. In return, I must bolster their power as an agent of Desire." She laughed a little, and looked back down at her plate. "Essentially, I became prettier. My face is the only physical part of me I still recognize. My singing voice got better, though if I may say so it was already pretty good. And... I have to have sex with someone at least once a week, or Kami comes to collect."

"Sounds pretty good to me," Sumner said and the rest didn't immediately motion otherwise. In fact, Durante nodded. After all, stories of their past victories made it clear that they were not chaste. They had standards, clearly, but they didn't shy away from the subject.

"I know I need to say it because they think I will be disappointed with them if they suggest it," Alces started. "If you are in need, I know that we would all be more than happy to help you."

Sumner was visibly relieved.

"However," Alces continued loudly, making it very clear that he was being serious, "you are part of our party for now, until you wish to leave. That does not change. We will fight with you, protect you, and celebrate with you in any way you are comfortable with. Nothing alters this."

"I... thank you," she said, laughing a little, though mostly at herself. "You are all quite attractive and it has been an interesting struggle with myself to not say anything. I'm not certain I entirely succeeded. But I've also been alone for a long time. I enjoyed our camaraderie, and was afraid to strain it." She glanced up at them, her gaze flicking from violet eyes to green to pink, then back at her plate.

"I will... be more honest in the future. Though if at all possible I would still like things to progress... naturally?" She furrowed her brow not sure how else to say it. "And...a re you all right with me... that is, if I say yes to someone on one night and someone else on another...?"

They all looked at each other for a moment, started to snicker a little, then started laughing. Well, mostly Alces laughing, which caused something in the grass to startle and fly off, and Sumner, who cackled. Durante quietly snickered but nodded.

"Let us say it would not be the first time that has happened," Alces finally said. "But you are our friend. I do not see that changing. You have my word upon the Spree Spirits, my honor as a knight, and my blood of the dragons."

"As long as I get a turn, I'm good," Sumner said with a shameless grin. Alces slapped his shoulder lightly but chuckled.

"We trust each other," Durante added, "and I'm enjoying our chats. I'll enjoy your company in any setting."

Octavia smiled and leaned back into Nutmeg. "Thank you. It sounds like we understand each other. Good." She glanced down at her plate and sat up again. "I suppose I will stop talking, finish eating, and then get my chest and bag out of the tent so that we can pack up and go."

"This conversation," Alces started, glancing towards Sumner but also smirking a little, "is at your discretion, Octavia. Otherwise, we continue as we have been. May our times together be filled with light." To emphasize his point, he popped one of the roasted birds in his mouth. The whole thing. Chewing happily.

"Uh, yeah, I'll finish with the rest of the eggs and pack up the food," Sumner said. "We wanted to make time before the mist this place is known for rolls in."

"Don't worry," Durante said, holding up a compass, "we're not going to get lost. It's just annoying."

And that seemed to be that. The three men went about life as if it were just another morning, and Octavia followed their example. She had Alces help her back to her feet after breakfast was done and managed to saunter back into the tent long enough to coax Matilda out and grab her satchel. She told Durante how to collapse the tent. Alces hoisted Octavia up onto Nutmeg's back. She found the elk was amazingly comfortable, even without a saddle, and his back wide enough she could stretch out and rest against his ruff. It didn't take long for them to get ready to go, douse and scatter the fire, and be on their way.

Octavia snuggled into Nutmeg once they started out. "No, it's too late, I do love you," she murmured sleepily, hugging him again before settling into a more stable riding position. The elk sort of whickered pleasantly at her. She snoozed for a good part of the trip, not really coming to full wakefulness until the midafternoon, well after the fog had rolled in.

Yawning, she picked up her head and looked around. Durante was at the front of the small company now, with his map and compass out, the other two following cautiously.

"Oh, Gods," she murmured, "it's so heavy."

"Yeah," Durante said, adjusting his compass. "The canyons aren't much better. It spills in from the plateau."

"Fog is a challenge," Alces said, slowing his step to walk next to Nutmeg. "The light reflects off of everything, making it harder to see. There is a trickery to it that is almost worse than darkness."

"I dunno, I always kind of liked it," Octavia said with a small smile. Alces turned to look at her. "When I was younger, and the fog would roll into the bay, I imagined what wonders hid within it. Mermaids, swan maidens, ghost ships full of treasure and stories, lost princesses." She yawned again, still sleepy. The dragonkin looked at her for a moment, a soft smile on his face, something fond twinkling in his eyes.

"I know it's different when you travel," she added.

The wind shifted direction, and Alces sniffed and unhooked his shield. "There is something in the mist," he said. Octavia felt a tingle, an energy she hadn't felt before.

"What is it?" Durante asked, pausing in his walk.

"It smells like old magic," Alces said. Sumner pulled up the masking cloth he had around his neck and drew his sword. Durante went to tuck away the map and the compass and pull out his device.

Alces suddenly turned his head and roared. White arctic winds blew from his maw and in the mist there suddenly formed a shape, howling. That helped Octavia shake off the rest of her fatigue. She sat up on Nutmeg, and swung her bag around to the front so that she could pull things out if she needed. Sumner dashed forward, coming up behind the creature and ran his blade into it. It howled out again and then wriggled off Sumner's blade, fading into the mist again. Her eyes darted around, but the mist was very difficult to see through.

"Elementals," Alces snorted. "Probably drawn to the residual power of the primordial. No matter. Tough, but manageable."

A sudden gust blew through the group and Alces raised his shield against it. Resounding thumps pounded against it and they could see the apparition through the swirling mist. Durante fired his screwshot and while the blue streak slammed into the creature, it also seemed to go right through. The elemental was definitely perturbed by the attack and turned towards the pale man.

"Ah, skuffs, wrong charge," Durante said and started to shuffle through his bag.

The elemental grew closer as Durante kept digging. Octavia brought up her hand and sent a bolt of arcing blue power at the elemental. The blast definitely hit it. It did not seem stunned like a humanoid would have been, but a wind-like roar told her the blast still hurt. They were doing well keeping it distracted. It couldn't tell who was the biggest threat yet, so it kept getting turned around. With the momentary pause in attacks, Alces roared out and smashed his mace into the elemental. There was a sudden burst of light when the weapon connected, and the creature wailed yet again.

"Sumner!" Octavia called out as she cast, blue fire leaping from her hand to wreath his sword in flames. If her blast made it hurt, this definitely would.

"Good call, Tavi," Sumner shouted, whipping the sword around him before striking down on the elemental again. "Die!" The fire licked at the air creature, carving through it. There was a sudden smell, sharp and pungent, like when lightning strikes too close.

Maneuvering with surprising deftness in spite of his size, Alces placed himself and his shield in between the flailing elemental and the others. Durante found the glass tube he was looking for and hooked it up to his contraption. Taking aim, he fired another shot - this one a streak of black that impacted and blew a piece of the elemental off.

"We're wearing it down," he called out.

The wind seemed to screech as the mist suddenly swirled around them. Alces turned and shouldered Sumner out of the way as the wind whipped around, buffeting the dragonkin and nearly tearing the shield from his arm, but his grip held true. Octavia could see his claws grip into the dirt to keep him upright. She brought up her second hand and sent two beams of energy into the elemental this time. Her shot staggered the creature and stopped it from continuing the blows smacking Alces around, then Durante tilted it to the other direction with his own shot. Dropping to one knee, Alces planted his shield into the ground, bracing his shoulder against it and leaning in. Sumner ran up the knight's side, springing off his thigh, then leaping off his shoulder. He sailed through the air and came down on the apparition with his flaming blade.

"I said fuckin' die!" Sumner shouted. Pinned to the earth by the flaming magic, the elemental thrashed then quieted, its form dissolving and dissipating into the mist once more. With the elemental gone, the wind also died, leaving them in an unsettling quiet.

SEVEN

"Well done," Alces said, shattering the silence and sliding his leg back underneath him so he could stand upright. He looked around and pulled his shield from the dirt. "I think we missed the others. Should be relatively safe now."

"That would have taken a lot longer without that blade enchantment," Sumner said, giving Octavia a wink.

"Or if I remembered to just slot my screwshot charges," Durante said with a grunt.

With a relieved sigh, Octavia slumped forward on Nutmeg and the fire around Sumner's blade died. "Is everyone all right?"

"Oh, I'm good," Sumner said, checking his blade before sheathing it. "I'm real good."

"Frustrated but I'm fine," Durante added.

"Not a scratch. Pummel as much as you like, wind isn't blowing this knight down," Alces said with aplomb. "How fair you, brave Octavia?"

She laughed. "Good! Nutmeg stood stoically and I'm more ranged anyway." She reached down and rubbed the side of the elk's neck. "Feeling very awake now, we'll see how long it lasts."

Nutmeg chuffed again and leaned its head to the side so Octavia could rub more.

"Yes, yes, you're very brave," Alces laughed, addressing the elk. "Run away and keep the pretty girl safe. Very strong."

"Don't listen to him, you were brave," Octavia said, leaning over to hug Nutmeg's neck again. "And you didn't run anywhere, you stayed right here and didn't startle when I cast spells, and you were such a good boy." She gave him more rubs.

"You're going to give him a big head. You have not been hearing him bragging all day. Insufferable," Alces said but patted the elk on the nose and turned towards Durante. "Continue on, wise Durante."

Durante was busy slinging his screwshot and pulling the map and compass back out of his bag. He looked like he was still stewing over his misstep. Sumner made a clicking sound with his tongue. "Don't I get some praise this time?"

Alces laughed. "Of course, quick Sumner. Without the true strike of your blade, we would still be fighting."

Looking up at Sumner, Octavia grinned. "You were also a good boy."

Sumner grinned back and raised his eyebrows at Octavia. "I was, wasn't I?"

She gave Nutmeg one last rub, then sat up. "How much further today, do you think? I've lost my sense of time in all this."

"I'm hoping we can get off the plateau before nightfall," Durante said, getting his bearings again and starting to walk forward. Everyone else moved at his pace. "Another couple of hours, at least."

Octavia nodded. "All right." As they moved through the fog, she shivered a little and leaned down against the warm beast beneath her once more. Tomorrow she would need to dig out her coat.

Durante's calculations were pretty good, and they were able to get off the plateau before nightfall. This led them off the slope and heading back towards one of the main roads. Durante paused the group as he looked over the map.

"Okay, we have two choices. We've got a natural arch up ahead that we could camp under, or two hours back we have Boxende town and an inn. How're we feeling?" he asked.

"Back? As in back where we came from?" Octavia looked at the others. "I don't know anything about Boxende, so I'm not sure if it's worth the lost time. But if you'd prefer somewhere to get a drink I won't protest."

"In the opposite direction, yes," Durante said. "I'm keen to keep traveling, especially with that nice tent of yours, Octavia."

"I am as well. The sooner we get to the Drukankor Tower, the better," Alces stated.

She nodded. "I'm good to make it to the arch." She thought for a second, then laughed. "And I may have mead in the tent."

"Perfect," Sumner said, "let's gooo."

"Sooner we make camp, the sooner some of us can lay comfortably without worry about attack or jostled travel," Alces commented. Nutmeg chuffed and Alces patted his nose. "Yes, we know, mighty Nutmeg. You did a great job, and that is all I'll say,"

Octavia giggled. She couldn't ride Nutmeg everywhere, but this was pretty fantastic and he was so magnificent. She kept that to herself, though, in light of Alces' comments. Also, as much as it was easier than walking, riding Nutmeg was still doing a number on her already strained hips and thighs.

They arrived at the arch in good time. It was massive, spanning several hundred feet across and sixty or so feet above them. It would be an amazing natural bridge if it wasn't so steep. Still, nestling the tent up against the edge of it also hid it from the road, the scrub and low trees keeping it quite hidden.

Alces helped Octavia down. The great elk nuzzled Octavia once more, then chuffed at Alces before strutting down the path where he disappeared in a puff of purple light. Sumner and Durante got everything inside. Soon they were all in softer clothing and set up in the sitting area with the leftover eggs and birds and a few other sundries they had packed away. Octavia headed over to a chest off to the side of the room, its pale wood almost the same color as the tent, making it easy to overlook.

"Gods, what was I even thinking," she muttered to herself as she sorted through a number of dry goods that were all in excellent shape due to the nature of the tent. She set aside the biscuit tin and also withdrew two bottles of mead and a rich red wine. It looked like she had more alcohol than anything in there.

"Ohhh, this is when I did all that work for that tavern," she murmured, moving the bottles around. "We can save the harder stuff for another night, I imagine."

Standing back up, she walked over and handed a bottle of mead each to Alces and Sumner. "A bit tame compared to your last post-battle celebration, I know, but it's not bad."

"This is perfect for our celebration," Alces said, accepting the bottle and nodding to Octavia. "A wee battle gets a wee celebration. Barely broke a sweat, so we'll only break one bottle!"

"What the big guy said," Sumner said, looking his bottle over. "Thanks. Still good to relax, but we got a handful of days left hiking up a mountain."

Fishing out some glasses from her trunk, Octavia came back and handed one to Durante before cracking open the red so they could share. "Thank you," Durante said, settling on the couch so they could sit close enough to share the bottle. "Also, the weather is starting to change. We really should break out the winter gear tomorrow. Or at least make sure it's at the top of our bags."

Octavia folded herself onto one side of the couch with a groan. "I was thinking that today, actually," she said, gently swirling the wine in her cup. "That I would need to dig out my coat, I mean. I'm happy to say that the temperature inside the tent remains the same, regardless of the environment outside. Well, mostly. It can get a little colder if there's enough snow, but I promise it's always warm in here."

She sipped her wine. A pleasant drowsiness was seeping into her limbs. While snoozing on Nutmeg's back had been very nice, it hadn't been enough to make up for her evening with her patron. They ate, and she watched them quietly, her lack of sleep slowly starting to catch up with her.

"Tomorrow will be tougher. We should sleep soon," Alces said, looking at Octavia with a softly amused smile. His bottle of mead had already disappeared along with the eggs and part of a bird that had been left.

"I know you're going to wake me up early, good hunting around here. We should get something bigger to last us up the mountain," Sumner added and Alces nodded in agreement.

"Prod me, make sure I don't sleep too late," Durante said to the room.

Octavia yawned and stretched. "You can always wake me up if I oversleep. I try not to. Sometimes Comicha wakes me up." She set her cup down. "So far the sound of voices has been enough. Not used to it." She was about halfway through her second glass of wine, and leaning heavily on the arm of the couch, most of her weight on her hip. Her feet had slowly inched down the couch until they were resting against Durante. She shifted, and one foot slid into his lap.

"Little cutie seems to have made herself scarce since last night as well. Something happen, or she's taking it easy like Nutmeg does?" Sumner asked.

"A little like Nutmeg, I think. Technically she's only supposed to come out when I summon her," she said, rolling her eyes. "Sometimes, though, she just...appears. I think it's because she's more intelligent and has more autonomy than a regular imp. I'm probably going to call her up after I go to bed and have her work on this ache in my thighs. She'll forgive me when I pass out on her."

She folded her arms on the scrolled arm of the couch and laid her head on them, her hair spilling down the side. She had started to absently rub her foot against Durante's leg.

"Um… Octavia?" Durante's voice quavered slightly with uncertainty. Sumner snickered.

"Hmm?"

There was a beat of hesitation. "Um… nevermind," Durante murmured.

"Octavia, if you are still not up for walking, it will be no trouble to summon Nutmeg again," Alces said as he stood. "Tonight we sleep well. Tomorrow will be when things start to get hard."

"Yup, good idea," Sumner said, hopping up and stretching. "Morning is going to be early and annoying."

"Especially because I'm not letting you sleep in. You have work to do," Alces added before giving a wave. "All, sleep well. Will see you in the morning."

"Sleep well, Ser Knight," Octavia murmured, her eyes closed, foot still absently rubbing Durante's thigh.

"Should be for all of us," Sumner said, the laughter in his voice barely contained. "Right, g'night you two."

"Night, Sumner." Octavia's words were slower, barely pronounced.

There was a long moment of silence, and then finally a hand nudged Octavia's calf. "Hey, Octavia, unless you plan on sleeping on the couch, you should probably head to bed too, yeah? W-weren't you going to have Comicha give you a massage?"

"Hm? Wha?" Octavia picked her head up and blinked, then looked over at her legs. "Oh! Sorry." Yawning, she pulled her legs out of his lap, then leaned over and kissed his cheek. "Thank you. I'm so tired, I just… yeah. Night, kitten."

Durante sat and smiled, touching his cheek a little. "Good night."

Pushing herself up out of the couch, she stumbled back to her room. Pulling the curtain, Octavia yawned again. "Comicha?"

The little imp appeared with a pop and a smile. "Yes, Mistress?"

"Shh, quietly." Octavia took off her lounge clothes. "My thighs still hurt a lot. I'm hoping you can rub them out. But I'll probably fall asleep."

"Oh, yeah, the boss did a number on you," Comicha said as Octavia fell into bed. Flying over, she landed between Octavia's legs and pouted a little. "Just a massage?"

"Just a massage," Octavia repeated, her eyes already closing.

The little imp sighed, "Yes, Mistress," and got to work. Octavia, true to her word, was asleep in minutes.

***

"Wake up, my friends," Alces cheerfully called out through the tent, his booming voice easily penetrating the thick curtains and startling Octavia awake. She flailed in her blankets for a minute as she struggled to sit up. "Breakfast is ready soon, and then we march! The mountains await!"

She sat in the bed for a moment until she got her heart to calm down, then got up and got dressed. Heavier pants, a typical shirt, heavier socks, and she dug out her coat from the bottom of the chest. The ache in her legs was much improved, and a day on Nutmeg meant her feet were doing fine. Hair twisted back up into a bun, she grabbed her coat and went out to see what everyone was up to.

It seemed that Alces and Sumner had been busy that morning, with a whole goat hanging to drain, and another that had been dressed and had parts cooking over the fire. There was also a selection of pome fruits sitting on a bundle of cloth.

Sumner gave her a wave as he rotated a pair of goat haunches. Alces turned to see who Sumner was waving at and smiled broadly. "Ah, there she is, our wondrous Octavia! The smaller bits of goat are almost cooked, and we found some fruit trees."

"Good morning," she said, pulling her coat on but not fastening it yet. She could still feel the ache in her legs as she walked but it was much better.

Taking a chunk of goat that had not been cooking, Alces blew on it, frosting it solid and tucking it into a thick leather bag. "Oh, that's clever," she said as he froze and stored the extra meat. "Very practical. You have many talents, Ser Knight."

"Blessed by the spirits, my lady," he said with a nod.

Sumner shaved off some pieces of goat meat and sliced up what looked to be a pinkish tan apple, placed them on a tin plate, and handed it to her. "Have you seen Durante yet?" he asked as he did so.

"Thank you." Octavia took the plate and stepped to the side, out of the way. "Um, no, not as I was leaving."

"I'm here, I'm here," the nobleman in question said as he stumbled out of the tent, pulling his coat on. "I was making sure I was packed first."

"Will you need Nutmeg's assistance this day?" Alces glanced back to Octavia, brows arched. "He's rather insistent, but I don't want to encourage him too much."

"I should try to walk for a while first, but I may eventually need Nutmeg," Octavia said, flexing the muscles in her legs and feeling the sharpness of the ache increase. "Walking will be good for me, but...well, I'll be honest, I'm not used to walking this much even without the other night's activities. But at least until lunch I'll do my best to go on foot unless I start holding us up."

"You start to waver, you let us know. It is best for you to be rested and prepared than to tough things out," Alces said. "We take care of each other."

"Yeah, I mean, if it was all about how hard you could push yourself, we would have left tubby here ages ago," Sumner said, pointing to Durante.

"Hey," the noble said, narrowing his eyes at Sumner.

"Brother, clearly a joke. You've trimmed up a lot since we first took you on. You're doing good," Sumner said with a smile, handing him a plate of food.

"Well, okay then," Durante said, playfully sticking his nose up at Sumner but took the plate just the same. Alces laughed at the exchange. Octavia giggled.

"I'm pretty sure I've got more chub than you do, and less endurance," she said. She took a bite, and considered. "Well, for walking, anyway."

"I would quantify that there is a distinct difference between chub and curves," Durante said, then his eyes went wide. "Oh, I'm sorry, I didn't mean to offend."

Sumner was clearly struggling not to laugh. Octavia stepped over and bumped Durante with her hip. "I'm glad it's in places you approve of. And I'm very difficult to offend." Durante gave her a pretty genuine smile and nodded. She stepped away before being too close to him made him flustered again.

"You're getting there," Sumner said with a grin and then made his own plate. Alces had finished freezing the remaining goat and tucked it away.

"Alright, we leave soon. Make sure everything is packed and you're ready to go as soon as you're done eating. We want to take advantage of this summer sun as much as we can," the knight said.

Octavia finished eating and helped clean up before she headed back to call Matilda out of the tent. After everything was out she collapsed the tent once more, putting it away, and fighting the urge to ask Alces to call Nutmeg now.

The first day up was a change of pace to be sure. There was a road up to the tower, but it was old and hidden. Finding where this place was had probably been an adventure all on its own. Disuse, lack of maintenance, erosion, and plant growth made the road little more than close-knit marker stones. That, and the incline up into the mountains, she could now understand why they still had another two or three days to travel.

The chill was starting to come down as well. The mountains were snow-capped and the wind seemed to be coming right down off of them. Octavia bounced from hot to cold, the warm summer sun being countered by the occasional blast of cold wind. Mostly through stubbornness, She made it to about lunch time before she was unable to keep up. The thinning air as they climbed wasn't helping, either.

"Alces!" She called out as they reached a short bit of the path that leveled a touch.

The three stopped, and the silver-scaled knight turned with a smile. "Yes, elegant Octavia," he said, "are you alright?"

She jogged up and stopped, bending over and setting her hands on her legs as she panted for a moment. "I'm sorry," she said after she'd caught her breath, "I think I need Nutmeg."

"There is nothing to be sorry for," Alces said, putting a hand on her shoulder. "Stand up straight. There is no shame, and we are here to support you. Give me a few moments to summon him. Find a stump to rest."

Octavia caught up to the other two and found a boulder to sit on. "I see," she began, her chest still heaving a little bit as she caught her breath, "that I did myself a disservice taking a carriage everywhere."

"Oh, don't be too hard on yourself," Durante said, nibbling a piece of meat. "I did as well. As Sumner pointed out so astutely this morning," he said with a grumpy growl, "I was not in any hiking shape when I first joined them either. But, if you continue adventuring after our agreement is done, I would recommend more walking. Helps a lot." Smiling,

Durante patted his gut.

After our agreement is done. There was something about those words that made her a little sad. She didn't dwell on it, though, and just smiled and nodded.

"You know," Durante started, "sun's pretty high. Could be a good time to get some lunch."

"Still have some of the fire cooked goat left," Sumner said, bringing his bag around. "I don't really want to make a fire right now, but here." Fishing out a parchment wrap, he opened it up to reveal about a pound or so of goat meat shavings. Easily enough for them to share. Alces wasn't there to devour the whole thing in one bite.

The dragonkin had moved a ways off path and was summoning his elk companion. A summon that sounded a lot like a mix of elk calls and ethereal chanting. Octavia watched, fascinated, as they ate. She didn't have a lot of experience with other types of magic. For all that it seemed that Alces also shared a bond with a primordial, the type of bond was decidedly different.

"So," she said after she'd had a few bites, pulling her eyes away from the summoning, "am I allowed to ask what we're hoping to find in the tower?"

Sumner glanced at Durante. Tilting his head back and forth, Durante made a thinking noise, then nodded. "Sure. You've already figured out most of the things, so why not. We're... trying to figure out a way to fix what I did," he said, sighing. "The tower belongs to Vaztus Drukankor, a mage that dabbled in a lot of alchemy and transmutations. I'm hoping there will be some research in there that may help me reverse this, well, curse that I bestowed upon myself."

Octavia's brows rose in surprise. "You did this to yourself? I'm sorry, I assumed...well. I'm guessing you didn't mean to do this to yourself."

Durante sadly nodded and gave her a little shrug.

"So we're breaching a mage's tower, specifically." The corner of her mouth quirked a little. "That will be fun, provided no one gets killed."

"That's why we have Alces," Sumner said with a grin. "Things get dicey, he's our wall. And escape route."

"Don't think we'll run into ghosts," Durante said, "but who knows how many of his experiments might still be alive. Or what sort of traps still hang about."

"You know, I don't think there will be that many traps," Sumner said, leaning against a tree. "Think about it: we got information about this place, we got a basic idea as to the layout, meaning someone else has been here. And if one person has been here, surely more people have been here. But the path isn't cleared or showing use, so not a lot of people. How many you think came in and already set off those traps or got eaten by mutants?"

"Okay, that's a grimly positive take away from that," Durante said.

"A strange thing to hope for, certainly, but if we're lucky." She found herself studying Sumner for a moment. He was very practical, and kept people on track. He often seemed the voice of reason. Or at least common sense.

"Shame on you," came Alces voice from the woods, distant enough to not be part of the current conversation, as he walked back with a Nutmeg along side. "I will do no such thing. Now, go on."

Nutmeg trotted up to Octavia and settled himself down on the ground right in front of her. Alces shook his head. "You have broken him. I need a new mount," the knight said with a laugh. Although Nutmeg did look back at Alces and narrow his eyes at him. This only made Alces laugh harder.

"I'm sorry," Octavia said, even as she reached down and started petting Nutmeg. "You don't mean that though, do you? I can't have broken him that much, and he's so nice, and look at how majestic he is!"

"You keep that up, and I don't think the woods will be able to contain his ego," Alces said, then shook his head. "Of course not, I will never replace Nutmeg, even if he is no longer my mount and has pledged his services elsewhere."

The look of kicked-puppy sadness that Octavia turned towards Alces was probably unfair. "No, I didn't mean to take him from you! I'm sorry!"

Alces bellowed out another laugh that caused something in the woods to dash away with great speed, and he smiled down at Octavia. "It is quite alright, he has a good reason, even if it is selfish," he said. "Besides, I am the one who offered his services, and I would not go back on my word."

Nutmeg seemed rather proud of himself, and the two others were laughing. Sumner took out another package of meat and handed it to Alces, then dusted off his hands and got up. "Don't worry, you can't actually take Nutmeg from him. Especially since Alces is the only one who knows what he's saying," he said.

"Okay," was all Octavia said, still feeling a little guilty, but she did go back to actively petting Nutmeg.

Alces unwrapped the pack, smiled and nodded to Sumner, then dumped it into his maw. To his credit, it didn't disappear immediately. He chewed and savored the flavor, he just did it all at once.

Octavia leaned against Nutmeg and hummed to herself as everyone finished lunch and prepared to start again. She wasn't sure if she should climb on his back now or wait for Alces to boost her up after, so she petted him and waited, watching the three of them as she did. It was fast becoming her favorite activity, observing them together and trying to learn more about them from it.

Sumner did some more stretching and Durante massaged his shoulder where the screwshot had been hanging from. Nutmeg seemed quite happy to lay there and let her dote on him.

"Are we ready to go, my friends?" Alces asked as he finished off his snack with a glug of water from a skin that looked like it could hold a few gallons.

"Yup," said Sumner, shaking out his arms.

"Yeah," Durante said, sounding tired but determined.

"Yes," Octavia chimed in, getting up and giving Nutmeg room to get on his feet. Even with the sun, the cold was starting to get to her, so she buckled up her coat. The wide fur collar framed her cleavage once everything was cinched in.

Looking down, she sighed a little. "Everything I own," she muttered to herself, but didn't dwell. There were worse things.

"Oh, you didn't need to get up," Alces said, walking over and scooping Octavia up, placing her on Nutmeg's back. "He's strong, you can get on him and he'll stand. Unless you like me picking you up." The dragonkin gave her a wink and patted Nutmeg's flank.

"I might," she said with an answering smile. In truth, she did, but experience had taught her you didn't just say that. Once settled on Nutmeg's back, she leaned down and gave his neck a rub before they got going.

EIGHT

As the wind came off the mountains, everybody else started to put on their gear. Both Sumner and Alces had fur-lined cloaks, Sumner's was smaller and black while Acles' had bright white fur lining it. Of course, Alces also wore his thrown back over one shoulder, implying it was more for fashion than function. Durante had a thick coat and gloves that he pulled from his bag, buttoning up as they went. As they headed further up the mountain, she took her gloves out and pulled them on. Octavia's winter gear was of excellent quality. Having been made before she was kicked out, it weathered the past eight years with minimal wear and tear.

She found herself humming as they traveled. She did it often while on her own, but less around people. A sign she was relaxing more around them. Alces paced beside her while Sumner was up front, finding them the best ways through the path and calling for Alces when a tree trunk needed moving or something along those lines. As they moved past the timberline, Alces looked Octavia over.

"Lovely Octavia, while I certainly am impressed by your fashion and choice of clothing, are you not cold?" he asked, concern in his voice. "That is still a lot of skin to expose to the elements."

With a laugh and a sigh, Octavia shook her head. "So, let me tell you a little story. It took about a year for my body to become what you see now. I grew into it, like a strange second adolescence. After that year was up, everything I wore altered itself to me within the span of a day. My shirts, my pants, my coat - they all became more form fitting, often lower cut. This was most strange with my coats, because to me they feel the same as they did, despite how they look."

"That does explain a lot," Sumner laughed, "I didn't want to say it, but your clothes did seem impractical for travel."

"Oh, horribly impractical," Octavia agreed with another laugh. "I look like I just left my pampered house yesterday and have no idea what I'm getting into. Wait until you see what it did to my sweaters."

"'Made perfected'," Durante muttered, "that's what your patron meant."

She looked over at Alces and leaned down with a teasing smile. "If you are worried, I invite you to put your hand to my chest and see that it is still warm."

"Who am I to deny such a charming woman's request," Alces said with a grin, reaching out and doing as she had suggested, placing three clawed fingers gently against the exposed tops of her breasts.

She hadn't expected him to do it, if she were being honest. She thought he would laugh and defer. She let out a little gasp as he touched her, as his own hands had been chilled by the elements. The pads of his fingers were soft and smooth, the scales pliable and flexible.

"Oh, apologies," Alces said, withdrawing his hand, "I thought it would protect against my cold fingers. But true you are, warm and soft, as it should be." The dragonkin smiled again and continued walking with them.

Sumner rolled his eyes and chuckled. "That's what you get for asking," he said, "if you ask him to do something, he's going to do it if it seems like it'll make you happy."

"I will–," Alces started.

"Be the light of the world," Alces, Sumner, and Durante all said at the same time.

"You are certainly that, Alces," Durante chuckled.

Octavia smiled and sat upright again. "I will remember that. Though I hope you won't do something you don't wish to, regardless of whether or not it will make someone happy."

"Certainly not," Alces said. "Although, you will be hard pressed to find that, for if I can do it, and it doesn't bring darkness to someone else, I will be happy doing so."

"Alright, we're past timberline, so it's going to get colder regardless, and I don't know if the weather is going to change up here," Sumner said.

"And who knows what magicks Vaztus caused that could make things worse," Durante added.

"Right, so how good is your tent keeping out the weather, Tavi?" Sumner asked as he guided them around some loose rocks and onto a more stable path.

"Pretty good," she answered. "If it snows it may get a little colder, but nothing that we need to be concerned about. I got caught out in a blizzard once, and had to grab extra blankets from the other rooms, but I was also alone. There's more of us, it should keep the tent warmer."

"Heavy snowfall and it won't collapse?" Sumner asked.

She nodded. "It definitely won't collapse."

"Alright, so we don't need to find a cave," he smiled.

They continued up the mountain until the light started to fade. At which point they found a clearing and started setting up a firepit with the wood Sumner had gathered as they had gone up.

"Glad your walking trunk was able to handle the terrain okay," Durante said, patting the funny magical construct.

"She's a good old girl," Octavia said, reaching out to Alces for him to help her off Nutmeg. Once on her feet, she gave the great elk a hug and a pet on the nose, thanking him for carrying her again. Nutmeg nuzzled her, the cold nose going straight into the exposed cleavage. She let out a little shriek and a laugh but gave the elk more rubs. The elk strutted away and she went and opened up her chest and got the tent out, finding a good spot and getting it set up. Once the tent was set up, people started moving their things inside. Sumner stayed out to build up the fire and get the goat cooking. She led her trunk inside but then came back out where Sumner was getting the goat on spits.

"Do you mind if I sit out here with you for a minute?" she asked.

Sumner gave her a toothy grin. "Not at all. Better looking company than those two," he said. That made her laugh. She knew he found her attractive, but she was not immune to honest flattery.

The fire had already been sparked up. and he was slowly feeding a few broken bits of log into it. It was a simple ring of stones, but it was doing the trick. She wandered over closer to the fire, and looked up at the swiftly darkening sky. "How much longer, do you think, until we get there? If the weather holds."

"Weather holds, hopefully tomorrow. If not, the morning after," he said, glancing up the mountain. "Best guess, of course. We haven't been there before, just got instructions and ideas."

Nodding, she followed his gaze. "I am a little worried about the tower. Old magic is unstable. Not so worried that I think we shouldn't try, it's more that I want us to be cautious." She looked over at him again and came around the fire to stand closer to him.

"We're mostly cautious when it comes down to it, but I appreciate the note on that," he said honestly.

"You're like the ringmaster of this little circus, you know that," she commented, smiling. "You all look to Alces, but you're the voice of common sense keeping everyone under budget and on time."

Sumner laughed. "I suppose. I feel more like a herder of some sort. I mean, Alces is definitely the leader. He's the most experienced, the toughest, and he's always on or has a mission. But, yeah, sometimes I need to pull the reins a bit. And they're both terrible with money."

"I'm not a lot better," she admitted, sheepishly. "Better than I used to be, certainly, but I like luxury. Fine foods. Good wines. Soft beds. Handsome men. Pretty women. The good brothels get expensive." She grinned and tossed her hair back.

"Don't I know it," Sumner laughed again. "Alces doesn't care, he sees money all as fleeting so saving doesn't mean anything to him, and Durante was like you, once. Used to those things."

"In my limited defense, I do need to be careful in cities," Octavia said, leaning back against a boulder. "I have to keep my patron happy, but I can't go into a tavern and bat my eyelashes. That's an easy way to get drugged and sold. It's safe in smaller towns, but then I spend a lot of time educating virgins or near virgins." She sighed and looked off to the side, muttering, "My kingdom for a steady partner with some experience."

Sumner smirked and raised an eyebrow at her. "You know, I don't know how long you plan on travelling with us, whether it's just for this gig or if you'll stick around, but I think your patron did mention a little disappointment that you hadn't batted your eyelashes at us."

"Oh, they were awful about it," Octavia said, pushing off the boulder and stepping close to Sumner. "They kept prodding me to pursue any of you, chastising me for not acting on my attraction." She was fairly close to him now, in his space but not touching. She felt a flush despite the cold as she looked into his gleaming, catlike eyes.

"But I was so thrilled you came looking for me and wanted me to travel with you, work with you, that I didn't want to ruin it," she said candidly, with a softer smile. "And maybe I wanted you all to like me enough to think about keeping me around a little longer. Maybe I'm tired of doing this alone."

"Well," he said, scooting over a little so she could sit next to him on the rock, "I can probably speak for the rest of them when I say I think we'd enjoy having you around. Lots of advantages having a spell slinger around. Such a beautiful one to boot. You get places we can't, know things we don't know, have abilities well beyond our ken - like reading any language ever."

The conversation was briefly interrupted as he had to rotate the spears of goat meat so they didn't burn, but then his attention was right back on her. That attention did seem to be growing in intensity. Or maybe Octavia was imagining it.

"And what about that other part of traveling with me?" she asked with a wry smile. "The part where I need to be physical with someone at least once a week? More is better, you know. Not just because more sex is often more fun, but because the more I indulge Kamvasana the more power they bless me with."

"A very lovely added bonus," he said with a smile showing a touch of fang. "Bonding. Comradery. Making sure you're top of your game. Save us all a lot of money on brothels."

Snickering, Octavia pulled off one of her gloves and reached up and cupped the side of Sumner's face, her thumb lightly brushing across his bottom lip. "I don't know, I'm a lot better at this sort of thing than your average barmaid." She looked up in his eyes again. "You might get spoiled. Do you want to risk that?"

"I don't mind a little spoiling," he said before catching her thumb in his lips and licking it gently. It was at that moment she noticed his tongue was textured. Not rough like a full cat would have been, but certainly more than a normal human's. "But I'm far more experienced than your average near-virgin, think you'll be okay with not teaching but learning a thing or two?"

"I love learning new things," she murmured as she leaned in closer, letting her fingertips drift down the side of his neck. Then she pressed her lips to his.

Sumner leaned into it and kissed her far more fully. There was a soft moan as he deepened the kiss, and she pressed herself into him. His tongue teased hers and his hand reached for her hip. He knew what he was doing, there was nothing awkward about the kiss, it was tender and the right amount of depth, and he pulled away with a little tug of her bottom lip in his teeth. Octavia swore she heard a tiny bit of a growl come from the back of his throat. That growl sent a tremor through her. It was full of promise.

"How is dinner coming," Alces called out as he stepped out of the tent. He paused as Octavia and Sumner looked at him, still in each other's arms, and grinned. "It's going great, it seems. I'm sorry, please continue." Bowing slightly he stepped back into the tent.

Octavia muffled her laughter by pressing her face in against Sumner's cloak. After a moment she sat back and looked up at him grinning. "He's like the most encouraging older brother," she said, trying not to giggle again. "I suppose I should head inside and let you finish dinner. Without distractions."

"As long as that's not the last time we do that," he said, smirking at her. Another breath, and he let go of her with a sigh. "Tell Alces to get out here and take over. He's a better cook and the cold doesn't affect him; he should be doing this."

Octavia stood but bent down to kiss him lightly before heading inside. "This is only the beginning. And I'll let him know."

Ducking into the tent, Octavia immediately started to unbuckle her coat as a wave of heat rolled over her. "Alces? Sumner says that you're immune to cold and the better cook, so he'd like you to take over."

"Of course," Alces said with a grin. He was just inside the entrance, so he towered over her as she came in. "He asks me to take over for the boring part." He laughed and patted her on the shoulder as he stepped outside to do as he was asked.

Durante was sitting on the floor, fiddling with Mathilda when Octavia stepped further inside. "Temperature dropped fast when we lost the sun, huh," he said, not looking up.

"It did." She hung up her coat on a series of hooks near the entrance and got her boots off before she walked through, pausing to run a hand through Durante's hair on the way. The kiss with Sumner had her warm and excited, and that meant she was more affectionate. There was an immediate relaxing of his shoulders as she played with his hair, a soft sigh, and he looked up at her with a smile.

Lifting his eye glass contraption off his face, he watched her pass by. She moved to her room to change, but didn't close the curtain all the way so they could continue to talk. "I'm guessing one way or another we're hitting snow tomorrow. Hopefully it will remain light."

"That's always the hope," he said. "Given that we're still in the last parts of summer, hopefully it'll hold off for another couple of weeks, at least."

"Is the season why you were all so urgent to get up here?" Octavia asked, leaning over to look at Durante as she did. The curtain hid most of her body, but it was also easy to see that she was not yet wearing anything. "Trying to be done before the snows start?"

Durante was caught for a moment, his eyes skimming the hip and thigh that were visible, but shook his head a little and nodded. "Yeah. Travel would be mostly impossible otherwise. Combine winter with whatever twisted or failing magicks might be up there, and forget it. Maybe Alces could do it, but good luck getting him to do anything alone."

"Honestly, this doesn't strike me as the type of thing anyone should do alone." Octavia came out in a dressing gown, one that was on the sheer side, and walked back through, pausing to play with Durante's hair again. He had fantastic, thick hair with a deliciously silky quality to it. She could happily play with his hair for a while. He leaned into her hand.

"I'm going to bathe real quick before dinner," she said, reluctantly pulling away. "We all might want to tonight." They were all fragrant from the road, and she was fairly certain she was dragging at least one of them into her bed this evening. Sumner was currently the most likely candidate, but she was open to other possibilities.

"Oh, okay," Durante said, giving his head a little shake again. "Probably for the best. I keep forgetting this tent has a bath."

"Aww, what'd I miss," Sumner said as Octavia's butt disappeared behind the curtain to the bathroom.

"Nothing. Octavia's taking a bath before dinner, we should probably all do the same, was the suggestion," Durante replied. "How's dinner coming?"

"Fine, now. Tonight's goat will actually have a little seasoning on it. I honestly don't know why he wants me to cook so much," Sumner said, flopping down in a chair.

"Practice?" Durante asked with an obviously unknowing tone.

"Didn't we just have a brief discussion about the merit of learning things," Octavia called out from behind the curtain, certain they would hear the smile in her voice even if they couldn't see it. She tapped the large wooden tub in the washroom, and it filled almost instantly with steaming water. Her soaps were already in here, so she had what she needed, and slipped into the hot water with a content sigh. It wasn't really a tub for relaxing, but it was still nice.

"Fine, fine," Sumner said, but it sounded like he was also smiling. "Hey, need someone to scrub your back?"

"Sorry, I'm trying to make this a quick bath." Even the most naïve girl in the world had to know what would happen if Sumner came in here to scrub her back. "Also, isn't dinner going to be done soon?"

"Yeah, yeah," he said, laughing so it was clear he wasn't hurt by the rejection.

She grabbed her soap and got started. The smell of honey, spices, and musk floated out through the gap in the curtain. She could hear the sounds of movement, and a metallic shuffling that told her someone was pulling out those tin plates.

"You know what this set up needs is a table," Durante commented.

"We could buy one," she called out as she soaped up her hair. "Any furniture brought in stays in. Though I might be able to modify it a little. I'll have to dig out the manual."

Octavia grabbed the pitcher by the tub, pouring water over her head until the soap was gone. She squeezed the water out and stood up, using the pitcher again to sluice off any lingering soap on her body. She then tapped the spot on the tub again, and the water drained away as she stepped out and started vigorously toweling herself off.

Robe back on, she flipped over her hair and gathered it into a scarf, tying it off loosely to let it start drying. She wandered back out into the main room and sat down on her favorite spot on the couch, legs tucked up, still in her robe. "Bath is free if anyone wants it. You tap the silver plate in front once to fill it, and twice to drain it."

"I suppose that would be me," Durante said, and put a hand in his bag, producing a small garnet. He focused on it for a moment, taking out a metal stylus and inscribing a small rune upon it. Giving it a little press, metal started to form around the gem until it looked like a tiny mechanical lobster with fine pinchers. Octavia leaned forward, watching with fascination.

Setting the tiny lobster down on Mathilda, Durante stood up and stretched. "I think I have the enchantment weaves figured out. Snippy there will try to align them and get them reinforced. It'll take all night, I'm guessing, but by morning Mathilda should be pretty close to new. Not exactly, but at least in better shape where I can figure out what else is wrong," he said, smiling over at Octavia.

"Thank you, Durante." She smiled brightly at him, with a small amount of awe. She didn't know he was capable of that kind of enchantment.

"Now for that bath." Taking his bag, Durante headed into the bathroom.

Sumner seemed about to say something when Alces stepped in with a stone covered in seasoned goat meat. The smell was tantalizing, and Octavia became aware of how hungry she was. She thought she heard Sumner's stomach growl.

"Dinner is ready, my friends. Eat up. I think we still have fruits left as well," Alces said, setting down the stone in the middle of all the plates.

She unfolded from the couch to find a clean knife to slice up some of the fruit. Sumner watched her as she moved through the room. Unless she had completely misread him, she was fairly certain that he was going to occupy her evening. The idea that something might finally happen with any of them was strangely exciting. There was a level of anticipation that she wasn't used to.

Settling in with food, she mentioned the bath to Alces and told him how to make it work if he wanted. They determined that first Alces, then Sumner would bathe after dinner. She also promised to dig out the manual and see if maybe tomorrow night she could make sure there was a table.

They all set in. Today had probably been one of the most strenuous days of walking they'd had since they started and tomorrow was going to be worse. As such, appetites were pretty high. About halfway through dinner Octavia undid the scarf and let her damp curls spill down to finish drying. The curls were tighter in their natural state, giving her hair a wild feel. Her robe gaped in front, but it was natural, not staged. She felt comfortable. Alces looked at her with open admiration but didn't leer. Sumner's eyes, however, devoured her as surely as he did his dinner.

"What is on your mind, dear Octavia?" Alces asked, smiling over at her.

"Not much," she said with a little shrug, "just that I'm enjoying this time with you all. You are not the first group I've ever traveled with, but I have never felt this at ease. Now, that might be because you all know my dark secret," she grinned playfully, "and so I don't need to hide so much of myself."

"I do not think your secret is dark," Alces said. "Quite the opposite. You bring light in your own way! True, the timing is forced upon you, and that is unfortunate. However, as you have said yourself, it's something you enjoy doing, and I guarantee whoever does it with you greatly enjoys it as well. No, we are much alike, and we are most happy to have you with us." It was a little difficult to tell if it was the royal 'we' being used there, but the sentiment was certainly nice.

She set down her empty plate and leaned on the arm of the couch. "Thank you. Ah, I hope he'll forgive me for revealing as much, but Sumner suggested that... maybe you might enjoy having me travel with you once we're done in the mountains?" She arched her brows with the question.

Sumner had his mouth full, but the corner of his mouth quirked up and he glanced towards Alces. Alces laughed, and it was a joyful sound. "But of course, beautiful and learned Octavia! You would be most welcome to continue travelling with us. I did not wish to make assumptions. You have already granted us the boon of your traveling home and your company. You would be a delight," he added.

"I second that," Durante said from the bathroom.

"Fird," Sumner said, snerking a little as he talked around his goat meat.

For the second time in their association, Octavia felt blood rush to her cheeks, and she felt strangely shy but also delighted. "Thank you," was all she said.

Durante finished, coming out in his lighter clothes that looked freshly laundered. He cleaned up nicely, and he sat down to dig into the meat as well. Sumner had finished by this point and took the time to head back outside and check on the fire. Alces stood and excused himself for his bath.

NINE

It was quiet for a minute as Durante ate and Octavia considered what she had done—she'd asked them if she could stay, and they all said yes. So they would be traveling together for a while. That was good. Though she didn't completely understand the fluttery feeling it caused in her stomach.

"I suppose if you're going to be adventuring with us a little more long term, you might have questions," Durante offered as he slowed down. She picked up her head and focused on him. He didn't eat as much as the others, but it was probably because of his other dietary needs.

"Yes and no," she said, brow furrowed as she considered. "The answers are coming. I'm getting to know the three of you as we travel. Though, I am curious, what's the goal?"

"The goal of what," he said, tilting his head to the side. "You went over all the things we wanted out of life. Was there something else?"

Octavia giggled. "I'm sorry, you're right, that wasn't clear. Do you intend to travel together indefinitely, a band of brothers taking on the world? Will you go your own way if you find your cure, or is this camaraderie more than that to you?"

"Well, that's certainly a lot," he laughed, settling into his seat on the couch a little more. "I mean, I was disowned. Cured or not, I still have nowhere else to go. Alces will never retire, so he'll travel onward forever. I don't really see a reason to separate from that either. It's fulfilling in that we're helping people, and I think we're making okay money. I honestly don't know. Sumner handles the wherewithal of our finances, and he won't tell us how much we have. Only if he thinks we can afford whatever we're asking for."

He looked thoughtful. "I don't know about Sumner, either. Before the takeover, he was fond of the circus he was part of. Had a real family there before things went south. I'm sure that's what he's looking for, so he'll probably settle down at some point, but this is all speculation."

"Hmm." Octavia let her gaze unfocus as she took in Durante's words. In their way, they were all looking for their place. All four of them. Durante wasn't worrying about it yet. Alces would quest forever, it seemed, though she remembered him talking about how he sought love. And it sounded like Sumner was looking for a family he once had, but it was also possible he had found it in his companions. It would be interesting to see what the future brought, if her presence would alter their paths.

She brought her gaze back to Durante. "And now that we're alone for a breath, are you certain you're all right with me remaining with you all?"

"Absolutely," he said, smiling up at her. "You seem paranoid about people wanting you around, which seems preposterous, but I suppose we all have our hang-ups. You're smart, skilled, powerful, and, yes, outstandingly gorgeous, but that's an added bonus, really."

"Oh." Octavia felt herself blushing again and was very confused by it. "I don't think I'm paranoid, I just... it's important that I understand the reason someone might want me around. And..." she sighed, considering, but nodded to herself. "What I am. Who I have a pact with. It has driven people away. I have been rejected because it was 'too strange.' It has shattered potential relationships because they couldn't bear the idea of me being with either my patron or someone else should I need to be. Some of the people I've traveled with in the past sent me on my way because they were bothered by my 'promiscuity' for one reason or another. So I just... I want to be sure that Alces isn't speaking for all of you. Which is why I ask."

"We're not exactly the 'normal' crowd either," Durante said. He sat comfortably in the chair and met her gaze without stumbling or looking away nervously. "We're not chaste, we're not stationary, we're all odd folk in one way or another. So I'd say 'too strange' is just right, especially with us."

"I guess we'll put that to the test," Octavia commented, smiling a little. "All right, another question. We'll be at the tower soon. Do you need...something stronger to drink before we go in there? To keep your strength or your energy up, I mean. How often does your curse make demands of you?"

"I've never been able to figure that out," he said with a shrug, "it's random, I can't control it. The thirst pops up every now and then." He looked her over, and seemed to grow a little shy again. "I'm sure it would keep things in check longer, but I don't think it's necessary."

"I've...donated my blood before, to an individual in need," she confessed with a little smile. "I was surprised to discover that I rather enjoy being bit. Although, do different types of blood do anything to you? Because the last individual I was with informed me that my blood was a little different. I think because of my patron."

"Oh, yes, actually. Different blood does affect me differently. Like, in emergencies, I've taken some from Sumner, and that's okay. I can take some from Alces but it puts me in a rage. I think it's the dragon blood that's in him. Yours, and considering your patron," he said, sinking back in the couch a little more with a slight smirk, "I'll need to try that at night when I don't have anything planned."

"More like a kitten on catnip from what I've seen," she commented, still smiling. "But don't worry. Should it happen, I will take very good care of you."

"I'd like that," he said it so quietly it almost got lost in the sounds of movement and fabric shuffling when Sumner came back holding a nicely charred goat leg and a fruit wrapped in a few wet leaves that were currently steaming.

"Alright, have Alces' dinner. Is he out of the bath yet?" he asked.

"Almost," Alces called out, "the tub is a bit small, doing what I can. Don't worry, nothing has broken."

Getting off the couch, Octavia walked over and leaned down next to Durante, murmuring, "I know you will like it, Kitten." She kissed his cheek and straightened up, adjusting her robe so that it closed properly again. Durante melted a little on the couch and made a slight whimpering noise. Sumner raised a brow at Octavia but didn't pry.

"I'll be right back," she said, heading to her room to retrieve a small clay pot that she brought back out to the couch with her.

"What's in the pot?" Sumner asked when she came back out.

"Lotion," Octavia said, settling on the couch and carefully hiking up her robe a bit while tucking it around her legs to expose the skin but cover what needed to be covered. "Incidentally, if you're not a fan of my current fragrance, you're going to have to deal with it until I find a big enough market to do something about it."

She opened the little pot and carefully dipped her fingers in, taking out a small amount that she started to work into her feet. The faint fragrance wafting from Octavia was the same blend of honey, spices, and musk that scented her soap.

"Think that goes both ways," Sumner said, then sniffed the air. "Although, no complaints from this side."

"Terribly sorry," Alces said as he appeared holding a towel in front of himself, at the waist so that it covered what hid beneath those kilts he wore, but wearing nothing else, "I forgot to bring a spare change of clothes. Ignore me." To his credit, even if he had said nothing, they would have noticed. He was huge, the tent was cozy, things were going to get seen.

"I don't think anyone could, Ser Knight," Octavia noted as Alces walked across the tent to his room. He was a wall of muscle. A barrel of core muscles surrounded by legs and arms made of steel cables. Curse the towel for getting in the way. As he turned into his room, she noted that his ass was also magnificently sculpted and firm. She watched him go by unashamedly, noting that he would probably break her if and when his turn ever came, and she would probably love it.

After the fabric of Alces' door fell in place and blocked her view, she went back to her task, slowly working up her legs. She was aware that she was not entirely behaving, but it seemed she was aggressively aroused this evening.

"How much you want to bet he did that on purpose?" Sumner said after a minute.

"It's possible, I'm definitely doing this on purpose," Octavia said quietly, trying not to smile. Sumner winked at her, clearly hearing her.

"I'm going with not at all," Durante said, speaking a little more solidly but still sunk in his seat.

"Your bet?" Sumner asked Octavia, smiling at her.

She considered. "Betting money or something else?"

"Can't really bet money when Sumner has it all," Durante said.

"I mean, I've still got a small pile of teardrop sapphires that I was going to sell off once we were back in a town with a lapidary." Octavia got a little more lotion and carefully reached into her robe to apply it to her shoulders and upper arms. "So I could bet one of those. Unless there was something else you wanted to wager for."

"Money seems like a silly thing to wager. Do you have a suggestion, since you brought it up?" Sumner asked, stretching out on the chaise.

"No," Octavia said, switching to the other side, her robe falling down off her shoulder this time. "I'm reasonably certain I could get what I wanted from you without gambling for it." She looked over and stuck her tongue out at him.

"Then I think we're at a stalemate," Sumner said, sticking his tongue back out at her then licking one of his incisors. She felt a pulse through her sex when he did that.

"What are we betting on?" Alces asked as he stepped out from behind the curtain, dressed in loose pants and no shirt, plopping down on the floor before the goat shank.

"We're taking bets on how many of us are being shameless on purpose," Octavia said, the corner of her mouth quirking as she finished and put the lid back on her lotion pot, "but Sumner and I couldn't agree on a wager. And honestly, I'm always shameless. It's part of my charm."

"Doesn't shameless imply you have reason to feel shame for what you are doing?" Alces asked.

Setting the pot down, Octavia leaned back on the couch. "Many people would argue I should. I hardly behave the way polite society thinks a lady needs to. And that was true before I found Kamvasana. It's only gotten worse since."

"I meant in general, but certainly one should accept themselves and how they act. While I would say you should not force others to experience what they don't wish to, as long as it is easy to avoid then the problem is theirs, and not your own," Alces said with a nod.

"I mean, true. Not much reason to feel shame here, is there?" Sumner asked, putting his hand behind his head and wriggling around to get comfortable.

She waved her hand dismissively. "We're arguing semantics. I was still addressing the previous conversation and you were speaking more broadly. But for what it's worth, I don't feel shame for being...," she rolled her hand in the air as she considered her words, "a sensuous creature. I call myself shameless lightheartedly, because it doesn't bother me even if it bothers others."

She stretched out her legs. "And I try very hard not to impose on people. Some might call me paranoid about it." She smirked at Durante.

"Well, I hope no one here feels shame," Alces said, waving to the group before picking up the shank and taking a large bite out of it.

Sumner lifted up his cup in a toast then drained it. "I guess it's my turn for the bath then," he said, sliding his way up to a sitting position, then standing. "Got to make sure I'm all clean."

"I'm exhausted," Durante said, finally sitting upright. "I'll let Snippy do their thing and head to bed. Good night, all."

"Good night." Octavia smiled up at him as he headed to the room he shared with Sumner.

When it was only herself and Alces, she crossed over to the chair closer to the dragonkin and perched in it, leaning on the arm. While she knew Alces could be a mess while eating, something like a haunch also wasn't inherently sloppy. She was pretty sure she'd be safe.

"I don't want to interrupt your dinner," Octavia said, "but I have a question or two, whenever you're ready."

Rising his brow ridges at Octavia, he smiled, chewed, and set the flank down for the moment. Picking up a napkin that had been tucked under the plate, he dabbed at his mouth and wiped off his fingertips. "Of course, Octavia, what can I do for you?" he asked

"From talking to Sumner and Durante, it sounds like you rove out in search of light and love," she said, propping her hand up in her chin. "I was wondering if that was accurate. Do you just go where you feel guided to?"

"That is accurate," he said with a nod. "The spirits guide me to wherever I am needed, where the light needs to shine. I am blessed to have companions that wish to adventure with me."

"What are you three to each other, may I ask?" She tipped her head to the side. "Sumner called Durante brother, but I know that's not by blood. Durante says he hasn't been traveling with you as long as Sumner has, but it does seem like you've all been together for at least a few years."

"Brothers in arms and deeds, dear Octavia," he said proudly. "I do believe they have been traveling with me for, well, a dozen seasons at least. Sumner a few more than that. Time flies. We have been through many trials, tribulations, victories, and celebrations together."

That made her smile. Alces' joy and sincerity were utterly delightful. She felt that flutter just under her ribcage again.

"I hope my inclusion brings only more celebration," she said. "I'm looking forward to it."

Alces reached out and caressed her cheek with a single claw, the blunt side against her skin. "Wonderous Octavia, you walk in the light. We all stumble, we all fall. But, when we are together, we pick each other up. We learn, we become better. To leave people behind is to leave them in a shadow. You may walk with me, with us, for as long as you wish."

She leaned her cheek into his touch, and her eyes shone as she felt herself tear up. Not enough to cry, but...Gods, there was something about him that touched her in a way she really wasn't accustomed to. She remembered Kamvasana's frustration over Alces being "principled" but...his principles were beautiful.

"Thank you, Ser Knight," she said, smiling.

"My utmost pleasure," he said with a nod. "Now, there is a bit of ceremony if you wish to join us. As I assume you wish to travel with us for longer than a few months or so? Or is this a trial?"

She grinned. "I'm entirely too impetuous to say this is a trial. Honestly, I assumed you would want to see how I managed the tower or something before you elected to let me stay."

Alces grinned. "You make a good point. While I have no doubt in my mind, you must be sure yourself. So, we will hold off, but we shall celebrate and make it official after the tower."

Nodding, Octavia reached over and set her hand on Alces' arm, giving it a soft squeeze. She didn't take her hand away immediately either, her thumb gently rubbing over his scales. She'd never really spent time around dragonkin before. Had certainly never had her hands on one. There was a fascinating suppleness to them.

"I look forward to it," she said, then finally took her hand away and sat up, leaning back in the chair. "Finish your dinner. I'm sorry I kept you from it."

"Do not apologize for gracing me with your company, Octavia," he said, picking up the shank. "Conversations with you are just as fulfilling." Another smile and he took a sizable bite out of the shank. The rate he was going, the leg would disappear in short order.

Octavia left her seat long enough to retrieve her journal and then returned to it as she jotted down some notes, observations of their journey, and chronicled the important bits of her most recent bout with Kamvasana. As frustrating as her encounters with her patron could be, they were also almost always learning experiences. And given their similarities in size, if Alces did ever find his way into her bed, there were a few things she wanted to remember.

As she jotted down her notes, she sang softly to herself. Alces began to sway lightly with her song, his crunching getting softer. It was an old song, about lovers meeting in secret in the night, supposedly written by a bard in honor of an ancient god they trysted with. Octavia had always been somewhat dubious about the origin, but it was a beautiful song, with an arcing chorus that made good use of her clear soprano voice. She was singing softly, clearly relaxed and focused on her task. She had shifted in the chair, her bare legs over one arm, her head leaning against the arm closer to Alces, blonde curls spilling down the side.

When she was done, Alces chuckled so as not to be too loud. "I have always wanted a bard to join us, but you are much better," he said, his plate now bare of any scraps.

"Hm? Oh!" She shifted so that she could tilt her head back and look at Alces. "I do sing a lot when I'm on my own. I wanted to be a bard when I first struck out, but it turns out their colleges require money." She smiled wryly. "Or you have to find someone to teach you, but there were concerns with that as well. I can't play an instrument, other than a hand drum, and not all that well. I just sing."

"The voice of the ethereal," he said with a smile. "I do hope you sing whenever it strikes you. Your voice is divine, and I am once more blessed to have you with me."

She felt that fluttering again, and her cheeks went pink once more. "Thank you." She turned back to her journal, sheepish and pink, and tried to refocus on what she had been doing. After a little while, she started to sing again. A lullaby from Rupaiya, not sung to a child but to a lover, of a courtyard with pomegranate trees, a sparkling night sky, and the ocean in the distance.

Alces had long finished his dinner and had cleaned his hand with Durante's solution, but her singing kept him in place. As the song ended, Octavia closed up the journal and stretched, then looked over to see Sumner, clean and wearing only his soft pants, perched on the arm of the couch. "Oh! I didn't hear you come out."

"Didn't want to interrupt," Sumner said.

"With that melody in my ear, I believe I am to bed as well," Alces said, standing and setting his dish with the others. "Thank you for your gift, dulcet Octavia. I shall see you in the morning." Alces gently patted her head. "Same for you, Sumner. Do not stay up too late, you two. Tomorrow will be strenuous enough."

The imp-like urge to say "Yes, Daddy," in response rose up in Octavia, but she managed to beat it back down.

Nodding, he stepped out into his bedroom and closed the curtain.

TEN

Sitting upright, Octavia focused on Sumner. "Enjoy the bath?"

"It was very nice. Hadn't had one in a bit, but I'm all clean now. How're you doing?" Sumner asked, stretching out.

"Also very happy to have had a bath," she said with a smile. "I told Alces I must feel very relaxed around you all if I'm singing. It's been a nice evening. Though I am hoping you might not want to go to bed right away. Or rather, you might want to come to mine instead."

Sumner raised an eyebrow and smiled, sitting up on one elbow. "I was hoping there would be more than that wonderful kiss," he said. "Shall I escort you back to your room, then? Can you cast silence?"

"Unfortunately, I cannot cast silence," Octavia said, scooting to the edge of the chair. "However, when everyone is in their rooms, it's surprisingly hard for sound to travel between them. It's not completely silent, but it is on par with a building that would have actual walls. It's only when you're in the main area that sound travels like it would through canvas."

She leaned forward with her arms on her knees, her robe gaping in front, revealing more of her breasts than he had yet seen. "Shall we test it?"

"Oh, yeah," Sumner said, reaching out and gently running a finger down the valley of her cleavage. "Suppose we'll hear about it in the morning."

Smirking, the blond, gently bronzed man offered her a hand and gestured in the direction of her room. The soft pants he wore were already starting to show his intentions. Unfolding, Octavia accepted his hand and let him pull her to her feet. Before immediately heading to the room, though, she stepped into Sumner and kissed him again. Her free hand slid slowly up his back, and she pressed herself against him, nothing but silken robe and warm flesh. His free hand found its way behind her and palmed a healthy amount of her ass. Sumner kissed deeply, seeming not so reserved as they had been outside.

As the kiss ended, Octavia pulled back with a soft gasp and looked up into Sumner's eyes. She smiled and stepped away, but held onto his hand, leading him to her corner of the tent.

Octavia's room was different from the others, mostly because it was more personalized. It had a tapestry pinned to one wall, a bookshelf full of books and little baubles that she'd collected along the way. Most importantly, though, it had a larger bed. One that would easily and comfortably fit the two of them.

"I like what you've done in here," Sumner said, "very cozy." A toothy smirk and Sumner's hands went to the edges of her robe. Taking a firm hold of it, he pulled her close. Octavia's brows rose, and her breath came a little faster.

"I tend to be very hands on," Sumer said, watching her face carefully, "a little more demanding than most. I have a feeling you won't mind."

She smiled and slid her hands up over his shoulders. "No, I don't think I'll mind at all. Anything in particular we need to discuss before we begin, or would you prefer to learn each other as we go?"

"I do like learning," he said, "but you tell me. Anything you want to say to signal I'm being too rough?"

Her eyes grew wider, and she felt her body flush. After months in small towns with barmaids and farmer's sons, someone who maybe needed a safeword had her tingling a little in anticipation.

"Orchid," she said, and had a feeling Sumner wouldn't be surprised that she understood and didn't need it explained. "If I say it once, slow down a little. If I say it twice, stop."

"Orchid it is," he said, giving her that feral grin again, then pulled her robe open with a sharp tug, exposing her to his gaze. His eyes moved over her body, and then he dove in. He took hold of her, one hand at her waist, the other grabbing her ass. He kissed at her neck and bit at her shoulder. Moaning softly, she let the robe fall away before she reached for him, sliding eager hands over his skin but also careful not to get in his way.

"Goddesses above you are delectable," Sumner growled, nuzzling into the curve of her neck. "You're gorgeous, you smell like spiced honey, and fuck are you soft." He started to move her towards the bed, even as he bent his head to hungrily nip and lick at her chest and the tops of her breasts, moving down slowly as he savored her taste. She gasped and trembled in his hands as he moved across her skin.

The room was still small, and it didn't take long before Octavia's calves encountered the edge of her bed. He released her and smiled, then gave her a little push so that she sat down. Once she was seated, he dropped to one knee and lifted a single leg. She was panting softly and bit her lip. It was like she could feel her blood thrumming in anticipation. He leaned in and nibbled against her inner thigh, moving slowly inward. She could hear that rolling growl in the back of his throat, and the muscles in her thighs felt like harp strings from the tension.

"Tonight, you're mine," he said with a smirk, "and I plan to enjoy all of you."

"Yes," she whimpered.

This time he bit down a little more firmly on her thigh, and sucked hard, causing the skin to bruise. She cried out and fell back on the bed, her legs spreading further for him. She had told Durante earlier that she liked to be bitten, but that was a lie—she loved it. Pleasure spiked with a little pain traveled from her thigh through her pelvis. A heartbeat later, Sumner's mouth was also following that path. The first thing he did was drag his textured tongue up the length of her pussy and across her clit.

"Oh, Gods, your tongue!" That was a new sensation, and an amazing one. More texture would have been too much, but his tongue was rough enough to punctuate the pleasure running through her. She twisted a little, still panting.

Sumner moved in on her, placing her thighs on his shoulders then sliding his hands up her body. The tongue graced in and out of her, lapping up the length of her entrance to tease her clit, then driving back in to taste deep of her. Even with the relative soundproofing between the rooms, Octavia had a feeling there were going to be comments in the morning because she could not be quiet. His hands glided up her body, caressing her sides until he came upon the soft, heavy curves of her breast. Wrapping his hands around them, he squeezed firmly, gently raking his nails across her tender flesh. She reached down and ran a hand through Sumner's hair as she whimpered. She loved everything he did.

The nails against her skin brought forth a sharp cry and the hand on the back of his head tensed as her pleasure built.

There was something determined and relentless about the way he pleasured her. His hands kneaded her tits and teased her nipples, then scratched down her sides hard enough to leave marks. Sumner's tongue danced and dived, trying to lick every centimeter of her while lingering in the areas that made her quiver. It felt like he wanted her to come, and he wanted her to come now.

Octavia lifted off the bed as she arched sharply and cried out. She gripped his hair for a moment then let go as the peak ebbed and she gasped. It was a delicious start.

Sumner drew out his tongue and nibbled along her non-marked thigh, sliding back as he did until her legs were back down and her feet were on the floor. Standing up, he left his pants on the floor and now Octavia could see him bare.

Getting her breath back, Octavia pushed herself up again but stayed on the bed. It seemed the shifter in him changed more than his eyes and things that would alter when he felt like it. She let her eyes slowly drift up his body, pausing to take in his unique cock. It looked human enough, but it was bumpy and had little nubs circling the underside of his crown. They were small, but they'd be noticeable when it was inside her, that she was sure of. She wet her lips and let her gaze continue upward until she was looking into his eyes once more.

Sumner smiled down at her. He'd been hard since they kissed, and after she'd come for him, he was rock solid now. "So, now you're going to show me what you got, then I'm going to fuck you," he said, reaching out to run a hand through her hair, "and I'm going to keep fucking you until we both come again."

"Yes," she murmured, running her hands up his thighs before leaning in and sliding her tongue up the length of his cock. She took the head in her mouth and let her tongue feel over those bumps she'd seen. The cock throbbed in her mouth, and he rolled his head as she teased the strange bumps.

"Mmm, that is a good start," he said, reaching down to continue caressing her hair,

She started to take more of him, sliding a little further down his cock then back up to the head to swirl her tongue over those strange bumps again, then back down. He was soon nudging the back of her throat, and she looked up at him, her hands still caressing him as she sucked at him.

"Good girl," he groaned. The hand on her head sifted through her hair once more before tightening his grip on it. He wasn't holding her firmly in place, but every second or third thrust he pushed down into her throat.

She matched him easily and started taking him to his root as his hips moved forward, alternating her breath as he pulled back. The pace was still relaxed enough that it wasn't hard to catch those breaths. Still, a proud voice in the back of Octavia's head murmured that outside of maybe a brothel Sumner probably hadn't often experienced being swallowed whole.

"Ah, fuck," he grunted in approval. Now both of his hands were on her head, hair tangled in his fingers, as his pace picked up. With his hold on her, he made sure he was completely down her throat and held himself there for a second or two before letting up. This repeated several times and she could feel the shaft jump as she throated him. She moaned and closed her eyes, relaxing into it. Sumner wasn't as demanding or overwhelming as Kamvasana - she could keep this up for a while. She enjoyed the grip he had on her hair, the way he was obviously enjoying himself. She never stopped caressing him, encouraging him. She also wanted him to cum, but she wanted it when he was ready.

She could feel him getting close not only from the way the growl grew in volume or the telltale sign of his shaft swelling, but all those little nubs and bumps became more firm. Holding her head, he thrusted quickly until he couldn't take it anymore, then shoved himself as far as he could, her nose buried in the little patch of fur above his cock, as he came. The growl rumbled through his throat, and she felt the spurts deep into her.

He held her there until the jumps in his cock subsided and he slowly released his grip, taking a step back and sliding out of her mouth. She panted hard for a moment, catching her breath, and licked her lips as she looked up at Sumner again.

Smiling, quite pleased, he ran a hand through her hair, brushing the stray bits out of her face. "Mmmm, good girl," he praised, the words drawn out with pleasure.

Something in her loved that praise, though she wasn't sure she should tell him how much. Scooting a little further to the edge of the bed, she leaned forward to kiss at his thigh, her hands still caressing what she could reach. He had already told her what he wanted. And that meant she needed to make sure that he got hard again.

"That was well done," he said, stretching once more, "but you said you'd spoil me for other women, and I want to get a taste for that."

She let out a soft laugh, and bit into his thigh before standing up, sliding her body up his as she did. "And you're going to tell me every other woman you've been with can do what I did? But fine. Let me show you how good I can be."

She turned them both around and pushed him back onto the bed where she had been, but pressing him all the way back until he was laying down.

"I never said every other woman," he said, his grin taunting as she crawled over him. "Maybe a few, though."

She didn't answer but kissed him hard, drawing it out until they both had to gasp for air. A second kiss, shorter and less deep, then she drew her mouth across his jaw, licked at his earlobe, bit it lightly before nibbling down his neck. Her tongue traced his collar bones, and she left teeth marks in his shoulder. She kissed and licked across his chest, traced her nails down his sides, her soft curls trailing behind like an extra caress. As they touched, though, small sounds of pleasure echoed from her. There was no masking that she was enjoying his body, and everything she did to him turned her on more.

"Goddesses above, you feel amazing," he moaned happily. "Everything you do is a tease."

She slid her body back up his, kissing over him again. "That first night, when I followed you outside," she murmured between the licks and bites she was leaving on his neck. "I wanted to be the one who followed you back to your room. I dreamt about it. You on top of me. Those teeth in my shoulder as you fucked me."

"This time I followed you back to your room," he said, his hands sliding down her form to grab her ass. She kissed him again, sucking at his tongue, moaning into his mouth. Her hands slid into his hair and caressed his face. She was eager and hungry for him and wanted to please him more than anyone had.

Sumner pulled back and looked into her eyes. "I think it's time to make your dream come true." With a pop of his hip and a twist of his legs, he rolled her over onto her back and was on top of her in an instant. He rose up enough to grab her by her thighs, lifting her legs up as he knelt, resting his shaft against her mons.

"You're pretty flexible, right?" he asked, giving her a very feral grin. His hair had gotten a little shaggier, those spots had appeared down the sides of his face and along his shoulders. His arms and legs were longer, with fur appearing on the tops of his hands and forearms. Octavia could also swear his cock had gotten bigger as well, with the bumps more pronounced, and she had clearly succeeded in getting him hard again.

"Yes," she breathed, looking up at him. She was so absurdly wet with want, and she knew he could feel it as he rested against her. "However you want me." She squirmed a little beneath him. "Please…"

"Good, because I'm going to fold you in half," he said with that grin she liked more than she should. A small adjustment with his hips and his head sank into her entrance. His hands, gripping the backs of her knees, pushed her legs apart as he sank himself into her wet pussy. She folded as if it were nothing. Sumner let out a snarl of pleasure as he completely sheathed his cock into her in one long, slow thrust, his weight on her as he pressed himself down, her ankles on his shoulders as his face was against hers, jade green cat's eyes looking right into her sparkling blue ones.

"Yes!" She reached up and ran her hands through his hair again, kissing him hard before falling back with a gasp.

"Fuck yes," he growled, "your pussy is amazing." He stayed there for a moment, nuzzling into her, lingering in the feel of their connection. Then he started to move.

The ridges and bumps of his shaft massaged her walls and caused sensations she'd never experienced before. Each time he pulled back, she could feel those firm nubs along the head of his cock rub against her in just the right way. There was a firm rhythm to the way he fucked her, each thrust causing their bodies to crash together and the matress doing its best to support it.

"Goddesses," she gasped, shuddering. "Your cock feels so good… fuck, Sumner, I'm going to cum again!" Her voice was so sweetly desperate, and her muscles trembled under his hands.

He kissed her hard as she came, his tongue wrestling with hers before he parted with a gasp. With stamina to spare, he tightened his grip on her thighs and arched his back, putting everything into the movements of his hips as he started to piston his cock in and out of her. Their bodies slapped together as he drove himself into her; deep, hard, and fast. She cried out as he pounded into her, her hands curling around his shoulders, the nails digging in. She didn't warn him when she came again, but he felt it from the tensing in her thighs to the way her cunt gripped him like a vice as her voice spiraled up. Octavia was swimming in sensation, his magnificently strange cock triggering reactions in her that she wasn't certain anyone else could. She hoped he would want this again as much as she did. She already knew that one night would not be enough.

"More," she whimpered, still twitching around him. "Fuck, you're so good!"

"Fuck yeah, more," he growled. Giving her a dozen more deep thrusts, he pushed off of her, releasing her legs. "Alright, you little vixen, on your knees and show me that ass."

She whimpered when he pulled away, but rolled over onto her knees quickly, arching her back and presenting to him like he asked. She looked back at him, her gaze a little unfocused, panting like she was in heat. "Please..."

"Happily," he said, grabbing her hips with both hands as he lined himself up, then pulled her back forcefully. There was no time to ease into things, he was immediately pounding into her, making the bed rock with their movements. As he continued to bounce her ass off his pelvis, his hand slid up her back and slid fingers into her hair, grabbing a healthy portion of it and pulling her head back, making her body bow even more than she already had. She moaned and bent easily for him, still loving everything he gave her. "Fuck, you feel so good. How are you so fucking tight and wet?" he growled again.

It had been a very long time since someone (other than Kamvasana) had been rough with her, longer since she'd been with a man with Sumner's stamina, and his ridged cock continued to rub her in places she didn't know she'd wanted. The wet slap of him thrusting into her dripping pussy filled the room, almost as loud to her ears as her own cries.

Sumner gave her ass a sound swat, then rubbed it firmly to ease the sting, followed by another swat, and a firm grab. "Moan for me, Tavi. I want to hear you more," he growled again, that voice filled with feral intent. He hadn't slowed down in the least, either. He continued to spank her, timing the swats between thrusts of his hips. She did moan, louder with each smack, the heat and sting radiating through her.

She could feel the ridges and nubs becoming hard as he pounded into her. Sumner was getting close. The growl in his voice sent a shiver through her.

"Fuck," he rumbled in his throat again. Sumner started to pant, this thrust getting harder but slower. Moving to have a firm grip on her hip, he pulled her hair back against, making her arms lift off the bed to follow him until her shoulders were almost pressing against his chest.

"Fuck!" he exclaimed, stretching the word out until he grunted and bit down hard on her shoulder. She cried out sharply as his teeth came down into her flesh. This! This was what she'd wanted, what she'd fantasized about since he first smiled enough to show his fangs. His hips slammed into her as he buried his cock completely, and he came hard. Much harder than when she went down on him, the build up coming to its peak as she felt him erupt inside her.

One down, two to go, she heard in her mind. Kamvasana sounded very pleased. Octavia was absolutely not letting her patron's taunting spoil this moment.

Sumner wrapped his arms around her, still keeping himself buried and their bodies pressed together, for a long moment. He was...purring. She melted back against him. Releasing the bite, he licked where he'd bit her then started to kiss and nibble up to her ear.

"Yes, I believe I'm going to want to be horribly spoiled by you," he said with a gentle chuckle.

"You're incredible," she said, panting. "Anytime."

"Good," he said, giving her a nip on her neck. "Oh, the things we are going to do together." Sumner released her enough to glide over her body, finding her breasts and squeezing them firmly. "Sadly, I think Alces is right. We really should get some sleep," he muttered, kissing the ridge of her ear.

She laughed softly. "I guess I'll be good, then. Will you stay here with me?"

"I would love to," he said, releasing her breasts and sliding his hands down her body to her hips. Carefully he extracted himself and kissed the back of her neck.

They both climbed off the bed long enough to clean up—they had both freshly bathed, after all, no reason to mess themselves and the sheets. She pulled back the covers and climbed back into bed, stretching out with a content sigh and looking back at him with a smile.

"That was really fucking good," he said as he slid into bed next to her, stretching out one more time, and getting comfortable on his back. "I could get used to this."

"It really was," she agreed, grinning. She rolled onto her side and set a hand on his arm. "So, curling up next to you or staying on my side?"

"Whatever is comfortable. Having your softness pressed up against me might be the best sleep I've ever had," he said, then looked at her and grinned, "or the most frustrating. Won't know until we try."

Giggling a little, she slid up close to him, stretching her body against his, hooking one leg over him, pillowing her head on his shoulder. "The real question," she said teasingly, "is whether or not I accidentally start groping you in your sleep."

"One can only hope," he said, his hand sliding down her back to cup her ass and hold her close against him.

Reaching down she grabbed the blanket and pulled it over the two of them, and let out a content sigh. This was very nice. Teasing as they had been, it had indeed been a long day, and Sumner fell asleep with relative ease. Octavia wasn't far behind. She found sleep more easily than she expected. While she liked sharing a bed with someone, she hadn't done it very often, and most of the time she didn't sleep well. Something warm welled up in her as she was pressed against him, though, and she found herself slipping into dreams to the sound of his steady breathing and a softly rumbling purr.

ELEVEN

If she was to travel with them, Octavia would either need to learn to wake up earlier, or get used to Alces' voice doing it for her. "Rise and shine, my friends," Alces called out, although it didn't seem as resounding as the day before, "breakfast will be ready soon. I will see you outside."

"Yeah, yeah," Sumner muttered, stretching. Then his eyes snapped open, and he looked over at Octavia with a smile. "Oh, yeah, last night happened." The shifter leaned over and kissed Octavia's neck, giving her a squeeze. Yawning, she rolled into him and nuzzled at him sleepily, leaving a little trail of kisses over his jaw before falling back.

"Yes, it did," she said with a soft smile. "I hope you didn't forget it so quickly."

"You weren't the only one dreaming about what could be. Maybe I was dreaming again," he said with a raise of his eyebrows, then leaned in and kissed her. "Nope, that's very real." Letting her go, he stretched once again and started to wriggle out of bed. "Alright, as much as staying in bed sounds ideal with present company, we shouldn't keep the big guy waiting."

"You all are going to turn me into a morning person," she said with a regretful groan, getting up as well. "That, or I'll start sleeping with Durante and you'll have to drag us both out of bed."

"You might start shaking some things loose in him if you did," Sumner said with an easy grin, clearly unbothered by the possibility. "You know, he's actually quite a night owl. When we didn't have this tent, and we slept mostly outside or in our little tents, he'd take first watch because he could stay up for hours. He's almost the opposite of Alces like that, not to the extreme, but you know."

She yawned again and glanced in the mirror. "Oh, hells, I'm going to have to fix what you did to my hair." She giggled - it didn't look bad, exactly, but it did look more wild than usual and somehow managed to hint at the previous night's activities.

"Oh, your hair is always perfect," he said as he pulled his pants on. "Just, like, shake your head or something."

"Shake it. Sure. Oh! One question before you go, though," she said as she started to carefully untangle her hair while still trying to maintain its curl. "How comfortable are you with me being...casually affectionate with you? I find it's something I want, once I share myself with someone, but I don't want to unsettle you or the others."

Sumner paused at the curtain and thought about it for a moment. "You know, I think it depends. Like, if you meant what you said, and you do plan on getting with all of us, then I think I'd be okay with it," he said, with an uncharacteristic softness to his smile, "but, if I ruined you, and you only want me," he started, giving her a fangy grin and a chuckle, "then, I might feel uncomfortable you doing that around others. Well, mostly Durante. Alces, he'd love it."

"I don't want to break your heart, but I don't think you ruined me," she said with a wry smile. Then she paused and turned towards him, more seriously. "I do mean what I said...you each appeal to me differently. I know it's a little odd, but you seem genuine when you say it doesn't bother you."

"Well, like I said, you're not the first woman we've shared. Mind you, that was in a more casual, service-exchange heavy environment. But, also, because you seem genuine," he said, turning away from the curtain and towards her. "You're not going to use it against us, or pit us against each other for your affection. And I don't need to throw in a casual threat, because I have a good feeling that I'm right."

Stepping up close to Sumner, she took his hand, her eyes earnest. "I would never. Never!" She had known women like that. Her mother was like that. She would never be.

Sumner gave her hand a squeeze and leaned in to kiss her cheek. "I know, that's why I'm okay with all of it. So, sleep with Durante first, then you can lay your affections on me whenever, as long as he and Alces get some too."

She snickered. "I'm pretty sure I'm going to have to order Durante into my bed. I don't see him taking the initiative. But I..." she considered, and smiled a little, looking away. "I am learning more about the three of you and find myself... very charmed with each of you in your own ways. If Durante will have me, if Alces will have me, I will have no problem showing my fondness for any of you." She let go of his hand, feeling shy again, and got that strange flutter under her ribs once more.

"They will have you. They want you," he said matter-of-factly, and that flutter in her chest was becoming alarmingly familiar, "but yes, you will have to order Durante to do it. He gets nervous around women, if you couldn't tell. Mostly ones he finds attractive. The fact that he's speaking more easily with you is good, means you're getting through. See, brothels are a whole different thing for him. It's transactional, and he knows how to deal with that. Kinda. But when it's casual, emotional, nope. Not going to happen."

"I could tell. I have...maybe had a little too much fun teasing him," she admitted, glancing up at Sumner. "Though I also don't make promises I don't intend to keep. And perhaps he doesn't realize that."

Sumner chuckled and kissed her gently on the lips. "Speaking of, I should get dressed and make sure he's getting up. Not that I want to leave you." Sumner snickered for a moment, "unless you want to wake him up."

"I can wake up Durante." She reached up and caressed his face. "You'll have to tell me, sometime, how they became so important to you that you care more about keeping them happy than keeping me to yourself. And I don't say that because I think I'm so amazing, I say that because I've known my share of men."

Sumner shook his head a little as he smiled, then reached around and squeezed her ass. "You'll learn for yourself if you stick with us. You won't need me to tell you," he said, then wandered out.

Alone, Octavia looked in the mirror again and sighed. "Comicha!"

The imp appeared with the usual pop. "Mistress! Look at you! Someone very enthusiastically messed up your hair! The boss is quite pleased."

Octavia sighed. "Yes, I heard them last night. Please help me fix it."

"Yes, Mistress!"

About half an hour later, a composed Octavia, her hair once more in the perfect curls from the night before, sauntered out into the main room in heavy pants, her boots, and the aforementioned sweater. The knit garment hugged her figure like a second skin, and while it was one of the only items of clothing she owned that still came up to her neck, it somehow made her chest look larger.

She set her coat on the back of the chair and headed over to the room Durante and Sumner shared. "Knock knock," she said, parting the curtain enough to peer inside.

Sumner was gone but Durante was there, sitting on the edge of his bed wearing just his breeches. He was clearly waking up, running a hand through his hair that was standing up at odd angles. His shoulders and chest were well developed—he didn't have the mass of muscle that Alces did, but he wasn't whipcord and wire like Sumner either. There were stretch marks on his stomach, and he had that sag to the skin of his abdomen that people got when they lost a lot of weight. There was still a little roundness to his belly. Honestly, Octavia wasn't certain why he was so insecure about it. He looked very touchable, in her opinion, and those shoulders were a damn bit more impressive now that they weren't hidden under a flouncy shirt. He was very pale, but there was nothing sallow or unhealthy looking about his skin.

Yawning, fangs extended, Durante looked up and realized he had an audience. "Oh, hi Octavia. You missed Sumner if you're looking for him," he muttered, pointing out the way she was standing.

"I was looking for you, Kitten," Octavia said with a smile, stepping into the room. She walked up to him and ran a gentle hand through his still rather upright hair, to which he made a happy noise and leaned into her touch. Based on the texture he probably used a pomade to keep it slicked back during the day, which would explain why it was standing up so well now. "I promised I would make sure you were awake. You seem to be coming around. Need anything?" She didn't stop playing with his hair as she spoke, which she suspected was fine until he woke up a little more.

Blinking, he looked up at her again, eyes clearer now. "I, uh, oh, no, I'm fine, thanks. I need to get dressed. Have you checked on Malthida?"

"Not yet, no, I just got dressed and came looking for you," she said, and caressed the side of his face before taking her hand away and stepping back. His head tipped into her touch, but he stayed put. "I'll see how breakfast is going, since you seem to be up. All right?"

"Uh, yeah, thanks," he said, leaning into the touch as well. "Sorry."

She paused at the curtain, a mirror of her exchange with Sumner earlier that morning. "Why are you apologizing? You've done nothing wrong. I just came to check on you."

"For… for needing to come and get me and seeing me like this. It's—," he started, then sighed and shook his head.

Arching a brow, she stepped back up to Durante and put her hand under his chin, tipping his head up to make him look at her. "There's nothing wrong with me waking you up, or seeing you like this. I'm going to see how breakfast is going. Don't apologize, Kitten. We'll talk about this more tonight." Leaning down, she kissed his forehead.

"O-okay, we'll talk tonight." He never pulled away from her touch, or seemed bothered by it. He just seemed uncertain in her presence. "I'll be out in a minute. Thanks."

Leaving the room, she grabbed her coat and headed outside. She had come to a decision when talking with Sumner. Originally, she had wanted each of them to come to her in their time. Yes, she kissed Sumner, but he had been direct and flirty from the start, and she was certain her overtures were welcome.

With Durante, though, while she had teased him, she assumed it was something that would figure itself out eventually. But Sumner was insistent that she would need to be the one. Sumner also implied that it might hurt Durante if he thought she favored Sumner over him, or at least cause him to withdraw more. Maybe she did, maybe she didn't, but she would need some time alone with him to figure it out. Finally, if he was still skittish after being in bed with her, then there was no hope for the boy.

Her coat was still over her arm as she stepped outside, though she pulled it on quickly when she saw the light dusting of snow and felt the bite to the air. It wouldn't impede their progress, and the sun was starting to peek out of the clouds.

The fire that Alces and Sumner had built helped. It was a large blaze, much bigger than last night, but that seemed partially due to Alces cooking the entire extra goat they had, and it looked almost finished. It seemed Alces did not get much sleep at all. Sumner stood near the fire, wrapped in his leathers and his cloak, and smiled at her as she walked out.

"There is our wondrous Octavia," Alces said joyfully as he raised his arms in greeting. "Good morning! Sumner was informing me that you were making sure Durante was up. I expect to see him in due time if you are here. Breakfast is almost ready."

"He's awake," Octavia said as she buckled her coat against the morning chill. "He promised to get moving when I left him. Looks like the snow wasn't too bad."

"Not in the least," Alces said, rotating the goat once more. The edges of the meat looked like they were getting nice and crispy, and she could smell seasoning in the air.

"Gotta admit, as nice as the enchanted tent is, there's something special about a cold morning by a campfire to wake you up and get you ready for the day," Sumner added to which Alces laughed and nodded.

"You can always sleep outside if you'd rather," Octavia said with a smirk. "I would never want to force you to miss these experiences if you prefer them."

"Who's missing it?" Sumner asked defensively. "We're doing it right now."

"Besides, who would turn down an invitation from you, sweet Octavia," Alces said, "stalwart Sumner has never been more chipper in the morning."

A small laugh bubbled out of Octavia. So they were going to talk about it like she and Sumner had spent the evening playing chess. Well, that was all right. A little refreshing, actually, given how she usually had to dance around her evening activities with people. Sumner stuck his tongue out at Octavia, curling the tip at the end.

Grinning, Alces produced a sizable knife, carefully slicing off a piece of goat that steamed in the morning light. "Try some?"

"Yes, thank you." She saw the short stack of places and grabbed one before accepting a slice of the goat. Sumner also took a plate and held it up for Alces to fill. "I suppose I'll have to see if I can improve the rest of your dispositions as well. Though I don't know how you could be more cheerful, Ser Knight."

"You are most welcome to try," Alces laughed. "The light can always be brighter. Ah, there's our wise Durante. Come, sit and eat."

Durante was coming out of the tent, dressed in his fine winter clothes but still seemed to be getting used to the idea of morning. "Thanks," he said, stumbling over and grabbing a plate as well.

"I do have good news and bad news. The good news is, we have plenty of goat meat for the trip, as it's all nice and cooked now," Alces said, filling plates with shaves of meat, "the bad news is we're out of firewood and we'll probably not encounter many more trees. So, thank you again for the use of your tent, Octavia."

She nodded. "Glad I could be of help." She found a place to perch and eat, and looked up at the mountain. "Sumner, did you say that you thought we'd reach the tower by the end of today?"

"That is the plan, yeah," he said, looking up towards the mountain as well.

From their angle, it was difficult to see if a tower was up there. What they could follow of the trail, even with the snow covered, appeared to be several switchbacks and a couple of peaks high above them. With any luck, the tower would be in the col and not require actual climbing.

"I assume we're not going in tonight," Octavia said, looking back at the three of them. "If nothing else, we'll need to make sure the grounds are actually safe to camp in. Unless we're forced to, I very much recommend not camping in an abandoned wizard's tower."

"Oh, no," Durante said, shaking his head. "Abandoned wizard tower, at night, exhausted and unsure of the grounds? Sounds like a cautionary tale I don't want to be a part of."

"Yeah. Get there, camp out, scout the place in the morning, enter around noon-ish where we should have the most light," Sumner said. Alces may have had a comment, but he was working on a rack of ribs at the moment, so he nodded in agreement.

She nodded. "So long as we're all on the same page." Finishing her serving, she licked her fingers and got back on her feet. "Alces, can I ask you to call Nutmeg again?"

Alces grinned and she felt a nuzzle against her neck as a great elk nudged her and then bugled above her. "He was rather insistent," Alces laughed after swallowing his bite. "Nutmeg was wandering around."

Laughing, Octavia turned and gave Nutmeg a hug, a nuzzle, and scratches around his ears and antlers before letting go. "I'm going to read through the manual for the tent while we travel and see if it's possible to make it more comfortable for a party of four."

"Our own rooms would be nice," Durante said, "despite Sumner being an okay roommate."

"That, and Alces always gets his own room. Big ass dragon," Sumner laughed.

"All right," she said, "I'll go dig the manual out of Matilda and coax her out of the tent so we can finish packing up."

"I checked the progress Snippy made," Durante said, nibbling on his piece of goat. "Just reach out to her, she should come now. The attunement enchantment was still intact, so I was able to reinforce it."

Octavia blinked. "Really?"

She reached out, and felt Matilda again, as she hadn't in a while. The trunk came lumbering out of the tent at a more energetic waddle than it had in years. Octavia let out an excited sound of delight, and ran around the fire to hug Durante and kiss his cheek. "Oh, thank you so much!"

Durante smiled shyly, but he didn't move away from the affection. "Yeah, of course," he said, reaching out and rubbing her back. Sumner raised his eyebrows, and Alces grinned.

Letting go, Octavie smiled brightly at Durante and then skipped over to her trunk. She gave the top a little rub, like it was a pet she was proud of, then popped the trunk open and started to dig through it, eventually pulling out a small but surprisingly thick book bound in leather with a picture of the tent etched on the front cover.

"Okay," she said cheerfully, "everyone eat, get your stuff, and then we'll figure this out." She was already flipping through the book. "Comicha! I'm gonna need you today!"

"YES!" The imp popped into being very excitedly, zipping around. She looked everyone over, and drooped a little. "Awww, you're all dressed. You don't need me for fun things, we're going to have to actually work today, aren't we?"

"You okay in this weather... naked?" Sumner asked Comicha as she appeared. While he probably could do it, even Alces wore something out in the cold weather.

Comicha blinked. "Yeah. You're not?" She fluttered around and glared at Nutmeg. Nutmeg grunted at Comicha, snorting at her, then settled himself in front of Octavia until she was ready to get on.

Durante finished eating, as he always had a relatively light meal, and hurried inside to get his pack and gear. Sumner and Alces needed to take a little longer, breaking down the goat and wrapping the pieces before tucking them away in the bottomless bags, then needing to put out the fire and bury the pit. Before they buried the pit, Octavia gathered a pouch full of ash and tied it off carefully, tucking in the pocket of her coat.

In due time, everyone was geared up and the camp had been broken down and cleaned. It was time to head up the mountain, and so far the weather was holding. Alces effortlessly scooped Octavia up and placed her on Nutmeg's back, and Durante handed her the collapsed tent. Engrossed in the manual, she kept the cube that became the tent between her legs, but upside down. On the underside was what mostly looked like your typical magical circle, but very small. Octavia kept sending Comicha to fetch her things, which she then fed into the circle on the underside of the tent. This included the pouch of ashes, chunks of ice, as many scrubby twigs as Comicha could find, rocks small enough to fit through the little circle (a lot of rocks), and at the end, ten sapphires from Matilda. Alces was keeping himself paced with Nutmeg and watched as Octavia and Comicha worked.

Dropping the sapphires in, Octavia sighed. "At least it's cheaper than buying a new one," she muttered. After the sapphires went in, the cube sort of...hummed for a moment, and then changed from the sort of golden brown it had been to a deep, night-sky purple.

He smiled. "I will ask Sumner to recoup your loss," he said, "you are doing us a favor, but it should not be putting you out. I'm sure we can cover it."

"Cover what?" Sumner asked from ahead in the trail.

"Ten blue gems," Alces said back.

"You're going to need to be more specific."

"Sapphires. And you don't need to," Octavia said, waving her hand in negation as she closed the manual with a snap and handed it and the tent to Comicha to put back in Matilda. "They were left over from Kamvasana's charming humiliation ritual. I had been intending to sell them. But it's fine, this is a better use."

Sumner whistled. "That's a hell of an initiation prize. Sadly, don't think we can match that," he said. "Think Kamavsana is looking for others to serve?"

Alces laughed, hard, patting Nutmeg's haunch in the process.

"What?" Sumner said with a pseudo-innocent grin.

Alces glanced over at Octavia. "If I'm piecing things together the right way, that's going to include some caveats he's not going to like, yes," he said, hoping he was guessing right.

"Well, for starters, I'm pretty sure that Kamvasana only accepts warlocks attracted to multiple genders," Octavia said with a smirk, as she was fairly certain that Sumner was solidly only attracted to beings of a feminine persuasion. "And remember, if you don't keep Kamvasana happy, you pay the forfeit. And before you think, 'It's just sex, I can do that once a week if I can't find a partner,' I would like to remind you that it's actually you becoming Kamvasana's toy where they do whatever they want to you for 8 hours."

"Oh," Sumner replied with a grunt.

"And," Alces said, "I do believe your weekly requirement that Octavia has pointed out many times could no longer be met with other followers of Kamvasana."

Octavia giggled. "It's true. As much as Comicha would love for me to be able to use her to satisfy my pact, the partner cannot be another bound."

"Yeahhhhhh," Comicha said, fluttering back over with a pout. Octavia snickered and undid her coat, opening her arms to the imp, who let out a happy squee and zoomed in for squishy cuddles.

"Yeah, fuck it, the ol' rogues road for me," Sumner said, throwing up his hands in forfeit and continuing to scout the trail.

TWELVE

It was a little after noon when the tower came into view. It was, indeed, in the col, so they would not need to climb the actual peaks. From what they could see, it was several floors and had clearly seen better days. It also looked frozen over, with rings of ice every dozen feet or so. While the mountains were cold, it appeared the tower was going to be worse.

"Oh, wow," Octavia murmured to herself as they approached. For all that she attempted to be a voice of reason, she was also very excited to explore this place. This far removed meant that the wizard valued their privacy, which meant that it definitely wouldn't be trapless, but maybe Sumner was right and enough people had already disturbed this place. Then again, it was so frozen over, maybe no one had considered it worth the effort.

"This may complicate things," Sumner said.

"With sections of the tower frozen, that means there's a good chance they're undisturbed," Durante added, hefting himself over a rock. "Which means unsprung traps. Or, one could assume." It seemed they were on the same wavelength as Octavia.

Octavia nodded. "We'll perhaps have to go a little more slowly. That should be all right. There are still things to hunt this far up, and getting back down the mountain will be easier than getting up. And with the upgrades to the tent, we don't need to worry about camping too long in the cold."

"No matter. We are together, those that came before did not have us," Alces said with a grin.

"Definitely going to be cautious. Even with Alces, we don't want any major injuries," Sumner said.

"Incidentally, what all did you do to the tent?" Durante asked. "I'm curious how the metaphysical dimensional transcendence glyphs function and are activated."

"Four rooms instead of three," Octavia began, listing things off on her fingers, "merged the two beds in the first room into one for Alces though the gem 'upgrade' should make all the beds a little bigger, an icebox, a brick oven, a table in the lounge area, though it'll be a low table because I didn't have the materials to turn it into a dining area, and...I think that's it. It'll be a little nicer, because the only gems I had that many of were sapphires, so it changes the aesthetic and feel a bit."

Sumner whistled again and Durante's eyes lit up. "When we have downtime, I'm going to want to thoroughly examine this tent! And the manual."

"We may need to find another one for you to experiment with before you start messing with Tavi's home," Sumner said, calming him down a bit.

Alces laughed. "An oven! Oh, the things we can make! I'm going to need flour when next we're in town," reaching over he patted Octavia's thigh. "Such a wonder you continue to gift us with. My thanks!"

Octavia found herself glowing, very pleased. "Well, I did put all my money into it, essentially. It's the nicest tent I could afford at the time. I remembered that the proprietor had said I could make changes, but I didn't think much about it until now. It took a lot of raw materials and more in gems than it cost me initially, but if it makes everyone happy..." she trailed off, feeling that strange flutter again.

"You have made us all very happy," Alces said, and the others agreed. "We will make it up to you. To give you back happiness tenfold in exchange!"

"Tower first," Sumner said, pointing up. Durante rolled his eyes and Alces shrugged at Octavia.

The continuing march up the mountain was starting to get a little more dicey. Both Alces and Sumner had to slow their pace, though they still moved steadily. Nutmeg seemed pretty sure of his steps but Octavia had to hang on around his neck in some particularly steep parts. Surprisingly, Durante had the swiftest ascent, climbing almost lightly up the incline. She could only assume there was something about being a dhampir that made the climb easier.

Night was starting to creep in as Alces stepped on something solid. Looking down, it was a bit of armor and a skeleton inside it. Clearly a failed expedition had encountered issues here. Alces had his light up, making their trek as easy to see as possible.

"Are we close?" he asked.

Sumner nodded and they moved around one more switchback to an area that had either been naturally carved from glacial movement, or magically levelled. Either guess could have been accurate as they now found themselves at the base of the tower. It was too dark to see past the first couple of floors, but the great doors seemed held tight, and they could make out the bottom of the first ring of ice.

Grotesques of great bestial creatures, roaring out at any who approached, flanked the doors and the steps leading up had crumbled and were barely functional. A couple more stripped bodies lay about, but Sumner couldn't find any more than that.

"Chances are, this was a while ago," Alces said. "I don't feel any immediate darkness encroaching around us. Octavia, can you sense any magicks?"

"Nothing out here," Octavia said, closing her eyes for a moment so that she could extend her concentration. "Everything outside is... normal. But," she opened her eyes again and looked to Alces, "I can't penetrate the tower. I have no doubt magic remains within."

"So, relatively safe out here. Inside, not so," Sumner said. "Okay, set up camp over there. I'll set some traps and alarms in case something out there decides to get curious. Nutmeg, try not to trip over them if you go wandering." The elk grunted and turned his head.

Octavia had Alces help her down, and she gave Nutmeg his usual pets and a kiss on the nose for carrying her that day.

"Oh, hush, it's not a competition," Alces said to Nutmeg as the elk chuffed and danced on his forelegs. "We're going to be here for a time, so say goodbye." Nutmeg wandered over and rubbed his forehead against Octavia and nibbled playfully at her sweater. The other two gave Nutmeg some pats and then he wandered off, disappearing in that swirl of violet smoke.

The tent was quickly set up. It mostly looked the same, though much like the cube, the warm brown canvas was now a blend of dark purple and blue. Otherwise, it seemed to have the same footprint it always did and did not look much more remarkable on the outside than it had.

Durante took Sumner's bag while he was out and headed inside the tent. Alces held the flap for Octavia, waiting for her to go in before following suit. Once inside, it appeared the layout of the tent had changed with the altering of the primary spell. The "rooms" were now two to each side, the icebox and brick oven were in the main area near the entrance. The bathing area was now dead ahead, though aside from location it was the least changed.

The rooms that could be claimed by Sumner or Durante now contained more reasonable sized beds. The bed that was clearly Alces' was the largest in the tent, and certainly large enough for the dragonkin to stretch out - maybe even with someone else. Octavia's room was also largely unchanged.

Glass lanterns with sapphire blue panels had replaced the previous simpler lamps that had hung in the tent, adding soft blue shadows in addition to the brighter light. The furniture in the lounge area was mostly the same, though now with a large low table that they could all eat at.

"Wow, this is amazing," Durante said, looking around. "The enchantments and metamorphosis interweaving needed to create this in a few hours must be incredible." He continued muttering as he walked through, checking the rooms one at a time and quickly retreating when he stumbled upon Octavia's.

Looking around, Octavia privately reflected that yes, the tent had definitely been worth trading three generations of her family jewels for. She wondered briefly if her mother had noticed that Octavia had stolen them when she ran. It wasn't worth dwelling on. She'd never find out.

Alces set his things in his room, then went back to look over the ice box and the brick oven. "Will items always stay cold?" he asked. "Do we need firewood or is it a magic oven?"

"Hm? Oh, I'm not sure." Heading over, Octavia looked over the oven. "I mean, yes the icebox will stay cold. As for the oven, I don't know if we... oh!" Her fingertips passed over the image of flames stamped on a metal plate in the front, and the oven immediately roared to life.

"Oh ho ho," Alces exclaimed, "perhaps our journeys will be too relaxing! We'll have to take on more perilous tasks to balance it out!" Grinning at Octavia, he went to work stuffing the ice box with the leftover goat, minus pieces for dinner, and various other bits they had hidden away."

"I need to prepare some things for tomorrow," Durante said, "I guess come get me when dinner is ready."

"That we will, ingenious Durante," Alces said from over his shoulder.

Glancing over at Durante, she watched him disappear into his room. Good that he was dealing with this now, because if she had anything to say about it, he had plans later. She felt a little guilty about contriving this plan of hers, but only a little. Besides, based on everything she had seen, Durante was very receptive to a woman who was firmly insistent. She wondered if that was something he had encountered before, in their various trips to brothels. It was certainly something you could find at the right brothel, but given the other two, Octavia suspected it was more likely that they'd found women who were patient and sweet.

She laughed a little to herself as she directed Matilda over to the spot next to her bedroom. She intended, whatever happened, to make sure the evening was unforgettable.

Sumner came in later and was thoroughly impressed. After checking things out, and finding out he got last dibs on rooms but it didn't much matter, as the room next to Octavia's was Alces'. After putting his own things away, he went to the new kitchen area to help the large knight prepare dinner. Alces wasn't shy around magical trinkets, it just took him a moment to understand them. As such, he was quite pleased when he was able to control the temperature of the oven and shoved something in from his pack. Soon, the small tent started to smell of baked bread along with the warming up goat.

"Oooo, is that bread?" Octavia looked up from sorting through Matilda, very interested. Despite Durante's assurances that her pudge was all curves, she had seen her share of other women naked, and knew that she had a rounder belly and more give than the average woman. And that could be blamed entirely on baked goods.

"It is a loaf I have kept frozen since Gravemont. I have been waiting for the opportunity, and this is perfect," Alces said, producing the crusty loaf from the oven and adding it to the table along with the steaming pile of trimmed and seasoned goat meat.

"That smells amazing," she murmured, looking at the beautiful loaf. "Alces, can you...make tarts?"

"I've met many in my day," Alces laughed.

"Yes, he can," Sumner said with a chuckle as he started to slice the loaf with his knife. "Honestly, if he wanted to, he could go to Buadier Cique and challenge any of the chefs there. But this is the life he chose."

"If you can make tarts, I will follow you into the hells," Octavia said with what may have been an unnerving amount of sincerity.

"I'd be a terrible baker if that's where my tarts took you," Alces said, mirroring her sincerity.

"I'll go get Durante," Sumner said with a shake of his head.

The loaf sliced and the goat served, dinner was fully available at the new table. Durante came up behind Sumner and sat down with everyone else. Octavia scurried back to Matilda long enough to produce a jar of whipped honey, which she set down on the table with a spreader (also from the chest). Time to eat.

It was easier to sit on the floor to eat around the lower table, but at least it was a table, and the lounge area was set on a rug made from the fur of some great beast. Octavia got a slice of bread and spread the whipped honey on it, and made a few noises not normally associated with baked goods as she ate it. She was so very happy to have something fresh baked in her hands, and enjoyed dinner more than she had in a while. She finished her food, made sure everyone had bread already, and got a second slice. She was good, though, and stopped there, even though she probably could have finished the loaf on her own. But that hardly seemed fair, that bread would be fine tomorrow, should save the rest.

When they finished, she helped clean up and put things away. She took the cups and hopped outside to fill them with fresh snow. She brought them inside to melt and leave them with something cold to drink.

Today was a long day of hiking, perhaps even worse than yesterday, so everyone was keen to turn in. Bidding everyone good night, they all retired to their respective rooms. As Durante moved to head to his chamber, Octavia's hand wrapped around his arm, gently stopping him. As if through an unspoken plan, Alces and Sumner were gone.

"We still need to talk," she said, gently but firmly, "and we have already determined that we cannot brave the tower before the sun is fully up. Come with me, Kitten." She slid her hand down his arm until she reached his own hand, grasping it.

He smiled a little shyly. "Um, okay, Octavia," he said, following her. "So, what did you want to talk about?"

She didn't answer right away, leading him into her room and making sure the heavy curtain was pulled behind her. "Sit down, Kitten," she said, in that same voice, soft but commanding.

Durante did so, almost instantly, despite it being her bed, in her room, where he had avoided pretty solidly up until this moment. He looked surprised with the ease in which he obeyed her.

"Good boy," she murmured, running a hand through his hair. He leaned into her touch like he was hungry for it.

"We need to talk about you and me, Kitten," she said, looking down at him, "and I need you to be honest with me. You get very skittish around me sometimes. You apologize for being yourself, which cannot stand." She ran her hand down the side of his face, and tipped his chin up. "Why were you so embarrassed when I came to wake you this morning?"

His pink eyes met hers, and he sighed. "I feel like sometimes I'm a chore," he said after a long moment. "I'm not as athletic as Sumner, or strong as Alces. I'm soft and slow, and freakish. They're different, but all in good ways. I'm pale as a sheet of paper with these pink eyes that make people squeamish. I'm always worried I'll say the wrong thing and upset you, and I like having you around."

"Oh, Kitten." Octavia leaned down and kissed him, slow and soft, caressing his face and letting her hands slide down to gently slip into the collar of his shirt. It wasn't awkward. He'd kissed before, and while he may not be as passionate or experienced as Sumner, he was tender and sweet. She pulled back and looked him in the eyes.

"You are not a chore," she said, authority in her voice. "And it is a shame you do not realize how handsome you are. You are clever and creative, and I would guess smarter than both your companions. Your pink eyes do not bother me in the least. They're like roses." She smiled. "I love roses."

"You really mean that?" he asked, surprise and a touch of disbelief in his voice. But there was also hope there, and the way he was looking at her melted her heart.

"Of course I mean it," she said, and she began undoing his shirt. "When I said I felt desire for you all, I didn't mean everyone except you." She started to smile again. "I've thought often of what I would do when I had you to myself. Would you like me to show you?"

"Um, yes, I think I'd like that," he said, feeling better and still loosening up for her. "Do you need me to do anything?"

"Promise to be a good kitten and do as you're told," she said, drawing her hands through his hair again. "If I do something that is too much for you, you need a word you can say to stop me that makes it clear I have crossed a line. If you say it once, I will pause. If you say it twice, we stop entirely. Do you have one?"

Durante thought for a long time, then smiled. "Emerald. It's the opposite of a rose in the color spectrum," he said. "But I don't think you could possibly do something that would make me want you to stop."

"Oh I *could* but other than being a little demanding I don't intend to push your boundaries tonight," she said, and bared her teeth at him playfully, which got a little surprised laugh. Then she stepped back. "Stand up, and undress. Let me see you."

"Oh, um, okay," he said, standing up as she instructed. He undressed quickly, there was no showmanship to it, though she really hadn't expected any. She doubted Durante had ever actively seduced anyone. He also didn't seem to be physically aroused yet, though he was likely too nervous.

Every inch of him was pale white and hairless aside from his brows and what was on top of his head. She walked around him, reaching out with one hand and gently touching his shoulder. She let her hand wander, feeling his skin, even squeezing his ass, which got another small laugh.

"Now," she said, coming back around before him, "undress me. You may touch me as you do, but not more than that."

He nodded and tilted his head to the side. "Okay."

It seemed that setting parameters and giving orders was taking the anxiety out of their interaction. Octavia could see that the tension in his shoulders had lessened. He knew what to do and what was expected of him. He wasn't rushed, either. As he pulled up her sweater over her head, he made sure her arms were in the right position, he lifted the material before exposing her breasts; he was very conscientious of what he was doing and what would be comfortable for her.

Rather than casting the sweater away, he folded it and set it aside. He did the same for her underclothes. Her upper body now exposed, he tentatively touched her breasts, running his fingertips along the curve and caressing them gently. There was something almost reverent in the way he touched her, how he exhaled as if in wonder. Mindful of her instructions, he didn't linger, and knelt to help her out of her pants. One by one, he lifted her leg, taking off her shoe and sock, then standing back up to work her pants and small clothes off her hips until they were on the floor.

"You are astoundingly beautiful, Octavia," he finally said as he folded up her pants and set them aside with the rest of her clothes.

"Thank you, Kitten," she said, smiling warmly at him. She drew him in and kissed him again, still slow and sweet. He melted into it, and as their bodies pressed together, she could feel that he was responding to her physically as well. She gave his lower lip a tug with her teeth as she pulled away. Letting go of him, she sat down on the bed.

"Kneel, Kitten. Right here." Her voice was ever soft, but the expectation that he would be quick about it was clear.

"Yes, Octavia," he said, kneeling before her as requested.

"You've been very good these last few days," she said, reaching out to pet his hair again. "You outpaced us all on a hard climb. You fixed my poor Matilda. So tonight I am going to tease you, and play with you, but when it is all done, I will ride you until you come for me. Would you like that?"

"Oh, wow," he murmured, his eyes growing a little wide. "I'd love that, Octavia. Thank you. What can I do for you?"

She caressed his face, and ran her thumb lightly over his lower lip. "I know you're not completely inexperienced. But have you ever gone down on a woman?"

"Once or twice, but I was afraid of biting them," he said, but moved a little closer. "I'd be happy to try with you, if you're willing."

"Oh, I insist," she said with a grin. Before he inched too close, though, she lifted up one leg and set her foot on his chest. "Start at the ankle. Work your way up. I expect you to use your mouth and your hands. When you reach your goal," she leaned back on one hand and stroked her sex with the other hand to emphasize her point, "you will keep on your task until I come. I'll give you guidance if you need it. And Kitten, if you get hungry," she moved her hand over and drew her fingertips over her inner thigh (conspicuously opposite the mark Sumner left), "you bite here."

"Of course," Durante said, lifting her leg with the utmost care, one hand on her ankle and one hand on her thigh, keeping her supported as he leaned in and started kissing.

As he moved, his kisses got a little more involved: gentle sucking, a brush of his fangs, and a slight bit of tongue. The tease of his fangs sent a tremor through her. When he had reached her inner thigh, he was nearly giving her more hickies with each kiss. Nearly. His efforts were rewarded with soft cries.

Durante reached his goal, smiled softly up at Octavia, then lowered his head and started to kiss her sex. His tongue caressed the length of her entrance. As he began to lick into her, she let herself drop back on the bed like she had with Sumner, spreading her legs wider to be all the more accessible. His tongue explored deeper and deeper until he was stretching it out as far as he could with each drive. Something in her flavor made it all the more exciting for him, and he was getting hungrier and hungrier with his motions, face pressed firmly against her pelvis. She was warm and flushed and moaning, and very aware that Durante didn't seem to pause—he didn't pull back for a breath, and it didn't seem to bother him.

"You're doing so good, kitten," she gasped out at last. "It feels amazing, but I need you to focus on my pearl now."

Durante wrapped both of his arms around her thighs and moved up, using the tip of his tongue to find what she wanted him to play with. What he lacked in skill he made up for in enthusiasm. He started licking her clit like it was the best ice cream he'd ever had, and he wanted more. His mouth pressed against her, and she shuddered again as those sharp ivory daggers brushed her very sensitive skin. She reached down to run a hand through his hair.

"Good boy," she moaned. It was perfect. It was what she needed. She tightened her hand in his hair and cried out as she came.

The fervent licking didn't stop, and the arms around her thighs tightened their grip. She could feel how strong he was, how he kept her in place even as she started to twist beneath him. He started to suck at her clit, no longer just licking it, his fangs pressing into her soft skin. She came again, crying out louder, and he still didn't stop. She hadn't told him to.

"Ohhh, Kitten, you did so good!" She shuddered again, nectar dripping from her and coating his chin. "Easy, let me catch my breath!"

Durante paused and then pulled away slowly. She pushed up enough to look into his eyes again, and saw that the pink had begun the shift to red. She shivered again, and tried to contain her anticipation and excitement.

"Do you want to feed on me, Kitten?" Pleasure still pulsed through her, and it was hard not to squirm.

"Yes," he said, his voice taking on a darker tone, but he was controlled, and he licked the spot she told him he could bite. Still, he was waiting for permission.

"It'll make you more tactile, but also easier to command," she said, wanting to make sure he understood. "You'll want me even more, and you'll do anything I say."

"I don't know if I could want you more," Durante said, licking the spot once more. "I would already do anything you asked of me."

His words sent a delicious shiver down her spine. "If you trust me, then do it. Bite down. Take what you need."

"Of course I trust you, you have been nothing but good to us." He nuzzled her thigh and licked it once more. "Thank you." Gently, softly, and with the utmost care Durante's fangs sank into the soft flesh of her inner thigh.

It stung, of course, but that sting was soon replaced by a tingling warmth that radiated out. Durante moaned, loudly, and held fast to her thigh. Octavia also moaned, a shudder running through her. Three, no more than four, pulls later, he eased his fangs out of her but stayed close to her thigh, licking the spot to stop the bleeding, then again as if to remember the taste. He whimpered, as if he were utterly taken by her flavor and what her blood was doing to him.

"You taste so good," he muttered. "You feel so good. Everything about you... so good."

"You're a delight," she said, panting softly, and reached down to run a hand through his hair again. "Come to me, my kitten. Come up on the bed with me. You've been very good, and I have a promise to keep."

Slowly, and a little unsteady, Durante picked himself up off the floor and moved over to her. It was a touch different, as Durante was about six inches taller than her and Sumner, and he was much more pliable. He slid against her, climbing up onto the bed and pressed against her as he lay on his side, holding her to him. His hands moved over her, caressing her thighs, squeezing her breasts, touching as much as he could as he held her to him.

"Please," he begged softly, kissing her shoulder, her neck, her cheek, wherever he could reach.

"Soon, Kitten," she murmured, "but first, I'm going to kiss you. And touch you. And you can do the same to me."

She cupped his face, turning his head towards her and kissed him deeply. It wasn't rough like it had been with Sumner, but it was no longer gentle and sweet as it had been when they first started. It was thorough, and building. Her hands moved over him, she moaned into his mouth, and she hoped he remembered all of this tomorrow. Remembered how much she had enjoyed him and wanted him. He kissed her softly but deeply, leaning into it and hungrily sucking on her tongue, his hands moving over her body in slow, grabby circles. She was so soft and his fingers sank right in.

They stayed there for a while, kissing and touching, the kisses getting less restrained by the minute. Not that they were terribly restrained to begin with. Octavia kissed around his face and neck, and bit gently into his shoulder. She wanted to leave a mark if she could. Nothing that would show when he was dressed, but something to see when he was alone. A reminder that this had been real. Finally, she pushed him onto his back and climbed atop him. She trapped his cock between the two of them, rubbing her wet sex against it.

"Are you ready, Kitten?" She was teasing him again. She knew the answer, but she wanted to hear it. "Do you want this?"

If he had been a little more disobedient he could have slipped right in. He held his hands to his eyes, elbows up, as he rolled his head back. "Please, Octavia, I want you so much," he muttered. "You're amazing."

She reached for his hands, pulling them away gently. "Look at me, Kitten," she said, and let go of him to set her hands against his shoulders for balance. Now when he met her gaze, his eyes were pink again, but they seemed to shimmer. "I want you to look into my eyes as you sink into me."

Lifting up, it was actually easy to twitch her hips a little and sink back down without having to use her hand to guide him. His hands dropped down and rested on her hips. She moaned as he slid into her, and finished with a small, punctuating cry as she came to rest against his hips. His head rolled back again and he called out her name.

"Tell me how it feels, Kitten," she said softly, sliding her hands over his chest.

"It feels amazing," he groaned. "You're so warm and wet, yet tight and clinging. I can feel you pulse around me as you flex, and your weight on me is so nice. Like I'm safe under you."

She felt like someone squeezed her heart, and she smiled down at him. "My kitten," she murmured, reaching up to caress his face, "you're always safe with me."

She bent to kiss him once more, then pushed herself back up and began to slowly move her hips, up until it was almost too far, and then back down until she was grinding against his pelvis. And again. And again. Durante was squeezing and massaging her thighs as he wriggled a little underneath her. As speed and rhythm built, the motion became less teasing. Little cries came out of Octavia every time she dropped her hips and he sank into her again. Durante was being surprisingly vocal, which may have been an effect of her blood, making him supremely sensitive. As she rode him, he started to press his hips up as well, and she could feel him growing more inside her. His time was coming.

"Yes," she gasped, clawing lightly at his chest as she kept up her steady bounce. "Are you going to come for me?"

"Yes, Octavia, yes," he cried out, the last word a hiss as he arched his back and thrusted up with his hips, driving into her and releasing. She could feel him flood her vessel as he throbbed and came for her, his grip on her thighs tightening. When his orgasm passed, he collapsed onto the bed, his hands gently caressing her flesh.

Moaning, Octavia dropped herself down to kiss him, her hips grinding against him as she did. She was close enough, she could absolutely get herself off like this, and she suspected he would enjoy it.

"Do you want to feel me come?" she asked him, her voice breathy as the kiss broke. Her hips rolled against him, and she squeezed the cock still inside her. Almost…

"Yes, please," he said, whimpering again as his sensitivity had increased. "Let me help. Let me…," he added, trailing off a little as he kissed down her face to her neck, brushing his fangs against the sensitive skin with every tender kiss. She shivered at the feel of his fangs. There wasn't a lot he could do from this position, but his hands caressed over her back and squeezed her ass. Durante's hips moved in opposite of hers, trying to give her as much stimulation as he could.

"I love the way you feel, Kitten," she murmured, her legs starting to tense. "Your body beneath me, your cock inside me, your fangs on my skin. It's…it's perfect…oh, Gods!"

She clenched hard around him as she came, head dropping down and moaning loudly into his shoulder. The sensations cascaded through her, then let go, and she went soft against him, still laying on top of him for the moment, panting. He continued to caress her, holding her as she lay atop him. There was no reason to move, no urgent need. Nothing to do but linger in their shared afterglow.

After several minutes, Octavia picked her head up and kissed him lightly. "I'm going to get up and clean us off real quick," she explained, smiling softly at him, "and then I will be right back, and you can hold me and kiss me as much as you like. You'll stay with me tonight. All right?"

She didn't wait for a response and gently extracted herself, whimpering softly as he slid out of her. Durante nodded as she did and stayed put. She wasn't sure he could get up if he wanted to, drunk on her blood. As promised, she was quick and wiped them both down before climbing back in bed next to him and pulling the covers up. She pressed herself up against him and ran a hand through his hair again. He curled up against her, his leg sliding along hers, hands touching her everywhere he could, lips scattering kisses over her face and shoulder. She felt that squeeze around her heart again and pulled him in closer to her, returning his kisses, playing with his hair, rubbing his back. As they relaxed, her movements became more sleepy and languid, but she didn't stop him, didn't tell him they needed to sleep now. She was there for him until he was fulfilled.

Durante did slow considerably, but it seemed like she ended up falling asleep with him caressing and gently kissing her. It was soothing at this point. She couldn't say how long the night owl stayed up touching her, but her dreams were vivid enough to give her some idea.

THIRTEEN

Sometime in the night Octavia woke from her lurid dreams, panting and aroused. Rolling over, she kissed Durante into wakefulness and pulled him on top of her, wrapping her legs around him and kissing him until she couldn't breathe as he thrust into her, surprise and wonder written on his face. Or... she thought she did. Maybe she dreamt it.

All she knew for certain was that when she started to wake in the morning he was spooned up against her, nuzzled into her neck, holding her close. She smiled in her half-awake state. This was... lovely. She had never been with someone so sweet, who couldn't stop touching her. Sure, part of that was the effects of her blood, but it was still wonderful.

"Good morning, my friends! Who is ready for adventure?" Alces' voice roused Octavia further. With the upgrades to the tent, the curtains were thick enough that his voice almost sounded conversational. "Breakfast soon." The great knight mumbled something else after that but it was lost.

Durante's response to this was to squeeze Octavia closer and mumble incoherently. If she was a cat she would've purred. Part of her thought she needed to help wake him up, but this felt so nice, the way he was pulling her closer after having spent the night kissing and petting her. She didn't think she had ever felt so...wanted. Not sexually, Durante wasn't about to rip her clothes off, he was sleeping and comfortable and wanted her closer.

After a moment, Durante did start to wake. He had a brief start, then blinked and looked at Octavia.

"Tavi," he asked, still waking up, "did... last night actually happen?" It seemed surprise and disbelief were a common morning-after experience in this group.

She rolled over so she could look at him. "You called me Tavi," she said with a smile, reaching up to caress his face. She giggled. "We're in bed naked together, and we're sticky. What do you think?"

Durante smiled, and he leaned in, kissing her softly, holding her close once more. "Maybe next time I won't be so blood drunk that I'll remember it more clearly, but I *do* remember that it was incredible. Did you have fun? Was I good? Please be honest."

Nuzzling into him, Octavia smiled again, and laid kisses across his shoulder. "I did, and you were. You were so sweet, and wonderful." She nipped at him lightly. "Do you remember when I pulled you on top of me in the middle of the night? Do you think I would have done that if I didn't enjoy myself?" She was fairly certain that was not a dream at this point.

"Mm, that did happen, too. Good," he said, and playfully nipped back. She shivered a little at the nip, a soft little moan escaping. "Thank you. I'd really like to stay here with you. I've never woken up like this, it's really nice."

Looking up at him, she smiled. "You don't need to keep thanking me. I didn't do it *for* you, I did it *with* you, and I enjoyed it too. I've woken up with someone before, but never someone who just... held onto me like you did." Was she blushing again?

"Well, I'm very glad I could do something new for you as well," he said. "We should really get up, though. While I'm almost positive Alces has been awake for a couple of hours, and he probably gave us more time than usual, we shouldn't stay too long. But, maybe someday we could stay in really late?"

She nodded. "Maybe after a celebration, some time when it's expected." Impulsively, she leaned in and kissed him, then let go. "All right, get up," she said, shooing him away with a smile.

"Okay," he smiled again and got out of bed. He took a moment to find his clothes, and since he never made it to his own room he still had his bag that slung over his shoulder. Pulling out one of his bottles, he splashed a little bit on the part of him that was sticky and offered it to her. "Clean up?"

"Oh! Sure." She took the bottle and dribbled it carefully where it was needed, and found any residue removed with nothing left behind.

"Fascinating."

Getting all the way dressed, he moved in once more for another kiss, then made his way out so that she could get ready in peace. Once he was out of the tent she continued to sit on the bed for a moment feeling warm and happy. And then the voice of realism asked what the hell she was doing.

"Oh, Goddess of Mercy," she murmured, running a hand through her hair. She had feelings for him. That...that was that squeezing she felt around her heart last night, that sensation, that want to cherish him and make him feel appreciated and adored. Her emotions towards Sumner were fond, and maybe deepening, but he was careful and cautious. Durante was shy, but once you bridged that…

"Oh, what am I doing!? It's been two weeks! If that!" She ran her hands over her face and took a deep breath. There was no reason to panic. Everyone already thought she was very nice, and they would be travelling together for a while. She could...she could figure this out.

Two down, one to go. Delightful, my little protégé, the voice came once more. It was hard to tell if Kamvasana was praising her or mocking her. Really, it could go either way, or both. Her patron probably was unbothered by Octavia's emotions on the issue, so long as she kept taking Sumner, Durante, or whomever was available to her bed regularly.

Groaning, Octavia ran a hand over her face again. It was hard to say why Kamvasana's encouragement was so annoying. She started to get dressed, and pulled her hair up in a bun. They were going into the tower if they could manage it. She needed clothes and hair that wouldn't catch on anything. Everything in place, she headed out into the main area.

Alces and Sumner were warming breakfast at the new stove. It was pretty much just the goat and the leftover bread with the last couple of fruits. It wasn't much, but it was hearty and it would keep them going for the day.

"Good morning, dear Octavia. Are you ready for this quest?" Alces asked as he set the last of the dishes down on the table. Durante was sitting near the table already.

"Good morning." Octavia smiled, a little awkwardly. While she wasn't ashamed of what she had done with Sumner or Durante, this was the first time she'd sat down to breakfast with two people she'd slept with. "I am looking forward to seeing what awaits us, and how I can help."

"I think you'll be invaluable," Durante said, "most wizards use their own language, or lost languages, to notate things and place reminders. There's a good chance we'll need you constantly."

"Never worry about your worth, brilliant Octavia," Alces said, "we wanted you for a reason, and we knew you would be the best."

"You know, I don't know that I ever asked," Octavia said as she layered goat on a slice of bread, "but how did you find me? How long were you looking for someone?"

"It wasn't easy," Sumner said, leaning back and eating a piece of meat.

"It's true," Alces said with a nod, "we found a family you translated documents for. I don't remember the name, but they were surprised you could read any of the manuscripts they had in their old, dusty basement. I think their grandfather had been a collector."

"It was the Hazelmennings," Durante offered.

"Right," Alces exclaimed and clapped Durante on the shoulder, "easy description, though. The most beautiful woman you've ever seen who does not look like she belongs wherever she is."

"The Hazelmennings," Octavia repeated, then laughed. "Gods, that was...years ago! I'm surprised they remembered me. I remember those manuscripts, though, if I had been less ethical I probably would have left with five or twenty of them."

She was thoughtful for a moment, taking a bite and staring off into space, then laughed again. "Beautiful woman who looks like she doesn't belong where she is. I don't imagine I look like I belong anywhere. Certainly feels like I don't most days." She shook her head.

"Well, you certainly don't look like you belong with us," Sumner laughed. "Not that that's a bad thing."

"True," Alces said with a grin. "You look much better."

Durante had to shrug in agreement as they worked on breakfast. Octavia waved them off and focused on her own food. She didn't have the heart to tell them that, for all that she was enjoying traveling with them more than she ever expected, she didn't quite feel like she belonged yet either. She was getting closer. And it really hadn't been that long. Maybe after they were done with the tower.

"So what is the plan?" Octavia asked as they started to clean up. "Sumner, you scouted last night, see anything important?"

Sumner shook his head. "I just set traps and alarms. Didn't notice anything other than really old marks of fighting, camping, and death. Everything else was too dark, even with my eyes. Best to check it out now."

"Yes, we waited for the sun to be high before looking, but now we shall check, we'll go in, and we will go carefully and hope for the best," Alces said.

"Wizard towers are really hard to prepare for unless you have a lot of history on them," Durante said. "We had bits and pieces, but most of it is speculation. Monsters were this guy's primary research, so that we can expect. Not so many explosive glyphs and ghostly servants."

Nodding, Octavia headed back into her room to grab her satchel and came back out. "Well, I'm ready to give this a whirl when the rest of you are. I've even recharged twice this week, so... should be in good shape." She laughed at herself a little over that.

"Is that what you call it," Sumner said, raising his eyebrows. Durante looked a little shy but smiled. Alces ate what was left and the rest grabbed their gear and got themselves ready. It was time to take the tower.

Heading outside, the sun had almost reached its zenith. The tower was somehow more imposing in the daylight; now they could see the top of it high above them. The ice was interesting, in that it was near perfect rings every twenty feet or so, all the way up. The last ring they could see blocked their view of the top of the tower.

"Experiment gone wrong?" Sumner asked.

"I don't know," Durante said. "Nothing ever mentioned him studying weather or ice spells. Maybe a rival?"

"Definitely unnatural," she murmured, pulling on her gloves and making sure her satchel was settled and out of the way. Getting through the ice would add to the challenge of navigating the tower. It could double the amount of time they thought they were going to need to be there.

They headed to the entrance, and Octavia could see the scorch marks and remains that Sumner had mentioned. Someone had certainly come here at some point. Possibly multiple someones, though it seemed it was a very long time ago. Once more the party encountered a large set of doors that hadn't been opened in years, possibly decades.

The doors appeared to have no discernable lock or latch. Sumner examined them thoroughly, looking for a hidden catch or a bespelled keyhole, and found nothing. Durante attempted to apply his cleaning solution to the hinges to make sure they would open, carefully dripping the liquid down a length of wire through the narrow gap on the edge of the massive doors, but it was hard to say if it did any good. Finally, for lack of any better ideas, Alces grabbed the painstakingly tooled handles and pushed the massive doors open. His muscles strained, but unlike the door in the mausoleum a week or so ago, this one didn't break and offered only initial resistance before swinging wide open.

They were immediately met by a pair of creatures that looked like someone had armor plated giant moles and given them the heads of sharks. With impressive speed, Sumner drew his bow and fired off a shot, which scuffed off the armor. However, neither of the creatures moved, they simply retained their menacing appearance. The blue crackling energy had started to form in Octavia's hand, but she dismissed it quickly, shaking the lingering tingle out of her fingertips.

"Taxidermied or frozen?" Durante asked after everyone took a breath.

"Comicha," she murmured, and the imp popped into being next to her. "Can you tell if they're still alive?"

The imp nodded, and flew up to one of the creatures, close but also high up enough to take off quickly if it came back to life. The little imp flew around for a moment, then shook her ass at them. When they didn't respond, she flew closer and knocked on one of their heads.

"Nothin'," she said with an exaggerated shrug. "Either stuffed or magicked into just... this." She presented the creature with an outthrusting of both her hands.

"Maybe a distraction or scaring off novices," Durante suggested and started to step inside, Sumner close behind. Alces didn't take his eyes off the creatures and held his shield up, just in case. Octavia stayed behind Alces.

"It certainly isn't welcoming," she commented, staring at the creatures for a moment. "A statement to visitors. It would mean different things depending on the visitor."

"Well, looks like we got stairs that go up and that's about it," Sumner said, looking around.

The main foyer was basically a large, round room. Old tapestries hung on the walls, and the years hadn't been kind. Without some care, it would be impossible to see what was on them under the dust and fading. There were a number of trophies around the area, heads of fantastical creatures, many no one had seen before, all looking into the room. Octavia looked warily at the heads lining the walls. With careful steps, she approached one of the tapestries and murmured a spell quietly, gently touching it. The dust disappeared, leaving the tapestry pristine and clean, though it couldn't reverse the march of time. Comicha hovered nearby, curious and ready.

The first tapestry was relatively faded. What words on it were lost. The image was a dissection diagram of a creature she encountered before. It appeared to be a frog, but slightly more humanoid by standing upright and with opposable thumbs. It was a surprisingly thorough anatomical diagram.

"Vodaman," Durante said, looking up past Octavia at the tapestry. "Kinda rare up here in the mountains. Looks like Vaztus was a collector."

Wrinkling up her nose, Octavia made a moue of distaste and moved to the next tapestry, performing the same spell, revealing another dissection diagram. She stepped carefully through the room, cleaning the different hangings in turn, assuming once they were all clean they could then see if there was any pattern or purpose to them, other than a slightly gruesome display.

"Kitten, if you ever get into dissection, I'll smack you," she muttered.

"I'm happy to say that is not an interest of mine," Durante said, looking over the tapestries as she went. "Just what the parts can be used for. Let's see; wyvern, greater tunnel squid, I... don't have a clue what that is, and that's a mountain blood ape."

"What are the chances we're going to run into any of those going up the tower?" Sumner asked, starting to step up the stairs, carefully peering up the stairwell.

"Maybe the blood ape," Durante speculated, "because this is closest to its natural environment. But I have no idea what Vaztus may or may not have been doing to these creatures."

"Perhaps it is best if I go first this time, brave Sumner," Alces said, moving towards the stairs. "If some mismatched hell beast is going to jump out, I'd prefer it jumps out at me."

Looking around, Octavia shuddered. For all that she used magic, and understood all the good it could do, she also was very clear that it could do horrible things. Kamvasana may annoy her, but their machinations were comparatively harmless.

The tower was designed in such a way that it had an opening through the floors in the center, but the ice was currently blocking the floor above. Alces went first this time and slowed when he got near the top.

"This does not look good," he muttered, then glanced down the stairs, "Brilliant Durante, come take a look and tell me when you see. But be quiet about it."

Durante carefully pushed past Sumner and moved up next to Alces. He muttered something under his breath then motioned for everyone else to be quiet but move with them.

Topping the stairs, the next room looked as if it had been infested. The walls were coated in organic resin of some sort and there were round orbs, roughly the size of pumpkins, scattered about in clusters. As they paused near the top, they could see the stairs leading up, and through the first ring of ice, on the opposite side.

"Oh, deepest hells," Octavia muttered. She looked around the room for a moment, then reached into her bag and pulled out a scarf, wrapping it around her hair. She sensed deep in her soul that if anything did hatch, it would get squishy very quickly.

"Okay, I don't know for sure," Durante whispered, "but this looks like a tunnel squid nest, but the eggs are... very big. Vibrations can set them off to hatch, so if they're somehow still alive, we should be very quiet getting across to the other stairway."

Alces moved to the side and waved for the others to go first. He was the biggest, most lumbering of them so if anyone would set them off it would be him. Sumner went across without issue, the nimble thief moving through the craggy flooring without much of an issue. Durante motioned to Octavia. Nodding, she moved carefully through the room. She wasn't a rogue, but she had been raised with the hopes of a noble alliance. Grace had been drilled into her from a young age and her time with Kamvasana had only enhanced that. She was capable of a light step.

Durante followed closely behind and seemed overly cautious, but he made it to the foot of the stairs as well. Alces took a breath and started to trod across. This took the longest time, as his footsteps were naturally heavy, and if he tripped and fell, well that would be a whole different event. Thankfully, despite a couple of steps that were worryingly heavy, the large knight also made it to the stairs with nary an egg twitching. If that's what they even were.

"I took a look up the stairs. It seems someone tunneled through the ice, it goes all the way up to, I guess, the floor past it," Sumner said, waving them upwards.

"Given everything we have seen, isn't it far more likely that some*thing* tunneled through there instead of someone?" She turned a questioning look to first Sumner then Durante, but she kept moving.

Durante made a noise as he thought, then shook his head. "Normally, I'd agree with you, but this tunnel is too uniform and at the matching angle of the stairs in the same spiral. Not random enough or direct to be an animal of some sort," he said, pausing. "I hope."

The next floor they reached was more of a hall. A series of tables and chairs, with a larger almost throne-like chair set by itself before a round table. Part of the room was cut off by a wall with a pair of doors on either side of where the looking hole in the center would be.

"Huh, crazy wizard actually had guests," Sumner stated with a rise in his voice, a little surprised at the very idea.

"That does seem surprising, given the remoteness of the tower." She approached the throne cautiously, looking it over. Vaztus' decorative taste seemed to derive from his work, with the throne seeming to be made of bone and a rich leather. She could feel a slight hum of magic from it. It was very slight, though. Possibly fading out.

Sumner moved towards one of the doors and glanced in. He suddenly backed up, grabbing for his sword. "Shit, shit, shit," he said, getting progressively louder.

Alces turned, shield up and ran in his direction as the door burst open. Several beasts came snarling out. They looked like someone had given giant wolverines a worse attitude, beady eyes, and massive canines. "To arms," Alces rumbled, "beasts about." Taking his mace, he clanged it against his shield, making sure he kept their attention.

The throne would have to wait. Octavia dashed forward and threw down an arc of sparkling sand in front of Alces. "Don't step into the fog," she cried out as a dense mist roiled up before them around the charging monsters.

Ravenous growling echoed through the room. As the first creature entered Octavia's fog, the swirling mist darkened and erupted in a heat they could all feel. Blue tentacles whipped out from the darkness, grasping the creature and pulling it in. It roared as it started to burn.

The second was already mid-lead and passed through the darkness a little singed and dazed, which was enough for it to crash against Alces' shield, who came down on it with his mace, smashing it into the floor. The other two skittered around the darkness, one coming for Sumner, the other headed right for Octavia. Sumner had his blade drawn already and was backing up while Durante was trying to unsling his screwshot and steady it. Octavia flung out her hand, and blue fire leapt to Sumner's sword once more. As the beast came at her, she mentally scrambled through her bag of tricks and ultimately decided getting out of the way was step one. She had to keep focused on the darkness to keep the spell up, waiting for the beast inside to succumb or break free. She waited until it was lunging and dove to the side.

"Fiends," Alces growled out in a surprisingly vicious way. The creature below him took another several blows, trying to scramble out from underneath the dragonkin but failing as the hulk of scaly muscle landed strike after strike with the mace.

"Had to fuckin' be," Sumner said, rolling over a table and flipping up onto his feet as the other creature came after him. "Let's send 'em back to the hells!" He kicked the table into the creature as it leapt for him, causing it to spin when it struck its back legs. It sprawled before Sumner, who stuck it with his blade. The fiend screamed out, thrashing as the blue flame licked from the blade and started to engulf the monster.

In a smooth, practiced motion, Durante produced a red cylinder from his pouch and slapped it into the receiving catch on the side of his screwshot. Leveling the firearm, he aimed for the creature lunging at Octavia and fired. A red streak slammed into the monster, twisting it in the air and having it skid near her, injured and angry. Octavia leapt as the beast spun and had to roll to get further away from it, the trajectory changed by Durante's shot. The roiling darkness fell away as she was now more focused on the angry beast directly in front of her. Blue power crackled from her hands and two bolts shot at the snarling fiend as she scrambled back to her feet. It spasmed, stunned by the attack, and looked at her wild-eyed. It was enough time for Durante to fire again, hitting the beast in the shoulder and knocking its wounded leg out from under it.

Two seemed down at this point, with the one that had been trapped in Octavia's spell left on the ground, twitching and charred, and the one at Alces' feet beaten to a pulp. Alces stood and started looking for the next one to fight. Sumner was squaring off with the one that had attacked him, blue flames licking over its fur and his blade.

"C'mon you dumb, ugly bitch," Sumner shouted and the beast charged once more. Sumner parried the attack, rolling with it as the creature wasn't little, and it required both his hands to counter. Unfortunately, the other claw raked his side, cutting through the leather and leaving a trio of nasty gashes. Holding his side, Sumner hobbled back away from the beast and held his sword at the ready. Injured, but not out of the fight. Not yet.

Quickly murmuring an incantation, Octavia braced herself as tendrils of blue-tinted darkness erupted from her, lashing at the fiend still trying to get back on its feet before her and leaving searing marks where they had touched before dying away.

"Please be dead," she murmured, giving her head a shake. She hated that spell, mostly because of how aroused it left her. It was a weird setting to suddenly want to fuck someone. Unfortunately, damaged as it was, it still twitched and threatened to get up.

"Fire going out," Durante said as a warning as he pulled a glass sphere swirling with reddish orange energy and chucked it at the monster. The orb shattered on impact erupted into a ball of flame. With its injuries, it couldn't get away and started to burn.

The beast on Sumner jumped at him again and snapped its maw, its teeth closing inches from his face. It had been stopped cold by Alces grabbing its tail. All momentum lost, it crashed to the ground and Sumner was aware enough to stab it again, the flames starting to build. Alces wasted no time and stomped down on it, his toe claws digging in as he pinned it to the floor. Between everything else, Sumner's stab, the blue magical flame, and Alces' mace exploding with a brilliant bright light against its skull, there was nothing left of its life.

As the magical fires burned away, the creatures' bodies turned to dust. The only one left was the first one Alces had beaten down. It was quite dead, but its body remained.

Panting a little more than she should given her level of exertion, Octavia walked towards the remaining beast, stepping through the ash. "Those weren't illusions, they had...substance. But this is the only one that was real?"

"They were all real," Alces said, moving towards Sumner and setting his hand against the bleeding wounds. Closing his eyes, he started to chant again and they could feel it reverberate through them. Sumner winced as his skin started to stitch back together under Alces' healing spell. The magic soon soothed the pain and he breathed a sigh of relief.

"I think they're weak to fire," Durante said, walking up and placing a hand on Octavia's shoulders to see if she was okay. "The flames seem to eat at them."

Unthinking, Octavia leaned into Durante's touch a little, unable to help it. She stopped herself before she turned towards him. She had mostly gotten pretty good at ignoring her body after spell casting, but that was before she started traveling with three people who, by their admission, were all very willing to either wreck her or be wrecked by her. She clenched her jaw and took a deep breath.

"The flame blade thing is proving to be a very useful trick," he said, giving Octavia a wink. The wink didn't help.

"Ah, thanks. I'm... I'm going to go look at the throne," Octavia said, gently stepping away from Durante, but not so quickly that he would think something was wrong. "It's definitely bespelled, but it also feels like it's fading."

"Alright, be careful. If fiends are here there is no doubt other terribleness still afoot," Alces said, taking the remaining mangled body and pushing it down the icy slope. Durante nodded and kept his screwshot out, wrapping the sling around one arm so he wouldn't drop it and it would be easier to steady.

"Those things are out," Sumner grunted, standing to his full height and brushing the spot where he'd been hit. Now it was just a bloody patch on his leather jerkin, the wounds healed and the jerkin repaired, "I'm going to finish looking in that room."

The throne did have some magic still left in it, but Octavia couldn't derive what it did. It was too faint. As she examined it more closely, she was able to discern a single hot spot of magic. A trigger, and it was on the outside of the left arm of the throne.

"It looks like only one spell is left intact," Octavia said, turning her head a little so her voice would travel back to the others. "And unless one of you can figure this out, I suspect there's only one way to know what it does."

Durante came over and crouched down next to the throne. Pulling on his eye glass set, he started to look it over. Hemming and hawing, he tilted his head and finally shook it.

"I wish I could, but all I'm seeing is a trigger spell. It'll do something somewhere else," he said, looking around, trying to trace it, "but where, I can't tell."

Octavia nodded. "That's basically as far as I got. Do we risk it? I doubt it's immediately destructive, given that it's linked to his chair. Though maybe don't sit in the other chairs after triggering it."

"No sitting for us yet," Alces said, keeping an eye down the stairs. Durante gave her a shrug.

"Near as my research told me," Durante said, straightening up and taking a step back, "Vaztus Drukankor was into alchemy, chimerization, and bestial research. I don't think it'll make anything explode, but it may open some cages somewhere else in the tower."

"Anything that's in a cage should be long dead," Sumner said, coming back out of the door. He pointed back behind him. "Looks like a kitchen and pantry. Torn to pieces. Probably why those fiends were so starved. I expected them to be a lot harder to fight."

"This place has been abandoned for years and years," Octavia murmured, coming around to the side of the chair with the trigger. "Why are these beasts still here at all? How are those eggs in the other room still gestating?"

"Who knows," Durante said. "Magical stasis? Or hunting and using the tower as a nest? As a well studied alchemist, I can assure you that magic does weird stuff sometimes, especially if it's horribly broken."

Sighing, Octavia nodded. "Okay. Be ready." She looked at the rest of them, then touched the trigger. As her finger brushed over the trigger, there was a pulse that was felt through the tower, then nothing. There was this sense of tension that everyone was feeling by the way they looked around, but nothing seemed to be happening.

"Maybe it's broken?" Sumner hoped.

"We may or may not find out later, friends," Alces said, moving towards the stairway that went up along the wall, "for now, we have to move on. There are still books to find."

Nodding, Octavia straightened up. She looked over the chair for another minute but finally turned to follow Alces. Thankfully, the mysteries around them were easily overriding the spike in her libido brought on by her patron's power.

FOURTEEN

"Fiends cannot starve to death," Alces started to say as they headed upstairs. Octavia found herself behind him with Sumner behind her, and Durante bringing up the rear. Given the threat of the unknown, they were very close together. "If there are more of them, they would be weak but frenzied. Dangerous, but easier for us to kill."

There was an unfamiliar rancor in Alces' voice. As they walked up the stairs, Octavia briefly set her hand on Alces back. It bothered her to see him so angry, he who was so often their light. She felt a strange want to make him happy. She had no idea how. He looked back and caught her hand, giving it a small squeeze, but remained focused and unsmiling.

As they reached the top of the stairs, they found themselves in a lab. Between the cold and the age, any smell of rot and gore had long dissipated. It was likely the fiends from down below had already eaten any organic remains on their way through.

A massive table sat in the center, with bolted clamps running along the edge. More shackles and cages lined the walls, some with skeletons of creature still trapped inside them. More tapestries along the wall and a shelf of scrolls, along with two boards of tools hanging in place, ready for horrific use. They could see a ring shell of ice on the floor above and the stairs leading into a carved tunnel.

"Well, this is a room I'm certainly glad we didn't come into years before," Durante said.

"Goddess of Mercy," she murmured, pausing before the wall of tools. There never seemed to be anything good about the types of wizards who hid themselves away like this. "I would love, just once, to hear about a remote wizard's tower full of beneficial plants or something like that."

"I know of one," Alces said, his voice softer but still severe, "I'll introduce you, sweet Octavia."

"This might be it," Durante said, moving towards the scroll shelf, the diamond-shaped cubbies holding nearly a dozen scrolls each. Carefully, he extracted one of the scrolls and started to unroll it. "Well, I have good news and better news. Good news is, they're vellum, so they're in fine shape. Better news, I can't read it so, Tavi, I'll need your skills."

"The fact that they're vellum really isn't surprising," Octavia said as she walked up to Durante. "He probably made it himself."

Octavia closed her eyes for a second and stifled a moan as Kamvasana's power flowed through her. Clearing her throat, she opened her eyes to look at the scroll. Her eyes, which were now glowing, and looked like they were dotted with stars, but a very careful examination would reveal that it was actually a scattering of runes and glyphs.

The scroll was a treatise on the various uses of a pixie's body parts. "This one is on everything you can do with a pixie, from the wings to the blood to the ground meat," she said, wrinkling up her nose. "I might be here for a minute. Kitten, is there something in particular I'm looking for? Something that will indicate if I've found what you're after?"

Sighing, he looked around and then leaned against a wall. "Anything on vampires or creatures that have vampirism," he said, sighing as he glanced over. "Sorry to make you read through these things. I don't know exactly what I'm looking for, just more information. OH!" He exclaimed and took her hand, "I remember! Look for anything on strix or striges, if you can find it. I think that's the blood I used."

She looked up at him and nodded. "It's alright. If I come across anything too gruesome, I'll find a way for you to make it up to me." She flashed him a playful grin, and squeezed his hand. "Strix or striges. Got it."

Letting go of Durante, she reached for the next scroll and unrolled it with care. He shied away, but not nearly as much as he had previously. The other two were looking along the walls and under various work benches. Alces was sniffing at the air from time to time, trying to sense something.

To be fair to the mad wizard, Vaztus was very clinical in his explanations and descriptions. The truly gruesome part came from the imagination of him getting the information and the means to go about doing so. None of this prevented Octavia from wanting a bath when they were done.

"So, Kitten, huh?" Sumner commented as his exploration brought him back around. "Thought if that was to be someone's nickname, it'd be me." He flashed her that toothy grin, his spots still on his face and down his neck from the fight below.

"You're not sweet enough," Octavia said matter-of-factly as she pulled down another scroll. "I'm still thinking of a name for you. Ringmaster is too long. Beast is too inspecific. Jaguar has too many syllables and doesn't... feel right."

"Yeah, those don't fit me at all," he said dismissively.

"I won't be having you take my nickname," Durante said, poking him with the butt of his screwshot.

"All yours, brother, all yours," Sumner laughed.

Octavia smiled and felt that flutter under her ribs again. "Give me time, I'll come up with a good one."

The next scroll had similar information about shimmer hounds, dogs of the fae. She'd heard stories about their intelligence and loyalty. Kind animals that had rescued many a lost traveller from the Wilder Woods and beyond. Octavia's smile dropped.

"What kind of monster dissects shimmer hounds," she muttered to herself, and set the scroll aside looking very unhappy. She reached for the next one.

"Shimmer hounds are good dogs," Alces said. "Good fae. Rare among their type as they're not tricksy. Honest and honorable." There was no good news in this tower for Alces. He posted up near the stairs, just in case something decided to get frisky.

"I will say that even if we find something here, we should probably look through as much of the tower as we can," she said as she spread out the new scroll. "While I don't want you all leaving me behind, per se, you could maybe check the next floor. I don't want to make you pace while I read through all these."

"While I appreciate it, I think it's probably best if we stick together," Sumner said, looking over the tools. "Never know what might be upstairs or what might come from downstairs."

"Never split the party," Durante said with a smirk.

The current set that she was flipping through didn't seem to be what she wanted. More fae of various types. Unless there was a red cap variant among this pile, these scrolls wouldn't be useful to Durante, at least not for his current problem.

"These... are all fae," She murmured, and rolled up the scroll she was looking at before loading them all back into their square. "At least it's organized. Okay." She withdrew a scroll from one of the other sections and spread it out. If he kept things organized, finding the right category would speed up the search.

"I'm conflicted," Durante said as he watched her flip through them. "On one hand, I want to set it all on fire because it's disturbing what he did to get this information. On the other, I want to collect and publish all this information so no one else does the same experiments to find this out. But, if this knowledge is known, how many of these creatures will be hunted for their valuable parts?"

It took Octavia a few tries, but she finally came to the cubby housing the 'flying beasts of the carnivorous variety' category, which hopefully the strix would be in. "People in the know are hunting them already," she replied, pulling a couple scrolls down to try to speed up her process, "but I don't think it's a good idea to make the information more accessible. Opportunistic hunters will go after many of these creatures because they read somewhere that they were valuable."

"So, keep or burn?" Durante asked, still conflicted. "Even if we don't share it, it's a significant amount of research and information that may be helpful in the future. But I'll trust your assessment."

"The market for magical components is already cutthroat," she murmured as she spread the scrolls out before her, eyes moving over them quickly. "You could keep them and make the decision later after more thought. Don't your bags hold everything?"

"They hold a lot, but not everything," Durante said with a chuckle.

"Although we've never hit the max. We just don't... keep that much," Sumner added.

Harpy, Griffon, Pit Fiend, Strix...Strix! "If you—oh, this is it!" She'd found it after all. Good grief, they were ugly. Like a demonic owl with a mosquito nose and a lack of feathers. She skimmed the scroll for a moment and nodded. "Yeah, those are hideous."

"Have we found the research our dear Durante seeks?" Alces asked.

"We have found a detailed study of a strix," Octavia said, turning to Alces. "I need to transcribe it for Durante to know if it's what he actually needs, since I don't know what he's after and only I can read it. If we wish to return to the tent, I can begin doing so. I don't know if you want to explore any further today. There is…probably a lot more to learn here, but…well you three should perhaps discuss it."

"So far, we are well. I don't see a reason not to continue," Alces said and the rest sort of nodded and shrugged.

"Leave no tower un-tilted," Sumner said with a grin. Well, they were professional adventurers, and while they had a goal with this particular raid, there really wasn't a sense to stop now.

"Just give me a minute," Durante said, deciding that it was best to take the scrolls and they'd go through them later.

"Wait, wait," Octavia said, stopping Durante before he dumped anything in. "I have an idea."

It took a few minutes, but Octavia flattened the scrolls she had been sorting through and rolled them all up together before pulling a length of ribbon out of her bag to tie off the large bundle. It was clunky and weird, but it kept all the creature types together and would also reduce the time it took to fish all the scrolls out of the bag again. She got Sumner to come over and help her as Alces continued to keep watch. Sumner and herself unrolled and stacked the scrolls, then rolled the whole bundle up and Durante tied them off and dropped them in his bag.

"Thanks, Tavi," Durante said with a smile before everyone situated themselves and got ready to move out. Alces nodded and started heading up the stairs. It had been relatively quiet, despite the fight downstairs. So far, the cave squid eggs, or whatever they were, seemed to be insulated from the noise.

The next room appeared to be the wizard's actual lab. Dusty equipment used for distillation and processing. Beakers overgrown with solutions that had gotten contaminated. There were containment glyphs, wards, and equipment that no one could identify. Potential volatility at this point could be incredibly dangerous. However, there were alchemical reagents that were sealed away that would be worth a hefty sum, all labeled in the language only Octavia could read.

"A number of these are probably still good," Octavia announced looking over the shelves of sealed reagents.

Ice covered the hole above them and the stairs up disappeared into another carved tunnel. It was odd that the ice seemed to only be every other floor. Certainly unnatural, certainly magical in origin.

Magical senses were also tingling here. There were items all over the shelves humming with fading power. Durante appeared thoroughly impressed and even Sumner was drawn in a little with the sheer variety.

Alces was the only one uncaring towards the room, but smiled at Durante's wonder. Octavia was interested, but also getting a headache from the constant hum. She pulled down two bottles of pale blue, shimmering dust that was actually scales from fey dragon wings. A pot of thick red liquid that was a suspension of pennaggolan blood. The cerebral fluids of two dragons in wax sealed carafes. And finally, a vial of phase beast seminal fluid.

"If these are still in good shape, they will sell very well." She said, stepping back. "I have no idea how to test them to see if the seals held well enough, and I don't suggest opening them, but if there's anything to take from this room, this is it."

Durante came over to take a look, his eyes scanning over the various items. "I can check them later. So far, they look okay. Nothing is leaking, so that's a good sign," he said.

Donning his eye glass set, Durante took a careful look at the items, deemed them safe for travel, then tucked them away. Looking around while he still had it on, he paused and gestured towards a rack that had contained drying plants of various types. Any that remained were now brown husks, unidentifiable.

"I'm seeing something against the wall there," he said.

Arching a brow, Octavia looked to where he indicated and headed over. She was reasonably cautious, but so far this room had not seemed overly hostile. She carefully pulled the long-desiccated plants from the rack, many of them crumbling to dust in her hands. Beyond, she could feel that same sense of magic she had from the throne two floors down. Another switch of some sort, connected to something beyond her ken. She carefully examined the rack, then pulled it away from the wall. It swung out of the way to expose a switch. Another glyph like the one on the throne, ripe for the pushing. That typically negative voice of reason decided to be helpful for once, and reminded Octavia that she should probably announce her intentions to the rest of the group.

"Another switch," she said. "I think it's linked to the one on the chair. It... the spell feels the same."

"Fuck it, why not," Sumner said, shrugging. "Nothing happened last time."

"Always be wary. It may expose treasures others missed, but it may release dangers," Alces said.

"Go for it," Durante said, but unslung his screwshot all the same. "I'm not going to jinx it, so I'm going to say outright it's probably a horrible idea."

"I'm going to get kicked out of the group if this is an elaborate self-destruct sequence, aren't I?" Octavia flipped the switch anyway.

"I'm sure you can make it up to us," Sumner said. However, it did not seem to be the case. A shiver of magical energy that they all felt went through the tower, but nothing happened. The tension they had felt before increased, but they couldn't figure out why or how.

"I guess it's too old," Durante said but didn't put the rifle away yet.

"Shall we continue?" Alces asked calmly but perhaps a touch impatiently. Octavia wasn't entirely certain it wasn't working the way it was intended, but she nodded and moved to follow Alces.

The ice tunnels were almost a calm separation between the gore and madness of the tower owner's machinations. Topping another set of stairs, they found what could only be called a storehouse. While the room downstairs had alchemical ingredients, this was where the results of his research truly were. Horrid amalgamate beasts hung from the wall in perfect stasis. Untouched by rot or age, they looked ready to lunge at them at any moment. However, not even a heartbeat or a flutter of hair was heard. Although, should that stasis become removed, they would have a vile fight on their hands.

Eyes wide, Octavia put a hand to her mouth to stifle the whimper of fear that wanted to come out. In all her travels, she had never seen anything like this. She stepped closer to Alces, but tried not to make it look like she was hiding behind him. This was still her trial run, after all. She imagined the visceral reaction she was currently having might not leave a good impression.

Amidst the beasts, there were shelves of specimens of smaller creatures or organs in jars. Between this and the scrolls they got before, there was a chance Durante could maybe accelerate his research by a dozen years.

"Immoral magicks, these must be destroyed," Alces said, looking up at a beast that resembled a polar bear with a wolverine's head, and its arms replaced by a half-dozen tentacles. He then turned to Octavia. "It is alright to hide behind me. I am the wall to protect you from darkness."

"It can save your life," Sumner said, looking up past them and around.

"I'm sorry," Octavia murmured, embarrassed that she was caught. She took a shaky breath as she looked around. "I just… I've never…" She took a deep breath and closed her eyes, pulling herself together.

Alces put a hand on her shoulder. "Do not apologize. These are grisly things," he assured her.

"Yeah, I want none of this," Sumner said, stepping back from a gangly horror with claws as long as Octavia's hands.

"Gods of Reason, this is horrific," Durante said but still approached, drawn by curiosity as he moved up towards a creature with a wyvern's body but a griffon's back half. The eye stalks were not doing it any favors in the looks department.

"Is there… um, is there a quick way to kill them?" She stepped a little closer to Alces. "Something merciful that doesn't immediately lead to a grisly battle?"

"I don't know," Durante said, looking over them with his eye glass set again. "I don't know what will trigger the stasis, or if we can do anything to them while they're like this."

"So, trying to slit a throat right now…," Sumner started.

"May wake them up immediately, or keep them frozen like that until they come out, at which point they will bleed out and die," Durante finished, being rather clinical in tone.

"Do we set fire to the tower as we leave?" She looked to the others. "Bar the doors and wait to take on anything that makes it out?"

"Magic," Durante said with a sigh, "no guarantee it'll catch fire. Otherwise, not a bad idea. A derelict of insanity and depravity, it would be best to bury it."

"Wisely said," Alces agreed, glancing up at another monstrosity. This one looked to be a reptilian centaur with the upper half of a hulking insect. Its arms had claws that looked like they could crush the stalwart knight. "I like a challenge but this may be too much for even me."

Looking at the creatures did not get easier the longer they were in the room. "So what do we do?" Octavia asked, focusing on Durante. "Attempt to deal with this now, hope the magic in the tower has deteriorated enough to let it burn, or maybe see if there's a better answer further up?"

It was quiet for a moment as he considered. "I think we move up," he said, reaching out for one of the jars on a shelf, then thinking better of it and putting his hand on the stock of his screwshot. "Hope for the best. I'd say we don't risk waking anything up in here, if it can be done. Thankfully, none of the switches we've hit went here."

Nodding, Octavia turned back to Alces, ready to follow him further up. Tentatively, they left the floor of horrors and headed up the stairs to the next floor. They had to be getting near the top, but there was still another segment of ice above as they entered into what was clearly the wizards library, but more than that. Aside from shelves of books, which had been picked at, there was a collection of trophies and cases. Some had already been emptied, their contents looted. Whatever had happened to the tower hadn't kept everyone out.

There was even a rather comfy-looking leather reading chair, although the age had done a number on it. There was even a book wheel with some heavy tomes atop it. They could spend days here trying to sort and decipher what was left.

"I could spend a week in here, easily," Octavia said softly, looking around the room. "If I could forget what I walked through to get here."

"I hope there's something good left," Sumner said, sliding past Alces and taking a look around.

"They left a good number of books," Durante said, glancing about, "chances are they didn't know what they were looking at or couldn't haul it all."

Ever cautious, Octavia approached the book wheel. It would be revealing, and possibly even more disturbing, to see what the late wizard had been studying. She blew the dust off the tomes but otherwise was careful not to touch them. The first book was countless years old, held together by magic so as not to fall apart over the ages. The language lost to all but the most dedicated scholars. What brief excerpt she was reading was not so much a summoning incantation, but rather a study on the methods behind such things.

"Well, probably keeping that," Octavia murmured to herself and turned the wheel to look at the other books on it.

Meanwhile, Durante and Sumner were going over the various artifacts, with Sumner asking if something was magical, then checking for traps, then tucking it away if it hit the marks in his mental checklist.

Alces was glancing about, looking more carefully at the trophies. Octavia wasn't worried about him, he would be fine once they were out of there, but she found herself concerned about his happiness. The tomb hadn't done this to him, even with the strange ghosts and the offsetting sensations. She followed his gaze up to the various gear mounted to the walls. High up were various weapons, shields, even pieces of garb that were mounted for display. They were not in pristine condition; these were items that had seen use.

"Old enemies, do you think?" she asked, as many of the weapons didn't seem like something a wizard would have used. "Friends he outlived?"

"I'd almost guarantee enemies," Alces said, gesturing toward a pair of notched cutlasses. "That's Karim the Bladesinger's swords. I'd recognize those decorative baskets anywhere. Mercenary, usually pitted himself to assist the dark horse in a battle. Was mostly in it for the thrill, but he wasn't a bad person. I guess this is where his tales ended."

Octavia's brows rose, and she looked up at the swords in question. "Oh." She looked around again and sighed. "I do not think I would have liked this man."

"I certainly don't," Alces agreed, setting a hand on her shoulder and giving it a squeeze before letting her continue on.

Turning back to the book wheel, Octavia quickly determined she wanted nothing to do with the rest of the collection. The remaining books in the wheel were about summoning, demonology, and descriptions of various fiends. Perhaps Vaztus was changing his focus of study, or needed to look into otherworldly sources of materials.

Rotating the book wheel again, Octavia looked over at the other two. "Sumner, when you have a minute, can you make sure lifting this top book won't cause anything to explode?"

Sumner looked up from the gem on a stand that they had been looking at and glanced over. "Hm? Oh, sure, yeah." Durante also stepped away. Clearly that gem was bad news, or at least enough trouble that they didn't want to take it.

She stepped away from the book wheel and started looking through the stacks. Her ability was coming in very handy. There were sorting indicators, numbers and letters, that were clearly coded but she was able to see through it and find the section she had been looking for. Blood, its uses, sources, and inherit abilities was a strong subject for the alchemist, if the shelf she was looking at was any indicator. Several of the books were still here.

"Durante, come here!" She called out. "I found the blood section!"

"Great," he said, moving towards her.

As he approached, she looked over with a smile. "I'll read any titles to you that you can't read, and we'll figure out what you want to take with you."

He stood next to her and started looking over the spines and covers. They spent the next few long moments translating and comparing, having Sumner check for basic traps. All in all, it appeared that the wizard didn't expect anyone to get this far. Traps were very few and far between, and the handful of ones they did find had already been triggered. Unsurprisingly, they did find the remains of bloodstains in the area of those traps, so it seemed the people who had raided before them hadn't been as cautious. With any luck, that also meant the items they really needed would still be here - along with any true treasure buried among the tomes and codices.

"I would encourage you to take anything that might have information you can use," she commented, sliding her fingertips along the spines to the first book she thought might be useful. "I think there's still a chance we're setting this tower on fire as we leave."

"I see you're still stuck on that path," Durante said, glancing at her and giving her a smirk. "With any luck, I suppose." By the time they were done, a majority of the shelf was tucked away in a magical bag, waiting for study at a later time. Octavia added some books she was interested in as well—she could get them later, and might as well not weigh herself down.

"These are stories that deserve their ending," Alces said abruptly, nodding to the trophies on the wall. "I'll take them, then we can finish this place." Tall as he was, Alces was able to reach up and pull the various arms and armors down, tucking them away in his own bag, along with the plaques if they had any.

Finally leaving the stacks, Octavia looked over at the stairs. "This... should be it. The last floor. Are we ready?"

"I think I'm good," Sumner said, setting his hand down on a bust of someone no one had recognized. It seemed in all their looking, they hadn't noticed the small bit of magic on that particular item, and they all felt that wash of magic and sense of tension that, ultimately, didn't seem to lead to anything.

"Um... oops," he said with a shrug as all seemed still and quiet.

Octavia tipped her head to the side. "Same magic. Still tense. The release must be on the last floor, if there is one." Sighing, she turned to Alces. "Ready, Ser Knight?"

"Yes, let us be done with this place," he said, grunting but giving Octavia a smile. He turned and started up the carved ice tunnel. Whoever had made them had ensured that not only was the ice a dry freeze, but it was textured for a slight grip so no one was sliding unless they wanted to.

Reaching the top was a longer set of stairs until they'd reached the pinnacle room, but at long last they had reached the peak of the tower.

The wizard's quarters.

If there was one thing you could say for Vaztus Drukankor, it was that he had a sense of grandeur. Horror show below notwithstanding, the view was incredible. There didn't appear to be any walls, yet they felt no cold from the mountains. They could see out along the mountain range and the valley below in the dying light of the late evening. Only six support pillars on the outer edge seemed to be holding up the roof above them. A sensible bed and other pieces of furniture that one would expect were there, of high quality but of sensible nature. It painted the picture of a lonely, crazed magician who would stare out into the void of nature and little else.

Looking around, Octavia started to search for that magic signature again. "This doesn't feel right," she murmured. The rest of the tower was too staged. He may have been a lonely old nutter, but he was also full of himself, and surely his bedroom would reflect that level of self-aggrandizement.

"Everything feels better than right," came a voice that they all had to look around to find. A voice old, and gravely, that chilled your spine with the viciousness it hid.

FIFTEEN

There was a throne on one edge that hadn't been standing out until just now, its shape blended with the room divider next to it. "Tell me, intruders, how did you make it this far? All the way to my chamber, the peak of my domain?"

Alces already had his shield out and standing before everyone else. Sumner had drawn his sword and crouched down near a piece of furniture, becoming still and hiding in its silhouette. Durante unslung his rifle and held it at the ready. Octavia stayed as she was. Her eyes flicked to the throne, but also continued to comb the rest of the room. This still didn't feel right. It was possible that the wizard was still alive, that he had been the one to carve out the path through the ice rings, but then who had raided the trophy room? Why was there a layer of dust everywhere as if nothing had moved through this place in ages? Was he really there, or was this an illusion of some sort?

"Your tower is a decrepit testament to your madness," Alces said, bouncing the weight of his mace in his hand. "There is little to keep us out and little reason for you to be here."

"This is my tower, of course I'll be here as long as my tower stands," the voice retorted. "Surprising with a leader so large that you creeped in so quietly. Didn't even wake my pets. Now how did you manage that?"

"I'm not sure they'll ever wake again," Durante puzzled aloud, less as a response.

Looking the room over, Octavia wasn't picking up on any illusions. The room seemed as it appeared. There were subtle magicks everywhere, probably small housekeeping spells and the like, but nothing major enough to hide an entire room. The only major magic was the throne, that was easy and obvious enough to spot now that she was looking.

Brows furrowed, Octavia murmured, "Comicha." The imp popped into being behind her, quietly. Octavia nodded towards the divider, and mouthed the word "Look." The imp nodded, and flew up and over cautiously. The small creature floated up and over to the divider, looking down over it. She fluttered back and forth for a moment, then stopped.

"Another fiend for me to play with," said the voice and Comicha froze completely. Not even her little wings were beating but she was remaining in the air. "Such a gift. This one is an odd little creature. Touched by the fae, even. It does make things more difficult."

Octavia's eyes grew wide, and she felt her heart pound in her chest. She also felt power crackle down into her hand. She took two steps forward, a blue shimmer started to form around her, but then stopped herself. It wasn't just her. Sumner was right there, Alces was ready. She was panting and power burned in her hand with her rage.

Alces stepped up and raised his mace towards the throne. "You will release our friend, or your life is forfeit and this conversation is over," he said.

The touch of fae might have been what was stopping Comicha from being completely overtaken. Octavia could see fear in her eyes, and she was twitching, fighting whatever was trying to dominate her.

"Say the word and I'll slit this fucker's throat," Sumner said quietly, inching towards the divider to come in from the side.

"Their parts are quite useful," the voice continued and Comicha floated closer to them, but was still held in whatever spell was trying to control her. "The wings can be used in levitation spells. Their tail contains a powerful toxin. Even their little horns, ground into powder, contain enough hellish essence to be used in burstfire oil."

Alces stepped forward with heavy stomps and grabbed the throne, twisting it so it faced them, knocking over the side table and the room divider as he did so. The room divider seemed to only be hiding a dresser and small stool. Sitting upon the throne, however, was a corpse. Not an animated corpse, a ghoul, or even a lich rising to meet them; but a very long dead skeleton with clothing threatening to fall apart at the slightest breeze.

"Careful, knight. You don't want to do anything hasty," the voice continued and Comicha made a whimpering noise as her wings started to spread. Alces looked back at Octavia, a touch worried as what his next step should be.

It was then that Octavia noticed another glyph, on the arm of the throne, much like the one all those floors down. It had to be another trigger, and possibly the last one. "Be ready," was all Octavia said, and then the silver blue mist consumed her in a blink before she reappeared next to the throne, bringing her hand down harder than she needed to on the glyph.

"Oh, let's see if that'll work," the voice said, followed by a haunting laugh. Suddenly the tower shuddered, a rumbling shook the entire building and they could hear cracking and shattering below them. That tension that they had all been feeling was now building up to a peak, and it was unnerving.

Something snapped below them and the tower lurched to one side, causing the furniture and everyone to start sliding. Alces reached out his arm and grabbed Octavia, holding her close to his body. His other hand snapped the mace to his belt and then reached up and pulled Comicha out of the air, pulling her in as well.

Octavia turned towards Comicha, pulling the imp in against her even as she clung to Alces. "I'm sorry, I'm sorry," she whispered to the little creature, torn between wanting to cry and wanting to rip the room apart.

Sumner slid and braced himself against one of the supports, reaching out and catching Durante before he went too far. Just as it seemed they were going to spill off the side of the tower, something else erupted below them and it over-corrected, tilting back the other direction. The throne seemed to have bolted itself to the floor when this occurred and did not move.

"Curses," the voice shouted, only now it was a little distorted. "That vile witch and her entanglements!"

Alces crouched down to keep himself centered and his weight lower when another shudder happened. Sumner and Durante went skidding in the other direction but came to a stop when they caught Alces' foot. There was a final cacophony of shrill explosions, and everyone's stomach dropped as the floor suddenly became very heavy.

A moment later, the room stopped and everyone flew up off the floor by a foot or two. Sumner landed on Durante when he hit the ground, while Octavia and Comicha were well protected in Alces' arms as his body took the blow. The furniture was tossed up even further, with the decrepit skeleton, having nearly no mass left at all, flew out of the throne and smashed against the ceiling. The only recognizable part left was the skull, which was now cracked with a bit of the top missing.

"Are you all alright?" Alces asked, worried first about his friends.

"I'm fine." She looked down at the imp in her arms. "Comicha, are you with me? Please, little one!" She looked over at Durante and Sumner, panic and rage still coursing through her.

"Ooof, good thing you hadn't gotten rid of all your padding yet," Sumner chuckled, patting Durante's gut as he moved off of him and stood up quickly.

"Yeah, yeah," Durante said, groaning as he, more slowly, started to get up.

Comicha stirred and reached out for Octavia, wrapping her little arms around her neck. Octavia let out a relieved sob and held her familiar tight. "Yeah, I'm 'kay. The bad energy disappeared when the big boy grabbed me," she said softly.

Alces hugged Octavia close, then released her gently before standing back up, staring at the skull. "What has happened?" he demanded.

"Look around, you group of idiots," the voice berated them. "You triggered the tower's security. Everything went off at once!"

"Oh, shit," Sumner said, completely unrelated as he looked down the stairs. The floor had been a completed one on this part of the tower, no hole to look down.

"What?" Durante asked.

"We're... up."

"Goddess of Mercy," Octavia groaned, looking around again. It appeared that they were much further up than they had been before as she could see the peaks of the surrounding mountains now. Well, that was it, she'd ruined everything, they were definitely getting rid of her after this.

"You're all interesting specimens. I wish I could have observed your movements more, or had you play with my pets," the voice said.

Gritting her teeth, Octavia shifted Comicha to her hip then stalked straight up to the skull, picking it up and examining it. "Where are you really, you vile piece of shit?" The voice seemed to laugh, a rather assured laugh. Resting in her hand, she could see a gem inside the skull where an empty cavity or a rotten brain should have been.

"I'd threaten to destroy everything you ever loved, but I'm fairly certain you've never loved anything in your sad, overly-long life," she muttered, examining the gem.

"Actually, I was pretty pleased with my life. Got a lot of work done," the voice said, which was definitely coming out of the skull as she held it.

"We could jump," Durante offered.

"I will say, I am quite done with this place," Alces added.

"Do we have a way of not hitting the ground and dying if we jump?" Octavia asked, walking back over to Alces.

"Yeah, no problem," Durante said, pulling back his coat and indicating a gray leather belt he was wearing. "For emergencies. This seems like one."

Octavia nodded. "All right. Also, Kitten, unless you've got a reason not to, I'm going to have Alces crush this," she said, indicating the skull. "While I'm curious about which witch and what those machinations might be, don't really trust him to keep him around and find out."

"Sure, crush me. Right now," the voice said, the skull having no animation or look to it, but she could picture the smug face that matched the voice.

"Don't get too excited, you pompous twat, I'm not that stupid," Octavia said, hooking her fingers through the eye sockets to make it easier to carry. "Let's be on our way, then. Comicha, can you fly?"

The little imp nodded, and popped into the air, but perched on Alces' shoulder instead of staying aloft. Honestly, she really couldn't blame Comicha, she also enjoyed Alces' shoulders and the feeling of safety they brought. Durante slid his finger over a rune on the belt. The grey leather belt made a screeching noise and then glowed gently. Around the belt was a few wound pieces of catgut that he undid and handed to everyone. Wrapping her hand around the catgut, she felt lighter in the foot.

With a careful step, Durante moved everyone to the edge. "Alright, let me go first, but don't fall too far behind. As long as you hold onto that, you should be fine," he said.

"All set, brilliant Durante," Alces said, stepping to the edge.

"Let's go," Sumner said, "fuck this place."

Octavia nodded.

Durante jumped off and the rest of them followed. Sure enough, they fell, but at a slow, controlled float. As they drifted, they could see what had happened: at every part of the tower, where the ring of ice had been, it had separated and suspended above itself. This was probably meant to be done in stages but instead happened all at once.

"That's what the ice was for," Octavia murmured. "The witch, whomever she was, knew about the tower's defenses."

As they drifted down, they were hearing ungodly noises coming from the tower: monstrous shrieking and roaring. It seemed the puzzled horrors had come out of stasis after all and were very unhappy.

The skull seemed quite amused by this. "They're free and awake," it cackled. "Oh, let them play. I cannot wait to watch them tear you apart!"

"And what keeps them from turning on each other in their panic?" She highly doubted Vastuz allowed his creatures any level of elevated intelligence. "Also, are they going to survive when we crush your skull and the tower collapses?"

"Like I would allow panic to grace my creations. If anything, they are hungry for intruders," the skull said.

"You don't think they're panicking now?" She looked back to the tower. "With all that movement and noise? You're adorable."

"You could drop him and see what happens," Durante suggested.

"Or chuck the undead fuck into the tower," Sumner added.

"Eh, chucking him into the tower won't do anything. He's a skull. There's also a chance he still has some limited control over that menagerie," Octavia said, then looked down. "Dropping, though, could be fun. But we'd have to find the gem afterwards to make sure it shattered properly."

"Hold on close to it," Alces said, glancing at the skull. "I will crush it myself."

"Do you really think that's the best idea," the skull said as they started to near the ground. "You don't know what'll happen if you do that. Horrible spells are keeping me alive."

"Oh, of that I have no doubt. After all, you're a horrible person." She tilted the skull again, examining it, trying to see if the magic felt infernal or not. "Though it's very thoughtful of you to consider poor Alces' health."

"Counterpoint: I have no reason to care for his health. I'd have killed him and used him for parts. Do you know what I can do with dragonkin hide? Also, male, lot of money in his seed as well," the skull cackled.

"For someone who is supposed to be a mad genius, you're not smart enough to detect sarcasm." Octavia released the catgut and looked around for a moment, trying to find a good spot. "Pity. I hope we didn't waste our time collecting your research. I'm no longer convinced of its reliability."

The skull grumbled, seething at the slight to the only thing Vaztus seemed to care about. The others were looking at Octavia, quite amused.

They had touched down at the bottom of the tower, on the other side from where their tent was. She moved closer to the base of the tower, at the foot of the stairs, and set the skull down.

"Time to say goodbye," she said coldly.

"I've been forced to be alive for a terribly long amount of time with no body, no way to move, and no sense outside my tower," the skull said with finality as she set it down on the ground and walked away. "Do me the favor."

She counted out ten paces from it, then two more to be safe. "There are a lot of enchantments on that skull. Do you...can you call on the light to protect you?"

Alces crouched down next to Octavia and put his shield out in front of the two of them. "I can protect us both," he said. She could feel an actual tingle from his presence, something that was indeed shielding her, although not greatly but enough that she felt safe.

"It is time," Alces said, squeezing Octavia's shoulder once more then standing. Comicha left his shoulder and hugged onto Octavia's back, nearly hiding herself but peeking over her mistress's shoulder.

Alces stepped up and bounced the mace in his hand as he did so, the runes wrapped around the head starting to glow. "Your tale ends here," he said, raising his mace high above his head. He roared out and brought the mace down with a thunderous retort. The dust exploded outward and white light burst from the impact.

There was a pregnant pause in the cool mountain night, only the echo of the impact sounding off. The ground then started to shake. As they looked up, they saw the many segments of the tower start to fall. Alces dashed back to the rest of them and motioned for them to get down while he held his shield up high, his arm sweeping to keep everyone close and under him. As the segments crashed to the base, deafening noises filled the col. Crashing rock, death roars from creatures unknown, and debris exploding outwards.

It was a lot of material, and dust was being kicked up as the floors shattered on impact. Alces started to scoot them further and further from the base, stones and brick impacting onto his shield with resounding force, but he held strong. It felt like an eternity before the destruction finally stilled. There was a resounding silence afterwards, but the tower was well and fully destroyed along with the gem and the wizard it contained.

Slowly, Alces lowered his shield, and they all stood back up, surveying the remains. Octavia was quiet for a long moment. "I wonder how much of his sanity he retained after all this time," she said softly. "It sounded like someone else put him in the gem. I have no doubt he deserved it."

"Whoever froze his tower, no doubt," Durante said, brushing himself off.

She turned back around and looked them all over. "Is everyone all right?"

Durante nodded. "I'm good, thanks."

"Yup, all good," Sumner said, sliding out and rolling into a stand. "Definitely adding 'destroyed a wizard's tower' to the story of my rise to power."

Octavia snickered. "I'm glad you're already composing the epic retelling of your adventures. Maybe we'll find you a real bard to put it to song. Alces? Are you all right?"

Alces slowly put his shield and mace away, nodding to Octavia. "Yes, sweet Octavia, I am fine," he said, giving her a slight smile.

She was relatively certain that Alces was only reporting his physical condition, but didn't want to push. "Dinner and bed, then? I can attempt to help make food, though my value there is mostly as an assistant."

"There is not much but to cook the rest of the goat," Alces said as they started moving towards the tent. "We will go into town tomorrow, get better supplies. I believe I owe you tarts."

"Now, I need to set a mess of traps and try to camouflage the tent," Sumner said as he looked around again. "We do not need anything surviving that collapse and getting the jump on us."

"Given its new color, once night falls completely I think it'll already be fairly camouflaged, it's just a matter of extinguishing the lights," Octavia pointed out as they moved towards the deeply blue tent. She looked over at her familiar and gave her a gentle pet. "Comicha, you can return home, if you wish."

"Yeah... yeah, I think I will until you leave this place," she said with a little shiver. She flew in for a squishy hug, then flew towards the tent but popped back out of this plane on her way.

Once inside, Octavia put away her coat and gloves and then headed over to the kitchen to attempt to assist Alces.

"I will be back to help in a moment," Alces said, rolling his shoulder and disappearing into his part of the tent.

"I need to start sorting through things," Durante said, "I'm sure I'm going to be very busy for the next few days, whenever we get a moment."

"I'll help you transcribe if you need me," she offered, then grinned a little. "Starting tomorrow."

Durante nodded and disappeared into his own room. Octavia was left alone for a long moment before Alces came back. He had doffed his armor and was back to only wearing a pair of breeches.

"Much better. Cooking should be enjoyed, not labored by wearing armor," he said with a smile and moved to the kitchen area to pull out the goat meat and start trimming it and slicing it into proper cuts for the oven.

Octavia mostly cleaned things as Alces finished with them. There really wasn't much she could do, particularly given their limited resources up on the mountain. She paid attention, though, and tried to learn a little as Alces worked. Because she was paying attention, she noticed that he had a sizable bruise occupying the majority of the shoulder of his shield arm and parts of his back. It was almost difficult to see, as the silver scales hid it, but there was some definite discoloration. On a human, it would have been deep purple, but on Alces it seemed like a dimming of his bright scales and a slight bluish tint.

"You're hurt," she said quietly, setting delicate fingertips on his shoulder. It was clear he didn't want to bring attention to it, but she couldn't ignore it.

"Just some bumps," he said with a grin. "Falling chunks of a tower are pretty heavy."

The scale was definitely softer in that area, almost tender. Alces would probably say a missing appendage was just a scratch.

"I'm sorry." Octavia sighed and took her hand away. "I should have thought of that. He was just... horrible. I wanted to be rid of him. I didn't want him to come up with a reason to convince us otherwise."

"Do not apologize," he said, petting her hair gently. "I would have done the same. You did nothing that one of us probably wouldn't have done as well. Better to collapse the tower now instead of waiting to see how long it stays floating, how long until the monsters inside escaped. It's all part of adventuring."

Alces paused cooking and wiped his hands on his pants before taking Octavia by the shoulders into his hands. "You have done good this day. You were wise with your spells, skillful with your caution, and protective of those you cared about. I am proud of you."

With some horror, Octavia felt color rush to her cheeks and tears prickle her eyes. She could not remember the last time someone had said they were proud of her. Well, Kamvasana said it sometimes after a particularly energetic evening, but that really wasn't the same.

"Thank you, my knight," she murmured, and then blushed even more when she realized "my" slipped out instead of "ser."

Alces grinned and then reached under her, scooping her up and hugging her with his arms around her. "I hope you forgive my impulsiveness, but I felt this was needed," he said, giving her a firm but incredibly comforting squeeze. She was surprised, but she did wrap her arms around him, and leaned her head against his. Then he winced, hissed, set her down slowly, and chuckled. "Right, falling tower bits."

As she was set back on her feet, she suddenly had an idea. Something to make Alces happy, to be a joy for him. It would wait until after dinner, though. As he finished cooking, she cleaned up and set out plates and cups at the table.

SIXTEEN

Sumner came in roughly around the time they were ready to eat, with the freshly roasted goat and a few other sundries they had squirreled away. It was a little bit of a struggle getting Durante away from the scrolls and back to the table, but they managed to assemble everyone for dinner. While they stated they'd celebrate more fully when they got to town, they still broke out some mead and cheered to their victory.

As Octavia sipped her mead over the remains of dinner, she felt that warmth in her chest and the flutter under her ribs again. No one had chastised her for the security system, and Alces had gone out of his way to say that she wasn't to blame for the crumbling tower. They had a wealth of information for Durante to sort through. This felt like more of a victory than the tomb had. The tomb where they found the book she still needed to study. She stifled a groan. The book had been forgotten in the wake of everything else. Well, in time. She imagined Durante would be keeping her busy with translations for a while longer.

After a day like this, they were all exhausted. Durante excused himself first after dinner, as he wanted to sort as many of the scrolls as he could before bed. Sumner helped clean up while Alces happily finished off the goat and his extra helping of mead.

Octavia excused herself for a moment and darted into her room. She got undressed, and used the basin to clean herself off before trading out her gear for one of the pieces of lingerie Alces had spotted on the bed that first day, a chemise that technically reached her knees but was cut up high over her hips. It was perhaps a bit much for an activity that wasn't meant to end in a night of passion, but… she wanted to look nice for him. She pulled her robe over it and took her hair down, shaking it out. Finally, she fetched a pot of salve from her trunk before heading back out into the main area.

Octavia came out as Alces was heading towards his own room. Sumner must have departed as well, as they were the only ones left. "Did you forget something, fair Octavia?" Alces asked, looking back to see if she had left her pack or something.

"No," Octavia said, stepping towards him, the squat jar in her hands, held forward almost like an offering. "Um, I have this…it should take the sting out of your scales. If you like, I thought I might follow you to bed and work it in for you. I can be gentle."

"That is very thoughtful of you," Alces said with a smile, giving her a nod as well. "Of course, between that and your touch, I'm sure I will be cured if not physically, certainly in my soul."

She smiled. Of course he would say something like that.

Alces led her back to his room. It had only been a day since the tent was expanded, so there were no decorations aside from what Octavia had left in there previously.

"How do you want me?" he asked in all innocence.

Any other night, Octavia would have had detailed instructions for him. Tonight, though, she smiled. "Get comfortable. You may fall asleep, so you should be in whatever state you would normally be for that."

"Of course," he said and laid down on his bed on his stomach, stretching out with his arms folded under his head. There it was, the broadest expanse of back, cut with muscle, that Octavia had ever laid eyes on. She could curl up on him with room to spare. Maybe. She ignored the flush of desire.

Removing her robe, she hung it from the bedpost and climbed onto the large bed next to him. As she set the pot down and scooped out some of the salve, the room filled with the fresh, green sweetness of calendula, the faint honey of beeswax, and a sprinkling of cinnamon. She rubbed the salve on her hands to warm it and started to hum. As she hummed, Alces smiled. By the time she set her hands against his shoulder, she was singing another sweet song, about being guided by one's heart and turning away from cruelty to focus on the beauty of things.

He started to growl, low and long. It rumbled through him in a way that reminded her of a purr. She could feel it through his chest, and it made the entire bed flutter with its bass. A smile slowly grew on

Octavia's face even as she continued to sing. Her soft fingertips worked the salve into his scales, and she was once again intrigued by the feeling and how unexpectedly supple they were. There was some hardening on the shoulder ridge, like natural armor, but she worked up to it and let her fingertips find their way around it.

It took a little while - he was enormous, and she was thorough. Alces continued to emanate happy, growly noises. His breathing got deeper and steady, his muscles no longer twitching when she pressed hard. Finally, it was done, and she was absently rubbing the last of the salve into his scales. The large dragonkin eased into the bed and sighed with contentment.

"Blessed light upon you, sweet Octavia," he rumbled softly. "Your touch and voice are a salve to my being."

"I, um..." she looked at Alces, and shifted off of her knees and onto her hip. "I'm glad. I know...I know what you saw today upset you, and then when I saw your shoulder... I wanted to help."

Slowly, Alces rolled onto his side to look at her. A gentle smile, even with the teeth, and he reached up, cupping her face. "Your presence only brightens me," he said quietly. "Fiends, most fiends I should say, are creatures of darkness and chaos, who only wish to inflict such on the world. They are antithetical to whom I serve and what I want the world to be. As such, they are enemies sworn. Of course, I say most, Comicha is friendly and a delight, she is a bright little light and is welcome always."

"Would...would you like me to stay?" She felt so oddly out of her depth. This wasn't a seduction, she understood that wasn't what was needed, but she was also embarrassed to realize she didn't really know what to say or do if she wasn't trying to seduce someone.

Tilting himself a little more, he opened his arm to her. "I would be so lucky if you would stay with me and share in your light. I can only hope I comfort you half as well as you have me."

Octavia slid into the bed with him and settled in his arms, laying her head against his chest and closing her eyes with a sigh. "Thank you, my knight."

"Of course, gentle Octavia." Alces pulled her close and moved his arm such that he could pet her hair while she laid against him. "Speaking of, if your little friend ever needs comfort, I welcome her as well. She had a scare today."

Nuzzling into him, she giggled softly. "Ah, I will let her know, though Comicha would want to...repay you for your comfort. Which I'm not sure any of you are ready for yet."

Alces couldn't help but chuckle a little, refraining from his usual booming laugh. "I suppose she is locked to her nature. I fear I would break the poor creature," he said, shaking his head slowly. "I shall always offer her a hug or a shoulder. As to you as well." His hand moved from her hair to slide down her back, cupping her hip.

She wondered, as she felt herself unwind against him, how she felt to Alces. If she was as soft to him as Sumner and Durante seemed to find her. If he felt the difference between her skin and the silken chemise. He felt warm, smooth, and solid, with muscles so defined that she could feel the shape of them even when he was at rest.

"Thank you, again, Octavia," he said, settling in a touch more. "You have already assisted us greatly and brought a bright light to our group. I do hope you decide to stay with us."

"I'm glad you still want me," she murmured, her voice sleepy and quiet, though there was a depth of emotion in those words.

Alces said nothing farther, just held her close against him and closed his eyes, smiling as he slept. Cradled as she was, Octavia also dropped into sleep after the long day. It was a calm sleep, a comforting sleep. One that she had only gotten from deep exhaustion and the rare times she felt secure, even despite the events and terrors of the day.

When morning came, Octavia found herself alone in Alces' bed. How he was able to slide out without waking her was impressive. She yawned and pushed herself up slowly, feeling small in the center of the large bed.

Didn't even cop a feel, came Kamvasana's voice in her head. *Very disappointing.*

"Oh, learn to read the room," she muttered at her patron as she climbed out of bed and pulled her robe back on.

The room reads me, *darling,* the voice returned. *In due time, I suppose.*

Rolling her eyes, Octavia yawned again and headed out into the main area of the tent. It was currently empty. Alces was no doubt outside, possibly hunting. That was fine. She headed into her room. If she was going to keep traveling out in the world with them, she would need to invest in some items she hadn't previously worried about. Like a teapot. If Alces was going to keep waking her up early, she needed tea. She got dressed, brushed out and braided her hair, and headed back out into the main area. Glancing around, she headed over to Durante's room.

"Kitten, are you still in there," she called through the fabric, then peered in. "Did you sleep?"

It was dark in his room, and he snorted a little when she called for him. Lifting his head from his pillow, he blinked and smiled a little. "Oh, Tavi, it's you," he said softly, yawning. "Is it morning already?"

Smiling, she let herself in, walking over to the bed and sitting down on the edge. "It is morning," she said, looking at him fondly. "I'll admit, I half expected you to have stayed up all night. I'm glad you slept." She paused and tipped her head to the side. "You did actually go to sleep, yes? You've been unconscious for more than an hour?"

"I don't know," he said, moving enough to wrap his arms around her waist and rest his head on her thigh. Her brows rose and she felt that squeeze around her heart again. She started to pet his head. "Probably. I couldn't read most of the book covers, so I couldn't sort them too much." Sighing, he nodded over to the piles along one wall and the mess of books surrounding them. He'd need bookcases or something. Or an actual home and lab. That last one would probably be required eventually.

"Well, I can help as soon as there's time." Her fingertips slipped through his hair, playing with it lightly. "I'm guessing we want to get out of the mountains quickly."

"Yes. And to the town. Need supplies, maybe see if we can offload things so we can pay you. Find a quest to do, as we need money," he grumbled, rubbing his face into her thigh a little. "I think we need money. Sumner would know."

"Gods, you're adorable," she murmured, unable to help it.

"I'm not, I'm just very tired and you're so very comfortable," he muttered and bit at her pants, giving the fabric a little tug with his teeth.

"I would guess we need money," she said more conversationally. "It's a little wild to me that you both let Sumner handle that, but if it makes sense then it makes sense. And it's not like he's going to run off and abandon you or anything." She knew that, with certainty. Sumner was loyal.

"Alces understands the whole exchanging money for goods and services, but he has no thoughts about long term. Evidently, I'm just bad with money." The more they talked, the more Durante was starting to wake up. He turned his head and looked up at her. "Are you okay after last night? I know things got a little tense." His voice was soft and concerned, and she felt that flutter again.

"I am," she said, and smiled a little sheepishly. "I stayed with Alces last night. We didn't—I mean, it was a mutual comfort thing. I noticed he was pretty bruised from the rubble that fell on his shield, so I rubbed some salve into his shoulder, and then we cuddled. He...well, he was clearly upset in the tower, and I felt guilty that shattering the gem gave him such a beating."

"Probably would have happened anyway. He can be impulsive, and Vaztus was a piece of work," he said, letting her go and rolling on to his back to stretch. "That was nice of you. I know he still gets something, light or whatever you want to call it, from being around people, erm, enjoying each other but he can use the care sometimes as well. Even if it's not that kind of care. Holds the weight and happiness of the world on his shoulders."

She nodded. "Hard to be the light of the world if there isn't also someone to be there for you." She bent down and kissed him lightly. "But thank you for caring, Kitten."

Durante sighed happily. "That's so nice. I'll happily take more of those when you have the time."

Giggling, Octavia turned more so she could press up against Durante, kissing him again, though still light and soft. He melted into the second kiss, moaning a touch.

"You let me know if there's anything else you'd like more of from me," she said, then picked herself up. "Right now, though, we should probably pack up and get ready to head to town."

"Damnit, you're right. Later, though, please?" he asked, making the movements that he was going to get up and get ready himself.

She paused and reached out to caress his face. "See? Adorable. I'd climb back on you right now, but we need to get going."

"Oh, that's not fair," he groaned and resigned himself to getting up and getting dressed.

She headed back out with a smile. Going back to her room, she followed her own advice and got packed up, and started making an actual list of things she would want to buy in town. In the middle of her packing, she could hear noises from the main room. Most likely it was Alces and Sumner returning from their morning venture for food. Pausing in her task, Octavia peaked in the mirror for a moment to check her hair and make sure she looked presentable. And then stopped.

"Why do I care?" she asked herself quietly. Sure, she was vain, but Kamvasana's patronage meant that she was always fetching. Why was she checking how she looked for breakfast? Shaking her head, she headed out into the main area.

"Well, hey there, beautiful," Sumner said with a smirk as Octavia came out into the main room. Alces gave him a bump and bowed to her.

"Good morning, fair Octavia. I hope I did not wake you when I got up this morning. You seemed to be sleeping quite peacefully," he said before returning to the prep area where he was chopping up some root vegetables.

"Oh was she," Sumner said with a glance, then looked back at Octavia.

Octavia found herself smiling again. She was doing that a lot this morning. "Good morning, gentlemen. Ser Knight, I was impressed by your ability to slip away silently." Looking back to Sumner, she shrugged. "He took a beating yesterday. I worked on his shoulder and stayed for cuddles. Much needed cuddles, I might add, yesterday was full of the most horrible things I've yet witnessed and also being terrified I had sent my familiar to her death."

"I suppose that would be a good reason for that. But we're calling it cuddles now?" Sumner said with a laugh, clearly teasing.

"Please," Octavia leveled a look at Sumner. "I was giving an honest accounting of the evening. I don't skirt away from or lie about that sort of thing." And then she raspberried him.

"The party stays and lives together," Alces said with a nod as he looked back at the preparations. She glanced over at him, realization dawning. This felt natural to Alces. All of them together. And anyone's needs, whether emotional or physical, could be met by any one of them, it seemed. It was something to think about.

"So how far is it to the town?" Octavia asked.

"I think we can make it in a day," Sumner said, wandering over and sitting down. "Going down is a lot faster than coming up."

"Of course, it is your choice, but Nutmeg would like to carry you down the mountain. I told him you need to walk to keep your legs in shape. However, it is up to you," Alces commented as he put four bowls of something in the oven and turned around.

"Aw, I don't know if I can deny Nutmeg," Octavia said with a grin. "And I could start translating that scroll for Durante if I ride down instead of walking." Her gaze slid over to Sumner, and the grin became more suggestive. "I'll find another exercise to make up for it." Sumner raised his brows at her and grinned but didn't say anything else.

"Morning," Durante said as he emerged from his part of the tent. He was dressed and looked maybe a little more awake than he would have normally.

"Good morning." She turned towards him. "Apparently Nutmeg is requesting to take me down the mountain. If you give me the strix scroll, I can start translating it."

"I can do that," Durante said and started to shuffle through his bag to find the roll of scrolls that contained that particular diagram. "Do you need lead and paper?"

She shook her head. "No, I'm well supplied there. I'll have Comicha help me. She's a surprisingly proficient secretary." Durante nodded and sat down, still shuffling through the scrolls.

Alces took a seat in one of the chairs and stretched out a little. "Breakfast will be ready in a few minutes. We are short meat. Slim pickings this far up, and I trust nothing from the tower," he commented. "But I think you will find it tasty."

"I'm sure you're correct, everything you've made so far has been delightful." Octavia dropped onto the couch, tucking her legs up underneath her as she was wont to do.

Sumner rubbed the bridge of his nose. "The remains of the tower are a mess and highly unstable. I hope everything got crushed when it collapsed. Nothing seemed to be coming out yet," he said.

"Not too late to set it on fire," Octavia said, trying not to laugh. "Though I don't really want to sit up here while it burns to make sure it doesn't spread."

"It'll take care of itself in time," Sumner said with a yawn, "creatures will starve, adventurers will come along to clear out the wizard tower, another wizard will try to take it over, something."

"You'll let me set something on fire eventually." She giggled that time.

"Oh, I promise I'll let you set lots of things on fire," Sumner laughed.

Standing up, she walked over to Alces and gently squeezed his not-bruised shoulder. "I'll finish packing real quick, I was almost done. Just holler at me for breakfast."

Reaching up, Alces squeezed her hand and nodded. "I will do so," he commented. "It shouldn't take too long."

Heading back into her part of the tent, she wrapped up her packing and sent Matilda back into the main area. She also adjusted her satchel to make sure paper and her favorite enchanted pens were easy to access. She had two - one for herself, and one for Comicha, who had smaller hands. She came back out as Alces was pulling breakfast out of the oven. Four bowls, steaming hot as he placed them on the table. They seemed full of oats and berries, a deep purple in color.

"Used what leftover grains and a bit of sugar we had," Alces said as he placed spoons down, "so, it's not as good as it could be, but it will be enough energy to get us into town tonight."

"It smells delicious," she said, genuinely.

It was almost like a fruit crumble, with the top being a touch crispy. Sweet, fruity, and full of grains. It could have used more sugar and definitely some cream, but it was still plenty tasty. Octavia helped clean up after breakfast, got the scroll from Durante, and headed outside with Matilda. She looked at the remains of the tower while she waited for the others.

It was a mess. Several levels of tower, all crashed down upon itself with rubble strewn over the mountainside. It was a miracle none of it had landed on the tent with the radius of destruction she was overlooking. But it was done, she couldn't feel any more magic coming from it. Whatever had been there was tied to the wizard's soul, and with the gem destroyed that, too, was scattered to the wind.

Sighing, she shook her head. "What is it about power and magic that makes people awful?" She knew that wasn't fair. Not all powerful magic users were awful. But it seemed many of them were.

She crouched down and picked up something metal winking in the sunlight and dust. It was a short cup, the kind alcohol was served in, carved into the likeness of a snarling beast. There was nothing special about it, other than the fierce visage, and it wouldn't fetch much. She would keep it. A reminder.

"Comicha," she called, and the little imp popped into being next to her.

"Hi, Mistress!" The little imp seemed her usual smiling self.

Reaching out, Octavia ruffled the imp's hair. "How are you feeling?"

The imp made happy noises, and flew up to give Octavia a snuggle. "I'm okay. Yesterday was scary, but nothing bad happened, so it's okay. The big guy's strong! And... full of light? It tingles."

Octavia giggled a little. "I'm glad you're feeling good. Think you can help me with a translation today? I need you to play scribe."

"Yes, Mistress!" As ever, Comicha was just excited to serve.

Octavia felt a sudden nuzzle against her neck and some rubbery lips nibbling on her shoulder. It seemed Nutmeg had arrived. The great elk chuffed at Comicha, who glared at him. Laughing, Octavia turned and rubbed Nutmeg's nose.

"We are ready to go now, yes?" Alces said as he stepped up to Octavia and also reached out to pet Comicha's head.

She looked up at Alces. "All ready." Comicha made happy noises. The other guys looked packed up and ready to go, as well as Durante deactivating the tent and folding it back up.

"You're utterly spoiled," Alces said to Nutmeg as he picked up Octavia and set her down on his back. Nutmeg grunted at Alces and the dragonkin shook his head. "You're lucky she does."

Durante walked over and handed Octavia the cube that had been their tent and then patted himself down to make sure he had all his gear on him. Sumner was already starting down the hill.

"Killing daylight, let's go," he said, circling his finger in the air. Alces rubbed Nutmeg's nose and then started down the hill as well, the rest of them following suit. Octavia rolled her eyes at Sumner, but she imagined she would get used to it eventually. Part of the issue was not being used to consider others' schedules. She would have to make some adjustments as they continued to travel together.

SEVENTEEN

Octavia bent to her task as they made their way down the mountain. Comicha sat behind her, their backs together, as the imp wrote down everything Octavia described. They had done this many times before, and Comicha asked the occasional clarifying question about what footnotes Octavia wanted her to include.

The evening light was descending on Boxende as they approached. The town looked more like a fort, with high stockade walls, watch towers, and staged gates.

As they approached, they got a rather short response. "State your business," the guard called out from his spot on the wall.

"Greetings, I am Ser Alces Brightrain, Knight of the Spree Spirits," Alces called out, hooking his hands into his belt and standing proudly. "My compatriots and I wish to find room and board and purchase supplies for travel. Possibly conduct trade."

There was a discussion above them where they couldn't make out what the guards were saying, but they seemed to come to an agreement.

"Very well. Pass granted for two nights. You and your party will be out by noon on the following day," the guard said, and the large doors started to open.

"Two nights," Octavia repeated, mildly offended. "Thank goodness we didn't need to get something repaired, or a horse re-shoed, or were grievously injured."

"Little rushed but not bad," Alces said with a shrug.

"They're nervous," Sumner noted, "but I don't think about us."

She turned her head to address the imp still leaning against her back, where the guards wouldn't have seen her yet. "Comicha, I'd hide. I'm not sure what they'll think of you, and they're apparently already not feeling terribly hospitable."

"Ugh. Yes, Mistress." Comicha popped back to her den.

When the doors were fully open, Alces set his hand on Nutmeg's neck and started to lead them in. Nutmeg didn't want anything to do with the town, and once they had cleared the gates and made it into the main square, Alces helped Octavia down so that Nutmeg could wander off into the ether. As they moved through Boxende, things seemed dour, but it was still functioning. They found an inn that was clean and available, the proprietor was mostly quiet but accepted their coin, gave them keys, told them when dinner was and so on.

Alces took a moment to step out and look around, trying to get a feeling of what was going on while Durante went to take their things upstairs. Octavia elected to help Durante. Sumner decided to be careful but still disappeared down an alley to take a look at things. Alces voted to stay outside and wait, looking at the people in the town and getting a sense of the situation.

The rooms were nice enough. Linens and a feather tick instead of straw. That was something. Nothing fancy, but should be comfortable enough while they were there. All two nights. She made a face at that. She'd never been told there was a limit on how long she was permitted to stay somewhere. Then again, she'd also never arrived with a group of men who could clearly do damage if they felt inclined to. Perhaps that was part of it.

Octavia changed out of her travel gear into something more appropriate to wear about town, and unbraided her hair, shaking it free to fall in waves down her back. She left her satchel in the room, locked away inside Matilda, and pulled out a purse that could be worn around her neck and disappeared in her cleavage.

Coming back down into the inn once more, she found the keeper and smiled her most disarming smile. "Is there much to do in the evenings here?" she asked.

"Lady pretty as you," the keeper said, shaking his head. "Not normally. Especially now. Those your friends you came here with?"

"Yeah, they're with me," she said, keeping a pleasant smile on her face.

"If you trust them, keep them close. Pretty things like you are starting to disappear," he said. "Just about anyone young, actually."

"Oh." She let the smile fall, replaced with concern, and leaned forward. "Do you know what's happening? Are there monsters from the mountains?"

"Hard to say. Been a few days now, but I'd suggest you finish up your business and go when you can," he said with a nod.

She nodded back. "Thank you, sir. We'll be careful." She turned and headed towards the door of the inn. She needed to talk to Alces about this.

The draconic knight was still on the porch of the inn. "Good evening, gentle Octavia," Alces said without turning, glancing down the road into the center of town. The knight was still standing out front, like he had been before. Given the grim feeling, he was almost like a literal light in the darkness of the town.

"Good evening, Ser Knight," she said as she stepped up close to him. "I talked briefly with the innkeeper. I heard a little about what has the town on edge."

"People missing?" he asked, but the tone was almost like he already knew. Almost. His head rotated to look down the other road, still staring off. It's like he wasn't trying to see something, but rather sense something.

"Yes," she said, "particularly the young. The innkeeper advised me to keep the three of you close while we were here. How did you know?" She wasn't surprised that he had an inkling, but she was always up for learning how to read these things.

"It's the shadows that cover this town," he said, gesturing a little vaguely. Maybe there was something, but it was hard to tell. "I've felt it before, been to places that had something similar happening. They're mostly a fort, a protector against what is in the canyons, so when something happens to them it hits twice as hard, you understand?"

Alces finally turned to her and set a hand on her shoulder. "He is right, keep us close. Not that you're not powerful and adept in your own right, but we can watch each other's back this way. Although we may have more insight soon."

"I'd rather avoid a fight on my own if I can help it," she commented, and leaned into Alces a little. "I guess we won't be celebrating yet."

"Not yet," he said, sliding his hand around to hold her against him as she leaned on him.

"But definitely soon," Sumner said, dropping down off the roof of the building. She managed not to startle, though barely. "I think I know what's up."

"I was curious when you'd come back," Alces said with a grin, "what did you find, sneaky Sumner?"

"Eh, I think you could have done better than 'sneaky' but I'll let it slide."

"Subtle? Sly?" She continued to lean against Alces, not yet seeing a reason to move.

Sumner ignored her for the moment. "I figured whatever is going on is coming from the canyon, or we would have seen something on the way in. And I checked away from the gatehouse, because they also would have found something. Sure enough, I found a tunnel leading past the walls near one of the stables. Who or whatever is causing this, is probably going in and out through there."

Octavia arched a brow. "Any idea what it might be?"

"Nope," Sumner said, putting a hand on his hip. "Everyone's on edge, so I don't want to add to it by creeping around too much. However, I also don't recommend we look into it right now. I've got an idea, though. Need to talk to Durante. You two, uh, continue keeping watch or whatever." Sumner gave her a wink and headed into the inn.

Octavia rolled her eyes at Sumner but stayed as she was. He reminded her a little of her brother—the teasing, specifically. The thought made her a little wistful. She wondered where he was now. She didn't know why he'd left, other than (much like herself) he'd disappointed their parents and been shown the door.

"That's good," Alces said with a nod, bringing her back to the matter at hand. "It means it's physical. A person or a creature with thought. Not spirits or devils or unseen horrors. Just people being awful, which is easier to fix."

"I wonder if this plan is going to involve me being used as bait," she muttered, looking across the quiet streets.

"I wouldn't believe so, or he would have asked you. Also, if the brigands or whatever are at least nominally intelligent, you would put off an aura of 'trap' if we tried to use you for bait," Alces said rather matter-of-factly.

"I don't know, it's worked before," she said with a wry smile. "If I've learned anything in the past seven years, it's that plenty of men are perfectly willing to believe that I am too pretty to be smart or anything but harmless."

"Perhaps I give them too much credit," Alces said, looking down at her. "A woman as beautiful as you just happens to be at a border fort town, right as people start going missing—well, I would think it a trap. Perhaps you are right, though."

"Because you are not like other men, my knight," she said with a smile.

"That is quite true," Alces said with a laugh and gave her a squeeze.

"Right, here we go," Sumner said, holding a small mechanical beetle in his hand as he walked back out of the inn. "Let me go put this near the hole, and I'll feel a little better sleeping tonight."

Leaning over, Octavia examined the beetle. "Is that like Snippy? Is it some sort of alarm or something?"

Sumner nodded, "Yeah, something like that. A little bit of an alarm, but also a tracker. It'll try to attach itself to whatever comes out of that hole, if anything does. I need to get it over there before it gets much later."

"We will stay here until you get back," Alces said. "Be quick, or we'll come looking for you."

"What he said," she chimed in.

"Remember me fondly should I go missing," Sumner said with a grin, then leaned in and gave her a firm kiss.

"Mmph!" She felt a rush as he kissed her, her hand instinctively coming up to cup his face, and then he was walking away, headed down the street in the growing darkness. It seemed all the more odd as she was still leaning into Alces.

"I... was not expecting that," she murmured as she watched him disappear into the night.

Alces grinned. "Well, he has said that to us before, dramatically, but he has never kissed any of us."

Moving his hand up, he ruffled Octavia's hair gently, then returned to holding her close as she leaned against him. "So, we can go over what we know while we wait for Sumner to return. Most likely what is happening is a kidnapping, mostly of young people, especially woman. The two major groups that reside in the Southmist Canyon are the Black Crag Clan of bandits and the Grummork tribe. Both worth avoiding if possible, but that may change. Thoughts?"

"Bandits make less sense," Octavia said, considering. "They would be ransoming people back, not continuing to take more. What do we know about the Grummork tribe?"

"Grummork tribe came about when the goblins and the orks in the canyon banded together, finding a common enemy amongst man and the other noble races," he said, filling her in. "They've been like that for a decade or so, I believe. So far the alliance is holding."

"Hmm." Octavia considered. "I suppose it depends on how young those being taken are. You'd think they'd be smart enough to find travelers on the road and leave the town be. It's hard to keep raiding if the town dies off and there's no traffic anymore." She considered again, and smirked. "I've heard orks like human women, but honestly I assumed that was lurid romance fodder."

"The canyon is a known, dangerous place. Hence why Boxende and Fort Shroauxdover were built on either end to serve as protection. They run escorts through, but some people want to chance it. Either can be hit, depending on how feisty the denizens are feeling," Alces explained. "So, travel is sometimes light. But, it could be either of them. The Black Crag for ransom, the orks for... other reason, mayhaps. Either for labor? Mystery at the moment."

"So what do you think?" she asked, looking up at Alces. "You're better traveled than I am, and have most certainly fought more foes. Does this feel more like bandits or the Grummocks?"

"I think bandits," he said with a nod. "Sneakier, more organized, more controlled. The Grummorks would be louder, more brash. They don't understand subtle. The why, though, I can't quite figure out."

"What if the bandits are trading the people to the Grummorks?" She wasn't sure if a clan of gremlins and orks could be sophisticated enough for such an arrangement, but what did she know?

"Now that is a thought," he said, looking down at her with a smile. "Very astute, brilliant Octavia. Perhaps they seek to band together as well. That would make a truly formidable presence in the canyon."

"We figured it out already?" Sumner asked as he stepped towards them silently.

"You are a sly one, aren't you?" She looked him over with admiration, smiling. "A theory. Alces says there are two powers in the canyon, a bandit clan and an alliance of goblins and orks. The bandits make more sense as the kidnappers, but why? So I proposed that they're taking people and selling them to the orks."

"As good a theory as any," Sumner said with a shrug. "Bug is placed, so let's head in and rest up. I can't believe I'm saying this, but you should probably stay with Alces tonight. Should those guys try anything, they will definitely think twice if you're staying with a dragonkin."

"I'm also surprised you're saying that," she said with a playful smile.

"I'll assume you'll make it up to me later," Sumner said and turned to head inside.

"You are always welcome with me, dear Octavia," Alces said humbly at the proposal.

She looked up at Alces. "Well, Ser Knight, if you'll have me."

"I do believe I just offered," he said with a tilt of his head but he was still smiling. He offered Octavia his arm, which she took with a smile, and they followed Sumner inside.

When they went upstairs to the rooms, Durante stuck his head out wondering how things were going. Sumner gave him the summary of the theories and the hope that his little automaton would give them some more light in the morning. As Sumner updated Durante, she flitted briefly into her room for a couple items and then returned to Alces' side.

"It appears that our supply and business day will be delayed," Alces said as they talked in the hall, "however, if we are able to get back all those that had been taken, a better reward awaits us."

"Oh, I'm sure they're going to pay nicely to get them back," Sumner said.

"I'm thinking Alces means everyone will be in a much better mood and we can stay without limits," Durante suggested in a dry tone.

"That, and with a town saved, we can celebrate properly," Alces said much louder, a broad grin on his face. Octavia smiled quietly at the three of them while they talked. She was enjoying these moments, the way they interacted, their easy brotherhood.

"To a proper celebration, then," Sumner said, "D, let me know if your buggy picks up anything. Otherwise, I'm knackered. Walking down a mountain, then sneaking around a town twice is exhausting."

"Will do. Likewise. Goodnight," Durante said.

"Good night," she said to the both of them, then impulsively kissed first Sumner then Durante. "See you in the morning." Both the guys seemed pretty pleased getting a kiss goodnight and disappeared into their rooms with a smile on their faces.

"To bed with us as well," Alces said, "and you are not obligated to serenade me to sleep this time, although I will not turn it down."

As she followed Alces into his room, she contemplated what she intended to happen tonight. She wasn't sure. She wanted him, but...she wasn't sure. Despite Sumner's assurance that Alces desired her as much as either of them did, she wasn't certain that he actually did. She had no doubt he would say yes if she asked, but was it because he wanted her specifically or because she was pretty and he liked keeping people happy?

Alces moved off to the side and started the long process of detaching and pulling off his armor and padding. "If you need to change, I promise to look away and not turn until you tell me to," he said honorably.

Octavia sighed. "Of course." She laid her robe and chemise down over a chair off to the side. "You know, I normally don't wear anything to bed, but I brought something." She took her boots off and started to unlace her pants. "I promise I won't...I mean, I don't have any expectations. I can sing you to sleep and leave you be."

Alces chuckled a little. "Octavia, you should never have to second guess around me. If you wish to wear nothing, then do so. But I'm not one of those paladins that is celibate, I admit I will certainly enjoy seeing you that way," Alces grinned, but it was an amused, honest, and gentle grin. "If you wish me to match, I shall do that as well. Also, I'm unsure if you can just leave me be, the bed is not that big, we'll be quite close all night."

Sighing again, Octavia looked back over her shoulder at Alces. "I... you're too accommodating. Sumner's desire was very easy to sense. He's direct and unsubtle in his wants, for all that he's excellent at going unseen when he needs to be. Durante was also easy to gauge. He is shy, he never would have reached for me on his own, but he wanted to and it was easy to tell. You..."

She turned pink, looking unsettled but determined. "You want to make people happy. Whatever...whatever may pass between us, I do not want it to be because you thought it would please me. I need it to be something you want. And you're gallant, and kind, and I feel a flutter in my chest every time—" She stopped. That was too much. That was more information than she had planned on giving.

Alces crouched down and motioned for her to come near. He was still halfway through getting his armor off, so he didn't want to rattle and make a mess. She slid her pants off before walking over - they were already mostly undone and it would have been awkward. More awkward.

"Glorious Octavia," he began as she set her pants aside, "you are a beauty among nymphs, your kindness has shown in the many days we have known you, you are smart and thoughtful. Yes, I try to bring light wherever and however I can, but as I have said, you bring light to me. Whatever you wish between us, know that I would relish in it as well."

"I have bumbled more around the three of you than I have anyone else in years," she muttered, pink cheeked again. She walked over in her shirt, which barely skimmed her thighs. "And I have had several thoughts about what I would do with you if given the chance."

"You are more than welcome to share those thoughts with me," he said, still grinning as he finally got his breastplate off and pulled off his padded jerkin, leaving only his bottom half dressed at the moment. His silver scales reflected softly in the dim candlelight of the room, his violet eyes nearly glowing. "Never feel shy around me, never feel like you must avoid saying the wrong thing. All I ever want is honesty, in whatever form, in word, thought, and deed."

"You know, I never have, before," she confessed, smiling sheepishly. "Felt shy, I mean. After seven years in Kamvasana's service, I didn't think I was still capable of it. I... I don't know what it is about you that suddenly makes me uncertain."

"I'm not certain as well," he mused, "but it does show a level of vulnerability that I am charmed by. You are so beautiful, yet moments like this you are also adorable. Yes, those things are different and they touch my heart differently."

She looked up at him, her blue eyes luminous. "I have never...been with a dragonkin before. There's a curiosity there. But also..." she reached up, and cupped his face. "You are endlessly charming, my knight."

He raised his hand to press hers against his face, leaning into it. "My sweet Octavia, I am yours to explore," he said, then released her hand. "Once I get this armor off, that is."

Snickering, Octavia stepped away to finish getting undressed as well, folding up her clothes on the chair. Alces grinned again and stood up before her, working on the latches and straps of his boots and thigh plates. There was still work to do, as clearly hopping into bed with this particular dragonkin would never be a speedy affair. She left the chemise next to the robe, and moved naked through the room. She sat down on the far side of the bed and began to brush her hair, and started to sing as she did.

Alces smiled and swayed gently as he finished pulling off his armor and setting it aside carefully. Looking over at Octavia, he smiled further, and moved to match her level of undress. His breeches didn't pull on, due to his clawed feet, but wrapped around and so it was easy to pull them off, leaving him naked and towering in the room.

EIGHTEEN

If her first time with a dragonkin was to be with Alces, she had quite the specimen before her. Tall, incredibly muscled, and a seasoned warrior with a handful of scars on his shining silver scales. Now, however, she could see her prize, which may have been the largest phallus she had ever seen outside of livestock.

It was scaled to the base, then the scales thinned leaving starkly white skin with a silver gray… well, marbling, for lack of a better descriptive term. The shape was a little more tapered, with no clear crown, but there was a firm ridge that seemed to spiral around the shaft in a wandering manner. There was a thick ridge along the base as well. He wasn't quite hard yet, but it wouldn't take much to change that. He took a moment to stretch out his back, his hands going up until they hit the roof, then slid along to the sides until he could fully stretch out his arms. Octavia set down her brush and her eyes widened a little as she took him in. She hoped Kamvasana would bless her with the ability to take everything the dragonkin was capable of giving her. Considering how impatient her patron was for her to cross that threshold, she figured they would.

"You really are magnificent," she said, her voice and gaze full of admiration.

"My scales pale in comparison to the beauty you present," he said, bowing slightly and offering her his hand. "I am at your whim, my lady Octavia."

Taking the hand, she rose from the bed, and he drew her closer. She slid a hand up his chest, and tipped her head back to look up into his eyes. She felt very small next to him and wondered fleetingly if this was what Comicha felt like all the time.

"The texture of your scales is so different than I expected," she said as her hand continued to gently caress his chest, the other one still held by him. "Does my hand feel much different than, say..." she leaned in, trailing kisses across him.

"You are exquisitely soft," Alces commented, his free hand sliding up her side and down her back, claws caressing the tender skin. He continued to hold her hand, almost as if they were dancing together, and squeezed it gently. "You are blessed, as life on the road usually leaves one rough and callous."

"Part of that is Kamvasana," Octavia said, "and part of that is not being on the actual road as much. Most of my travel has been by carriage or horseback, and specifically from town to town. I haven't been out in the wilds as much as the rest of you."

"It is true, but Kamvasana only blessed your form, your heart is your own," he asserted.

Tipping her head to the side, she grinned. "Pick me up, my knight."

"Happily." Reaching under her, Alces grabbed her by her plush and full butt and lifted her with no strain until their faces were even. "Would you do me the honor of a kiss, my lady?"

"I would love to," she said. She was curious as to how kissing would work—he had lips of a sort, though the structure of his mouth was certainly different. Well, if she started, he could finish. She pressed her lips to his, her hand cupping the wide curve of his jaw as she did. Alces returned the kiss softly, tenderly. His mouth was certainly large, and his lips a little rubbery, but there was little awkwardness, and they teased each other a little with their tongues. A deep kiss would be an experiment, but this was nice, and his tongue was very agile.

Octavia giggled softly at the initial stuttering, but she was happy to continue kissing him until they eased into each other. Kissing him was even more of a dance of tongues than with a human partner, but it was still intimate and exciting, and she found herself moaning quietly. Her hands caressed his jaw, slid down his neck, and her fingertips traced the firmer scales on the ridge of his shoulders. Parting from the kiss, Alces gently placed his forehead against hers. "I promise you, should I be so lucky for us to be like this again, I will take more of a lead. But you wanted to explore, so please tell me what you would like next," Alces said gently.

"Why don't you lay down on the bed," Octavia said, panting softly. "It'll be easier for me to reach more of you."

"As you wish," he said, gently setting her back on her feet while she was pressed up against him, letting her body slide against his. If the heavy shaft she felt between them was any indicator, he was more than ready for her at this point.

He gave her ass a little squeeze, then stepped over to the bed and laid down. What he'd said earlier was true, he occupied most of it. There would be no way they could lay next to each other separated. Octavia climbed onto the edge of the bed, then giggled and climbed all the way onto him, sitting on his chest and straddling him. This did mean he had an exceptional and up close view to all of her. His violet eyes drank her in, gazing over every bit of her and she could see the desire and appreciation in them. She tossed her hair back over her shoulder and planed her hands against his upper chest and collar bones. Alces smiled up at her and ran his hands over her thighs and up her hip, scaled fingertips caressing on their way up and gentle claws running over her flesh on the way down.

"So, my knight," she said with an impish smile. "You and Sumner have assured me that you are not celibate, and I think our current positions only reinforce that. I'm curious, though, have there been many human women in your history?"

"I'd say a fair bit. Bringing the light to many in many forms," he said with a nod. "Many have shied away after we undressed, but I brought them joy in other ways. Curiosity is certainly a strong agent of desire."

She shivered as his claws ran over her, a fine point of sensation. "I do look forward to the challenge you present," she said, and bent down, her hair forming a curtain around them. "Rest assured, my knight, I will not be shying away from anything this evening. But I hope you are enough of a gentleman to make sure I am ready for you."

"I am more than that," Alces said, both his hands coming up to her ass again, this time pulling her up his body even further until she was straddling his head. She let out a squeak as he moved her so easily. Opening his maw, he slipped out his firm, ridged, nimble tongue and started to tease her entrance. Clearly, Alces wasn't shy when he knew what was wanted of him, as only the barest exploration had started before his tongue started to push its way in, slowly but thoroughly.

"Yes," she whispered, reaching down and running her fingertips over his horns and the edges of his face. He had no hair to play with, but she could touch and explore.

Making a happy, growling noise that emanated right into her core, Alces drove his tongue in deeper and slathered it around her inner folds. Clearly, he was enjoying her flavor and was exploring deep within her to taste every bit. Despite its hunger, Alces was exploring, relishing, and making sure no part of her was untouched by that flexible tongue.

"Ohhh, Gods!" Octavia moaned and the muscles in her legs tensed and vibrated. Between Sumner's textured tongue, Durante's sharp teeth, and now Alces' astoundingly prehensile lingua, she had a delectable buffet of oral sex traveling with her. It was a heady thought.

At the moment, though, Alces was driving her to her peak much faster than she had anticipated. She cried out again and fell back against him, laying against his chest, her head on his stomach, her hair falling around the cock that was waiting for her.

"Yes, my knight," she gasped as her legs tremored. Soon.

Alces raised his head to keep going. Even with her cries, he didn't speed up or try to push her over the edge. Instead, he maintained a steady, deep exploration of her sex. His arms moved once more, one wrapped around her waist to keep her in place, the other sliding his hand up to caress and tease her breasts and sternum with his claws.

Whimpering, she twisted against him. The voice he seemed to enjoy so much sang to him in sweetly desperate cries. She grasped at his arms as if she needed something to hold on to, but did her best not to hinder him in any way. It seemed to just go on, the sensations building in her, riding on the edge but unable to cross it. He was strong enough that she could hold on anywhere, and he'd be unmoving, his arms solid wherever he placed them. There was a constant, pleased growl coming from him, which rumbled underneath her and vibrated the tongue inside her. And then, finally, she fell into the waiting arms of her orgasm. She cried out, her back arching, which pushed her wet sex against his eager mouth.

"Alces!" Her body remained taut and trembling until it finally let go, and she fell back against him again, panting hard, unable to move.

When Octavia's orgasm flowed through her, Alces relinquished his steady assault and drew his tongue out, now softly licking at her, enjoying her flavor and sounds. "You are delicious and a delight to please, my lady," he commented, his hands going back to gently petting her.

She panted and whimpered for a long moment, shivering in her afterglow. Slowly she pushed herself up and gently extracted herself from his hands so that she could rotate her hips and slide herself down his body to lay against him.

"My knight," she said, her voice warm and adoring, as she lay against him so that they were face to face.

"My lovely lady," he responded, smiling at her and caressing her body as she lay atop him.

She kissed him again. It wasn't awkward this time, but it was passionate, and she sucked at his tongue. When she wasn't sucking his tongue, he was teasing her mouth with it, drawing her in to kiss her more.

"Do you desire more exploration, my lady?" he asked as they panted between kisses. "I certainly hope so."

She moaned. "I am far from done with you." Another kiss, and then she pulled away gently to slide further down his body. When she felt his sizable shaft against the curve of her ass, she stopped. Pushing up from the bed for a moment, she rose up enough so that she could trap his cock between the two of them as she brought her hips back down.

"I am very looking forward to more," he said, and let out another rumbling growl as she teased him. Pushing up into a sitting position, she looked down at the fascinating cock. She rubbed herself against him, feeling the ridges against her slick cunt. It would feel very stimulating once he was inside her. As she started to stroke herself, he reached out to grasp her thighs, pulling her more firmly against him so the texture and ridges were more pronounced, harder against her sensitive sex. "Your warmth and softness feels amazing, my sweet lady."

She gasped and looked back up at him. "I think you can feel how excited you've made me. I... mmmm... I think I'm ready to try this, my knight."

Lifting her hips, she reached between her legs and grasped his cock, guiding it carefully into her eager cunt. As she pressed down, she felt him stretch her like no one ever had before, filling her completely, each swirling ridge feeling like it would leave a permanent, delicious impression within her.

Kamvasana, let me take this, she silently pleaded. *Let me be the most perfect woman he's ever fucked.* She wasn't certain why it suddenly mattered so much, but it did.

"Blessing of the Spree Spirits, you feel amazing. So tight yet welcoming, giving," he growled, his hands tightening on her thighs but making sure he did not impede her movements or pull her down too quickly.

Three out of three, my darling, Kamvasana purred in her mind. *You've earned this boon.*

Each time she raised and lowered her body, she was able to take more of him. After nearly a dozen slow, pressing strokes, she found herself sitting on his pelvis, his entire length sheathed snuggly inside her vessel.

Alces' head rolled back, his horns threatening to splinter the headboard as a roar of pleasure was held back through gritted teeth. "How," he moaned, "no one has ever taken me so completely."

"Thank you, Kami," she whispered as she sat against him for a long moment. She'd taken all of him, but the sensation was intense. Overwhelming. Finally, lifting her head, she looked up at Alces. Her hands slid up his abdomen, fingertips tracing the muscles she could feel. "By all the Gods," she murmured. "Are you ready for me to move, my knight?"

"Brightest light," he said with a smile. "Please, do. Move as much as you like, ride me to your content. I want all of you." That much was obvious, he was hard as a steel rod and throbbing. The thick shaft moved her slightly each time it jumped inside her.

She began carefully, lifting her hips up and then dropping back down slowly. He was so large that she could rise up almost completely on her knees without him falling out of her. It made him easy to tease. Soon, however, it became apparent that whatever her patron had done, she did not have to fear him hitting the end of her. She hoped it was permanent. It probably was. All of Kamvasana's changes had been thus far. The way those ridges felt inside her were amazing going slow. She kept herself from laughing as she realized how hard she was going to come once they really got going.

"You're like nothing I've ever felt," she said, her voice low and caressing. She shifted her hips a little, got used to the wider spread of her legs, and then started to move with a little more purpose, sliding up and down on his cock, working up to a steady bounce.

"Blessed Spirits, you are amazing," he said, his hands caressing her gently, not wanting to slow her down in the least.

Something deep in Octavia, something pleasure drunk and feral, was slowly taking over. She was panting and crying out, touching as much of him as she could. The first time she came, the ridges of his cock rubbing so perfectly inside her, she slammed her hips down against him and held herself there, just for a minute, just to catch her breath. And then she started to move again, harder than before.

Alces grinned, lifting his head to watch her body bounce, enjoying the way her softness undulated with each movement and drove him to wanting more. Reaching back, he grabbed the headboard to make sure his head wasn't hitting it, and as leverage when he started to pump his hips up to meet hers. That was when she came again, her voice spiraling up as she trembled, clenching hard for a breath before going back to riding him.

"Oh, my Octavia, you are incredible," he grunted, that deep growl rolling through him and her. The ridges on his shaft seem to get even harder as he moved with her, the dragonkin chuffing as they went. "You're so tight. I feel myself getting close."

"Yes," she gasped, feeling the burn in her thighs as she continued to work her hips up and down his cock with fervor. "I want to feel it! I want you to flood me."

She wished he was touching her, but she understood why he needed to brace himself. The bed was too small. Once they were back in the tent, his hands would be more free. She looked forward to their next night, whenever that may be. She hoped he wouldn't be afraid to pin her down. She didn't think he could break her, but she wanted him to try.

Right now, though, she was very happy to keep riding that ridged cock until they both came again. His thrusting became a touch more severe with her want. Soon, he was bouncing her body into the air with each thrust, his breathing becoming heavier as he peaked. When Alces couldn't take anymore, he released the bed and grabbed her hips, pulling her down atop him and buried himself completely into her. Holding her firmly, she got exactly what she wanted: a flood she could feel. It was surprisingly cool, perhaps from his draconic nature, but so filling. Her vessel was filled to overflow, excess squishing out where it could with the seal her pussy had on his cock. The firm thrusts sent her over again, and she came with a cry. The cool cum filling her made her feel like she would burst from the pressure, but she didn't care, it was overpowering and so good. As his grip and her body both eased, she found herself falling, splayed against his chest, panting and moaning.

Growling, he continued to hold her tight until it finally subsided, which took longer than she had expected, and he collapsed to the bed. The large dragonkin had a wide smile on his face and the firm grip, which had left marks on her hips, had eased into a gentle caress. "Oh, my Octavia, you are glorious," he panted, "a pinnacle of pleasure."

"So magnificent," she said again with a whimper.

They had made a significant mess, but Alces didn't seem to care. He was very content having Octavia laying atop him, his hands caressing over her back and rump, anywhere he could touch. His hips were having a hard time remaining still, but their movements were slow, lethargic. "Incredible," he sort of half purred, half growled.

After several minutes, Octavia picked her head up and looked up at Alces with a smile. "That was… I will need to become a bard to find the words to describe it." She dropped her head again and kissed across his chest. "I look forward to doing it again. I also look forward to seeing what it's like when you're leading." She bit at him a little, gently and mindful of her own teeth, and he growled softly.

"Perhaps we shall celebrate, together, later," he said, "and see why we sometimes get kicked out of towns afterwards." Alces laughed, which caused convulsing sensations to run between them.

Octavia pushed herself back up to sitting and looked down at him with a smile. He was still buried in her, and she found herself shifting her hips a little as she sat there. He felt so incredibly good. She could probably undulate herself to another orgasm if she felt so inclined.

"I appreciate that this is a manipulative time to ask," she said with a playful smile, "but does this mean I passed my test run?" It was mostly a joke, as she was fairly certain she had.

Alces couldn't help but laugh again, which did more of the squirming undulation between them. "I would say that you passed before this," he commented, giving her hips a squeeze in his hands, "and, if you want, you are welcome to stay with us as long as you desire. We will certainly want you to."

"I… suppose I should climb off of you so we can attempt to sleep," she said, lightly sliding her hands over his scales as she continued to slowly rotate her hips. "It'd be easier if you didn't feel so good."

Alces groaned gently as she moved and smiled up at her. "I admit, I do not feel like you need to climb off anytime soon," he said, growling again. Between the two of them, she could already feel that he was growing hard once more.

Octavia bit her lip. "Am I allowed to make a request of my knight?"

"Of course," Alces said, "what do you wish of me, my lady?"

"Can I ask you to pick me up," she said, bending to kiss his sternum, "press me against that wall, and thrust into me until I come again?"

"Oh, of course, my lady," he said with a grin and wrapped an arm around her waist as he moved. Swinging his legs off the edge of the bed, he sat up then placed his hands on her ass to hold her in place. Standing up, he carried her with him easily and did as she asked, pressing her against the wall with his hands on her hips, letting the wall, and his cock, keep her in the air.

"Is this what you desired?" he asked as he started to move his hips, slowly but firmly pressing her against the wall and sinking into her completely with each press.

"Yes," she moaned, her head falling back against the wall. "Gods you're so strong. And the feel of you is... is incredible!" She kissed and licked at his chest and collar.

"Then let me use my strength to let you feel even more," he commented as he guided both of her legs to wrap around his waist. One hand then took a handful of her beautifully round ass, the other placed against the wall, and he proceeded to pound her. Firm, deep, rhythmic thrusts against a surface with no give, forcing her to accept every inch of him.

That feeling rose in Octavia again. No thoughts, only this sensation of merciless, relentless pleasure. It was different from the nights when she was used by Kamvasana, and not just because the personification of Desire wasn't quite as large as Alces. Like before, Alces was in no hurry. These strokes were there to make sure she felt everything, not to see how fast she could feel it. Solid, steady driving into her core as he smiled above her, that happy growl rumbling in his throat. Her hands gripped his shoulders, and it seemed like in no time at all she was coming again. She added to their mess as she came in a flood, gushing over him.

His movements slowed after she came, slowly ebbing until he stopped, burying himself completely in her as he leaned down, lifting her chin with a single finger and kissing her softly. "Have I served my lady well," he asked, "or do you wish more of me?" There was a touch of naughtiness in his smile, as if he could keep going if she needed him to.

"You've served me so well," she said, nuzzling into him, "but I can't help wanting more. What do you need to come for me again?" She drew her tongue across the hollow of his throat.

"Just you," he said, leaning in and gently nipping at her shoulder. "Just let me hear you, that will be more than enough. And I will happily come for you as much as you wish."

He moved away from the wall, taking her in his arms and holding her up as he stood in the middle of the room. Alces was easily strong enough to hold her. Not only hold her up, but bounce her in his arms, thrusting up into her as she came down, gravity making the thrust all the deeper.

She held tight to him and filled his ears and the room with her cries. She came again, wet and dripping, kissing and licking and biting at him as she lost herself in it.

This time, he did pick up the pace. He did move faster and harder, moving her body up and down so she was feeling the full length of his cock. Alces' grip tightened on her ass and he drove into her, bouncing her body up with each pounding press of his hips. He chuffed and nipped at her shoulder again as he felt himself get closer.

"My wanton Octavia," he rumbled, "I'm going to come for you. Take my light, let us glow together."

"Yes," she whimpered, "please!"

Another series of deep drives into her, and he pulled her down on top of him, holding her tight as she felt him flood her once more. The shaft buried in her jumped with each spurt, sending sensations through her until he eventually subsided. He was so tremendous. She thought she had known what it was to lose herself, but not like this. It was delicious and exhilarating and a little frightening, or it would be later. Right now... right now she would let him break the bed with her if he decided he wanted to.

Another pleasant shudder, and Alces eased her up and off of him, setting her gently on the bed. "You are hungry for life," he said, leaning down to kiss her once more, "and you are all the more amazing for it. Thank you, my delicious Octavia."

She shivered as she laid there, pleasure and exhaustion leaving her soft and languorous. She had come so many times. If she had been less exhausted she would have reached down and slid her fingers through the combined essence pouring out of her, just to feel it.

"I have never... become so undone," she said finally, having come back to herself enough to turn her head and look at Alces. "I am humming with pleasure and I... Alces. My knight. You are magnificent."

Kneeling next to the bed, he laid his head down beside her where she lay, reaching up to softly caress her body, from collar to ankle. "You have allowed me to feel things I did not think possible. You have brought such bright light into my night," he said, taking her hand and kissing it, "you are truly the gift. But, if I am your knight, then I shall always be for as long as you'd want me to be."

She felt that tremor under her ribs again and reached up to caress his face. "I could want that for a very long time," she murmured.

"Us dragonkin live a very long time, especially in service of the

Spree Spirits." He grinned as he continued to pet her. "Are you ready to sleep, my sweet Octavia?"

"Mm-hmm." The longer she laid there, the more her body was content to take the thorough, delicious fucking she'd received and follow it with what would likely be the best night's sleep she'd had in a while.

"How would you like us to sleep together?" he asked, standing up and waiting before he crawled into bed.

"Do you want to hold me?" She asked and yawned. Her voice was soft to her ear, sounding younger than she normally did. Vulnerable.

"A sillier question I don't believe I've ever heard," he said, and slid into the bed beside her, smiling softly with a gentle warmth behind his eyes. She moved up against him and kissed him softly, then rolled over and wiggled back against him so that he could spoon her if he wished. Thoughtlessly, she cast the cleansing spell as they settled into place so that neither of them woke up a bigger mess than they already were. He wrapped an arm around her and pulled her close against him. His arm laid across her, his hand cupping her flesh, protectively. Nothing would harm her, she felt, as long as his arms were around her.

"Goodnight, wonderous Octavia. May the spirits bring you the sweetest dreams," he said, kissing the top of her head.

"Goodnight, Alces," she said sleepily, eyes already closed, blissfully snuggled against him.

NINETEEN

Dreams that night were intense. Some of the most she'd ever had. Being passed around between Durante, Sumner, and Alces; or having two or three of them at once. Any position she desired, intense feelings, and pure ecstasy. Through it all, she could feel Kamvasana watching, pleased. Very pleased, in fact.

When she awoke, Alces was still wrapped around her, holding her close and breathing deeply. He was awake, though, eyes open, looking at her and smiling softly. Groaning, she rubbed a hand over her face, and then became very aware that Alces was still in bed this time. She tipped her head back to look at him.

"Good morning, my knight," she said, and yawned.

"Good morning," he said, giving her a squeeze. "There wasn't much of a point in getting up early this morning, and with us so close I didn't want to chance waking you."

She yawned again and turned towards him. "You didn't need to stay here if you were ready to get up," she said, caressing him lightly.

"Well, you're awake now," he chuckled and leaned in to kiss her. Another squeeze and he slipped out of bed. Now, in the light of things, she could see why that would have been a problem. The bed rocked as he got out and shook her.

"We should get the others and get ready to go, we have people to rescue." Smiling he started to stretch, which involved a lot of flexing, for his morning routine.

Octavia enjoyed the show for a moment, then got up and got dressed enough to head across the hall and change into more sturdy clothing. She was all for rescuing people, but not in the ruffled silk shirt. While she changed, she heard Alces knock on everyone's door and wake them up, making sure they were getting ready. It sounded like it was a nice rest for everyone involved. No early morning hunts were needed, they were not preparing for long travel.

Octavia dressed quickly and braided back her hair to keep it out of the way. Soon enough she was down in the main room of the inn, looking for breakfast and the rest of her party. The only one there was Sumner. Grinning, he waved her over. Food hadn't been presented yet, so she wasn't late.

"So, did you have a good night," he said, smirking.

"Are you going to do that every time I spend an evening with someone else?" She asked as she sat, leaning forward with a wry smile. "That 'I know what you did' look, as if you weren't initially planning on being the one I spent the night with instead? And yes, it was lovely, thank you for asking."

"Hey, I like to know how you're faring, making sure everyone is living up to expectations," he said with a shrug. "Sounded like a pretty good night. You, ah, still going to want to have fun with me. Me or D?"

"Ah, I was loud. That's fair, he's a lot to take." She reached across the table and took his hand, bringing it to her lips and kissing his palm. "You each delight me in your own ways. If you continue to not mind sharing my attention, then I am very happy to share it."

"Nope," he said, holding his other hand up. "Deal is a deal. I mean, I'm always going to want to call dibs, but I also have a vague idea of what you can handle so I'm man enough to admit you'd probably end up killing me." He grinned again and took her hand in return, kissing it, then leaned forward and kissed her. She caressed his cheek as they kissed and smiled at him as she sat back.

"I don't think I'd kill you. Maybe you'd get stronger." She continued to hold his hand, giving it a squeeze. "Though... I can be louder for you," she said in a softer voice, one that wouldn't carry. "After all, we ended our first night early. And I got the impression you'd enjoy being, perhaps, a little rougher with me. Which we can also do."

"I mean, I think I'd like a little bit of ecstatic screaming, but we're in close quarters, we're worn out every day from hiking or fighting. I think we need a nice evening where maybe I could steal you away. Just, every once in a while. I won't be greedy," Sumner said, then paused as the inn keeper came by.

Sumner ordered a fair amount of food, an amount that impressed the keeper, but Alces would be down in a moment, so it didn't surprise Octavia. The innkeeper still seemed run down, but given the atmosphere and what was happening, that wasn't terribly surprising.

"With rare exceptions," Octavia said after the innkeeper walked away, looking at Sumner again, "one of you could keep me busy every night, if you were so inclined." A smile quirked the corner of her mouth. "You're the organizer of this group, work out a schedule. Though there are about three to four days in a month when unless you're there to rub my feet and brush my hair, you get to leave me alone."

"I'm well aware of how a woman's body works," Sumner said, looking smug. "Lots of women in the circus; I had a mother, you know."

"You know, we all have mothers, and yet..." she left the statement hanging.

"As for scheduling, that sounds like a lot of work," he laughed, "I'd like to think that we think of you as more than a nightly activity. So, let's vote on letting things happen naturally?"

Durante and Alces entered and sat down next to them, Alces back in his armor and Durante fiddling with a framed piece of glass. "I think we have a plan," Alces said as he settled in. "Provident Durante's little bug clung to something and we have a track. We'll head out after breakfast and scout it out."

Grinning, she held a hand up to Alces. "One moment, I have a point to finish making," she said, and looked back to Sumner. "Look, the schedule was a joke. And I know you think of me as more than an activity, or I wouldn't be saying this to you. Natural is fine. I just want you to know that you don't have to wait for me to come to you. If you want me...you can tell me. And I'll probably be very receptive."

"Can't argue with that logic, sounds good to me," Sumner said with a grin.

She sat back, looking to Alces and Durante. "Same goes for the two of you. Anyway. Proceed with planning."

Alces gave a shrug, "That was it, that was the plan."

Durante, however, held up a finger in question and leaned to look around the table. "Hang on, I think we missed an important conversation here. What?"

Amused, Octavia looked over at Durante. "Which part is confusing, kitten?"

It took Durante a moment as his brain replayed things, but it pieced things together and he sat down. "Nothing, I think I got it now," he said, shrinking down a little bit in embarrassment.

She reached under the table and squeezed Durante's leg. "You can ask for more details later, if you like."

Thankfully, a distraction in the form of food arrived and the party started to dig in. If anything, it was nice to have actual breakfast food, fresh bread, and even fruit instead of what they had preserved or foraged. She had a little too much bread, slathered in butter and fresh jam, and finished off a pot of tea on her own. Sumner paid the keeper, and they gathered their gear, heading towards the opposite side of town from where they had started. When they got to the gatehouse, Alces called down the head of the guard for the area.

"Good sir, we've heard about the plight. I noticed you did not have a request posted but do not worry, we will retrieve your people and bring them back safely," he told them. "My associate here has found the means of them getting in, which is a tunnel beside the stables. On the east side of the structure, under a bleuthorn bush. I suggest you close it right away."

Octavia laughed softly, more of a surprised exhalation, and leaned in towards Durante. "Is this what he's always like? I thought knights like this existed in tales."

The guards seemed hesitant, though one on the wall seemed quite happy to hear this news. He kept his words to himself, though, and they opened the gate for the group. It seemed Octavia was being pulled along into one of Alces' crusades. Given her desire to travel with them, it was bound to happen, so it was best to experience it now.

"He's a living tale," Durante commented quietly as they started to walk out of the town. "I'm not entirely sure who the Spree Spirits are, but they have a hell of a knight in their service. Mind you, I haven't really, um, interacted with many paladins, but if they're anything like him, the world may be okay. Hang on."

Producing the piece of glass he was looking at before, he held it up before him and looked around. When he waved it in a particular direction, Octavia could see a blinking green light through the glass. If she wasn't looking through the glass, she didn't see the light.

"Alces, we should be heading north-northeast," he said and Alces nodded.

"Quick Sumner, did you hear?" Alces asked and Sumner nodded as well, already several steps ahead of them.

She was reasonably confident she was going to get her ass kicked today. Well, so long as Alces could drag her out of whatever he was dragging her into, it would work out in the end. She wasn't quite as altruistic as Alces, but she had found that sometimes she landed in places that needed a little help. So if she could, she helped. For a price, sure, but sometimes that price was whatever they could afford to give.

Adjusting her satchel, she pulled on her gloves and summoned Comicha. The imp popped into being and flew straight up to Alces.

"You beast!" The imp said, gleefully. "High five!" She held her tiny hand up.

"Goddess of Mercy," Octavia muttered, running a hand over her face.

Alces looked confused, but he smiled and offered his hand. "I'm considered a Dragonkin. Cousin of the grand, noble dragons. But I have been called worse, friendly Comicha," he said.

"Oh, I was talking about last night!" Comicha beamed at him. "She lost her mind! It was awesome!"

"Fucking familiar bond," Octavia muttered. She glared at the imp and said, more loudly, "Comicha, you can stop now."

Alces' brow ridges raised up, but the smile held. "She was quite coherent. However, if things are to happen, I make sure I do my best to please those I am with," he started, then tapped her gently on the nose, "however, those are conversations for private company. More importantly, ensure it is a conversation those involved want to have." He purposefully glanced towards Octavia.

"I kinda thought that's what was happening," Durante said, refocusing on his sensor, or whatever it was in his hands.

"What, she doesn't—oh." Comicha glanced over at Octavia, and seemed genuinely surprised that her mistress was upset. She flitted back over to Octavia. "I'm sorry. Kami's just so proud of you, I thought we'd be celebrating? I'm confused."

Sighing, Octavia reached out and ruffled Comicha's hair. "We're off to save people. And not everyone is used to people airing their private activities as if it were casual conversation."

"Hmm." This seemed to be a lot for Comicha to consider, and she fluttered along next to them, looking thoughtful.

Sighing again, Octavia looked to Durante. "Thought what?"

"You and Alces," he said softly. "Lot of noise last night. Sorry, shouldn't have said anything." Durante looked conflicted. A weird combination of busy focusing on the issue, acknowledging the expected results, and maybe a little disappointed, but it was hard to say at what exactly.

Alces had walked a little ahead by this point, making sure he was keeping an eye on Sumner, who was much further ahead. They were scouting, after all, and they needed their quickest, sneakiest person in the lead.

"Do you also need reassurance that I still find you charming and handsome?" Octavia asked quietly as they walked. "That I still hope you want time with me? Sumner did, so I understand if you do as well. This is…a bit of an odd arrangement, I know."

"No, I know you're being sincere," he said, giving her a little smile. "I'm being silly. I'm happy with whatever time I get with you. But thanks."

She wrinkled her nose at him a little. "We'll talk more later. For now I imagine we should focus on the daunting task ahead of us." She did lean over and kiss him, though, quick and light, then moved to catch up with Alces.

"She really, really likes it when you bite her," Comicha stage whispered to Durante, who did seem happier having heard it, then followed her mistress.

Alces turned as Octavia caught up with him. "Thoughts on what's ahead?" he asked.

"I'm not sure," she said, happy to shift focus back to the matter at hand. "Honestly, I'm a little nervous about the numbers we will potentially be encountering."

"Numbers mean nothing if they are cowardly, weak, and untrained," he said assuredly. "So far you've faced hellish horrors and ghosts of questionable intent. I don't think a few bandits and orcs will cause you any issue. If all else fails, hide behind me. I will always be your shield." Those words caused that fluttering again. Which felt a little absurd, as she was fairly certain he would say that to anyone. But still…

Comicha flew up and quietly perched on Alces' shoulder. Octavia contemplated for another moment.

"They said the disappearances were recent," she said, considering. "With any luck, they're still gathering people and haven't made the trade yet."

"If what you're guessing at is true, which has merit, then I believe that will be the case," he said with a nod. "The question is, do we rescue those that have been taken, and hope they don't try again, or do we wait until they try to trade, and get them all at once?"

"The second increases the chance of someone being hurt in the chaos," she mused, and kicked a larger rock off to the side. She looked up at the canyon walls. "Though... what are the chances we'll be attacked trying to get there? I mean, I wouldn't take you on if I could help it, but Durante and I give the incorrect impression of being less dangerous."

"That's why Sumner is up ahead. If he sees anything, he'll let us know, and we'll move more cautiously. With the abductions known, they are probably looking for guard movements. We appear to be lone travellers, which could upset their plans. They would be unsure of us. Guards are a known quantity," Alces remarked. "However, I could be wrong, and we could be jumped at any moment, at which point we will need to deal with them before they warn the rest of the Black Crags. I'm more worried about running into the Grummorks, but they'd be much easier to spot."

There was a moment of quiet. "One of the guards lost someone," she said after a minute. "The one that lit up when you said we were going in. I didn't make the connection immediately, but now it seems so obvious." She looked across the canyon again. "So, why are you more concerned about the Grummorks?"

"Because they're less prudent, less picky of targets," he said, glancing up at the canyon walls.

Most of them were fairly sheer, but there were crags and places to hide among the reddish stone. Small creatures would dart between dry shrubs as they walked. The occasional hawk would call out from above them, but it was mostly quiet aside from their own voices.

"It does suddenly occur to me," Durante said as he trotted up. "Absolutely no offense meant by this, but with Tavi with us, the bandits might think we're a fairly tempting target."

"None taken, I made a similar observation to Alces yesterday evening," she said, waving off the implied offense. "They'll think I'm helpless, and you'll compromise yourselves to save me, so on and so forth."

"Honestly, I was thinking more that you look like a gorgeous royal with her knight and council," Durante said with a shrug. "Not so much helpless, as worth a hefty ransom." She smiled at Durante. She'd been told she was beautiful many, many times, but for some reason it made her feel warm to hear him say it so casually.

"I'm not wearing enough jewelry," she commented. "But I've got a good 'spoiled princess' outfit if you ever need me to look fancy or act as bait." She looked down at the glass in Durante's hand. "Still heading the right way?"

Glancing back down at his glass and moving it around, he took pause, then gave out a whistle, doing an admirable impersonation of a bird. From down the way, a whistle came back in response, then a few moments of silence. Octavia noticed they all had stopped walking.

Just when they seemed to be standing there too long, Sumner popped up near some shrubbery. "Hey, what's up, D?"

"Well, it looks like it's more north now. Keep a lookout for caves or hidden branches in the canyon," Durante responded.

"Got it. I'll whistle if I see anything," Sumner said, and ran off ahead of them. After Sumner disappeared again, Alces motioned for them to keep walking.

"The bait routine is a classic," Durante said, returning to the previous conversation. "Wish we'd thought of it sooner. Then again, we don't know how bad they are yet. Couldn't bear to have them hurt you."

She smiled at Durante again as they continued down the canyon. "I've only ever been bait twice. Was specifically hired for it, even. Same group both times." She shrugged. "The spoiled princess outfit mostly gets me into places I shouldn't be."

"Where on earth shouldn't you be?" Durante asked with, wait, was that snark? Had she been whittling him down?

"Places with a distinct lack of taste, no doubt," Alces said, then suddenly burst out in laughter which unfortunately echoed through the canyon. "However, she may be banned from more places now that she's with us."

Octavia giggled and turned pink like a maiden at her first party. How did they do that to her? "I'm good at playing the noble, for all that I never was one," she said, pushing a curl out of her face. "Sometimes I would get dressed up, crash a party I had no right being at, enjoy their hospitality for the evening, and possibly find someone to spend the night with. You can learn a lot."

"I once had an enchantress try to seduce information out of me," Alces said, turning back towards Octavia. "She thought I was a celibate knight. How does the saying go? 'She threatened me with a good time'."

Octavia snickered. "I feel like that would have been fun to witness."

"She was quite surprised. Learned a lot from her as well," Alces said with his charismatic smile.

"If it's anything like the stories I've read, I can only imagine," Durante said, looking through his glass again. Everything seemed on track for the most part, but he did look a little confused.

Glancing over at Durante, her brow furrowed. "What is it?"

"Well, the tracker is due north of us now, but we still haven't seen a break in the canyon wall and Sumner hasn't said anything," Durante said, and as he finished his statement, a bird whistle came from up the trail. "Of course. His timing, I swear."

On Alces' signal, they crept along the edge of the canyon to where Sumner was hiding.

"What did you find?" Alces asked.

"Break in the wall, about twenty or so lengths up. Hidden behind some rock outcroppings," he reported.

"If that is their entrance, it's no doubt trapped, and we should be wary of scouts. I haven't seen any so far," Alces said, and Sumner shook his head.

"Me neither. So, they're either depending on the entrance being hidden, or they're planning something," Sumner said.

"We can't delay much. As Octavia has said, if we risk waiting too long, people may get hurt. So, in we go, but carefully, unless someone has another idea," Alces announced, glancing around. Both Sumner and Durante shook their heads. Octavia also shook her head. She was as ready as she could be. Time to see if her theory was right.

Carefully they followed Sumner as he led them towards the entrance. A minute or so later they came across a hole in a fold of rocks, completely obscured from the road by outcroppings. It was incredible that Sumner even found it. Carefully, they went in, Sumner still in the lead. Reaching back, Alces took Octavia's hand.

"Both Sumner and Durante can see in the dim light. Us, we are not so lucky, so we stay together while they look for trouble," he said. Clasping Alces' hand, Octavia nodded and gave it a squeeze.

It was slow going, because the path was indeed ladened with traps and Sumner was having a slow time disarming them or triggering them safely away from everyone else. The tension was strange - she'd climbed through a few tight spaces in the past seven years, but she was always alone, and usually very clear about what awaited her on the other side. This was different. Their numbers were reassuring, but relying completely on Sumner and Durante to guide them safely was a strange and new feeling. One she would probably have to get used to.

It felt like hours before they saw light at the other end. Alces could have used his, but they didn't want to give away what they were up to. When they came out the other side, they found what seemed to be a box canyon that they were at the blocked end of. They had actually snuck up behind the Black Crag Clan encampment.

"It appears you found their secret entrance, not the main one," Alces whispered, clapping Sumner on the shoulder. A stroke of luck. "Alright, let's look around and see if we can find our captives."

Alces gave Comicha a little rub on her head. "You could help us out a lot here," he suggested.

Pushing up into the air, Comicha nodded, and then faded from sight. They heard the smallest of nearly silent giggles before feeling a quick, small breeze as the imp flew off to her task. Sumner started to sneak off and Durante, well, he carefully checked his equipment then started to climb right up the cliffside wall. No harness, no rope, and it didn't seem like he was in danger of slipping. Octavia blinked, and her mouth fell open in surprise. She gave her head a small shake and looked around. She was definitely out of her depth.

"Alright, brave Octavia, we're not the sneaky type," he said, then looked her over and her small stature, "well, I'm not. How would you like to go about this? Do you have any spells that may help us?" It was an honest question, as aside from a few choice things, Alces did not know her power.

"My spells will be more useful if we get caught," she said, looking a little sheepish. "I can probably enchant anyone who runs into me if they're alone, or I can start throwing around spells that do various amounts of damage."

"Then you have options," he said with a reassuring smile. "So, do you wish to stick with me, or go off on your own. I will say, if it is with me, high chance we'll get into a fight. I don't like these people, and I'm easy to spot."

"I am not Sumner levels of sneaky, but I have a light step and can be careful," she said, thinking. "I think we'll split up, and if I hear a fight break out I'll come running."

"You'll be fine," he said and looked for a nearby bush. "Perhaps I will be the one to hide and wait. If you start a fight, I will come running."

She nodded and then turned and headed towards the rest of the encampment, sticking to the bushes and short, shrubby trees that had been left in the back of the camp.

TWENTY

The Black Crag Clan encampment had clearly been here for a while, at least a handful of years, but she was seeing it from the back end. There were multi-story buildings, or what could be called buildings, made of reclaimed wood and canvas.

Where they'd come out happened to be near what she assumed was either the forge or the cook house as there was heat nearby. A particularly large building, possibly the leader's roost, rose up from the middle of the structures and could be seen from almost anywhere in the camp.

It was relatively quiet, she could hear people moving about but not many. Perhaps the group was out waiting for travelers, or maybe asleep since they'd been up all night kidnapping people from Boxende and possibly Fort Shroauxdover. However, she did spot a pair of bandits walking past wearing ruddy shawls and tunics with pants that blended in with the brush in the area. Their camouflage was good for being in the canyon, but with the black tents and dyed canvas everywhere, they stood out.

There was little chance they were going to get the victims out without rousing some suspicion. But a distraction may help. Octavia did know how to be a very good distraction, but perhaps not yet. She needed to find where they were keeping people so that she could be a distraction away from the prisoners.

She inched around the over warm building and tried to see if there were obvious cages or...something. Slinking around it, she did see that it was a forge. It appeared mostly to be used for melting down jewelry, as there were little splatters of gold and silver near the crucibles. For now, however, it was just providing heat. No one was working the forge. As she moved along the structures, she could pick up on what the two she had spotted were saying.

"How many did those damn greenskins want?" one asked.

"At least twenty. The more the better our trade position," the other responded.

"And after last night, how many do we have?"

"If you count the kids, sixteen. Thirteen otherwise."

Kids? Octavia clenched her teeth and looked around again. Only two were up and about. If she could get both of them... but then to what end? No, she needed to find where they were keeping everyone.

She darted quickly to the next structure, hiding behind it as best she could. So far she had gone unseen. As she moved around towards another building, she felt a rush of air and Comicha appeared between her and the tent, grinning.

"I did good, Mistress," she whispered with a sassy cock of her hip. "Found 'em. They're in the base of the big, tenty building thingy in the middle. Crammed together. Don't think they hold prisoners a whole lot."

Looking up, Octavia smiled. "Good job. Go find Alces and let him know, all right? Quietly, if you please," she added.

Comicha grinned and gave Octavia a salute. "Yes, Mistress!" With that, she disappeared and fluttered away.

So, if she was going to be a distraction, she should do it further away from the central tent. Theoretically this was something she could do. She looked up at the watchtowers, trying to see if anyone was currently on watch. Coming away from the canyon wall and more into the camp to see the towers, she was spotting a person in each one. There were only two, one on each side of the entrance, and they were looking the other way. After all, why would they be looking back into their own camp? As she moved, she started to hear people waking up and getting out of their tents and buildings. If they were going to do something, it should be soon.

She paused and considered her options for a moment. She had a fair amount of distance between herself and the main tent. She had an idea. She hadn't cast this particular spell in a while, but she had a feeling it would work. She straightened up and reached into her bag, taking out a pinch of glittering dust that she sprinkled over herself. It bounced over her and then clung to her, highlighting her hair, giving her exposed skin a golden glow. She then started to saunter through the camp, a swing to her hips, her head up, heading to the spot right between the watchtowers.

At first nothing much was happening. After all, she'd been back by the canyon walls and had just started to explore the camp. A few steps in and she caught at least one person's eye. They were stunned, shouted that there was an intruder, and ran after her. Once they got within the spell's aura, they stopped, blinked, then smiled, licking their lips as they started walking towards her.

The shout brought more out, with much the same results. They would charge out, become enraptured by the spell, and then approach Octavia making lewd suggestions and whistling at her. She even snagged the first guard in the tower, who dropped his crossbow and slid down the ladder to get to her. The interesting part of the spell was once they got within arm's reach of Octavia, they froze. Those behind them would shove the frozen ones out of the way to get in closer, only to have the same happen to them. She was surrounded by lust-hungry zombies, all wanting a piece of her but unable to touch.

The only one she hadn't snagged in her approach, because it was getting harder to walk, was the opposite tower guard. He saw what was happening and leveled his crossbow. Before Octavia could react, he was struck by a white bolt of light and collapsed. A half-second later there was a muffled crack, like a rock had hit the ground after falling off the canyon wall.

"Looks like that's my cue," she said, bringing her arms in tight to her sides. She turned her hands to present her palms, fingers outstretched as she chanted a short string of words few on earth would recognize. Then dark, shadowy, grasping hands erupted out from all around her, grabbing at the bandits surrounding her, planting searing ecstasy on their skin.

It was like being in the center of an orgy. Men and women alike moaning and screaming out before collapsing with ruined breeches. It certainly was attracting attention, as those who hadn't been caught in the spell were heading in her direction.

Octavia winced. "Oh, you all are louder than the last group," she murmured. She felt a certain amount of pride as she looked at the ring of bodies around her. "Lot more of you this time, though."

"What the fuck is going on," came a roar from the center of the camp. She could see the bandit leader making his way out of his tower in the center. The building had a wrap-around stairway on the outside, but also a ladder. It took Octavia a moment to believe it, but it seemed this camp was run by a ghastly looking minotaur with a shattered horn on his left side, and he was quickly coming down the ladder.

Octavia felt a flutter of panic, but it passed quickly. She wasn't alone, and she had options. She looked at the ones that were left coming after her. Aside from the terrifying leader, it looked like three more bandits had been outside the spell's reach. Blue energy shot forth from her hands at two of them, and she backed up out of the circle, glancing around. The two she hit stumbled and groaned, dazed and more than a little confused. The third bandit was hit by another bolt of white light followed shortly by another distant crack in the distance.

"Oh, a brave little magic girl, huh," the minotaur growled, producing two axes from his belt. "You're going to be a tasty one to break when I get my hands on you."

Octavia held up her hands and looked up at the minotaur with big eyes and a fear that wasn't completely fake. "I may have made a misjudgment," she said, her blue eyes glowing faintly as she spoke. "Is it too late to negotiate?" Her voice became unnaturally honeyed, and it appeared a button popped on her shirt, further displaying her impressive cleavage.

A grin split the minotaur's face and he licked his lips. "Oh, we can negotiate. Stripped down and on your knees and all is forgiven," he said, but had not put the axes away. The two she had blasted were still slowly approaching, but moving more so they were behind their leader. Her blast had definitely shaken them, and they didn't look ready to fight.

Another step back, and Octavia dropped down to her knees. "I just...I wanted to help the town," she said, eyes still big, though now it was getting a little hard to keep up the terrified girl act. "What...what are you going to do to me?"

"Oh, first I'm going to slap that pretty little face with my cock until you bruise, then you're going to get a hole stuffed for each one of my men you've tortured with your magic. After that, I'm going to shackle you up, and you'll be free use to myself and the rest of my clan until we get sick of you and sell you to the Grummork, who will probably do the same." He continued to grin. She could see a rise in the front of his loincloth as he imagined her punishment. Aside from the two behind him, she was starting to see more heads pop up from the noise. She definitely had the camp's attention at this point.

"Oh no..." she whimpered fearfully, until he was close enough to block her view of his remaining crew. At which point she dropped the act. "I'm going to have to decline your terms."

Arcs of blue energy shot from her hands into him, and in a blink she disappeared, leaving a misty outline in her place. The blasts singed the minotaur, who was none too happy based on the angry roar. They didn't stun him the way they had his subordinates, one could hypothesize a rage boner was a normal occurrence for this specimen.

She popped up on the other side of the bandit chief and the two flanking him, and started running towards the back of the canyon. The sudden sound of a scuffle behind her slowed her step, and she turned to see Alces dropping the last of the minotaur's immediate henchman.

"Your tale ends here, you vile excuse for a man," the dragonkin said. Before the minotaur could react, the knight slammed his shield into him, stunning him as his head rang out. This was quickly followed up by a shattering smash upwards to his jaw from Alces' mace. The impact rang out like a boom of thunder and tossed some of the approaching bandits aside.

The minotaur stood there, head cocked back, arms at his side, seemingly frozen. Alces grinned and pushed him in his chest with the mace, watching the large bandit leader fall to the ground. Turning, he looked at what of the bandit camp remained and banged on his shield.

"Which of you wish to test your mettle against a Knight of the Spree Spirits," he roared out gleefully.

Motion caught Octavia's eye, and she saw Sumner waving to her from the base of the bandit lord's tower. People were running past him and towards the rear of the camp. She had bought him time to find them and unlock the cages. Octavia angled her route towards Sumner. She wouldn't be much help to Alces right now, and she'd prefer not to risk accidentally hitting him.

"Is everyone still here?" she asked as she ran up. "Should be sixteen total."

Sumner shrugged as she came up. "I don't know, I wasn't counting. I was just getting people out," he said as another person ran past. True to what they had been told, most of them were young women with the occasional young man among them.

"Are they waiting in the back or fleeing straight for the fort?" She watched a girl run past, then looked back at Sumner. "Is the canyon safe without us?"

"I told them to wait by the cave," he said, "I don't want anyone jumping us or a trap I might have missed catching anyone. With the noise, there's a chance they already sent someone in."

Behind Octavia, she could hear quite a commotion as Alces was dealing with the rest of the bandits. At intervals, she'd hear that cracking noise that she now recognized as Durante's screwshot. It sounded a lot different in a wide canyon than it had in the confined rooms of a tower.

"All right, I'm going to check above us for anything useful, then head back to the cave unless someone says otherwise," she said, then impulsively kissed his shoulder and headed back up into the fallen leader's tent. Her adrenaline was up, but she wasn't afraid, and while the clan was clearly a bunch of bastards, there also wasn't the horror from the tower. She felt surprisingly good.

The bandit lord's domicile was a mess. Mostly piles of stolen goods, barrels and crates, pieces of destroyed carts. Mostly it was things the town guards could go through as she didn't have time to sort through it right now. When she got to his bedroom, it changed a little. More cleaned up, trophies of kills mounted on the wall, fine drapes and linens used for bedding. Most importantly, there was a young woman, chained and hanging from a cross beam, her clothing torn haphazardly but otherwise she didn't look abused.

"I'm going to castrate that fucker if he's still alive," Octavia muttered, running up to the girl. "Hey," she said softly, checking her over. "Are you from the town? Do you know where the keys are?"

"Huh," the girl said, then startled, but eased up when she saw Octavia wasn't wearing any of the colors of the bandits, and also appeared clean and taken care of. "Oh, yes, please! No, I don't know where the keys are. Are you here to rescue us? What happened?"

"Yes, we're here to get you out of here." She paused and looked the girl in the eye, her voice careful. "Did he touch you? Have they done anything to you?"

She shook her head. "Not, just a lot of threats and tearing my clothes. He… he promised to make an example of me tonight."

"Well, if he's not dead, he will be before we leave, so no worries there," Octavia said darkly, then started ransacking the room for a key.

"I might need to get someone to get you out if I can't find a key," Octavia said as she rifled through the bedside table, "but I'll cover you first if I do. I mean, we need to wrap you in something to get you out of here regardless, but I promise not to march anyone else in here until we get you covered."

"Just get me out," the girl whimpered. "I'd run out of here naked as long as I was gone from this place!" Thankfully, it didn't seem to be much of a search. Finding a jailor's key among finery turned out pretty easy, especially since it was on a table near the leader's bed.

"Love the practicality," Octavia said, holding up the key, "but thankfully not necessary."

She came over and undid the girl's shackles, easing her down. "Do you feel stable on your feet? Do you have a name?"

"Arms are sore but I can walk," she said, smiling at Octavia, her eyes getting even softer as she gazed upon her rescuer. "Satea."

"Hi Satea," Octavia said, smiling warmly, and she hoped reassuringly. "Hold right there for a moment, I'll get you sorted."

Darting around the room for a moment, Octavia took a sheet from the bed and cut it into a quick wrap dress, then folded the remains of the sheet to use as a shawl. She didn't remember women's fashions in the town very clearly, but she was fairly certain they were on the more conservative side.

"All right, Satea, are you good?" Octavia adjusted the shawl and nodded to herself. "Ready to go?"

"Yeah, I'm good. Thank you. Who *are* you?" she asked, holding the makeshift wrap and shawl close against her.

"My name's Octavia," she said, guiding the girl out of the tent. "Outside are Sumner, Alces, and Durante, and we're here to get you all back to Boxende. Come on, bunny, let's quit this place before the stench of unwashed bastard clings to us." She gave the girl a little squeeze as she bustled the both of them out of there.

"Thank you, Octavia," the girl said and followed close behind her. The way wasn't complicated, and soon Octavia found herself among a gaggle of people and Sumner, who was trying to calm them down and get them to stay together instead of taking off into the tunnel.

"Please, there may still be traps and we want to make sure we have everyone," he said, "you're perfectly safe here, we're taking care of the bandits."

"Hey, shhh shhh shhh," Octavia said as she came up, one arm still around Satea. The charm she'd used on the bandit leader was still active, this crowd should find her fairly persuasive. She released Satea and turned to Sumner.

"I'll take over, this is the sort of thing I'm good at," she said with a smile, that sparkling glow still in her eyes. "Go help clean up. Also, if there's even the slightest chance the leader survived Alces' attack, go castrate him for me, would you?"

"I'd rather not sully my blade, but I'll make damn sure he's down for good," Sumner said, then gave her a kiss on the cheek before running off to help Alces and Durante. The surprise attack and Octavia's mass charm double-cross seemed to be working well, as the noises were starting to die down, but she could still clearly hear Alces' shouts of victory and the reports from Durante's screwshot.

"What's happening?" one person asked.

"Can we leave? Why can't we leave?"

It was a mess, but thankfully it wasn't a massive crowd.

"All right, bunnies, take a breath, please," she said to those gathered, reaching out and setting a gentle hand on the most agitated of the prisoners. "Listen to me. We will leave as soon as we know we will not be followed. Alces and Durante are seeing to that now. We also need to be certain that there are no more traps in the tunnel. We need Sumner for that - I have no doubt many of you are competent and skilled, but you do not have the experience he has." As she spoke, she moved slowly, placing herself between the crowd and the cavemouth.

While her words may not have been penetrating, her demeanor, softspokeness, and her appearance made it very easy for them to at least calm down and follow what she was saying. There was probably more than one crush being formed as well, but that was something to deal with later.

Sumner arrived first, cleaning his sword and sheathing as he did. "Okay, we're good. We just need to wait for the others," he said, grinning slightly. "I'll go ahead and go in, get a head start on any sort of traps. Don't leave until Durante is back to take up the rear."

Sumner disappeared into the tunnel, but at a much more measured pace. Alces arrived a few moments later and clearly looked like he had been in a battle. Blood spattered his armor, arrows were sticking out of his back and shoulders, and his armor looked like it had taken a couple of hits. The crowd stirred when he arrived, a little dubious given his appearance and size.

"Easy, my doves, easy." Octavia walked through, touched shoulders, and ruffled the hair on smaller heads. "This Knight is your champion, the one who felled the bandit leader. He fought for you, and he will make sure we all make it back to Boxende." They were a little awed. But, if she said so, it must be true, and they calmed once more.

Turning to Alces, she winced a little. "Oh, Goddess of Mercy.

Should I pull out arrows while we wait or leave it until we get them back to the town?"

Alces grinned and shook his head. "No, caring Octavia, we shall tend to it later. Evil has been thwarted this day. It will be quite some time before the Black Crag Clan returns, if they ever do," he said, reassuring the group.

Durante suddenly dropped down next to Octavia, slinging his screwshot. "Okay, they're scattered and no one is following," he said, smiling at Octavia. There was a little stir, but at this point the crowd accepted that they were in an okay place, and these warriors, odd as their appearance was, were their saviors.

Octavia nodded and smiled in return. "All right. Sumner said we could go once you were here to watch the rear. If Alces goes ahead, I'll stick myself sort of in the middle to help keep track of everyone."

"Sounds like a plan," he said, moving towards the entrance but waiting.

"We are set. Come, my dear friends, let us away home. Carefully, and don't crowd up. The tunnel is dark and dangerous, but we will lead you through," Alces said, smiling and forming a bright ball of light in his hand. He set it on his shoulder, so that it would light up what was behind him as well as ahead, and started to move towards the tunnel.

In contrast to Octavia's charm, she noticed the three children, two boys and a girl, flocked to Alces and stuck close to him as he started to walk into the tunnel. It was no surprise that the children ran to him. She found herself smiling as they did. The rest filed in slowly, with Satea right next to her as they went, and finally Durante taking up the rear.

She helped shuttle people in, let Satea hold her hand, and kept a hand on the shoulder of a young man who had proven a little volatile. The ball of light made the tunnel significantly more pleasant to traverse. The trip through was much quicker this time. Most of the traps had already been dealt with. In fact, Sumner only found two that he'd missed because they were meant for people travelling the other direction. Soon enough, they found themselves in the late afternoon air of the canyon, a few hours away from home.

"We only have one more worry now," Alces said as people stretched and felt more at ease. "If one of the Black Crags ran to the Grummorks. However, even if they did, they won't get organized and after us before we get to Boxende."

"Good, because I'm out of mana, and while there's a solution to that, it requires fewer witnesses," Octavia muttered, smiling wryly.

Turning back towards the group, Octavia clapped her hands for attention. "All right, my doves! Home isn't far, but it's a bit of a walk, and we want the daylight. Let's keep moving! If you get tired, let us know."

There was a quiet chorus of acceptance, and they began to make their way out of the canyon.

TWENTY ONE

The walk back was a long one for the captives, but they made it without too much of an issue. By the time they reached the gates of Boxende all three of the kids were either riding on Alces' shoulders or being carried by him. Three of the more delicate women were on Nutmeg's back.

As they approached, the gates opened without prompting, and the guards rushed out amidst excited shouts. It was a strange melange of emotions. Octavia had helped people before, but there was only one of her. She'd helped a family, a shopkeeper, a parent. She'd never had the gates joyously flung open for her. She felt strangely uncomfortable.

The commotion brought forth friends and family all coming out to tearfully join their lost loved ones. The guard Octavia noticed before they left charged down the tower and scooped up Satea, hugging her close. "Oh, you found my daughter. Thank you!"

Octavia smiled at Satea's father. "I saw the hope on your face when we left," she admitted, a little awkwardly. "I'm glad we could bring everyone back."

"I can't thank you enough," he said, kissing Satea on the cheek and reaching out to squeeze Octavia's hand in thanks.

Most of the others went off with their loved ones after they'd all come back to say thank you and to congratulate them. Alces was beaming throughout, reassuring them and announcing the veritable dismantling of the Black Crags, explaining to the guard chief how they had routed the bandit clan and killed their leader. Octavia overheard a reward being put together, and an assurance that they were no longer expected to move on in two days.

Alces nudged Octavia. "Now you shall see how we celebrate. Right after I get this armor off and these arrows out of me, they're starting to sting."

"Yes, if we could, please," Octavia said, motioning back towards the inn. "Goddess of Mercy, Alces. And maybe wash the blood off? Just a thought."

"Well, yes, that's the easy part," he laughed then winced slightly. With the trip done, people mostly spreading out, and adrenalin starting to wear off, Alces would be feeling the wounds by then.

Sighing, Octavia ran a hand over her face. The adrenaline had washed out of her as well, and she was feeling a little unsettled. She was worried about Alces, even though he was clearly mostly fine. Durante had remained somewhere on the ridge the entire time—the bandits had thought that his shots were her castings. She'd gotten a good look at Sumner, he was fine. Comicha had popped away after telling Alces where the prisoners were. Everyone was all right, and they were victorious.

"Come on, big guy, let's get you patched up," Durante said and they all walked back to the inn. They had several people celebrating, including the innkeeper, who was talking animatedly with a woman holding one of the children they rescued. It turned out the little girl was his granddaughter.

"Whatever you want, on the house! Rooms are free," he said when they walked in, smiling and gesturing towards the dining hall.

"Soon, my good man. Get the fires on, we are starved," Alces said with a grin, then headed upstairs to his room. Octavia let Durante see to Alces—clearly they already knew what to do—and headed into her own room to check herself in the mirror and make sure she didn't also have stray blood anywhere.

Other than dust and grit, Octavia had gotten away rather untouched. Most of the bandits she had dealt with were hit by spells that didn't exactly promote rapid blood loss, and no one had touched her. Their plan of creating a distraction and then using that distraction to create a bigger distraction, went off rather well.

She peeled off her clothes and poured water into the basin to clean the dust off of her. She undid her hair and let it fall down her shoulders again. She considered her clothing - if this was going to be a celebration, she should wear something more fun, perhaps. Not the princess dress—

that needed a grander setting or purpose. She pulled out her clothes from Rupaiya, deciding on a skirt—the first skirt anyone would have seen her in—another cropped top with heavy embroidery at the sleeves and the bottom hem, and a long, sheer wrap that was pinned to one shoulder. The gauzy fabric technically covered her midsection, but the outline was clear to see. Sliding into what had essentially become her house slippers, Octavia stepped back into the hall. Maybe she'd see how the boys were doing.

Sumner was already out in the hall, leaning against a wall as he was looking into Alces' room. When Octavia came out, he looked over and his brows lifted. "Well, hey there, beautiful. Don't you clean up nice," he said with a grin. "Good job out there. Threw us for a loop, but you bought me time, since I knew you could handle yourself."

"Alces or someone had said something about creating a distraction," she said with a shrug, gliding over to him. "I haven't used that spell in...a while. I'm not often in situations where I need to do something about that many people. Though I'm guessing that may change." She smiled at him wryly.

"Oh, I'm sure you'll handle many people quite often," he said with a smirk.

She arched a brow at him. "I am not sure if I should be offended by that."

"And here I thought you liked us," Sumner said under his breath but was still smirking.

"Well, that could have been worse," Durante said as he stepped out of the room, wiping off his hands. "He'll be out in a minute, he's getting dressed."

Turning around, Octavia looked at Durante and felt a tension unwind from her shoulders. "Good. I suppose that sort of thing happens often?"

"Considering he refuses to let anyone get hurt, yes," Durante said with a sigh. "Half of my time is making healing salves and medicinal wraps for him. The platemail takes the brunt of it, but stuff still gets through. I think that battle would have been drawn out a lot more if you hadn't softened up and distracted that damn bull. You really did a number on him."

"Well, I can be very charming when I need to be," she said with a little smile. "Though can we work on a "anytime now, please" whistle or signal for me if we do that again? I mean, it all worked out very well this time, but some people aren't as easily taken in."

"Yeah, whatever you want," Durante said with a shrug, "I had you covered. Once the shouting started, Alces was already on his way."

She nodded to Durante. "They thought your shots were something I was doing, they weren't even looking for you."

"But that surprise, oof," Sumner said, shaking his head, "I'm honestly shocked it didn't pop his head off."

Alces stepped out of the room, looking freshly washed and not a drop of blood was on him. He was in a loose tunic and breeches and appeared about as comfortable as he could be while still getting ready to be seen in public.

Glancing over at Alces, she smiled. "Feeling better, Ser Knight?"

"I feel fantastic," he said with a grin. "Captives saved, bandits routed, town celebrating. How much better can it get? Oh, yes, a feast downstairs. Come, let us soak in the glory!"

"And that's our cue," Sumner said, motioning towards the stairs. "Now is your final test, Tavi. Alcohol tolerance."

"This is going to go so poorly for me," Octavia said with a sigh, but followed down the stairs.

It turned out that little Boxende was more of a happening place than had first been described now that the crisis was over. Now this was a proper celebration. This is what the three of them had been alluding to. Townspeople were happy, the guards were happy, the innkeeper, his daughter, and his granddaughter were keeping the food going and the ale flowing. The entire sense of the town had changed, and Octavia could feel the light that Alces always referred to.

Speaking of, the great knight was regaling the guards with the tale of their adventure, from the dark cave of treacherous traps, to the mass seduction of the bandits by Octavia and her spells which laid waste to those that dared to get near her. Mention was made of Durante's crack shooting from the canyon wall, sewing chaos among the bandit ranks how they were being struck down unseen. He stretched out the fight with the bandit lord, adding in more exchanges, especially with Octavia's ploy with faux innocence to draw him in.

Sumner jumped in from his current chatting up of some of the women who were there to remind everyone of his quick, nimble fingers that undid all of their locks and shackles and the way he escorted them away from the camp. Of course, everyone agreed that he had done his part quite well, and they may have been caught in the melee without his help.

People were enamored and fascinated, and Octavia had more than a few of the people they had rescued offering her drinks, food, and companionship. They also asked for more stories about what she had done, if she had been afraid, how she became such a powerful warlock, and so on.

Octavia found herself sitting on a table so that more people could crowd around her. She let people bring her drinks and food, though she didn't try to throw back those drinks too quickly—she already knew she would end up drunk before the end of the night, so there was no reason to rush.

At first, she demurred; she spoke of Alces' fierceness, Durante's precision, and Sumner's stealth and swiftness. By her third drink, though, she started to talk about how the bandit leader had towered over her, and she had pretended that she was out of spells and afraid for her life. How he had threatened to ravish her and pass her among his clan, and she'd feigned helplessness before striking and running because she knew the others would come.

Somewhere in the back of the hall, people started playing music. This brought out something Octavia didn't ever think she'd witness: Alces dancing. A lot. With anyone. It was enthusiastic, it was energetic and, yes, furniture was broken.

Durante, the only one who was sipping his one glass of wine despite offers, kept assuring the innkeeper that they would fix or pay for anything destroyed. The keeper seemed weary, but after Alces' demonstrated that he could clean up after himself—in this case, by magically fixing a chair whose leg he had snapped off—the man seemed less tense. The chair was almost immediately rebroken when Alces twirled and put his foot through it.

Sumner was being an absolute dog; drinking, hitting on anything with curves but not making any promises, and challenging people to drinking contests and various tavern games. The night was still relatively young. It seemed every now and then his anger would spike, but a look from Alces or a word from Durante, and he'd nod, apologize immediately, and start to calm down. It was a very strange ebb and flow, but it also made it relatively easy to deal with.

Octavia was getting everyone's eye and attention. By this point in the evening, Octavia was another two drinks in, though she had eaten to try to ease her intoxication a little. Satea had come back and stayed right by Octavia's side when she could. But girls gossip, as they do, and they started asking Octavia about the men she traveled with. Some of them were women that Sumner had hit on, and they were very curious about what Octavia knew.

"So," one woman with midnight hair said, leaning in, "have you... *known* any of your companions?"

Octavia arched an eyebrow. "Known... oh! You mean have I slept with them! Yes."

The blonde next to the other woman giggled. "Which ones?"

"All of them, obviously," Octavia gestured to the room with her drink. "If you are presented with a feast, you do not only eat the roast, and I don't care how good it is."

All the women around her erupted into scandalized giggles, so much that a couple others in the room got curious and came closer. Midnight leaned in again.

"So what about Sumner?" she asked. "What's he like? Worth the time?"

"My dearest girl, they are *all* worth the time," Octavia said with authority. She straightened up, and cast off her shawl. "Ahem. Now then. The question is, are any of them what you're hoping for? So. Who likes it rough? Be honest, no one is helped by lying right now."

There was another scandalized titter all around, but after a minute Midnight, a ginger girl on the edge of the circle, and a brunette on the other side of Satea raised their hands.

"Excellent!" The exclamation was perhaps a little too excited and loud, but no one was bothered at this point in the night. "You three will have a lovely time with Sumner. Happy hunting, may the best girl win, or if you can work it out amongst the three of you, everyone can win! Trust me, he has the stamina for it. Off you go!"

Well, with that sort of permission granted, the three girls in question strolled off to see if they could get their claws into Sumner. Given what she'd observed already, at least one would definitely have him this night.

The tone of Alces' dance changed once the parents of the children had decided that the evening was getting to be a little too enthusiastic, and lubricated, for them to be around. They whined at having to leave 'the big hero dragon' but they eventually gave in as sleep was beginning to take them. Now some of the girls were looking forward to getting twirled and tossed around like they weighed nothing.

"So... what about the dragonkin?" Blondie asked after her friend had wandered off. "He seems...well, intimidating, maybe... but surely if you've been with him…?"

"Oh, Goddess of Mercy, no, he would destroy you," Octavia said, setting down her glass. "Sweet girl, you who have lived in this delightful hamlet have never known the absolute pummeling necessary to prepare you for such a thing." Laughter roared around her—it seemed her theatrics had gained an audience.

"However!" Octavia continued, "If you are taken in by strong, dashing men who are gallant and will give you the most delightful of evenings, even if you are incapable of sheathing that sword, I still highly recommend him."

Blondie looked at Alces thoughtfully, as did another dark haired girl. As they both stood up at the same time, they looked at each other, and sort of nodded in some understanding Octavia was too drunk to discern, then headed over to join the dragonkin's line of dancing partners.

"So what about the noble?" another redhead asked. "He's very quiet, but seems comely enough."

"Oh, he's delightful," Octavia said with a smile, "but very shy. Needs a firm hand and patience."

The girl smiled. "I think I can do that."

"Wonderful." Octavia smiled brightly, then looked at Red critically. "Don't call him Kitten, though. Only I can call him that. I will hunt you down if you try."

The redhead laughed, and promised she wouldn't, before heading in Durante's direction.

Octavia's ring of admirers had thinned a bit—most of them having been sent off to entertain her companions—so she got up off her table for a little while. She had a dance with Alces, laughing as he tossed her into the air and twirled her about. Even drunk, Octavia moved with an enviable grace. She chatted up the musicians and sang along with them for a few songs, her voice floating through the inn. She danced on her own, and with anyone who came up and asked.

She also kissed a half dozen pretty girls and two of the young men. She made out in a corner with Satea, going as far as to reach up the woman's skirt and bring her to orgasm as they passionately kissed. She did the same for an aggressively flirty woman named Inaya after a very drunk Satea had to be escorted home. She flirted shamelessly and left more than one person aching with want. She could feel that Kamvasana was very happy with her.

And yet, as the last of the revelers were leaving, and Alces, Sumner, and Durante had already retired with their partners, Octavia found herself drifting into her rooms alone, gently refusing the last handful of attempts to accompany her. She closed the door behind her and leaned back against it, listening to the sounds of ecstasy from across the hall and sighed.

Comicha popped into existence in front of her. "Um, Mistress, are you okay?"

"Probably not," Octavia answered, taking off her dress. Her shawl was still downstairs somewhere. Oh well, a problem for the morning. "I need to not make a habit of sending them all off with someone after a party. Especially if...if they're what I want."

"You liiiiiiike them," Comicha said, giggling. Octavia's drunkenness was affecting her familiar.

"I do," Octavia conceded. "It's leaving me unsettled and uncertain of a great many things."

The doors of the inn muffled the sounds across the hall a little, but not completely. Octavia lay in bed and started to touch herself. She could hear each of their voices if she concentrated. Alces' shout. Sumner's growl. Durante's moan. She ran her hands over her body, imaging the feel of each of them individually, and also together.

"Mistress," Comicha said, a desperate little whine in her voice, "may I? Please?"

"Yes," Octavia murmured, and spread her legs. The eager imp was on the bed in a second, feasting on a pussy that was dripping from a night of teasing. Comicha rang two orgasms out of Octavia, but they were climaxes that ended in quiet whimpers rather than ecstatic shouts. Comicha left her mistress to fall into exhausted, drunken sleep.

Morning came quietly. Given the drunken revelry of last night, there was a really good chance she was the first to rise as it was definitely early. Things had calmed down. No music, no voices, just the sound of birds outside and some foot traffic. Nothing was planned for this day except maybe some shopping. With their restriction lifted, and the inn being effectively free for the foreseeable future, this would be the laziest day she'd had since joining the group.

Octavia threw on her the low, soft pants she typically wore around the tent and the top that went with them, and fished out one of those small sapphires from her trunk, then headed out. She felt a little lonely, but she wasn't upset - she had very literally done it to herself, after all. She hoped they all had a fun night.

Coming downstairs, Octavia found the innkeeping leaning against the wall and looking into the dining hall, arms crossed. Looking past him, she saw Alces tending to the furniture that had been broken last night, using his magic to make the chairs and two of the tables like new.

Turning, the keeper looked at Octavia and smiled gently. "Ah, the well behaved one. How're you this morning?" he asked.

Octavia snickered, unable to help it. "I'm not sure I'd say well behaved, perhaps more contained," she said with a little smile. "And I'm well, thank you. I was hoping for a bath? Also..." she reached out and took the man's hand, turning it over and setting the sapphire in it. "For your troubles. I appreciate your want to thank us, but they're a wild bunch and it shouldn't put you out."

Taking the sapphire, the innkeeper shook his head and smiled. "I'm only taking this because you insist, but the value of having my granddaughter back, safe, is worth more than a hundred of these. Thank you again. Yes, we have a small bath house in the back," he said, pushing off the wall and leading her back towards a doorway that was under the stairs to a back outdoor area.

There were some stone basins that had been sculpted into the sandstone with a set of sluices set into the wall. "The water comes in naturally from the river that runs through the canyon. I'll get the coals ready to warm the water. You could have breakfast if you want to wait," he smiled and nodded a little. "It takes a while, but I think it's worth it."

"That looks lovely," she said, smiling a little more genuinely. "And yes, happy to wait for a nicer bath. I'll go find an unbroken table and wait for breakfast."

"Very good. Just let Reyan know, and she'll get you fed," he said, crouching down to work on starting a fire under a metal plate that was covered in river stones.

She headed back inside, finding Reyan and requesting breakfast and tea before going back into the dining hall. Reyan didn't let Octavia go without a kiss on each cheek and a hug. It was her daughter that they rescued, after all, and she didn't normally work at the inn but she wanted to pay them back in whatever way she could. She promised a breakfast they wouldn't soon forget.

Octavia retrieved the shawl from the night before and wrapped it around herself before settling at a table clear of the carnage but close enough to talk with Alces should he wish to chat. Alces turned as she came in, grinning broadly.

"There's my magnanimous Octavia," he said, not quite as loudly as he had been known for. "You look beautiful as always. How was your evening?"

"Very pleasant," she said, smiling. "It was quite a celebration. It gives credence to Sumner's stories. How about you? How was your night?"

"Absolutely delightful," he said, giving her a nod. "It was very sweet of you to lead those women my way. We had a wonderful time, if I do say so myself. You can ask them whenever they wake up." Alces laughed and reached over, squeezing her hand. "How many did you share your delightful light with last night?"

"Oh! Um, I didn't take anyone to bed last night." She smiled a little awkwardly. For some reason, she hadn't imagined they would ask. "I danced, and sang, and kissed a number of charming people, but went to bed alone."

"You must have decided to do that, because I know there were many who would have gone happily," he said, then considered it a little farther. "Is everything okay? Were you injured and did not tell me because you felt my injuries were more severe? I can guarantee any scratch to you is much more of a worry than any arrow or blade that's struck me."

Octavia laughed softly and shook her head. "No, nothing was wrong. I just... the people I wanted in my bed were busy. And while there were several very charming offers, my...heart wasn't in it." She shrugged. "And you do not do that to another person. If you cannot give yourself without reservation, you don't give yourself. At least, I don't."

"To my understanding, you did for the others what you did for me," he said, picking up a cracked chair leg and adhering it to the chair it belonged to with his magic, "I certainly hope you weren't overly generous and directed one of those wonderful ladies to us when you wished to keep them company."

Snickering again, Octavia leaned forward on the table and propped her chin in her hand. "Not one of them, no."

"Well, whoever it was, you should snag them first before sharing," he said, setting the fixed chair down and reaching over to squeeze her hand. "You deserve all the happiness, and I will do whatever I can to ensure that. You just tell me how I can be your light."

"You are adorable," Octavia said, giggling.

Anything more was interrupted when Reyan returned with the breakfast she promised. It was thick slices of pan-fried ham, honeyed porridge with berries, fresh baked bread rolls, creamy butter, and wheels of a soft, sweet cheese. "For my heroes. Eat up," she said upon presentation.

"Oh, Reyan, this is the most beautiful breakfast I've seen in a long time," she said sincerely. "Thank you so much."

"Adept cuisinier Reyan," Alces began grandly, "your morning meal is a gift from the Spree Spirits themselves, and I look forward to eating it with much aplomb." The woman blushed and gave a little curtsey, then disappeared back into the kitchens.

Serving herself a small bowl of the porridge, Octavia took a bite as she looked at Alces again. "I would never be so gauche as to make demands on any of you on a night of celebration," she said as she gave the porridge a little stir. "I wanted you to do what you wanted to do. That you were all happy is all that mattered." Well, mostly, at least.

Alces looked at her for a moment, then realization crept in. "By the brightest light, Octavia, I am sure I speak for everyone when I say if you wanted to celebrate with one of us, that would have been wonderful. I will keep that in mind for next time. It would not be a demand in the least, and your happiness matters as much as ours. I told you, all I ever want from you is honesty, and that includes your feelings. Emotions can be tender, delicate things and if we can strengthen them, nurture them, enrich them then it should be done."

Sighing, Octavia poured herself a cup of tea. "I... care for you. The three of you. More than I have anyone. I'm not sure what to do about it, but it is not something I will burden you with."

"Once more, it is not a burden," he said, sitting down and taking a slice of ham. "We care for you as well. I'm sure they will say the same. You have not only shared yourself with us, you have proven yourself a smart, skillful, caring, and stalwart companion. I know you're going to say that I'd say this to anyone, and while I may to a far lesser extent, for you I mean it completely and to its fullest."

She looked at Alces with gentle skepticism but didn't comment further, sipping her tea and finishing her porridge. She also snagged a roll and covered it in an almost worrying amount of cheese drizzled with honey.

"It is fair that you don't believe me, loud and ruckus as I tend to be, but I am honest and true, and if you ever wish to burden me, know that I am here for you." Alces reached over and ran a hand through her hair, cupping her cheek. Her eyes closed as she leaned into his touch, turning her head enough to kiss his palm.

"Alas, I had furniture to attend to." Smiling, he leaned over and kissed her forehead. Standing up, he devoured the ham in one bite and knelt down next to a table that had been split in half and got to work. Octavia remained quiet and worked on breakfast.

There was a slow trickle of people coming down the stairs. First, it was Midnight and Ginger, two of the three women that she had sent after Sumner, then Blondie and the darker haired girl that had tackled Alces. Those two swung in long enough to giggle and kiss Alces and caress his horns before waving goodbye. Sumner eventually followed and entered the room at the same time as the innkeeper, who had come to tell Octavia the bath was ready.

"Damn, Tavi, how'd you find those," Sumner started, then got a little quieter knowing the keeper was right there, "fine young ladies that kept me company."

"I'm old, not stupid," the keeper said, shaking his head, "and as long as I don't have more furniture to fix, you all can have as much fun as you want as long as everyone agrees."

Octavia put a hand to her mouth to stifle her laughter, and looked up at the innkeeper before addressing Sumner. "Thank you, sir," she said. "I'll finish breakfast and be out."

After the innkeeper retreated she looked back at Sumner and shrugged. "Women talk. Some of the *many* women you approached last night asked my ... opinion about you. I did a quick canvas of the group and sent the three most likely to be happy with you in your direction." She poured herself another cup of tea.

"Well, you did amazing. You're welcome to join in next time," he said with a grin and a wink. Sitting down he picked up a roll and started to examine it. "How'd your night go? Who were the lucky guys or gals?"

"My night involved a lot of drinking and flirting, followed by a lot of sleeping," she said, looking amused. Apparently this was the normal post-celebratory conversation. "I went to bed alone."

Sumner was in mid-bite when he glanced over at her, more than a little stunned. "Why?" he asked flatly. It wasn't meant to be rude, he was just surprised.

Sighing, she looked at him for a moment. "Because you all were busy," she finally said, just as flatly, and popped the last bit of her roll into her mouth.

"Well, shit, definitely join in next time," he said, and set the roll down before tearing it open and helping himself to the cheese.

"Um, no, I am no one's afterthought or add on," Octavia said, picking up her tea. "You want to play with someone together and approach me first about it, fine, but you're not tacking me on after the fact." She finished her tea and set the cup down.

"Oh, no, oh Shadows, no, Tavi, I didn't mean it like that," he said, suddenly very embarrassed, looking up from his breakfast. "I'm so sorry."

"Good." She looked over at Sumner and sighed. "My beautiful storm. I'm glad you didn't mean it that way, because I was preparing myself to be offended and a bit hurt. More than a bit, probably. Instead, I will go take my bath and deal with my messy emotions privately." She rose to her feet and moved around the table, pausing to drop a kiss on his head.

Sumner caught her hand before she could leave and gave it a squeeze, kissing it gently. "You're amazing, don't forget that," he said, then let her go. She managed a smile, and headed upstairs.

It seemed the one she wouldn't have to chat with first was Durante, who hadn't made his appearance yet. Not needing to be up, it might be noon before she saw him. It was a relief, in truth. Sumner's careless comments had roiled something in her, and she was bothered by how upset she was. He had even apologized, made it clear it was a misunderstanding, and she was still upset! Where was the logic in that?

Grumbling quietly to herself, she fetched her things and then headed out to the baths as quickly as she could manage without looking like she was bothered.

TWENTY TWO

Heading back through the inn, arms full of bathing supplies, Octavia saw Sumner chatting with Alces, who looked to be done fixing the furniture and was eating. They were having a quiet conversation but it seemed serious. She would leave them to it.

The bath was filled with water from the sluices and the river rocks that had been fired were sitting in the bath, warming the water to a very toasty level. There were more rocks available, should she need a little more heat, and she could open the sluices to cool it down.

Octavia got herself in the water in record time, and then let out a sigh as the hot water seeped into her limbs. She let herself stew over her feelings. She had never felt this vulnerable before, and she did not enjoy it. Maybe traveling with them wasn't a good idea.

And yet...the way Alces had cupped her face this morning, and been so insistent that he would have happily spent the night with her. The way Sumner had kissed her cheek when they were freeing everyone. The way Durante smiled at her and had even teased her a little yesterday. She felt that strangeness in her stomach as she tumbled through those memories and others of the past week. It was like the tingling in her hands before she cast a spell, but with no way to expel it. It just lived inside her, growing in her chest, threatening to explode, but...into what?

"What is wrong with me," she muttered. Grumbling again, she sat up to grab the tongs and toss in another rock, then let the heat ease her muscles and a measure of her anxiety.

Eventually she got around to actually washing herself and moving through her usual routines. The water was soothing and soft, which made her soaps all the better at making her touchable and smell delightful. She'd have to remember this place, as they would certainly remember her. Breakfast was assuredly over by the time she was dressed and heading back inside to put all her things away. Tumultuous emotions aside, she did feel better, and was back to smelling like spiced honey rather than the dirt encrusted sweat of the road.

All three of the guys were in the dining area now, snacking on some leftover bread. It looked much better, in fact it didn't look like a raucous party had occurred in the least. Durante smiled up at her and patted the seat next to him.

"Good... almost noon, Tavi," he said with a shy smile. "Sorry I'm up so late."

She smiled. "Glad you got to rest for once. Let me drop these off, I'll be right back."

She darted up to her room and left everything on top of the trunk. She would deal with it later. A quick glance in the mirror, a sigh for her ridiculous vanity, and she was back downstairs and sitting down where Durante had indicated.

"Did they refill the tea?" she asked as she sat, pulling in her seat and settling herself.

"Asked for a fresh pot just for you," Sumner said and Alces nodded.

Smiling shyly, Durante reached out and gently patted her thigh. "So, anything you want to shop for today?" he asked as he nibbled on a little sandwich he had made from the rolls, ham, and cheese.

She smiled at Durante, encouragingly. "An iron teapot for travel, if there's one to be had," she said as she poured herself a cup. "And tea to go with it. Those are my big hopes for the moment."

"You wanted me to make tarts, yes?" Alces asked. "I will need the ingredients for that. Anything else you desire on our travels so that I can make sure I have what you need?"

Octavia shrugged. "I'm fairly flexible, and I understand that you all hunt and forage a fair bit. I like cheeses, fruit, and baked goods. I have enjoyed the meat heavy diet, though."

"I will be more adventurous. While I do not hold my breath for there being an array of spices here, some is better than none," Alces said.

"Honestly, being able to sleep in a bit and not go hunting first thing in the morning would certainly be appreciated," Sumner snickered.

"We can load up the ice box in the tent," she said, picking up her cup and holding it in both hands, letting the warmth spread through them. The room felt a little cool after the bath. "As far as I can tell, time doesn't exist for the tent when it's not in use, so anything packed in there should last a good while."

"Have I told you recently what a delight it is to have you with us," Alces said with a grin. "Being able to be on the road and cook proper meals! Blessed light."

She smiled indulgently at him. "I feel like that's the tent, not me, but I'm glad it makes you happy." She sipped her tea.

"Nonsense," Alces said, waving his hand. "The tent is just an object, the company is what's valuable. Sure, we could get a tent, but it wouldn't be the same. Not nearly as cheerful."

"It's true," Durante said with a nod.

She let out a soft laugh. "If you say so," she murmured, looking down into her tea again. "Though we should probably be about it, then. Shops aren't open all night and I'm not sure what else you've already discussed needing to find."

"If you are done with your tea, then we are ready to go. But there is no rush, as they're not kicking us out tomorrow," Alces said with a grin.

"That does make things easier," she commented, and finished her cup. "I can be done now. I'm sure I'll have more whenever we decide to have lunch." She set her cup down and rose to her feet.

"To the market, then," Alces said and stood, the rest following suit. Sumner snuck in and gave her a kiss on the cheek and a sneak squeeze on her butt, then skipped ahead of the group, waltzing out with his hands behind his head. She let out a small laugh as Sumner skipped off. Hopefully that meant that all was well between them. Her emotions still felt a little raw, but she wasn't sure that there was an easy answer for that.

As they moved to leave, Durante offered Octavia his arm and a gentle smile. Either he'd been told the conversation that had occurred, or he was quieter after a night like that. She blinked in surprise but smiled so warmly at him as she took his arm.

"I missed you coming down," she said quietly as they walked towards the market. "Did you have a good night? The redhead, was she good to you, or do I need to go tear her hair out?" She kept her smile, so that he would know she was joking. Or at least believe she was joking, because Octavia was certain she would take vengeance if he said otherwise.

"She was very nice. A little more demanding than I'm used to, but she wasn't mean about it. You're nicer, though," he said with a smile, squeezing her hand, "and far more lovely."

She smiled and kissed his cheek.

It was a relatively short walk to the market. While it certainly wasn't anywhere near the largest Octavia had seen, it wasn't bad. There was a fair bit of trade between here and the Fort on the other side, given they were owned by different kingdoms, so it was difficult to tell how good the prices were.

Finding a tea pot was a simple matter. Octavia even found one that was etched with serpents and vines. A lovely piece of work. Tea was a little harder to find, but eventually Octavia found a stall that had a few samples. That's about all it was, too. Samples for a trader that lived a few leagues away. She cleaned out their meager stock—maybe the inn might sell her a small tin's worth if she asked nicely. She tried to pay for the pot and tea, but Sumner waved her off and saw to it. Apparently, tea for mornings was an acceptable expense.

She also kept her eyes open for anything unusual or different. She'd learned some time ago that you could find the oddest things in smaller markets; items that a local had unearthed but wasn't certain of its value, shawls from weavers who were as gifted as any clothier in the cities or perhaps more so, local sweets that never became popular enough to sell elsewhere but were delightful and different.

The guys were also a lot more loose in the market. Alces was a discerning gourmet, trying fruits and vegetables, examining cuts of meat, gently sniffing spices. More than once he fed Octavia a fruit or some other delicacy to see if she liked it. He also purchased a number of treats the other two really enjoyed. Sumner had a penchant for these small spice cakes that were strong with cinnamon while Durante preferred dates that were stuffed with mincemeat.

Sumner was the money keeper, and during this particular event he didn't seem very stingy. At least when things weren't overly extravagant. Aside from that, he seemed more free. Occasionally cartwheeling, juggling fruit while he waited for Alces to choose something, and sneaking in a squeeze any time Octavia bent over, whether to pick something up or look over items at a stall.

Durante was more to Octavia's level as to what was interesting. Fine clothes and local artisan works. Together they did find a local leather smith that made gloves and harnesses for climbing, as well as satchels that crossed one's chest. Durante convinced Sumner to let him buy one, where he could keep bottles and charges for his screwshot in a much more convenient location.

Octavia's find was a jeweler that specialized in necklaces and pendants containing a rare crystal that, they claimed, could only be found in a cave within the canyon. It was a pale blue that seemed to swirl in the light. If their story was true, the Black Crags probably would have made a lot more money, and less enemies, if they just mined that out. Octavia held up one of the necklaces, one where the pendant dropped on a single chain down into the cleavage with smaller beads acting as catches to control the length. She twisted it around so that the light could catch it, oohing and aahing appreciatively, but set it back down. She technically didn't need any more jewelry, and she'd already gotten her teapot.

She enjoyed the market trip with them, seeing them be more themselves. It would be fun to be in an actual city at some point, should they all remain together long enough to make it to one. She wished this strange anxiety would see itself out.

Lunch was decided because Alces was hungry. They were able to find a nice place that catered to travelers and had simple, filling meals. Alces needed to order at least one of each just for himself. Octavia ordered a juice drink mixed with a light wine that seemed to be from the area, and something a little lighter for lunch after everything Alces had her try. Durante ordered the same, wanting to try Octavia's meal. Sumner got a meat and cheese plate that they offered. Alces insisted everyone at least try some of what he ordered if it looked good.

After lunch, they went towards the more serious shopping. Alces needed his tools tended to and Sumner needed some new arrows fletched and looked at some light armor. Durante needed alchemical components, gems (which seemed to make Sumner wince from the cost), and scrap metal from the smiths for his own workings.

Octavia looked over the alchemical ingredients and picked up a few. Most of what she needed to cast spells for Kamvasana, however, were based on old recipes. She mostly used sands and powders, and she had to make them herself. Well, Comicha helped.

Octavia did offer to sacrifice some sapphires for the greater good if Durante could use them. After all, they cost her nothing material, just a very long night of hard work. She'd already tested them, their origin wouldn't flavor whatever they were used for. Durante made it very clear that if she did offer the sapphires, he'd owe her. It was very open ended, because he didn't clarify past that.

It was a long day shopping, but Sumner had some new gear, Alces was happy with what would become a very full pantry in the tent, and Durante had plenty to experiment with for their future endeavors. Dinner was approaching, and Alces was content with heading back to the inn.

Arriving back at the inn, Octavia headed upstairs to deposit her tea prizes and change back into her lounging clothes for the evening. Perhaps it was presumptuous, but she didn't have a problem staying there for the rest of the night. She was sure this town had a tavern outside of the inn, but maybe she could explore that if they stayed another night. Instead, she changed back into her soft pants and her short velvet top.

Opening the door, Octavia saw Sumner in the hall, seemingly waiting for her. "Before we go down for dinner, I wanted to talk. Do you mind?"

"Oh!" She blinked in surprise but smiled at him and stepped back, motioning for him to come in. "Of course. I mean, I don't mind." She closed the door and sat down on the bed, which she had thankfully made. "What did you need?" She felt anxiety twist in her again.

"No, no, up," he said with a smile and offered her his hand. When Octavia stood, he twirled her playfully, pulling her close so her back was to him and her arm crossed in his. She sank back into his arms, unable to help herself.

"I have been told that I spoke poorly," he said gently in her ear, his hands moving to hold her hips, "my meaning was unclear, and I hurt your feelings. For that, I am sorry. I've been learning to apologize for my wrong doings."

"Oh, you don't—"

Sumner lightly pressed his fingertips to her lips. "Shhh. I'm not done." He nipped gently at her ear, just a little thing, as his hands glided up her back, caressing her gently. "So, this time, I want to make sure I'm very clear. You are an amazing woman. Possibly the best I've ever known or been with." Sumner's hands came up to cup her breasts, squeezing and pressing her against him. She trembled and gasped.

"You would never be an add-on or after thought. You would be my partner and reveler," he continued, releasing his grip but still caressing her skin, all the up to her neck where the pendant on a single chain, with smaller beads acting as catches, was held between his hands. She drew in a sharp breath in surprise. Just as softly, he slid the necklace around her neck and latched it, kissing her on the back of her neck right above where it rested.

"I do hope you accept my sincerest apology and this gift," Sumner said, taking her hips and gently turning her around to face him. "When we celebrate, we celebrate with the people, should they be amiable. I would never leave you out or ignore you."

Speechless for a moment, Octavia looked up at him. She had a glowing, rosy blush and her eyes were shining almost like she might be trying not to cry. She reached up and gently touched the pendant with her fingertips, looking down at it. She then reached up and cupped Sumner's face, kissing him deeply.

"I... of course I forgive you," she said softly as they parted. "I don't... Goddess of Mercy. I told Alces, I care more about the three of you than I have anyone I've ever known. I know you didn't leave me out last night. How could you, I sent them to you! I... wanted to give you what you wanted. But as the night went on, I started to realize that I... that I just..."

She laughed and shook her head, letting go of him and letting her hands fall to his shoulders. "I didn't want to make any of you deal with this, with me. But I feel this flutter beneath my ribs any time you're sweet to me, and it..." She trailed off and shook her head. She didn't have the words.

Sumner smiled gently, probably one of the few soft, gentle smiles he'd given her, and cupped her cheek. "You're with us now, which means we're dealing with that, with you, and happily," he said, then smirked. "So, you get first dibs. Or rather, I'll check with you to see what you want for the night next time we celebrate. I know the rules for the other nights already." Leaning in, he kissed her, long and tender. "Unless you decide otherwise, I think you're stuck with us."

She let out a soft laugh, and one tear slid down her cheek, which Sumner brushed away with his thumb. She felt her heart squeeze and held tight to him. "Does this mean you're free after dinner?"

"For you, I can make time," he said with a grin, and gave her rump a squeeze.

"Good." She kissed him again, more heated this time, not pulling back until she couldn't breathe. "We... we should head downstairs, probably."

"Before someone checks on us," he said, breathing a little heavier. Taking her hand, he led her out of the room and to the stairs. Sumner let Octavia go first, he walked down at a pace behind her. It was a little funny, because it was almost like they were hiding the relationship when, honestly, no one downstairs would care and expected it.

Alces and Durante were talking and chuckling about something as they approached and smiled up at them as they walked towards the table.

"Looking delightful as always, bright Octavia," Alces said and Durante offered her the seat next to him again.

Coming around the table, Octavia kissed Alces on the cheek, and did the same for Durante before she sat down. Her heart would figure itself out, but regardless, she was one of them. And they were hers.

I'm so excited to see what the future holds for your little coterie, Kamvasana mused as dinner was brought out and conversation picked up. *I think you'll serve me even better than you already have.*

Octavia was too content to be bothered by her interfering benefactor. Maybe, just maybe, the Essence of Desire was right.

The adventure continues in...

Changed for Desire

Coming in October 2025!

ABOUT THE AUTHORS

Clea Salar (she/her) is a bi, sassy freelance writer who spends most of her days glaring at her computer in between bouts of actually writing. She's a specialist in all things fantastic, with an impressive resume that includes such skills as spending recess and lunch in the library reading folklore and mythology books all through school, a familiarity with a variety of role-playing games, and regular attendance at every convention and Renaissance festival within driving distance. Clea loves bubble tea, tiny desserts, and the Oxford comma.

Tallis Salar (he/him) is a Jack of All (IT) Trades who would rather be diving, at least until "space viking" becomes a viable career path. He loves a good sci-fi, and is happy to explain why "Aliens" is the greatest film ever made. His creative background includes a staggering number of role-playing games, particularly as the GM. Tallis can be bought with video games, sour candies, and frozen drinks (this is a joke, he can't actually be bought, but he welcomes you to try).

www.ingramcontent.com/pod-product-compliance
Lightning Source LLC
Chambersburg PA
CBHW010610310726
48969CB00010B/2635